WESTERN

Rugged men looking for love...

A Valentine's Day Return

Brenda Minton

Their Inseparable Bond

Jil Weatherholt

MILLS & BOON

A VALENTINE'S DAY RETURN

First Published 2024
First Australian Paperback Edition 2024
ISBN 978 1 867 29969 1

THEIR INSEPARABLE BOND

First Published 2024
First Australian Paperback Edition 2024
ISBN 978 1 867 29969 1

Published by
Harlequin Mills & Boon
An imprint of Harlequin Enterprises (Australia) Pty Limited
(ABN 47 001 180 918), a subsidiary of HarperCollins
Publishers Australia Pty Limited
(ABN 36 009 913 517)
Level 19, 201 Elizabeth Street
SYDNEY NSW 2000 AUSTRALIA

Printed and bound in Australia by McPherson's Printing Group

A Valentine's Return

Brenda Minton

MILLS & BOON

Brenda Minton lives in the Ozarks with her husband, children, cats, dogs and strays. She is a pastor's wife, Sunday-school teacher, coffee addict and is sleep-deprived. Not in that order. Her dream to be an author for Harlequin started somewhere in the pages of a romance novel about a young American woman stranded in a Spanish castle. Her dreams came true, and twenty-plus books later, she is an author hoping to inspire young girls to dream.

Husbands, love your wives, even as Christ also loved the church, and gave himself for it.

—*Ephesians* 5:25

DEDICATION

This book is dedicated to Susan Gibson Snodgrass,
because she shared her beautiful words
about our words. She encouraged and she shone
her light so brightly in her faith and her marriage.
To Tom Snodgrass, who loved her deeply.
Romance written on our pages
pales in comparison to what the two of you shared.

CHAPTER ONE

THE TOWN OF Sunset Ridge, Oklahoma, had changed a lot since Mark Rivers left. He'd been eighteen the day he hit the road in an old pickup truck a lot like the one he drove today. A truck that smelled of oil and the farm, with cloth-and-vinyl seats and a faded red dash and more faded fake-wood trim. These days, he could afford better, but he'd bought this truck when his plane landed in Tulsa. A truck that took him back to his roots.

He pulled around the square, past Chuck's Café, past the thrift store and the antique store, then found a parking space a short distance from Kylie's Coffee Shop and Bakery. It was late on Sunday night. They weren't at home. Church had let out an hour earlier. He couldn't think of anywhere else they might be. His guess had been correct. The lights to the coffee shop were on.

He cut the engine, then he just sat there letting the cold January air seep in, not getting out, not confronting his past or his mistakes. Yeah, he guessed it might be true that he was a coward, but going in there wouldn't be easy. He'd hurt his wife, scratch that, his ex-wife, and his daughter, and he doubted either of them were ready to forgive.

He didn't blame them. There were times he didn't know if he could forgive himself.

From inside the truck, he watched as his… as Kylie hung cut-out hearts and white twinkling lights in the windows of her little shop with its green awning and bistro-style furniture. Through the big glass window, he saw her smile at their daughter, saw the light shimmer off her hair. She'd dyed it a silvery gray color. He liked it, even though he also loved her natural, dark hair color. Junie, now six, held the ends of the lights and said something that made them both laugh.

Junie. From birth, she'd had those dark curls and big eyes that made her daddy want to spoil her rotten and never let her cry. Too bad he'd been the cause of her tears.

Man, they were beautiful, his wife and daughter. They were the two biggest blessings in his life. He'd overlooked their value and picked the things that had landed him in the gutter.

He'd never get them back, he knew that. He didn't want them back, not if there was any chance that he'd hurt them again. No, they were better off without him.

They didn't need him. Watching them through the window, that seemed obvious. They were happy in this life they'd built for themselves. They were laughing and smiling, two things they hadn't done when they'd been with him. As he watched, Kylie twirled their daughter in lights, and then she took a quick picture of the two of them together.

They might not need him in their lives, but they did need for him to be a better person. They needed to be able to depend on him.

That started now.

He had to go in and make things right. He guessed seeing him clean and sober would be almost as surprising as the last time they'd seen him.

That hadn't been one of his finer moments. What he could remember of it. One thing he did remember, the look on Junie's face when he stumbled through the doors of the church, crashing into his brother's wedding. At the memory, his hands clenched on the steering wheel, seeing it as clearly as if it had just happened. Junie's expression had been branded into his memory.

A man had to get to a place of complete brokenness in order to get help. That had been his moment. He'd spent three months in rehab getting clean. He'd spent the past nine months out, living a sober life. All because of Junie and that day. He wanted to never see that look on her face, ever again.

He had to shed the persona of country musician Marcus Rivers, and he had to walk through the door of Kylie's shop a humbled man, seeking to make things right.

Casually, as if his heart didn't plan to beat its way out of his chest, he exited the old truck. He pushed the door closed, having already realized it didn't much like latching. The air was crisp, but not cold. It was the middle of January, and winter had settled over the countryside, leaving the grass brown and trees bare. The lights and tinsel of Christmas were gone.

He faced Kylie's little shop, the one he'd helped her purchase. She'd supported his dreams of becoming a country singer, so it made sense that he'd helped her gain her dream of having a coffee shop and bakery.

As he approached the door, his hands began to sweat, and he felt a little queasy. He'd never been as confident as he let the world think. His swagger and courage had come from the bottle, and now he had to find a new brand of strength. He'd found strength in renewing his faith. He guessed that eventually he'd even find a little faith in his own abilities.

From her perch on the ladder, she noticed him. It didn't take him by surprise, the way her dark eyes widened, the way she went pale. The shock turned to loathing in the space of a heartbeat. *Loathing,* that had to be the only word that fit the expression on Kylie's face.

Make amends, his sponsor had insisted. To move forward, this step must happen. It had to be more than an apology. It had to be about making things right. Not only for his wife and daughter, but for himself. He drew in a breath and prayed for more strength.

He entered the shop, the jingly-jangly bells ringing a cheerful greeting. Kylie stepped down from the ladder. Junie moved to her mother's side, her startled gaze shifting from one parent to the other. He'd thought of numerous greetings, but in the moment, he couldn't think of a single thing to say, or anything that made sense.

"Honey, I'm home." Not the greeting he'd practiced.

And yet he'd done it anyway. As the words slipped out, he closed his eyes and groaned.

"You still have a way with words," Kylie said. "What are you doing here, Mark?"

"I'm taking a little break." More than a break. "I came home to spend time with my dad." Those were also not the words he'd planned, because he hadn't planned on spending time with Buck at the ranch his brother Matthew had decided to bring back to life.

Dealing with Buck might be on the to-do list, but Kylie and Junie came first. He should tell her that, or something along those lines.

"Oh, I see." She pulled Junie a little closer, a gesture that hurt more than anything she might have said. "We were just closing up for the day."

He remained frozen to the cheery sunflower welcome mat, not daring to go any farther. He smiled down at his daughter. She was the best of the two of them. She had Kylie's dark eyes; her curls came from him, and that stubborn tip of her chin, well, it seemed a perfect imitation of her mother's at that moment.

In all the times he'd played this reunion through, he guessed he hadn't really pictured how they'd react to his visit. He'd thought about what he'd say and how he'd say it, but he hadn't thought about them. Again, he'd been thinking of himself.

That had to stop. This wasn't for him, it was for Kylie and Junie.

Kylie cleared her throat, and he shifted his attention to her. She'd lost weight. Because of him? It would make sense.

"I should have called," he said as he glanced down at the sparkly gift bag he'd carried in.

"Probably," Kylie said. "But you're here, so you might as well say what you've come to say."

He cleared his throat. "I'm sorry."

"Mark, please just..." she waved her hand, a gesture that told him to carry on. Junie had moved a little in his direction, her eyes wide with curiosity. It had been too long, and he'd not known the impact of the long months of separation until that moment.

"Hey, June Bug," he greeted as he went down on one knee to put himself at eye level with his daughter. No one wanted to be towered over, especially if the situation already felt dire. "I brought you a gift from Nashville."

Little teeth bit down on her bottom lip, unsure. He held out the bag with its tissue paper and multicolored ribbons. After a few long seconds, she took it, glancing up at Kylie to make sure she had permission. Curiosity overcame her, and she peeked inside. A smile grew as she reached into the bag and pulled out a music box. It was an intricate doodad that he'd picked up at a shop on Music Row. Probably the wrong gift for a little girl, but he'd thought it pretty when he spotted it inside the glass case at the store. She could shake it like a snow globe and cause tiny flakes to fall upon the Grand Ole Opry, or she could wind it up and listen to Loretta Lynn singing "Wildwood Flower."

On second thought, he regretted the gift and the song. A song of a love that had been misused and left by a wandering man who broke a woman's heart. The worst possible song—he'd just always loved the tune. He briefly closed his eyes.

"Nice," Kylie whispered, and he looked up just in time to see her swipe away a tear.

"I..." What did he say? "I'm sorry."

"For the music box?" Junie asked in a quiet voice that interrupted their conversation and reminded them of her presence.

Mark inhaled and prayed God would give him the right words for the situation. A situation of his own making.

"No," he started, looking from his daughter to her mother. "I'm sorry for so much—I don't know where to start. I should have written down all the reasons I owe you an apology and need your forgiveness."

"That would be a long list," Kylie said, her tone dry.

He studied her face, really studied it. The hint of amusement in her dark eyes reminded him of their early days. They'd been childhood friends and then teens falling in love. At seventeen, she'd joined him in Nashville, wanting the adventure and believing in his ability to succeed. He had found success, and then he'd ruined everything, including them.

Even at thirty-one, he still saw hints of the girl he'd known. She was tall, only inches shorter than him. She'd grown slimmer since leaving him. Junie, on the other hand, with her curls and rounded cheeks, seemed to be thriving.

"It would be a long list," he agreed. "I'm not sure where to start."

"Mommy isn't feeling well—we should go

home now." Junie spoke, the music box still clutched in her tiny hands.

"I'm fine," Kylie inserted with a firm voice. "We aren't going home just yet. I need to have these decorations up by morning. With Christmas over, we're moving on to Valentine's Day."

"I can help," Mark offered.

"No, we can do it." Junie again, her rosebud lips pursed in a perfect imitation of her mother. He smiled at her, wishing he had been a better father. Praying he could be a father again and make up for the times he'd failed her, for the years he'd lost.

"Junie," Kylie warned. "Always be respectful."

Junie opened her mouth as if to add something, but a quick look at her mother stopped the words.

"Excuse me," Kylie said as she pushed her hand to her mouth and hurried from the room.

That left Mark with his daughter.

"Junie, I'm really very sorry for hurting you and upsetting you. I haven't been the best dad." He paused at the expression on her little face. He didn't have a clue how he should talk to his daughter. "I've not been a dad at all. I hope to make that up to you."

She gave him a quick look, her head tilted to the side and her expression far too wise. After a few seconds, she nodded. "It's okay, Mark. I forgive you."

"Do you?" he asked, trying not to be hurt by the use of his first name.

"Yes, I do. We learned about forgiving in Sunday school. There's a verse I can't remember, but it's important to forgive."

"I'll look those verses up," he promised her. He glanced toward the door to the back of the shop. "Do you think we should check on her?"

Junie shook her head. "She'll be back. She's been sick all week, but she won't listen to Aunt Parker. Aunt Parker said she needs to go in and get checked. Aunt Parker is a nurse. You ruined her wedding."

He whistled soft and low at that. "Yeah, I guess I owe her an apology, too."

"She's the one who taught me about forgiving. If you ask, she'll forgive you." She leaned in close, as if telling him a secret. "Some wounds take more time to heal."

"Aunt Parker?" he whispered back.

Junie nodded.

Kylie still hadn't returned. He was caught between the urge to help and to mind his own business. She'd left him four years ago and made it clear he could see his daughter, but would no longer be welcome in her life.

"Should we go ahead and finish hanging these lights?" he asked Junie.

"I don't know," she frowned as she looked from him to the string of lights. "Maybe."

"I'll get on the ladder. You can hand them up."

She nodded, accepting the plan. He shouldn't have felt elated over the tiny hint of acceptance, but he did. Elated on one hand, worried on the other. Kylie had yet to return.

KYLIE LEANED AGAINST the wall, trembling, her legs weak. It felt as if a hot knife sliced through her abdomen, and the pain, unlike the other times, didn't seem to be abating. As she tried to take a step, the pain nearly brought her to her knees.

Of all the times for Mark to show up, why now? She didn't want him here to witness her illness. She didn't want to be doubled over in pain, feeling vulnerable, while he looked better than ever and smelled like an expensive trip to a Caribbean island.

He'd broken her heart. He'd used up all of

her loyalty, in the process destroying every ounce of love she'd had for him. She could forgive him. That didn't mean she wanted him in her life or her shop.

They shared a daughter. She had to remind herself that he had a right to see Junie, to be in her life. Junie wanted to see her father. Didn't every little girl? As a child who'd grown up with a single mother, Kylie knew the pain of missing out on a father.

It had been so much simpler with him in Tennessee and the two of them in Oklahoma. Absence hadn't made the heart grow fonder—it had just helped hers to heal.

Taking a few deep breaths, she found the strength to walk out of the bathroom. She would make this quick. She'd let him say whatever he needed to say, and then she'd go home to a cup of tea and her warmest robe.

As she entered the dining room, she managed to remain upright. The last thing she wanted was to collapse on the floor in a puddle of tears and sickness. *Bright smile*, she urged herself. *Pretend everything is fine.* She looked up to a scene that could have been on the front of a greeting card.

Junie stood by the window, the twinkling

lights wrapped around her body. Kylie's gaze traveled up. Mark stood on the ladder, his jeans low on his hips, his faded red sweatshirt snug across his shoulders. His hair, always curly, was more controlled these days. He hadn't shaved in a few days, or perhaps that was his new style, scruffy. She disliked that she noticed how cute he was or the way his silver-gray eyes sought approval when he caught her watching.

"Ky, you okay?" he asked, using the nickname he'd given her the year she'd turned twelve. They'd been riding bikes around town and then they'd headed to the creek to wade in the icy cold water.

"I'm good," she tried to reassure him and their daughter. She reached for the counter, doing her best to stay upright.

"Mommy?" Junie clearly didn't believe she was okay.

"I'm fine," Kylie repeated, to them and to herself. "I just need to go home and rest."

Mark hopped down from the ladder and moved to her side. Gently, he felt her forehead, as if temperature checking came naturally to him. Then he leaned and pressed his lips to her brow, the way she often did to Junie. "You're burning up."

"I'm not," she told him. "I'm good. It's just a virus."

"Aunt Parker says it's not a virus. She said you should go to the doctor." Junie said it with her chin up, a fight to be strong as tears filled her eyes.

"I promise you, I'm okay. I'm going to go home and rest. By tomorrow, I'll be good as new." She wiped a tear from Junie's cheek.

The last thing she wanted was to cause her daughter to worry. Her goal in life had been to give Junie a childhood without fear. A childhood. Period.

Kylie's own mother had stolen her childhood. Mindy Waters, Kylie's mom, had loved drugs more than she'd loved her own daughter. She'd loved drugs more than life. Raised by an addict, married to an addict. Kylie shook her head, freeing herself from the past and the pain of her childhood and the pain of watching Mark become a person she'd never expected him to be.

He gave her a long look and then slowly shook his head. "Don't." He leaned in and whispered the word close to her ear. "Don't go there."

He knew her too well.

"Junie, I'm fine. I promise." Kylie smiled

down at her daughter as she put space between herself and Mark. "Remember, faith, not fear."

Junie sniffled, but she nodded. "Faith, not fear."

"Let me drive the two of you home," Mark offered.

She started to object, but it didn't seem to be the right time for obstinance. If she were being honest, she didn't know if she could drive herself. "I'd appreciate the ride."

A few minutes and he had the lights off, had reset her thermostat and had grabbed her purse from under the counter. Junie followed him, giving him instructions on each thing he needed to do. Kylie couldn't help but smile as she watched the two of them.

As much as she didn't want Mark in her life, he needed to be in his daughter's life.

He finished all the details of closing up and returned to the table where he'd insisted she take a seat.

"Ready to go?" He reached for her hand and drew her to her feet.

"More than ready," she admitted. The pain had grown sharper, and she nearly doubled over as she stood.

"Maybe we should bypass the house and go

to the emergency room?" he suggested, still holding her hand.

"Please just take us home."

He locked the door behind them and helped her to the faded red-and-white truck parked next to her Jeep. When he opened the door, she stepped back, overwhelmed by "old car" smell. She couldn't imagine this scent ever being used in a diffuser. It was a combination of age, motor oil and farm.

"I don't think I can get in there."

"It isn't that bad," he defended.

"The smell." She put a hand to her mouth. "I'm not trying to be rude. I just, my stomach."

He looked a little bit hurt, but when Junie wrinkled her nose, he leaned in to check for himself. "I guess it isn't springtime fresh in there."

"Could you drive my car? I think it would be easier to get in and definitely more comfortable."

He grinned, flashing a dimple that matched the one in Junie's right cheek. "I suppose we'll just leave 'old red' here for now. Hopefully no one takes her."

"I think she's safe," Kylie assured him.

He took the keys she offered and opened the

passenger door of her Jeep. Junie climbed in the back and buckled into her booster seat as Kylie eased herself into the front. Mark leaned in to recline the seat, and then he gently eased the seatbelt around her waist. Her heart melted a little, and she had to close her eyes to distance herself from the emotions of having him so near, taking care of her. It felt reminiscent of the night he'd taken her to the hospital to have Junie.

Once upon a time, he'd been her handsome prince. He'd rescued her from a life of poverty and neglect. He'd put her on a pedestal. He'd even built her a castle.

He'd built it all, and then he'd broken her heart and left her empty. No, that wasn't true. He'd given her the best thing of all. He'd given her Junie. She would always have the best of him in their daughter.

A moment later, they were speeding through town in the direction of her new home. The house, formerly the Duncan place, had belonged to the lawyer in town. When she'd watched him with his family, she'd always wondered what it would be like to live in their two-story brick home with two parents and with children who always seemed happy and loved. His youngest daughter had even resembled Kylie, strengthening her childish fantasy.

A fantasy about a family that really had been hers, only they hadn't known she existed. She'd been the secret he kept with her mother.

Now she owned the house she'd never been allowed to enter. She'd thought to feel a sense of victory. Instead, she'd found peace and she'd let go of the anger she'd always felt for them.

Mark pulled into the drive, and she reached to push the button for the garage. "I'm sorry we left your truck. You can take my car for the night."

"I'm not crazy about leaving you alone."

"I'll be fine. If I need anything, I can call Parker."

He parked and took the keys from the ignition. "You can also call me."

She didn't have the strength to argue. Instead, she pushed her door open and tried to exit her car with some dignity, which didn't include losing more of her stomach contents on the floor of the garage. Unfortunately, she couldn't make it out of the car, not without his help.

"I can't do this," he said. "I can't take you inside and leave you. You need the emergency room."

The announcement made her want to cry.

She would have cried if she'd had the energy. She couldn't even argue with him.

"I know," she said. "I kept thinking I would get better."

"Let me help you," he said with a tender smile. "I know that I've done a lot to hurt you, to hurt you both. Trust me to take care of you tonight."

She leaned back in the seat and closed her eyes. "I forgive you. You don't have to earn that forgiveness."

"I know that. Maybe there is a purpose in my presence here tonight. Maybe, just maybe, God planned for me to be at your shop because He knew you needed me there to help you."

"Maybe," she said, letting a few tears slide free.

"I'm going to call Parker," he told her. "Let's see what she says."

Again, she nodded. She had no fight left in her. She couldn't even turn her head to make sure Junie was okay. As if she knew, Junie reached up and placed her hand on Kylie's shoulder.

"It's okay, honey. I promise it'll be okay." Kylie patted Junie's hand.

She closed her eyes and listened as Mark

gave Parker a brief rundown of her condition, and then he pushed the speaker icon, as if she needed to hear for herself.

"Mark, take her to the emergency room," Parker said. "We'll meet you there."

"It's just a virus," Kylie tried again.

Over the speaker, she heard Parker's sigh. "I think that argument has been lost."

"We'll see you there. And thank you." Mark ended the call. "Okay?"

She nodded, but words didn't come. She wanted to tell him thank you. She wanted to say how much it meant that he was there for her. The words wouldn't come, not because she didn't want to say them, but because she physically couldn't get the words out. She felt like the worst kind of sissy as she drew her knees close and curled up in the seat.

A strong hand touched her arm. She raised her gaze to meet his and saw all of the strength of the man she'd always wanted him to be. She didn't want to need Mark, but his nearness felt familiar and comforting. His strength, the strength of the Mark she'd grown up with, helped her to relax, to take a breath. She wasn't alone. Junie wouldn't be alone.

As much as she didn't want to depend on

him, for tonight, she needed to give up control and let him help. Not just for her sake, but also for Junie. It was much easier to let him help when she framed it that way. He was going to be there for Junie.

CHAPTER TWO

KYLIE SHIVERED BENEATH the paper-thin blanket provided by the hospital. The nurse's aide had seemed so confident that the "just out of the warmer" blanket would have her "feeling better in no time." Whatever the woman thought about those blankets and their ability to "make things better," Kylie had to disagree. And she knew, without being told, that she was being disagreeable.

"When is the doctor going to be here?" she mumbled, wishing she could sneak a sip of water or ask for a cup of tea. She'd already been told that both were off-limits because they were positive they'd be doing an appendectomy as soon as it could be arranged.

"Soon," Mark assured her. One side of his mouth hitched up, deepening those dimples that were almost, but not quite, hidden by the ten o'clock shadow that covered his lean and perpetually tan cheeks.

"I want to go home."

Another grin. "I know. This feels a lot like when you were having Junie. The two of us together in a hospital. You complaining that you want to go home."

"Me in pain, and you finding it amusing."

His grin dissolved. "I'm not amused. I'm just trying to cheer you up and make this easier."

"I'm worried about Junie."

"I'll take care of her," he assured her.

She sighed, closing her eyes. "I'm sorry. I'm not a good patient."

"No, but you always manage to make a cloth sack look like designer clothing."

She reminded herself that he'd always been charming. He should have saved all of that charm for her. He should have...

A light rap on the door shook her from the "should have" thoughts. Those thoughts had nowhere to take her but into the dark past of their relationship, and she didn't want to go there, not now. Now was a time for faith and hope, not darkness and depression. The door opened and the doctor entered, glancing at her, at Mark and then, of course, at Mark again. She almost groaned at the obvious reaction.

Dr. Janson cleared his throat, professionalism back on track. “Mrs. Rivers, we are scheduling your surgery. We’re going to try to get you back there as soon as possible.”

“And then I can go home?” She managed to sound more hopeful than she felt.

He gave her a clearly sympathetic look. “I don’t think you should plan on going home for a few days. We’ll know more once we get in there, but what we’re dealing with is a ruptured appendix and an infection.”

He continued, and she tried to focus on what he described as a situation that could have been much worse if she hadn’t come in when she did. She gave Mark a quick look and saw the downturn of his mouth and the way he drew in a breath.

“They’ll be in here soon to prep you for surgery. I expect things to go well, but you have to understand that you’re not going to be up and around in a matter of days.”

Mark’s hand had taken hers, and he gave a gentle squeeze. A reassuring, make-her-stronger squeeze. She didn’t pull back, not then, maybe later when she didn’t need him. They’d given her medicine for the pain; that explained the lowered defenses. Or at least that was what she told herself.

"I can't stay in the hospital. I have the coffee shop and Junie."

"You have yourself to take care of," Mark reminded her. "I'm here. I'll be here for you and for Junie."

"Parker and Matthew. I need to talk to them. Junie can stay with them. I know you didn't come here planning to stay and babysit. You probably have somewhere to be."

"She's my daughter, too, and it isn't babysitting." He brushed a hand through his hair and let out a breath.

"I have to know that she's going to be okay. She'll be worried. She's never been away from me."

"You have to trust me."

She looked away, unable to meet the hurt that she knew would be in his eyes.

He gave her hand a gentle squeeze. "I get it. Half the time, I don't even trust myself. I'll talk to Matthew and Parker. I'm sure Junie would rather stay with them. I'll stay with Dad. Is there anything that needs to be done at your place? Pets to feed?"

Kylie rolled over to face him, shivering beneath the white hospital blanket.

He knew she'd never had pets and still didn't. Her mom had brought home every stray she'd found, including people. The trailer she'd grown up in had always been overrun with mangy dogs and flea-bitten cats, as well as "friends" of her mother.

"No pets. And thank you for understanding."

"Trust me. With this, you can trust me." He sounded so sincere. "I'll be here as long as the two of you need me."

Trust him. What choice did she have? She closed her eyes on a wave of pain and worry. She didn't want to let the worry consume her. Didn't the Bible tell her that a person couldn't add a cubit to their stature by worrying? It wouldn't change her situation or the outcome to worry.

"Is Junie still in the waiting room?" she asked, an edge of panic creeping in. "I need to hug her."

"I'll get them," Mark spoke, his voice reverberating through her like the bass of a radio.

"Thank you."

The door snicked closed as he left, and for a few minutes, she had time alone, time to process the situation she found herself stuck in. She'd expected this illness to be just another virus that ran its course. She hadn't expected her ex-husband to waltz through the door of her coffee shop.

"Mommy?" Junie slipped into the room alone. Her dark eyes were luminous in her pale face. She stopped, taking in the room, the hospital bed, her mother.

"Come here, sweet girl. Let's cuddle." She held her arms open, and Junie hurried forward for the promised hug. "I'm going to be fine. They're going to do a surgery and take out my appendix, and in just a few days, I'll be good as new. Probably better."

"I don't want you to be gone."

"It's just a few days. I promise." Kylie pressed her lips to her daughter's brow. "And you get to have a sleepover with Aunt Parker and Uncle Matthew. You probably even get to sleep in Faith's room."

Junie pulled back, her expression troubled. "Not Daddy?"

"He'll be around. He's going to stay a few days with your granddad."

"Will I get to see him?" Junie asked.

"I'm sure you will." Kylie's heart ached at

the question. It had been so long since Mark had made an appearance. Now she knew why. He'd been getting sober. Junie was too young to process all of this.

The door opened. Junie sat up, watching to see who would join them. Kylie waited also, wondering if he'd stay, if he'd be there for Junie.

Parker and Matthew entered the room. No Mark.

"He's in the chapel," Matthew offered. "He needed a minute."

"Hmm," Kylie murmured. She couldn't say more, not in front of Junie. Matthew looked as if he wanted to say more. She wondered if he would defend his brother or give her words of warning as he'd done years ago, when she'd packed up her old Charger and told him she was going to Nashville to be with his brother.

Parker moved to her side. "Is there anything we can do, or get you?"

"I'd like water." Kylie smiled up at her friend.

"I wish I could." Parker winked at Junie. "I'm afraid no liquids."

"Where's Faith?" Kylie asked, hoping the conversation would keep her mind off the searing pain.

"She's with Melinda Carr. We'll pick her up on our way home."

Melinda, the church nursery worker and also a trusted babysitter for Faith and many other children in town.

"I'm so sorry you had to leave her and come out on a night like this. It's so cold."

Parker put a hand to Kylie's brow. "And you have a fever. Relax, we know that Faith is fine, and you're important to us. We want you well. It's good that Mark showed up when he did."

"Yes." She couldn't deny that fact. If he hadn't shown up, she would have gone home, the way she'd been going home for days, still sick and still believing she'd be better by morning.

After all these years, Mark was still coming to her rescue.

He'd been her hero, until he hadn't. She had no one to blame for that but herself. She'd looked to him to save her, to protect her from all harm. Unfortunately, he hadn't been able to save himself.

They'd been such a happy mess. Two broken people, trying to face the world together and be whole.

She didn't want to think they'd been a mistake. After all, they had Junie. Their daughter clearly was the best thing to come out of their marriage. Kylie could overlook the betrayal and heartache for the sake of Junie.

"Kylie." Parker said it gently, almost a question.

"I'm good, just tired of being sick. And don't say it, I know I should have listened to you."

"You are stubborn," Parker said.

Parker swooped Junie up off the bed and gave her bear hugs, and then she sat down in the chair next to the bed, still holding Kylie's daughter. "We're going to keep this girl busy, while you stay busy getting well."

Kylie nodded, fighting tears. When had she last been away from her daughter? Once, maybe, while she and Mark were still married. They'd gone to an award show together. Her best friend in Nashville had let Junie spend the night.

"Don't worry, we will be here to visit. We'll probably go home as soon as the surgery is over and you're in recovery. You won't feel up to visitors."

"I will," Kylie argued.

Parker shook her head, laughing just a little. "No, I promise you won't. But Mark is staying..." She let the words trail off.

"He doesn't have to," Kylie said. "After all, I won't feel like having visitors."

"He doesn't want you to be alone," Matthew said. "For that matter, neither do we. We'll all rest easier, knowing someone is here with you."

"Even if that someone is me?" Mark said as he entered the room, his cowboy hat in his hands, his smile clearly not meant for humor. He looked hurt.

She didn't want to care about his feelings.

"I'm glad you're staying," she assured him out of habit. Just habit, she told herself. She would have been just fine without him at her side.

He gave her a searching look. "Good, because I'm not going anywhere."

"Okay, we're going to say our goodbyes and go back to the waiting room." Parker stood, still holding Junie.

"Okay." Kylie held her arms out for one last hug from her daughter. "I'm going to be just fine."

Junie leaned in to hug her. "I know you are, Mommy. Mark will take care of you."

"Mark." Kylie glanced his way, and he grinned.

"We love you, and we're praying." Parker kissed her cheek, and then she was gone, leaving Matthew and Mark. The Rivers brothers looked uncomfortable with each other and the situation.

When had they last been in a room together?

"I'm going to pray," Matthew told her as he took her hand. Mark moved to her side and bowed his head, but his hand rested on hers.

The prayer was short but meaningful, bringing tears to her eyes. She'd needed those comforting words. She realized she needed the big brother hug that Matthew gave her before he exited the room, leaving her alone with her ex-husband.

"You really don't have to stay," she said, even as she realized she didn't mean it. As much as she didn't want to admit it, she needed for him to stay.

He'd hurt her, but before that, he'd always been her person.

MARK STAYED. NO way could he walk away and leave her alone in the hospital. He'd left her on her own one too many times, and this time, he could make the right decision. The decision to be there for her.

As they took her from the room to prepare her for surgery, he clasped her hand and leaned in to place a kiss on her cheek. She closed her eyes, her breath soft as she exhaled.

"I'll be here when you wake up," he promised.

She nodded and a tear squeezed free from beneath closed eyes. He caught it with a brush of his finger across soft skin.

"I'm afraid." Her voice trembled as she made the admission.

Her eyes, dark and shimmering with fear and pain, caught him in a devastating way, almost making him lose his grip on the courage that she needed from him.

"You're going to be fine," he promised. "I'm here, and I'm praying, and you're going to be better in no time."

"It's just a silly appendix," she said with a soft sound of mirth.

"We have to go," the orderly informed them.

"Junie," she rushed their daughter's name as they pushed her away from him.

"She's going to be fine. She's with Matthew and Parker."

"She's six, and she always tries too hard to be strong."

"Like her mother," he said with a wink. "You're going to be okay."

"I know."

And then the orderly pushed the bed through double doors with a sign that prohibited entrance by anyone other than medical personnel.

Mark stood in the hall, unable to walk away, still picturing Kylie's face, pale and exhausted, in pain. He leaned against the wall and waited for the strength to leave, to go find a place to sit and wait. A nurse walked past.

"Will they let me know how she's doing?" he asked.

"And you are?"

"Her husband," he said out of habit. And then he groaned because he wasn't her husband, not anymore, and he had no rights. "Ex-husband. But..."

"Sorry, we can only update if she gave permission."

"I understand, but I'm the only one. Can you find out if she gave permission? Someone has to be here for her." He jerked off his hat and brushed his hand through his tangled curls, wishing that he'd taken time for a haircut. Not that the style of his hair had any importance at the moment.

"You can have a seat in the waiting room," the nurse offered. "And I can check."

He nodded and scooted past her to the small room she indicated. Another waiting room with straight-back, vinyl-covered chairs, a television on low volume and dark windows looking out at a darkened city that he didn't care to see. He wished he'd asked Matthew to stay with him. They hadn't been close in years, but they were still brothers.

Years ago, the four Rivers brothers had been thick as thieves. They'd gone through everything together, and they'd done everything together. Mostly. Matthew, as he'd gotten older, took on the role of keeping them all out of trouble. They hadn't thanked him for that, even though it had been necessary. Someone in the Rivers family had needed to be responsible, and it sure hadn't been their dad, Buck Rivers.

Footsteps in the hall caught his attention. Boots, not the soft-soled shoes of the nurse. He moved away from the window to the coffee pot. As he poured a cup, the newcomer entered.

Not a newcomer. Matthew.

An unexpected feeling of relief swamped him, bringing the burn of unwanted tears. He focused on adding sugar to the hours-old coffee and then creamer that barely made a dint in the dark brew.

A hand touched his shoulder.

"I didn't expect you all to stay," Mark said, his voice catching.

"I sent Parker and Junie on home. They were both worn slick. I couldn't let you do this alone. Plus, I'm the hospital chaplain."

"So you're just here out of a sense of duty?" Mark picked up his coffee, and then he remembered his manners. "Want a cup?"

"No, thanks. That smells as if it's been here all day. Let me get us a fresh cup. I'll pour that out for you."

"I don't really want coffee," Mark admitted. "I just needed to do something to take my mind off worrying about Kylie."

He left the cup on the table and joined his brother, taking one of the orange vinyl seats that didn't encourage sitting for long.

"I'm here because you're my brother and Kylie is the mother of my niece." Matthew stretched his long legs, crossing them at the ankles. He didn't act at all put off by the furniture.

Mark could admit that he might have been taking his worry out on the chairs. He needed something to focus on, something other than Kylie being sick.

"Thank you," Mark said to his brother, "for

being there." He closed his eyes and said another *thank you*, this time to God, for giving him a brother who had a large quantity of forgiveness to pass out to troubled souls.

"No need to thank me."

"I'm sorry," Mark said. "That's why I came home."

"Here to make amends?"

Mark nodded and scrubbed a hand down his face. "Yeah. I guess you probably didn't question why I'd dropped off the face of the earth after last year."

"You did make our wedding memorable." Matthew said it with a chuckle, his dry humor still intact. "And Luke told us where he'd taken you. I waited, hoping you'd call."

"I had to deal with some stuff first. That look on Junie's face..." He felt another embarrassing sting of tears.

"Yeah, I know." Matthew put a brotherly arm around him and gave him a hard squeeze, then let him go. "We all survived, and it gave us something to talk about."

"I'm guessing it gave the entire town of Sunset Ridge something to talk about." He groaned. "I sang Garth Brooks for you."

"Something like that. Mostly you announced

that you didn't mean to ruin our black-tie affair. It didn't sound much like singing."

"That wasn't my best moment, was it? I don't know how to make it up to the two of you, to Junie and to Kylie."

"Mark, we forgive you."

He nodded, stunned, fighting tears and wishing he could be half the man his brother had turned out to be.

"Thank you," he said after getting hold of himself.

"How long are you here for?"

"I guess longer than I'd planned. I can't leave until I know Kylie is okay. She'll need help. I'll be here until arrangements can be made."

"Arrangements?" Matthew asked, his eyes narrowing.

"She'll need help with her shop, with Junie, all the stuff she won't be able to do after surgery."

"Oh, so you're going to hire someone?" The big-brother disapproval came through loud and clear.

"I doubt she'll want my help," he defended.

"You sure of that?"

"Positive. She only took my help tonight because I happened to be there." Mark stood, needing to move away from Matthew and from whatever lecture might be coming. "I need that coffee now."

"Let's go to my office. I can make a fresh pot, and we can talk."

"I don't think I want to talk. I need to find out how she's doing."

"Okay, we'll find out."

"I'm not her next of kin."

Matthew moved him toward the door. "We'll find out how she's doing."

They walked down the hall in the direction of the nurses' station. The nurse saw them coming. She looked up from her computer, smiling at Matthew, frowning at Mark. "I checked the paperwork."

"Is there a way we could find out how much longer?" Matthew asked. "I understand HIPAA. Unfortunately, her only next of kin is a six-year-old child."

"Let me see what I can do," the nurse said as she pushed back from her desk.

"We'll be in my office."

Matthew led Mark down the quiet halls of the hospital. The lights were dim; the rooms were dark. Everything was hushed and somber. He unlocked a door and flipped on the lights.

The room they entered had "Parker" touches. The soft, earthy throw rug, the oak desk with the office chair that looked comfortable but antique and two chairs for visitors that looked welcoming in shades of autumn red.

"This is better than the waiting room," Mark acknowledged as he took a seat and watched his brother start the coffee. "*Thank you* is starting to sound repetitive, but it's all I've got."

"You're welcome." Matthew gave him a steady look. "We're brothers. Thick and thin, we're here for each other."

"I know." Mark accepted the cup of coffee, not bothering to add sugar or cream. "I'd forgotten for a bit, but I'm coming back to myself."

"How are you doing?" Matthew asked as he took a seat behind the desk.

"Right now?" Mark sipped the coffee as he searched for the right response. "Right now, I'm holding on by a thread because this day has kind of shaken me. I'm good, though. I'm one year sober, and statistically, if we're looking at statistics, that's important."

"What's the plan for future you?" Matthew asked with a grin.

"Present me. I live in the present. Present me is a one-day-at-a-time person. I don't live in the past, or I try not to. I'm living my present life in hopes that future me is still sober. I'm going to focus on being a better version of myself, a better dad, a better ex-husband."

"Is that what you want?" Matthew asked, delving a little too deeply into things Mark preferred to not deal with.

"Yeah, that's what I want." It was what he trusted himself to do.

The last thing he wanted was to hurt Kylie again. He didn't want to hurt his daughter, either. But the kind of pain and humiliation he put Kylie through, that was something he couldn't do a second time.

He wouldn't. The only way he could guarantee he wouldn't hurt her was to stay out of her life.

A knock on the door interrupted the conversation.

"Come in," Matthew offered.

The nurse stepped into the room. "She's out of surgery. The doctor is coming down to update you. She appointed you as a contact person, but also gave permission for you to make decisions if she is unable to."

The nurse left, and a few minutes later, the

doctor found them. He gave Mark a tired smile as he stood in the doorway to address them.

"She's okay?" Mark stood, ready to go to her.

"She will be." Dr. Janson sighed. "She's fortunate that you brought her in tonight, or it could have been worse. We're looking at a pretty bad infection from the bacteria of the ruptured appendix. She's a sick young woman with a long road ahead of her. I'm hoping we can have her home by midweek, but it'll depend on how she responds to the antibiotics."

"Can I see her?"

"Soon," Dr. Janson answered.

The doctor left. Mark sat back down, feeling frazzled, useless and now exhausted.

"It's okay to feel overwhelmed. We all get that way sometimes."

"I know," Mark responded. He felt more than overwhelmed. He felt wound tight on the inside. The old Mark would have been searching for a drink. New Mark focused on taking a few steady breaths, and he said a prayer for peace.

"What are you going to do?" Matthew asked. The question meant something.

Mark closed his eyes, thinking of all his plans. He'd come here with every intention of leaving in just a matter of days. It was Thursday. He wanted to be back in Nashville by Sunday.

"What is that verse in Isaiah? 'My thoughts are not your thoughts, neither are your ways my ways, saith the Lord.'" Mark found himself laughing a little at the irony of his plans being interrupted.

Matthew also chuckled. "Isaiah 55:8. Verse 9 is also recommended. 'For as the heavens are higher than the earth, so are my ways higher than your ways, and my thoughts than your thoughts.'"

"Nice," Mark said. "Thanks for the reminder."

"God's word, not mine," Matthew reminded. "Plans change, Mark. Sometimes the plan and our path change at the same time."

"I'm not sure if she'll want me to stay," he admitted. "She has a lot of good reasons for not wanting me in her life."

"I know that Junie wants you here. She was worried you'd leave and not tell her goodbye."

Mark closed his eyes for a moment, just long enough to regroup.

"When you go home, tell her I'm not going anywhere yet."

"I'll let her know. And you should go check on Kylie."

"Thanks for the talk."

"That's what big brothers are for, to give unsolicited advice."

Mark hugged his brother, and then he left to go find Kylie. His plans had changed, but that didn't mean this new plan didn't have merit. Kylie needed him. He needed to be a better version of himself. For her. For Junie. For his future.

CHAPTER THREE

MARK LEFT THE hospital in the middle of the night. Kylie had insisted he should go get some sleep so she could sleep and so he'd be able to check on Junie. He drove her car back to Sunset Ridge and parked it in front of her shop, then he climbed into his old truck that smelled of age, motor oil and the farm, and he drove to the Rocking R. He realized one thing on the drive to the ranch: the truck didn't have much of a heater.

The old farmhouse he'd grown up in lay in silence. Not one light had been left on. Of course, Buck hadn't been expecting company.

Frozen, he searched the front porch, knowing Buck always kept a key hidden. He overturned planters, moved rugs and looked under the cushions of the patio furniture that looked newer than anything Buck had ever had on that old front porch.

No key. Since when did Buck lock doors and not leave a spare key? He stood on the porch, trying to think of another hiding spot. The porch light came on, and the door opened. Buck stepped out, wearing flannel pajamas and pointing a shotgun.

Mark raised his hands and stepped back. "Hey, whoa, hold on, Buck, it's me, Mark."

Buck lowered the weapon and stepped a little closer, peering at his son as if he'd just spotted a cockroach in the kitchen. "What are you doing out here making all that ruckus? Some people are trying to sleep."

"I was looking for a key. I needed a place to sleep."

"Get in here." Buck waved the gun in the direction of the front door.

"Do you think you could put that shotgun down?"

"It ain't loaded."

"Then what good is it doing you?"

"Scared you, didn't it?"

"Yeah," Mark admitted. "It scared me. Mind if I go to sleep?"

"I guess I don't mind. You could at least say hello and tell me why you're here bothering me."

"I didn't plan on bothering you. I had to take

Kylie to the hospital tonight. I'll be sticking around until I know she's okay."

"What's the matter with her?"

"Appendix." Mark scrubbed a hand across his face. "Could we talk in the morning?"

Buck pursed his lips. "Well, that's a shame. She's a good gal. I guess you can tell me more tomorrow morning."

"Yes, we can talk tomorrow." He was exhausted, and the conversation was buzzing around in his head. "I'm tired."

"I'm sure you are. Well, you know where your room is."

"Thanks, Buck."

"Yep, you're welcome." Buck headed down the hall, tall and stooped but healthier than he'd been in years. Sobriety did that for a person.

Mark didn't bother turning on lights. He knew his way to the room he'd slept in as a kid. He kicked off his boots and climbed into the bed, the lumps and bumps of the mattress familiar and strangely comforting. He pulled the quilt that smelled of time and dust up to his chin and went to sleep.

Hours later, or maybe ten minutes, he woke up to sunshine streaming through the room and foul breath heating his face. He pushed at the interloper, and the dog gave a soft woof. "Go away, you mutt."

The dog jumped off the bed and padded across the room to the open door. He woofed again, as if commanding Mark to get out of bed.

"I'll get up when I feel like getting up," he growled at the gray-and-white Australian shepherd. "Where'd you come from anyway?"

The dog sat down and gave him a wise look. He didn't like the look, not this early in the morning. A man didn't want to feel as if he'd been outsmarted by a canine.

The smell of chocolate and something baked came drifting through the open door. The dog didn't hold much sway over Mark, but his empty stomach did. The growling and rumbling pushed him from the bed, still in the clothes he'd been wearing for two days. He guessed he probably stunk as much as the cattle dog. He'd best take care of that before he headed down to breakfast.

A quick shower and change of clothes and he was ready to greet the day. He found the dog waiting in the hallway.

"Let's go." Mark gave a soft whistle, and the

dog followed him down the stairs. The aroma of chocolate grew stronger.

He walked through the house to the kitchen. Buck's kitchen, always a surprise. The chef's kitchen with the fancy cabinets and granite countertops had been installed almost thirty years ago, something Buck had done to try and keep his city-bred, country-club loving wife. Mark didn't call her Mom any more than he called Buck, Dad. But Buck had definitely earned the title of Father more than Isabel Rivers had earned the right to be called Mother.

At least Izzy had done right by the youngest Rivers child, Jael. The only girl had been born after Izzy left Buck. And Luke Rivers. The third of the four boys had sold out and moved to Tulsa to live with their mother. He'd waited until the rest of them had fled the state, but he'd gone to her, and now he helped run her family business.

Traitor.

The same traitor that had hauled Mark to rehab. For that, he'd be eternally grateful, even if he never found a way to get along with his little brother.

Sitting at the counter, perched on a barstool that seemed particularly large for a small child, sat his daughter. Junie was stirring something in a bowl she could barely see over the top of. She had a dab of chocolate on her face, and a grin split her dimpled cheeks in a merry way. She was the stuff that country songs about babies and puppies were made of.

"Hey, June Bug, I didn't expect to see you here." He started to give her a hug, but then wondered if she would even want one from him. "Mind if I give you a hug?"

Her eyes narrowed, and she made a face. "I like hugs."

He hugged her.

"What are you making?"

"Grandpa Buck is making chocolate chocolate-chip pancakes. They're my favorite. I get to stir."

"And eat chocolate while stirring?" he asked. She nodded.

"Coffee?" Buck asked.

"Sure thing." He rounded the counter and found a coffee cup already next to the coffeemaker. "Thanks. I didn't mean to sleep this late."

"It's just eight in the morning. You didn't sleep long at all." Buck wiped his hands on a towel and reached for the bowl that Junie had been stirring. "Let's see what we can do. We already have chocolate-chip muffins ready. They're on the cooling rack."

"Did you turn into a chef?" Mark asked as he grabbed a muffin so filled with chocolate chips he could barely see the cake. This explained the chocolate on his daughter's face.

"I had to do something to keep myself busy. I recommend baking—it's soothing."

Soothing? He couldn't remember ever hearing his dad use that word before. Not once. Ever.

Buck had never been a soother, more of a "pull yourself up by the bootstraps, shake it off and don't cry" kind of man. Being sober and having grandchildren had changed him.

Not in a bad way.

The muffins were mighty tasty.

Pancake batter sizzled on the griddle. "Why don't you grab the can of whipped topping out of the fridge," Buck ordered while focusing on cooking.

"Can do."

Junie cleared her throat and both Mark and Buck gave her a quick look. "What's up, June Bug?" Mark asked.

"I'd like to see my mom," she replied in a matter-of-fact voice that only hinted at tears.

"We'll finish our breakfast, take care of any chores your grandpa has for us and then we'll go see her."

"Is she going to be okay?" Junie asked, her voice holding a little more of a quiver.

"She's going to be just fine," he assured her. "She's going to take some time to recover, which means not working, but she'll get strong and soon be right back to making you do your schoolwork."

Her little nose wrinkled. "I like school."

"I'm glad you do."

"You'll have to help me until she gets better." Junie said it with a doubtful expression.

"I, uh…" Now what did he say to that?

"You're not staying, are you?" She sniffled, but put on a brave face, a face that should have made her grandpa happy and not had him glaring at Mark. "It's okay. I can manage."

"You don't have to manage on your own," he assured her. He was really out of practice at this parenting thing. He'd visited in the years since Kylie left him, took their daughter and hightailed it back home. He hadn't parented.

He hadn't drawn the connections before, but

he guessed that made him a lot like Izzy. His mother had become a visitor in their lives, not a parent. She hadn't been able to manage four wild Rivers boys and their father.

Izzy liked to manage. He guessed they differed there. He liked to avoid trouble and sometimes he avoided responsibility. Those were two things he planned on getting better at.

"Pancakes are ready," Buck said in a stilted tone that clearly conveyed his disapproval of his son. He put a plate in front of Junie, glared at Mark and went back to the griddle to pour more batter on the nonstick surface.

Step up and be the dad, his conscience told him. What if he couldn't? What if he failed and let her down?

But wouldn't he be failing her if he left and didn't help?

"Junie, I'll be here to help you with your homework. Until your mom is on her feet and able to take care of things, I'll be here."

"Hmmph," from Buck.

Mark brushed a hand through his still tangled curls and tried to gather his thoughts and skills as a parent.

"We're going to be fine. Your mom is going to be fine."

"Am I staying with you?" Junie asked. "Or Aunt Parker? She dropped me off because she had to work and so does Uncle Matthew. They have Faith. You're her uncle, but you haven't met her."

The baby girl, Faith. No, Mark hadn't met her, but he knew the story. About eighteen months earlier, the little girl had been abandoned in the back of Matthew's truck. Newborn, fighting for her life, and her mom, fighting her own poor odds, had left her to be found by someone who would care for her.

His thoughts had meandered like a kid on a country road. He realized that both Buck and Junie were staring at him, waiting for some kind of response.

"Oh, yes, of course you can stay with me." His heart gave a hard thump at the thought. There were so many ways he could mess this up, and she was the one reason to not mess up.

"Okay, that's settled," she said with a tilt of her chin. "Now we need to figure out the coffee shop. Someone is going to have to open that place up."

"I'm sure it'll be fine until your mom is up and around."

She gave him a hard stare and then proceeded to tell him why it wouldn't be okay for the coffee shop to remain closed. He listened, heartsick at the explanation about her grandma Mindy and the help she needed to be well. Of course Kylie provided the money and the help. Of course she needed the coffee shop up and running.

For years, Kylie had been his best friend. He'd promised to make her life better, to protect her, to cherish her. He'd let her down in so many ways.

KYLIE BLINKED A few times and then opened her eyes to see a little face peering into hers. She smiled and reached to touch her daughter's precious face.

"Mommy," Junie whispered, and then she cried.

"Oh, honey, I'm here and I'm okay. I promise you I'm going to be just fine."

Junie climbed into the bed with her, and Kylie didn't object, even though it hurt like fire to have her daughter curled against her side. She leaned in, pressing her lips to Junie's curly, dark hair. She glanced at the man who stood awkwardly near the window, not really a part of their lives and yet, somehow, a part of their current situation.

She was torn. She wanted him here because he'd always been with her in the hard times. She wanted him gone because she didn't want to start relying on him, only to have him walk away. Or worse.

"How are you doing?" he asked. "Are you in pain? Do you need anything?"

He was unsure, she realized. His confidence had taken a beating. It showed in his eyes, in the way he shifted and fidgeted. Once upon a time, she would have found his uncertainty cute. She could no longer care for him. She just couldn't allow herself to feel. Not for him.

"I'm doing okay," she assured him. "I have to get up and walk."

"Why?"

"They want me to keep moving." She didn't want to move. She wanted to stay still. Now she wanted to cuddle with Junie and pretend everything was okay. She wasn't okay. She was very sick. Weak and shaky with a fever that came and went.

"Let me help," he offered.

"Help me walk?"

"Of course." He smiled down at Junie. "Keep the bed warm?"

Junie nodded and curled up on her side, reaching for the remote. "I'll watch television."

Kylie didn't want his help. She didn't want to hold his hand and lean on him. How could she say no? He was there, at her side, holding her as she slid out of the bed, pushed her feet into the hospital slippers and pulled closed the robe that Parker had brought in a bag that morning. Parker always thought about the little things. A soft nightgown, a robe, sweatpants and T-shirts, toiletries. And chocolate.

There were roses, too. Those had been sent by Mark. The over-the-top bouquet had arrived just before he'd shown up with Junie. Roses, baby's breath and daisies. She understood the combination. He'd always said she was his classy country girl—daisies and roses, diamonds and turquoise.

"Take my arm," he told her as they walked. "Why the walking?"

"To make sure I stay moving. I don't need blood clots on top of this infection."

"Gotcha," he said.

They walked. She leaned against him, thankful that he was strong when she felt weak. He smelled good, too. A mixture of the outdoors, expensive cologne and minty toothpaste. She pushed away the memories of the two of them, how they'd made each other better, stronger. That had been a long time ago. They hadn't been together for several years, and it had been even longer since they'd been good together.

"I know," he said after they'd made one trip down the corridor. "I know."

What did he know?

"I'm sorry, what?"

"Junie is worried about the coffee shop being closed," he told her, his voice hesitant.

"The coffee shop will be fine," she assured him.

"The money you get for child support and alimony. She said it goes into an account for her, a trust. And it goes to a home for her grand-mother, Mindy."

This wasn't the conversation she wanted to have, not today. Maybe not ever. It had stopped being his business. Except now, Junie had made it his business.

"Mark, she's my mother." Not that she owed him explanations. "Junie doesn't go without. I don't take from what you send for her."

"I know that." He sighed, the sound filled

with frustration. "I know she's your mom, and I know you wouldn't take from Junie. It's just that I think of how she treated you and the danger she put you in."

"I can't punish her for being an addict."

They both faltered as they walked the hall. She felt his footsteps hesitate. Hers also slowed. They clung to one another, and she didn't want to cling. She couldn't undo their past, either, pretending it had never happened. Junie lived as proof of the love they'd shared. Junie was the reason Kylie needed real boundaries between herself and this man—because he'd devastated them once, and he could so easily do it again.

She wouldn't allow Junie to live the life she'd lived with her own mother. Speaking of Mindy brought it all back, reminding her of the reasons she'd left him.

"I'm sorry," he said. "I would have given you more had I known you were paying for her home. I'll take care of it from this point on."

"It's my responsibility," she argued.

"I know that I can't be the husband you deserve, but I can at least be a friend. Let me be that for you and let me take care of the cost of the home. Is it an apartment?"

She shook her head, again, near tears. Her

legs were weak, and her body ached. She made the slow turn back to her room, trying to order her thoughts, to think about how it would work out if he were her friend.

She knew they couldn't go back, but going forward, perhaps they could build a relationship that benefited their daughter and made it easier for them to communicate.

"It's an apartment in an assisted living facility for people who can live on their own but with daily help," she explained. "It's important that she is cared for. She is damaged, Mark. She's always been damaged. I don't know how I survived her, but she didn't survive her parents. It's a cycle that I don't want to repeat."

"I know." He kept a strong arm around her, supporting her. She relaxed, allowing herself to feel comforted by his nearness. "We will figure this out, Kylie. I'll make sure everything is paid for. I don't want you to worry. I just want you to take time to get healthy."

"I don't want you to feel as if you're responsible for this. I have the coffee shop, and I can afford to care for my mother."

"Stop being stubborn," he told her with that charming grin of his. "I want to help you. I owe you so much."

She took that back, the charming part. The grin, the expression, had changed. He wasn't carefree, charming the world with his music and his smiles. His eyes wore the tired expression of someone who had fallen hard. He also cared. No matter what had happened between them, he cared about her, about his daughter. He just hadn't been good at showing them that side of himself.

Maybe someday they'd be friends again. She might like it if that happened. He'd been a good friend.

"I'm going to hire someone to help at the coffee shop," he told her. All of her warm fuzzy feelings evaporated. "I stopped by and put up a sign."

"You can't do that. It's my coffee shop."

"And you want to keep it going. You're not going to be able to open, and you told me the town is planning a special Valentine's Day celebration."

"They are, we are. I can still do this."

"In a month, or however long it is until this festival, you think you can be healthy and able to do this on your own?"

She pulled free from his arms and nearly collapsed in the chair near the window. Her body trembled from the exertion of the short walk down the hall. Mark grabbed the extra blanket, folded at the bottom of the bed, and shook it loose to drape over her.

"Valentine's Day in Sunset Ridge," she explained. "It's another project to bring people to town. A tent on the square with lights and live music. A special dinner at Chuck's, also at my place. There will be vendors with different treats and crafts."

"I'll do what I can to help," he assured her.

"Thank you," she said.

"That wasn't so hard, now was it?" Junie said it from her place on the bed, a giggle punctuating the statement. She remained glued to the television, but she'd obviously been listening.

"Now where did you learn that?" Mark asked his daughter as he picked her up, tickling her until she belly laughed.

"From my grandpa Buck. He says it every time I do a chore for him."

"Grandpa Buck, huh?" Mark looked surprised, and for a moment, something like anger flashed in his eyes. "I'm glad he's teaching you to do some chores."

"Did he teach you chores?" Junie asked, all six-year-old innocence and trust.

"In a way," Mark answered. Buck hadn't really taught his boys; he'd just expected them to do what needed to be done. Junie didn't need those stories.

"Did he make you chocolate-chip pancakes?" Junie continued, unaware.

"He didn't. He made other things, though,"

"Like what?" Junie remained in his arms, her arms around his neck, her head back to watch as he replied.

"Hmmm, let me think." Mark paused for a moment, and then he grinned. "He made a pretty decent fried bologna sandwich. Matthew made the pancakes."

"Did you cook?" Junie quizzed, unwilling to let go of her father and the stories of his childhood.

"I did," Mark said with a grin and a wink. "Grilled peanut butter and jelly."

"What is that?"

"I'll make you one. Maybe if we can't find help for the coffee shop, we'll just open up and make grilled PB and J with coffee."

Junie laughed at that. "Daddy, you're silly. I'm glad you came home."

"Me, too."

Kylie watched the two of them, father and

daughter, so very much alike. Their conversation, carefree and sweet for Junie, brought complications for Mark and Kylie. She realized the implication of what her daughter had said. At six, she didn't see the heartache coming. When Mark left, there would be a hole. Their daughter would have to miss him all over again.

She should say something to prepare Junie for the day he would leave, but the words stuck in a throat tight with emotion. Mark gave her a quick look; perhaps she'd made a noise of protest. She managed to compose herself, and she kept her misgivings to herself. Mark was Junie's father. No matter what had happened in their marriage, Junie deserved a daddy who would be there for her, making her laugh and keeping her safe.

Kylie wished she could believe in his ability to be that person. Their marriage might be over, but she wanted him to be the father Junie needed.

CHAPTER FOUR

THE SUN WAS a red glow on the eastern horizon when Mark parked in front of Kylie's Coffee Shop and Bakery the Tuesday following Kylie's surgery. In the seat next to him, Junie roused, her eyes still sleepy and her hair tangled. She yawned big.

Man, he loved his daughter. It had taken six years, a broken marriage and a lot of therapy for him to grasp just what his little girl meant to him. No man should have to go that path to realize what mattered most.

Some people, he guessed, did have to go through the wilderness in order to find their promised land. If only he'd realized everything he really wanted had been right there in front of him and he just hadn't recognized it.

Too late, he told himself. He'd realized too late. Now, he knew he couldn't go back. He couldn't claim them as his, because the uncertainties of life frightened him too much. What if he failed them again? The thought made him want to run for the hills.

He'd accepted that they were better off without him. If he kept reminding himself of that, maybe leaving wouldn't hurt so much.

"I don't think you can do this on your own," Junie told him, with all of the wisdom of a six-year-old. She had sleepy eyes and a blanket for comfort, but a dimpled grin that wouldn't allow him to remain in the dumps.

"I'm willing to try," he assured her. He had to try. Kylie had made it pretty obvious she wouldn't take more money, so the only other option was to make sure she didn't lose income while she recuperated.

He would hire someone as soon as possible, but until then, he was the hired hand.

They entered the building, and he immediately kicked up the heat. Junie hunkered down in her coat and pulled a portable heater out from under the counter.

"You can plug this in until it gets warmer. I always sit by this and wait."

"Okay, let's get you warm and then I'll figure things out from here." Mark plugged in the heater and turned it on high. Junie pulled a stool back a safe distance and sat down.

"You have to start the coffeemaker."

"Of course, coffeemaker. I can make coffee."

"It isn't just making coffee," Junie said with a knowing tilt to her chin. "It's fresh roasted from a place in Tulsa. And Mommy knows all kind of tricks with syrups and frothy milk and sometimes cocoa sprinkled on top."

"It does sound fancy," Mark admitted. He was used to coffee from a can that he scooped into the coffeemaker he and Kylie had purchased soon after he got his first real paycheck in the music business.

"Sometimes Mommy makes Cuban coffee. I sip it from little cups she bought online." Junie reached under the counter and pulled out the dainty little cups. "Oh, my schoolwork is in there. Should I get that out, too?"

Coffee, schoolwork, all the little day-to-day things that he'd missed out on. The things he had no clue about. All of the things Kylie had been handling on her own. Guilt tasted bitter in his mouth, but he didn't have time to dwell on it, not with Junie staring up at him, waiting for answers.

"Schoolwork is a good idea." He was studying the coffeemaker, but he caught the look his daughter gave him. She knew he didn't know a thing about parenting, or about coffee. The machine in front of him seemed a lot more complicated than the discount-brand one he'd kept all these years, even though it was starting to clog up and make monster-under-the-bed kind of noises. "About this coffeemaker..."

Junie giggled as she watched him study the gadgets and buttons. "It's complicated."

"It's very complicated. I'm not sure if I can even pronounce the brand." He searched the small kitchen area and found bins of coffee, filters, cabinets of syrups and a cooler filled with all types of creamers.

His daughter moved a little closer to his side. "I'm not allowed to work it because it has very hot water, but I've watched Mommy. You push that button. And see, it makes espresso." She pointed to a button. "It also makes regular brewed coffee."

He saw the switch for that.

"Mommy also makes pour-over coffee and cold brew."

"I might have to stick to espresso and regular brewed coffee for now. I'm not a skilled barista."

The door dinged, and their first customer

walked in, a lady in a straight skirt and no-frills blouse with sleek, dark hair. "Is the coffee ready? Where's Kylie?"

"She's sick," Junie offered. "Hi, Mrs. Potter. We're just getting ready to make coffee. This is my daddy."

"Why, it certainly is. Mr. Rivers, it's good to have you in Sunset Ridge."

"Thank you, but hold the applause because I'm not sure how this coffee will work out for us."

"Do you have any of Kylie's quiche? I like the crustless."

Mark turned to Junie because, for now, she was running this show. She winked and hopped down off the stool. "I got this, Mark."

"Mark?" he called out to her.

"Dad," she called back.

She returned a moment later with a box; his tiny girl with her dark curls in a tight ponytail, compliments of Aunt Parker, had everything under control. "The quiche are in here. You have to put them in the microwave, and they don't cook for very long because they're eggs and eggs are sensitive."

"Sensitive," he repeated. He should have asked Kylie for a list of things to do here. But asking for a list would have meant telling her that he planned on trying to open for her.

"You can't cook them very long, or they get gross," Junie explained.

"Do you know how long?"

The coffeemaker had stopped, and he poured a cup for the customer. She gave it a serious look, sniffed and shrugged.

"If the quiche is a problem, I can make do with a muffin."

So could he, but he didn't have a clue about muffins.

"I think we can figure out the quiche."

He gave his daughter a questioning look, and she just shrugged and dug a quiche out of the box. She wore gloves that were too large.

"Any hints?" he whispered.

"I'm six," Junie told him in an exaggerated whisper. "I can't even ride my bike without training wheels."

The customer giggled.

"Okay, I've got this," he said with more confidence than he felt. "Do we have other food in the freezer?"

"A few things. Mommy usually bakes over the weekend."

She hopped down from the stool and hurried to the back, where the coolers and freezer were located. Mark peeked in at the quiche and waited for the microwave to stop.

When he'd been in rehab, they'd encouraged him to try something new. They'd suggested college classes or a hobby, something to refocus his energies, something other than just the obvious return to his career. They wanted him to challenge himself and also find ways to deal with stress. He'd never been a peaceful person. He'd always been high energy, chasing dreams and running from his past.

By "try something new," he doubted the therapists had meant for him to take on a coffee shop and bakery.

The smell of the overly sensitive eggs filled the air. It wasn't a pleasant aroma, and if he had to guess, he'd cooked the eggs too long. He glanced at the customer, and the look on her face wavered somewhere between sympathy and disgust.

"I think I'll have to pass on the quiche this morning. But the coffee is decent. How much do I owe you?"

"That one is on me," Mark told her. "Come back again, and I promise I'll have this figured out."

Now he knew, two minutes was too long

for a frozen crustless quiche. The only way to work this out was to try another and heat it in short spurts of time. He could do this. After all, it was just a quiche.

Junie returned. "There are six muffins and five scones. That won't last long. We have to find someone who can bake."

And then her little face dimpled, and her gray eyes lit with mischief.

"What?" Did he really want to know?

"We could make muffins!" she informed him with a frightening level of excitement.

"I don't know," he told her, aware of a flash of disappointment overshadowing her excitement. Baking definitely didn't top the list of hobbies he thought he'd like to try. Although his dad had said it was soothing. Whatever that meant.

The look on Junie's face, equal parts hopeful and disappointed, that look might encourage a guy to put on an apron and try his hand at baking.

The front door opened, and a group of ladies entered. They zeroed in on him with bright expressions.

"Mr. Rivers," the leader started, "I'm Marla Goode, and these two lovely ladies are my friends, Lena Pratt and Pearl Fedders. We are members of the Community Betterment and Growth Committee. If it's easier, you can refer to us as the committee." She gave him a quick smile and hurried on as if she feared he might interrupt or kick them out. "Kylie is a member of our group, as are several other local business owners. As longtime residents, we are working to preserve our small town."

"I see." He didn't, but he could guess that the introduction would end in some type of sales pitch. "I'm sure you know that Kylie is recovering."

"We are aware," said Mrs. Goode. "As soon as she is home, we will have a meal train ready to provide food. But until she's better, we were hoping you could help us with our February Sweethearts in Sunset. Isn't that catchy? We will have special meals at our eating establishments, a venue with twinkly lights, music and dancing, also craft vendors and a flower truck."

"Sounds to me like it's all planned. If you need a donation, I'll gladly help."

"It's planned, but we still have much to accomplish in the next month." This came from the taller lady in the business suit, Pearl, her short hair cropped and curly. "We need to finalize the menus for each restaurant and assign a committee to arrange the decorating of our dance venue."

"Dance venue?" He couldn't help but be curious.

"The old bank on the corner of the square," Lena Pratt responded. He remembered Lena. She lived in a big old house on the edge of town. As far as he knew, she'd never married, and her money came from a family trust.

"I'm still not sure how I can help," he said.

"We just need someone to help with a few things that had been on Kylie's list." This from Marla Goode.

"I'm afraid I won't be here." He shrugged as he said it. The last thing he wanted was to be on a committee with a bunch of women organizing an event for a town he'd said goodbye to sixteen years ago.

"Kylie will be out of the hospital in a day or two, and by the first of next week, I'll be heading back to Nashville."

As he said the last part, he glanced at Junie and watched as her expression fell. She blinked furiously and swiped away a tear that trickled down her cheek. He'd done it again. He didn't want this to be the relationship he had with his daughter. He didn't want to be like his father, always hurting the people who depended on him.

More than anything, he wanted to be Junie and Kylie's hero. He'd just never been hero material.

THE ROOM HAD grown smaller since she'd been admitted to the hospital five days earlier. Smaller, more confining, the bed more uncomfortable and the food less palatable. Kylie knew she was becoming a difficult patient. She just wanted to go home. She wanted to be with her daughter. She wanted to be in her coffee shop, visiting with her customers and making people happy with her baked goods.

The door opened, and she sat up, hopeful. And then she sighed and hunkered back down, pulling up the recently heated blanket.

"Sorry to disappoint you," Parker said. Parker, the woman who would have been her sister in-law, had Kylie and Mark remained married.

Matthew and Parker Rivers still claimed Kylie and Junie as family. They were her only family, because her mother, Mindy, was less capable now than she'd been twenty years go and the Duncans had never claimed her.

"I'm not disappointed. I'm just tired of being here."

Parker sat at the edge of the bed. "How do you feel?"

"Better today than yesterday. Now, I'm worried about Junie, worried about my business and the Valentine's Day event in town. I have so much to get done, and I can't stand being stuck here."

"All of that can wait," Parker told her in typical matter-of-fact Parker fashion. "And Mark will bring Junie in later. He's doing a good job, Kylie. She's safe, and she's having fun with Mark and Buck."

"Thank you," she whispered, and then she embarrassed herself by crying. The tears trickled at first, but then picked up steam as she tried to explain herself. It was serious ugly crying, but she couldn't stop.

Parker grabbed a tissue out of the box on the table and handed it to her. Fortunately, Parker didn't hug her; that would have taken the crying to another level.

After a few minutes, Kylie pulled herself together.

"I need to go home," Kylie repeated. "I know he can take care of her, but she'll..."

She didn't want to say it. She didn't want to be unfair to Mark or to Junie.

"He won't stay," Parker filled in. "That's why you're worried."

Kylie nodded and dabbed at a few stray tears.

"It isn't as if I want him to stay." She felt she had to explain. "He's been out of our lives, and we're used to the way things are now. I want him in Junie's life. It's important for both of them. I just don't want her life, and her emotions, in turmoil. I want structure. Ugh, I'm a mess. I just need structure."

Because structure had been sadly missing in her own childhood and teen years. She wanted it for herself and her daughter. She wanted to know that their home was a safe space, there would be food on the table, the electric bill would always get paid and there wouldn't be chaos. There wouldn't be emotional rages and intoxicated meltdowns.

"I understand," Parker said. "You're a great mom, Kylie. You're giving Junie what she needs."

"I hope so."

"Have they given you any idea when you can go home?" Parker asked, changing the subject.

"Maybe tomorrow. They're doing more bloodwork. I've been fever free since yesterday, and I've finished the antibiotics."

"That's all good," Parker acknowledged. "The last thing you want is to go home and then have a setback."

The door opened, and the conversation ended. Kylie brushed away any remaining traces of her tears as Junie raced to the bed and climbed in, careful not to bump her. Kylie wrapped her arms around her daughter, needing to hold her just as much as Junie needed to be held. She leaned in, sniffing Junie's dark curls and the familiar scent of their lavender shampoo.

"How did you get here? Did you drive yourself?" Kylie teased.

Junie laughed. "No silly, Daddy brought me. But he told me to come on up. He had to do something."

Kylie pushed aside negative suspicions.

"What have you been doing today? I expected you earlier."

"We were working," Junie explained. "I got my schoolwork caught up. Daddy isn't as bad at homeschooling as he thought he'd be. And we decorated, and I taught him to make coffee, but he..."

"Hey, don't tell all of our secrets," Mark said from the doorway, where he stood with a bouquet of roses.

"Oh, are there secrets?" Kylie asked, laughing as she tickled Junie in an attempt to free the secrets. Or perhaps she needed a distraction because Mark looked so good. He looked like the man she'd married, just older. Older, more mature, more attractive. He still had the too-long dark hair that had a penchant for curls, the laughing gray eyes that sometimes looked more like silver. Worse, he had that grin, the dimpled grin that undid her common sense.

"We burned the quiche and sold all the muffins, but Daddy can't make very good coffee."

"On that, I'm out of here." Parker leaned in to give her a quick hug and included Junie in the embrace.

Kylie watched her friend scurry from the room, and then she allowed herself to make eye contact with Mark. He stood just inside the room with the hospital bouquet in his hands. It was the typical glass bud vase, three yellow roses with baby's breath and a bright pink ribbon tied in a bow. He gave her a shy smile.

The smile took her back to their childhood and the little boy who welcomed her on that scary first day of school at Sunset Ridge Elementary. They'd fled Oklahoma City to escape her mother's abusive boyfriend, and they'd somehow managed to rent a tiny trailer in the local trailer park. Now she knew the money came from Roger Duncan, her father.

When they'd moved in, Kylie had been so happy. It had been safe and one of the nicer places they'd lived in. Her mom had made promises to eight-year-old Kylie, promises of a better life, of getting clean, of having food and clothes like everyone else. It was going to be so much better, Mindy had promised. It hadn't been her first promise, or the first promise broken.

"Aren't the flowers pretty?" Junie asked the question, dragging Kylie back. "They were for a baby, but Daddy asked the lady to take off the big baby balloon."

Mark's eyes crinkled at the corners, and Kylie felt a little lighter. All because Junie couldn't keep a secret.

"They're beautiful." She hugged her daughter close, loving her so much. "You've had a busy morning."

"Uh-oh," he said with a dimpled grin. "Are we in trouble?"

She shook her head. "As long as I still have a business."

"We didn't do too much damage," he assured her as he set the vase of flowers on the table next to her bed. He needed to stop buying flowers. As if he knew her thoughts, he winked, stopping her objections. "Junie helped me pick these out, and she was a big help at the coffee shop."

"You don't have to do this."

"Kylie, while I'm here, I'm going to help."

A soft knock on the door interrupted the conversation. Kylie called out for the visitor to enter. Dr. Janson entered the room, peering over the top of his black, wire-framed glasses. His smile, kind and reassuring. Fatherly.

"Mrs. Rivers, it's good to see you all here together. I wanted to bring good news before I leave for the day."

Mrs. Rivers. She started to correct him, but chose not to, not with Junie present.

"I like good news." Kylie sat up a little straighter, pushing aside thoughts of being Mrs. Rivers.

"Me, too," Junie chimed in.

Dr. Janson chuckled. "Well, I'm glad you like good news. I also hope you like going home. I'm going to release you today, but only if you have someone to stay with you."

She hesitated, relieved by the news but then worried about the "someone to stay with you" part. Who could she call? She couldn't drag Parker away from work and her family. She could possibly call one of the retired ladies from church. Maybe Lena.

"I'll take care of her," Mark jumped in to offer.

She gave him a quick look, then glanced at their daughter. Junie's face lit up.

"We can take you to Grandpa Buck's house. He's a real good cook. You can sleep upstairs in the spare room with me." Junie appeared ready to rattle on with her plan, but something in Kylie's expression must have stopped her. Whatever else she planned on saying faded away, and she bit down on her bottom lip.

"I'll be fine. And I have Junie."

"I know you'll be fine," Dr. Janson stated, his smile gone. "I have to insist that you can't be on your own for a day or two. I know that Junie is a wonderful nurse, but she's going to need help."

She wanted to go home. Kylie held her daughter close and, over her head, met Mark's steady gaze. He gave a slight nod.

"If we're at Buck's, Parker is close by if we need her." Mark made it seem like the logical choice.

She wasn't so sure, but she didn't have the strength to argue.

"Thank you," Kylie said. "We'll go to Buck's with Mark."

"That's good," Dr. Janson said as he typed something into his phone. "I'm sure they'll take good care of you. Call my office tomorrow and make an appointment because I want to see you at the end of the week. A nurse will be in with your paperwork. I know that you think you're released and you should be able to pack your bag and walk out, but remember, nothing in a hospital moves that quickly. Give them an hour."

An hour. She was going home; she could handle an hour of waiting. No, take that back, she was going with Mark and Junie to Buck's house. It wasn't the end of the world, she told herself. She could handle being with Mark for the next few days.

CHAPTER FIVE

THE WAIT FOR the paperwork seemed to take forever. Kylie knew it was just over an hour, but it felt more like ten. Eventually a nurse brought it and they were able to leave. Kylie found herself in the passenger seat of Mark's truck. Junie sat buckled between them, occasionally looking from one of her parents to the other. Kylie could guess her daughter's thoughts. A combination of hope and worry were darkening her eyes as she studied them. Kylie understood because she'd been a child always hoping, praying, for some stability in her life.

Kylie had given her daughter stability by leaving Mark in Nashville and starting a new life in Sunset Ridge. She sometimes worried what God thought of her because she'd walked out on her marriage, on her vows. She'd had to forgive herself for that, and she knew God wasn't holding it over her head like an angry parent, waiting to punish her for bad behavior. She'd done her best to protect herself and Junie.

She hadn't walked away without trying to help her husband. She'd prayed. She'd tried to reconcile. She'd begged him to get help. She'd already lived that life with her mother. She hadn't wanted to live it with her husband. She hadn't wanted Junie to live that life.

Mark had been in a place too dark to reach. He'd been too caught up in himself and in the bottle.

Yet here they were, together. She gave him a quick look. Heat rushed to her cheeks because he chose the same moment to glance her way. It still tied them together, the chemistry, the knowing each other better than they'd ever known anyone else.

He was better. She could see it in his eyes. For his sake, she hoped he stayed better. For Junie's sake.

"Thank you, for being here. I know this wasn't in your plans."

"It wasn't, but an appendectomy wasn't in yours, either."

Junie smiled at her father, and then she leaned back with a contented look on her face. Kylie knew the picture they represented to their daughter. A family.

For the first time in years, Junie had both of her parents together. What little girl didn't want to sit between her parents, believing her family could be whole?

The truck bounced along the paved road between Wagoner and Sunset Ridge. They were going east, and the sun, sinking now into the western horizon, was behind them. The orange glow settled over the interior of the truck.

"I really could stay at my own place and take care of myself."

Next to her, Junie let out a squeak, but then clamped her lips tight.

Mark gave her a too-cheerful look. "Doctor's orders, Kylie."

"I know," she muttered, not feeling as thankful for his help as she probably should feel. "All of this fuss over an appendectomy."

"It's just for a few days," he assured her. "And it was a bit more than your run-of-the-mill appendectomy."

"I'm better," Kylie argued.

"Yes, you are." He kept driving, and the conversation lagged.

Next to her, Junie's head dipped, and then

she swayed to the side, coming to rest against Kylie. Her lashes brushed her cheeks, and her lips parted on a light snore. Kylie put an arm around her and drew her closer, content to let the moment be, because moments like this were special.

The drive to the Rocking R took twenty minutes. The scenery was wintery and brown with only spots of green to break up the landscape. There were few houses, just long stretches of land. She knew the drive so well. She'd been on these roads hundreds of times, at his side, in an old pickup truck. In their teen years, she sat next to him, his arm across her leg as he'd reach to shift gears. This truck happened to be an automatic, so no shifting required. And this time, Junie sat between them.

He turned onto the driveway that led to the farmhouse that had been in the Rivers' family for more than a hundred years. In years past, the place had fallen into disrepair. But things were looking up for the Rocking R. The barns had been repaired, the fences were no longer sagging and livestock grazed the fields. Those changes had been brought about by Matthew Rivers, Mark's older brother and the new pastor of Sunset Ridge Community Church, a church that seemed to be busting at the seams since Matthew's arrival.

"Here we are," Mark announced as he pulled up next to the house.

He jumped out and hurried to Kylie's side, not giving her a chance to get out on her own. He reached for her hand, as if she couldn't manage.

"Mark, I'm fine."

"I know," he said with a shy grin, looking a lot like the boy she'd known. "I'm taking care of you."

"I can take care of myself," she said. She sounded rather ungracious, even to her own ears. "I'm sorry. Thank you."

"Let me help you," he said in a softer tone. He didn't mean from the truck to the house. She knew he meant to help her in other ways. The business. Her mother. Junie.

There was a danger in relying on Mark.

She slid from the seat, her feet hitting the ground and her legs going suddenly weak. Junie hurried from the truck, rushing to greet the Australian shepherd that Matthew had given Buck when his old dog had gone over the rainbow bridge. The new dog was Molly, or something like that.

The dog raced around in circles, tucking her tail between her legs when Mark commanded her to "settle down, Molly." Junie, like the dog, immediately went still.

Yep, Molly.

"I don't want the dog to bump into you," Mark told her as he reached for the overnight bag in the back of the truck.

"Mark," Kylie warned in a controlled whisper. "I'm fine. Don't scare your daughter or that dog."

He helped her up the steps to the wide front porch of the two-story farmhouse. "I'm not scaring anyone."

Junie and the dog were, again, racing around the yard.

"Do they look scared?" he asked.

"No, they don't." But she was afraid. Frightened by how good it felt to have him near, to lean on his strength, to feel protected by him.

She'd been strong for a very long time. Today she wanted to be a little weak, to lean on someone. It was just rotten circumstances that he happened to be that someone.

Maybe they needed this time together, to heal and to let go of the past, to forgive? When he left again, they'd be in a better place and more able to trust each other. The thought seemed logical and ridiculous all at the same time.

From the porch, Kylie turned to watch Junie with the dog. She tossed a stick, and the dog chased after it, not bringing it back. Junie giggled and called to the animal to bring it over. She said it in a loud, firm voice that the dog ignored.

Junie needed a pet. A dog, a cat, maybe a bunny. A pet, in Kylie's mind, meant messes. Pets could quickly get out of control. One pet led to two, or six. She shuddered at the thought. Her daughter needed an animal, but Kylie didn't know if she could let go of her memories in order to supply the need.

The front door opened, and Buck stood there, once a towering figure, now stooped with age and hard living. He motioned them inside.

"Get on in here. I've got dinner cooking, and I've made you up the spare room downstairs. Less walking that way." He patted her shoulder with a gnarled but still strong hand.

"Thank you, Buck. I'm sorry for imposing."

"Kylie, you're family. Now come on in and take a load off." Buck's way of telling her to have a seat. She would take him up on that.

The aroma of dinner cooking greeted them

as they entered the large, immaculate country kitchen. Mark pulled out a chair at the table, and she sat down. Junie had followed them inside, the dog panting next to her.

"Junie, the dog should be outside." Kylie motioned toward the door.

"No, she lives in here." Junie gave the dog an affectionate pat on the head. "Doesn't she, Grandpa Buck?"

"She does indeed spend part of her time here with us. Don't worry, she's a good little gal and doesn't make messes." Buck had already moved to the stove, where he stirred whatever he'd left cooking there. "I hope you don't mind homemade chicken and dumplings. I wanted something easy on your system and nutritious."

"It sounds wonderful after several days of hospital food, and it smells even better." Kylie didn't mind saying so. Her mouth watered at the delightful aromas that filled the kitchen. "I'd forgotten what a cook you are. I should have known, since you always bring something mouthwatering to our church meals."

"It's nothing fancy, but it keeps me out of trouble, and I enjoy it." Buck didn't have to elaborate. She knew he'd worked on sobriety the past couple of years. She glanced from father to son and noticed the dry expression on Mark's face. He didn't like the unspoken comparison or the reminder.

"Let me help you get this on the table." Mark didn't wait and started to move dishes to the table. "Junie, do you want to fill glasses with ice?"

Kylie watched as their daughter hurried to do as he asked.

It all felt very domestic, as if they did this every day.

They were sitting down to eat when they heard the front door close. The dog jumped up from her mat on the floor and ran to greet whoever had entered the house.

"Anyone home?" Matthew called out. His bootsteps on the hardwood followed the greeting.

"We're sitting down like civilized folk and having a meal," Buck called out in a growly and not-so-civilized voice.

Junie giggled, and Kylie shot her a warning look. Unfortunately, Buck gave his granddaughter a quick wink and brought on another burst of laughter.

Matthew entered the room, pulling off his cowboy hat as he did. He looked the image of an Oklahoma rancher, tall and lean, wearing blue jeans, a flannel jacket and dusty boots. This Oklahoma rancher happened to have a dark-haired little girl sleeping against his chest.

"What has you stomping around like an angry bear after a long nap?" Buck asked.

"I'm not stomping. I'm a big guy, and I sound loud, but I just got a call from our worship leader. He's leaving Sunset Ridge. His dad is having health issues, and he needs to be closer to his parent." Matthew's tone rumbled, but he'd lowered the volume so as not to wake his daughter. "How long did you say you're staying?"

Mark shook his head. "Don't look at me. I'll be leaving sooner than later. I have some meetings coming up."

"It was worth a shot." Matthew pulled out a chair and sat down, his hand cradling the back of Faith's head to keep her from being jostled. "We both know that I'm not in a place to do that job."

Buck had ignored the two of them. He grabbed a bowl, filled it with chicken and dumplings and sat it before Junie. He filled the next bowl and placed it in front of Kylie.

"Grab you one of those hot rolls," he told her

as he moved on to the next bowl. "You boys quit your arguing, and Matthew say grace."

Kylie quickly bowed her head. She listened to Matthew's prayer for the food they were about to receive, and she added her own prayer that Mark's departure wouldn't break their daughter's heart.

After saying "amen," Matthew returned to the conversation. Kylie wanted to tell him to just let it go, but how desperate would that sound?

"I heard you're helping with the Valentine's event in town," Matthew said between bites.

Kylie nearly choked on a bite of roll. "You're doing what?"

Mark's cheeks flushed a deep red, and he cleared his throat. "I just offered a few ideas and some assistance in pulling it all together."

"How did this happen?" she asked.

"The committee ladies came into the coffee shop. They were in a pinch without you there to guide them. It isn't a lot. I'm going to help them set up the music, find a band and arrange for tables to be delivered to the old bank. You know, that place would make a nice venue if someone had the money and time to buy it and fix it up. No reason it should sit empty."

"I've considered it," Kylie admitted. "I haven't wanted to take on more than I could handle."

"Maybe if we find you some decent help?" he suggested as the others listened.

She didn't comment; instead she told herself that he wanted to help and probably didn't see it as interfering. He'd put the sign up to make sure she had someone to take part of the load when he left.

He was temporary.

They were used to living life without him in it.

MARK KNEW WHEN to let a topic go. He hadn't always known, but in the past year, he'd gained some skills that had been sadly lacking for most of his life. Letting things go happened to be one of the new skills.

With that in mind, he changed the subject.

"Where did you say your wife was tonight?" Mark asked his brother.

Matthew had a silly grin on his face, the grin he always wore when Parker or their daughter, Faith, was mentioned. "Parker's working the evening shift. I came over to doctor a mare that got cut on barbed wire she found out in the field and to make sure our new foal is doing okay."

Family. Matthew had been given a beautiful family. He'd married his best friend, and they'd adopted Faith. Sometimes things worked out for a person. Things had definitely worked out for Matthew and Parker.

For other people, the path took a few rocky turns. Mark couldn't blame anyone but himself for the loss of his family and his marriage. Moments like this, his mind tricked him. It felt as if they were still whole. But they weren't whole, and Kylie was no longer his. She hadn't been his for a very long time. He couldn't walk back into his wife's and daughter's lives and take claim of them. He couldn't be a temporary father, a temporary husband.

"Need some help in the barn?" Mark asked his older brother as they finished clearing the table.

Kylie sat with Junie, going over the schoolwork their daughter had done that week. Their heads were close, one dark and curly, the other a shimmering silver with a touch of lavender. Her hair was straight and hung to the middle of her back. He had always loved her hair.

"I'd take some help," Matthew said as he put

plates in the dishwasher. "Dad, thank you for dinner. That was a lot better than the bologna sandwich I planned to have later."

"You know I always make plenty," Buck grumbled.

Mark chuckled at the growl in their father's voice. Buck might sound half mad, but there was an emotional edge to his tone. He liked having them home. The past five days had proven that to Mark. This house felt more like a home now than ever before.

"Daddy?" Junie's voice caught his attention. It caught his heart.

He had forgotten how that word felt. This past week, he'd heard it more than he had in the three previous years put together.

Matthew caught his eye and winked.

"Yes?" He had to clear his throat to get the simple word to come out.

"Can I go to the barn with you?"

"Of course you can come with me." He said it, and then he wondered if he should have given the answer more thought. He'd been playing at being her father for the past five days, but he still had a lot of catching up to do.

He had trust to earn back.

"If it's okay with your mom," he added a few seconds too late.

"We'll both go," Kylie said with ease.

"Should you?"

She sighed. "I need fresh air, Mark. I've been stuck inside for days. I need to be outside, and the barn always makes me happy."

"We can all go," Matthew interjected. "If I'm going to doctor that mare, it would help to have someone there to hold Faith."

Matthew smiled down at his daughter. She'd woken up, and she yawned loudly, reaching to touch his cheek. Mark felt an uncomfortable pain, something that had to be envy. Matthew had walked away from a church that had made him somewhat famous. He'd even written books about faith, about grief, about finding himself all over again.

And yet the smile on his face had nothing to do with anything he'd accomplished in life. His greatest accomplishment had dark eyes and dark hair and dimples in her cheeks.

"I'm going to rest for a bit," Buck announced. "You boys can take care of the farm work."

"Thank you for dinner, Cookie," Matthew said as he gave Buck a quick hug. "I'll probably head home after I take care of the livestock. I'll see you tomorrow."

"Maybe we can go to Chuck's for breakfast?" Buck said.

"We might just do that."

As the four of them, plus baby Faith, headed to the barn, Mark drew in a deep breath of country air. It was warm for January but still cool. The air was damp, and the clouds were low and heavy in the night sky. Maybe it would rain. Hopefully, it wouldn't snow.

"The place looks good," Mark told his brother.

"You've contributed."

Money, the thing he always had to give. Time and labor would have been appreciated, he guessed. He'd never enjoyed visits to the ranch he'd grown up hating. He'd wanted as far away from the place as possible. For most of his life, that had been his goal.

When it came down to it, maybe he wasn't so different from their mother. He didn't like to think about Izzy. Thoughts of her always brought a painful wave of guilt. His nine-year-old self had been the reason she left. Or at least the catalyst for her departure. He'd left her chickens out, and a fox or coyote had gotten hold of them. Izzy had told him he was as worthless as his drunken father and she was done with the lot of them.

Those words had stayed with him his whole life.

He'd only told one person, other than his therapist, about the pain those words caused, the scars they'd left. Kylie knew. Only Kylie. Just as he knew her secrets.

Matthew pushed open the wide doors to the barn and flipped on a light.

"This makes the old barn look pretty sad and decrepit," Mark said after a long whistle of appreciation.

"I hated tearing down the old barn, but with the money it was going to take to keep doing repairs, it made sense to rebuild. I built Parker a chicken coop out of the old barnwood. I wanted something of the place to remain."

"You're awfully sentimental," Mark said with more humor in his voice than he felt.

"Yeah, I guess I am." Matthew pulled Faith out of the pouch. "Kylie, are you sure you can wrangle her? She's mighty squirmy these days."

"I'll sit on the bench, and she can sit with us. Junie can help keep her entertained."

"Do I have..." Junie faltered, probably due

to the look her mother sent her. "I mean, I'd love to play with Faith."

"I promise if you help me for a few minutes, you can also help your uncle Matthew and your daddy with the horses." Kylie patted the bench, and Junie clambered up next to her, opening her arms to hold Faith.

Mark felt the embarrassing sting of tears as he watched his ex-wife and daughter snuggle together with Faith between them. He blinked away the dampness and found a smile.

"Do you need anything?"

Kylie looked up, her eyes brilliant and her face so at peace. Being in her presence loosened something inside of him, something tightly coiled and tense. He hadn't even realized he'd been that way until being around her undid it all.

"We're good," she assured him. "It's fun to sit and get baby snuggles and Junie snuggles, too. I've missed my girl."

"She missed you," he said. "I'm not too good at reading princess bedtime stories."

"You coming?" Matthew had entered a storage room, and he now held a bucket with supplies and another bucket of grain.

"Lead the way."

Matthew led him to the last stall. Inside, a pretty mare, deep bay with a white blaze down her dainty face, snuffled at hay and then brushed her muzzle through the water, blowing lightly.

"Pretty horse," Mark said as he entered the stall right behind his older brother. "You have some nice animals."

"I'm doing my best to build the place up. We owe our kids a legacy and not a rundown money pit with taxes due and fences falling over."

"I agree. Have you hired help?"

He thought about Junie, growing up in Sunset Ridge, perhaps someday having her own place on this ranch. A grown-up Junie with a solid and respectable life that included a good husband and pretty babies.

"I have a couple of guys that I call when I need them. You could always stay," Matthew said after a few minutes.

Mark held the mare's halter and soothed her with whispers and a light hand on her neck. His brother applied a salve to the numerous cuts that wrapped around her slender fetlock.

"She did a number on herself," Mark said, needing to move away from the topic of his staying. He needed to go, to get away from the tangled-up feelings that came with spending time in the presence of his wife—no, ex-wife—and daughter.

Matthew looked up, a searching expression on his face before he shook his head.

"Yeah, rain always manages to uncover old barbed-wire fences. She found this section somewhere by the east pond. Fortunately for her, I was out searching for a cow that I knew was about to calf. Smart little filly, she didn't fight the wire. She stood there, waiting for someone to come rescue her. She was trembling and about to fall down, but she never panicked."

"Would she make a good horse for a little girl?" Mark wondered aloud.

Matthew finished with the sticky salve, wiped his hands on a cloth and shrugged. The two of them had often been mistaken for twins. They both had the silver-gray eyes of their father and his thick, dark hair. Matthew kept his short. Mark preferred his a little longer. Or maybe his publicist preferred his hair a little longer. He could no longer remember what he really liked or didn't.

"She needs a little time under the saddle, but by the time that little girl is ready for a good horse, this one will be waiting for her. I'll make sure she's well-trained."

"Thank you."

"Or you could stay..."

Mark shook his head at the suggestion. "They're better off without me."

"Are they?" Matthew asked. He soothed the filly, rubbing his hand across her withers. "Charity. That's her name."

"Who named her that?"

"My wife." Matthew said it with a thread of warning.

"Good choice." Mark grinned. "I probably would have picked that name, too."

"You would have named her something like Renegade or Goober. I think you had a horse named Goober."

"I did, and he was."

"And yet you poke fun at Charity. Faith, Hope and Charity."

"When will you have a Hope?" Mark asked, now curious about the gleam in his brother's eyes.

"Now that, little brother, is something we haven't announced. How did you know?"

"You're glowing," Mark teased.

"We're adopting a little girl," Matthew admitted. "She's due in about six weeks."

Mark slapped his brother on the back, causing the horse, Charity, to dance a little. "Congratulations."

"What are congratulations?" Junie asked, peering over the top of the stall door.

"Hey, how did you get so tall?" Mark asked his daughter.

She giggled. "I have a stool, silly. Isn't Charity a pretty horse, Daddy?"

"She is indeed. I was telling your uncle Matthew congratulations for having such a nice horse."

"Faith is hungry."

"I'll finish feeding the horse if you want to take Faith to the house," Mark offered to his brother. "Maybe Junie can head on back with you?"

"What about Mommy?" Junie asked.

"I'll walk her back." Mark didn't know why he'd made the suggestion. Maybe the subject of babies had him sentimental? Maybe it was the January night and the full moon. The last thing he needed was time alone with Kylie. But at the moment, he wanted that time more than anything he'd ever wanted in his life.

CHAPTER SIX

KYLIE SAT ON the bench, feeling a little bit helpless as Matthew bundled up his daughter and took her daughter by the hand. She didn't like feeling this way, and it had happened too often in the past five days. Mark had a way of taking over.

"Why did you do that?" she asked as the door closed behind Matthew and Junie.

Mark sat down next to her. They were shoulder to shoulder, so close she could smell the horse scent combined with his cologne, a fragrance he'd always used. It was something wild and beautiful, like a walk through a pine forest to a mountain lake.

He shrugged. "Selfish, I guess. You should be used to that."

"Stop," she shushed him.

"You think I'm not?" He bumped against her, smiling down with a wolfish grin.

"Oh, I know you can be. I also know that you can be kind and giving, protective and..." She didn't want this conversation. It brought back memories of the boy she'd loved, before he self-destructed.

"I don't like it when you take over. Please, next time ask me my opinion on the decisions you make concerning me."

He nodded in agreement. "I can do that."

And then they were silent.

The soothing sounds of the barn surrounded them like a cocoon. Horses stomping, snuffling in their hay, overhead the soft tread of a barn cat running through the loft. It smelled of dust, hay and animals.

The air got cooler. Kylie shivered, and he drew her close to his side, wrapping an arm around her and holding her in a gentle embrace.

"I need to apologize," he said after a few minutes. "That's why I came back. Not to disrupt your life, but to tell you how sorry I am. If you could forgive me. Maybe not today, but someday."

"I've forgiven you," she assured him. "Have you forgiven yourself?"

"I'm working on that. I just need to make sure you are okay, and Junie."

"We're okay." She said it simply; it was what he needed to know. "We're happy in Sunset Ridge. We have our friends and our church. I have my business."

"I'm glad," he said softly. Maybe wistfully?

"So that's why you came to see us, to make amends."

"Steps eight, nine and ten. The rest have been finding my way back to God and my faith. But these three steps are important. You forgiving me is important. And step ten. When I'm wrong, I have to admit it. I think that's a hard one for me because I have to let go of that stubborn Rivers pride. I can't come into your life at this late juncture and take over. You were right to be angry. I was wrong to think I had the right to be in charge."

"This means a lot to me," she told him. "And I'm glad you can see a way forward. I'm glad you're doing better."

"Me, too. The last time I was here, I definitely wasn't my best self." He scrubbed a hand over his face. "I'm not sure if I've ever been my best self, but I'm working on it. For Junie. I guess for you, too."

"Mark…" How did she tell him that he didn't owe her?

"I know, there is no us, and you're not exactly waiting for me or wanting anything more from me. I didn't come here to complicate your life, Kylie. I know that you are better off without me."

She reached for his hand, lacing her fingers through his. It was a dangerous move, but he needed comforting, and she could give him that. She could also lighten the moment.

"About that last time you were here. Wow, you made an impact on some people."

He chuckled. "Yeah, not the best moment in my life. I sang Garth Brooks and fell through the doors of the church. Or so I've been told by my stalwart brother, Luke. I owe him."

"He made a decision that day to get you sober and to save your life." She removed her hand from his. It felt too much like the past, having his hand in hers. "I'm glad he did."

"Same. Do you think maybe someday we could be friends again? I've missed having my best friend."

"I think we can work on friendship. I think Junie needs for us to be friends. She needs you in her life. If we're grown-ups together, her life will be better for it."

"Could I visit?"

"You can visit Junie." She sighed. "I'm not quite ready to send her off with you."

"Wise woman," he agreed. "Let's go to the house. This has been a long outing for you."

"I am tired," she admitted.

Kylie allowed him to pull her to her feet. They left the barn, turning out the lights and closing the door behind them. The sky was midnight blue with a sprinkling of stars. They walked back to the house in the dark, in silence. Mark kept an arm around her, a protective arm.

She wanted to move away, but her heart told her to stay, just for the time being. She lied to herself, saying she needed his strength. She'd had surgery, after all.

When he stopped walking, she didn't protest. When he cupped her cheek with a warm, strong hand, she didn't tell him no. There was a full moon and brilliant, sparkling stars now that the clouds had drifted away. The January air had grown cold, and somewhere in the distance, a coyote howled. Memories were dangerous things. They drew a person in and reminded them of what they missed, reminded them of the good times. In a rearview mirror, everything looked distorted, different.

Mark lowered his head, capturing her mouth

in a kiss that made her think of their teen years and being in love. It was a love he'd misused. He'd wounded her, leaving scars that made love seem like a cheap gift, something disposable to be tossed away.

For a moment, she forgot the heartache. For a moment, it was just the two of them again. Two kids from Sunset Ridge, seeking a better life, the promise of forever, of being cared for and cherished. His mouth cherished hers.

The heartache of being left resurfaced, bringing with it a healthy dose of common sense.

"No," she told him. "I'm not doing this. We can only work on friendship if you don't do that again. I need boundaries."

He closed his eyes, nodding slowly. "You're right. Blame it on the moonlight."

"Or the past," she quipped.

"You're my most treasured childhood memory. I'm sorry that I didn't treasure you as the gift you were meant to be."

"No, you didn't treasure me." She put a hand to his cheek to soften the words. "I'll never allow Junie to grow up the way I grew up."

He whistled softly. "So that's how you see me?"

She nodded, a tear slipping free to trickle

down her cheek. "You're chaos. I won't have her growing up never knowing which Mark will show up. Right now, you're the sober, attentive man that I knew. Tomorrow..."

"I might fall back into the bottle. I know that, and that's why I'm determined to let you be. The two of you deserve the best, and if I can't be the best, then I can't be in your lives."

"You have to be in her life, Mark. For her, be your best self."

His thumb traced the path of the tear that had broken free. In his expression, she saw that he understood. What they'd been, they could never again be.

MARK WOKE UP early Saturday morning. So early the sun hadn't even broken the eastern horizon. The rooster crowed, and in the distance the cattle mooed, probably following a farm truck toward their morning grain.

He'd been sober—he looked at his watch—387 days. Not one drink. In over a year. There were times, like last night, that he wondered why he even cared to be sober. He couldn't have his wife. He could only have visits with his daughter. Three hundred eighty-seven days of clear thinking, rotten memories that couldn't be forgotten and loneliness.

Last night, he'd considered searching the kitchen cabinets for a bottle. He hadn't. He'd prayed. He'd reminded himself why he had taken this journey for the past year.

Sobriety was more than clear thinking and loneliness. It meant fewer embarrassing moments and not hurting the people he cared about. Sobriety meant living longer, watching his daughter grow up, maybe someday being a grandfather.

Last night, his dad had caught him sitting in the kitchen, talking himself into staying sober. It had been the hardest night in six months. He should have known better than to kiss Kylie. He needed to remember that his place in her life could be as a helper, not as a husband. Their marriage had ended, and now they were in a new stage, friendship.

Buck had prayed with him last night. It had possibly been the strongest father-son moment in their lives. It was a memory that would replace some of the fuzzier or harder ones.

He hit his knees again, needing the solitude of early morning prayer time. He had verses that he kept in his mind for moments such as this. He had the prayer that he knew he could always say when things got tough.

"God grant me the serenity to accept the things I cannot change and the courage to change the things I can."

The house was silent when he left for town. Buck might have been up and in the barns, but Mark didn't go searching for him. He drove to Sunset Ridge and parked in the square, just down from the coffee shop. There were lights on in Chuck's Café, which meant Chuck and Jenni were hard at it, getting ready for their breakfast crowd. Their place would fill up with the regulars, the farmers, the town business folks, the retirees. The coffee shop had a different clientele. Mostly, it seemed to serve the people on their way to work in towns other than Sunset Ridge, and it served the local ladies who wanted to gather in groups.

Mark unlocked the door of the coffee shop and switched on the lights. He started the coffeemaker; it had some type of heating-up function. He didn't know what he'd serve, but he knew what he was craving for his own breakfast. Grilled PB and J. Buttered bread and inside, creamy peanut butter and raspberry jam. It was too sweet and not exactly the best way to start a day, but it sure did taste good with a cup of coffee.

He'd just gotten his sandwich off the griddle when the door opened. A woman close to his age, probably a little younger, entered. She had short blond hair and a dimpled smile.

"Mark Rivers! I never thought I'd see you in here." She reached back to open the door. "I brought my dad in for breakfast. I didn't realize Kylie wouldn't be here."

"She's been sick." He probably narrowed his eyes as he studied her, trying to place her. She noticed and flashed those dimples again. She wasn't flirting, just friendly. She looked sweet, the kind of young woman that everyone liked.

"I hope she's better soon," she said.

He made a noise, and she gave him another amused look.

"Jennifer Bryers. I was a few years younger than you in school and not as cool."

Bryers? Ah, yes, pretty girl with dimples and far too innocent for any of the Rivers boys. And yet...

"Right, I remember. Did you date my brother Jonah?"

She turned a bright shade of pink. "Not really. We pretended to date."

"Oh." He'd been right, too innocent for the Rivers brothers. The brief flash of pain in her eyes said it had been important. To her. Jonah had never been good at relationships and still wasn't. Of course, the Rivers brothers didn't have the best role models. "I'm sorry if he hurt you."

It wasn't his apology to make, but it seemed that something needed to be said.

"I obviously survived." She reached to help the older gentleman to a table. Too old to be a father, or so he thought. He tried to remember what he'd known about Jennifer and realized it wasn't much.

"Do you have quiche or breakfast sandwiches?"

"Not yet. I'm going to work on that this afternoon. Cooking isn't my best skill."

"Whatever you have, it smells good." That came from the elderly Mr. Bryers.

"I made myself a grilled PB and J," he admitted as he showed them the plate.

"Is that on the menu?" Jennifer asked.

"I guess it is now."

"We'll take two and two regular coffees. The Kenyan blend if you have it."

"I'll see what I can find."

A few minutes later, he had coffee made. He'd found a big thermal carafe, and he filled it, hoping to serve it to customers if it stayed hot.

He carried two cups out to Jennifer and Mr. Bryers, and then he finished up their sandwiches and delivered those to the table. The door opened to three more customers. He greeted them and headed back to the counter. And so it went for the rest of the morning. Coffee, grilled PB and J, plus the occasional bagel and smoked salmon that he'd found in the freezer and thawed.

The door opened again. This time the customers were his father, his daughter and Kylie. Kylie glanced around the crowded dining area and made a face.

"What are you feeding people?" she whispered.

"Grilled PB and J," he said with a wink.

She put a hand to her forehead in a more dramatic fashion than was typical of Kylie. "You'll ruin me."

"Everyone looks pretty happy to me. I even learned to make a latte. The internet has videos for everything, even this crazy complicated coffeemaker. Now, if you don't mind, I have cupcakes in the oven."

"Cupcakes?"

"Yes, cupcakes. This coffee shop business is a breeze. A guy just needs the internet and some imagination."

"Uh-oh," his daughter whispered to her grandfather. No, not really a whisper, more a stage whisper followed by a definite giggle.

"What's going on?" Buck sniffed as he asked and leaned to look in the kitchen. "I don't smell anything burning. As a matter of fact, I'm going to have one of whatever he's cooking in there."

Kylie ignored them. She greeted a few of her customers and then made her way to the kitchen. Mark watched her go, amused by the worried pucker of her brow. She had nothing to worry about. It really hadn't been all that difficult to throw together some cupcakes. A few eggs, some flour and sugar, mix the ingredients and presto, cupcakes.

He'd enjoyed the process of creating. Maybe baking would be his new hobby.

"What have you done to my kitchen!" Her voice rose to a volume that made every head turn.

"Uh-oh, again," Junie said as she hurried around the counter to see what had her mother so upset. She glanced back at her grandfather.

"Have a seat, Grandpa Buck, this might take a hot minute."

"Hot minute?" Kylie said, releasing a breath between slightly clenched teeth.

Mark's hopes and dreams of winning a television reality show for his new baking skills evaporated. He stood in the doorway of the kitchen, Junie tucking herself under his arm to peer inside.

"Uh..." Junie started.

"Don't." Kylie raised a hand to stop the third *uh-oh* in five minutes. Her kitchen had been forgotten. He thought he had a reprieve, but then realized that wasn't the case. "Where did you get that slang?"

"It's my fault," Mark admitted. "Slang not allowed. I'll do better." And he meant it.

"That obviously isn't the worst thing she could say, but..." She closed her eyes just briefly. "It's fine. My kitchen isn't."

"I'm going to be a better man. And I'll clean up my mess."

The latter he said only for her ears, leaning in close. Close enough to feel the silkiness of that silvery hair brushing against his face, to smell the herbal scent of her shampoo. He'd never stopped loving her. He'd just been really bad at loving her the way she deserved.

What did it mean, he wondered, when the Bible said to love a wife the way Christ loved the church? He needed to do some research on that because he'd obviously fallen short.

"I know," she said softly, her expression matching her tone. She quickly drew herself together, obviously remembering last night and her conviction to not get tangled up in their past.

He had the same thoughts. He wouldn't go there. The last thing he wanted to do was hurt them. The easiest way to keep that from happening was to keep the boundaries between them.

"Back to my kitchen!" She shook her head as she surveyed the mess.

"I might not be the neatest cook, but I know these cupcakes will be amazing."

"But what happened!" She'd always needed her world neat and tidy. It came from living with her mother, Mindy. He hadn't expected her to show up and see the mess. From her perspective, he guessed it looked pretty bad.

"The flour exploded, and I broke an egg."

"The flour more than exploded. This is a

disaster." She grabbed a broom, but he took it from her.

"You're not allowed to clean," he reminded. "You're resting. I'm taking care of business."

"You're going to ruin my business."

"I tried to hire someone," he informed her. "One girl applied, and I didn't feel comfortable with the situation."

"Young?"

"Yes, and maybe infatuated."

"Well, you are cute." She closed her eyes and bit down on her bottom lip. "I didn't say that."

"No take backs," he said. "You're pretty cute yourself."

She walked away from him, swiping her hand over the flour-covered countertops. "Stop being charming and funny or this won't work."

"Got it, no funny or charming. I'll scowl and look unkempt."

"You could cut your hair," she suggested.

"Not happening." He swept up the floor while she wiped down the counters.

"One thing you have to learn is that when you bake, it's easier to clean as you go."

"Taking notes," he promised.

"Good," she said, and then her face scrunched up a little. She reached for the counter.

He hurried to her side and wrapped an arm around her too-thin waist. "Sit down."

"It was just a twinge."

He didn't buy that. "You have to rest. I've got this."

"I know you do." She looked around the kitchen. "Kind of. It's just, I need to get back on my feet before you have to leave because I'm sure you didn't intend to come here and play chef, or nursemaid."

"I'm up to the challenge."

"The longer you stay, the harder this is going to be. We can't pretend we're okay, or that we're the kids we used to be. Too much has happened."

"Okay." He had no choice but to agree with her. He had appointments in Nashville. She had good reasons for keeping the walls between them. "Then let's get the word out so we can find someone to help you."

"I will. I have a couple of women from church that I can call." She stood to get herself a bottle of water. He worried that the minute he wasn't watching, she'd overdo it.

The timer on the stove went off. He hurried to take the cupcakes out, praying they wouldn't be burnt and that she might be a little impressed.

"I don't serve cupcakes," she told him as he put the pan on the top of the stove.

"Well, this week you might have to because there's nothing else, except my special sandwich."

She wrinkled her nose at his creation.

"They're only a little brown," he defended.

"They're vanilla, right?"

"Yes, they are, but..." He laughed as she pried a cupcake from the pan. "This is why you have to hire someone. You can't have a coffee shop where your menu consists of burnt cupcakes and grilled sandwiches. In my defense, I followed the directions, even on the time they were supposed to be in the oven."

"I rarely follow those directions. I set the timer for five minutes sooner, sometimes ten, check the product and reset the timer accordingly."

"According to what?"

"To how done they are. Like these cupcakes. For these, I would have set the timer for fifteen minutes. The recipe probably said twenty or twenty-five."

"You are correct."

"When they're done, cupcakes and cakes bounce back when you touch them. So do pancakes."

"Got it, bounce back. Or the toothpick method?"

"Or that." She surveyed the brown cupcakes. "No worries, I'm going to stick around. Junie wanted to spend time with you, and she should."

He liked that idea, of Junie and Kylie hanging out with him. For most of Junie's life, he'd been an absent father, a statistic of the modern age. He hadn't read bedtime stories or said her prayers with her. He hadn't taken her to the princess dances or to gymnastics lessons. He hadn't done any of the stuff that mattered; he'd just sent the checks that paid for it.

Princess dances. The thought came to him with an idea because, just once, he should be here for the dance, to escort his daughter. He needed to be more present in her life. He could help create something that would make every little girl in town feel like a princess, including Junie. And he could be here to escort her, as a father should.

If he helped organize Valentine's Day in Sunset Ridge, as well as a princess ball for younger attendees, he'd have to spend time in Sunset Ridge. He'd have to spend time with Junie, and with Kylie. That meant he'd be back in a matter of weeks. He started thinking about the things he needed to take care of in Nashville, appointments that had already been set up. As fast as his thoughts went in that direction, he yanked them to a halt. Making amends meant doing things better, not just asking for forgiveness. If he played the game that way, he'd always be asking for forgiveness.

He needed to be present in his own life and his daughter's life.

For the past dozen years, he'd been selfishly drowning himself in booze and chasing a career that he thought made him somebody. He hadn't realized that the most important person he could be was the person Junie called Daddy. He should have been the most important person to Kylie, the husband she deserved. He'd lost that opportunity, but he still had a chance with Junie.

He guessed there was a song in there, somewhere. A song about the important things in life and the mistake of chasing after the wrong things. He would never love another, but he wasn't good enough for the one he loved.

"Hey, I could use some help out here." Buck stepped into the kitchen. "And there's a lady asking to talk to you about a kitten you wanted."

"I'll be right out." He avoided looking at Kylie. He hadn't expected the kitten to show up here.

Kylie gave him a sharp look and started to say something. He hurried from the kitchen to avoid having to explain.

In retrospect, the kitten might have been a mistake. A man making amends didn't want to just keep adding things to the list that he needed to apologize for.

CHAPTER SEVEN

KYLIE MADE THE decision to go home Saturday evening. It had been over a week since the surgery. Her follow up appointment had gone well, and she felt much better. She could manage on her own. She wanted her house, her bed, her comfy chair. She wanted her space. It had taken a bit to convince Mark, but she'd finally helped him to see that they needed to get back to their own lives.

When they pulled to her front door, her heart exhaled. Everything inside her relaxed. For the first time in days, she felt peace. She was home. She loved the grand old house with its curving staircase to the second floor, the high ceilings of the foyer, the dining room with floor-to-ceiling windows that overlooked the park-like backyard. The house had dignity, something her life had been sadly missing for so many years.

It was borrowed dignity; she knew that.

She'd bought this home, needing a place to call her own, even though it had belonged to people she envied and resented. A little part of her had thought that maybe owning this house would make her better, more acceptable…a part of their lives.

She tried to picture a cat in her peaceful world.

Cats looked dignified, but they weren't. Cats meowed in a way that sounded like the feline equivalent of howling. They also ransacked the house, shredded furniture and carpets, and they were picky.

"You okay?" Mark asked as he took his keys from the ignition of the truck.

They couldn't have this conversation. He noticed the direction of her gaze and so did Junie. She sat between her parents, the cat carrier in her lap. They'd picked the animal up after leaving the ranch. Her first inclination had been to tell Mark to keep the cat, but she'd caved because the kitten was important to her daughter.

Junie gave her a cheerful look, cheeks dimpling. "I promise to take care of her."

"I know you will," Kylie said, and the delighted look on her daughter's face made her decision concerning the kitten a little easier.

Once upon a time, before her mother started

hoarding animals, Kylie had loved kittens, too. Junie shouldn't have to pay the price for Kylie's own childhood trauma. It wasn't fair. She'd given herself that pep talk at the coffee shop when she learned that Mark had arranged for their daughter to have the animal.

"Let's go inside," she said as she pushed the door open. "I feel like we've been gone forever."

"We were..." Junie started, but then she clamped her mouth shut.

"You were what?" Kylie asked.

"We were going to..." Junie looked from her mother to her father. "I thought we were staying longer with Grandpa Buck and my dad."

Kylie had a distinct feeling that Junie had wanted to say something more than that.

"I'm sure Grandpa Buck will be glad to get his house back. And your father is leaving. We already discussed that."

"But I'll be back," he quickly added.

Junie started to pout, but she pulled herself together. Her liquid gaze focused on her father. "I liked doing school and baking with you."

"I loved it more than anything in life," Mark answered.

Kylie could see that he meant it. He'd been

gone for so long, and now that he had bounced back into their lives, she wanted him to be this person for Junie. She wanted him to show up and to do the little things, as well as the big.

He carried her suitcase up the front steps and waited as she unlocked the door. The cat cried from inside the carrier, and Junie hopped around impatiently. It gave her more than a little thrill to know that Junie had a home she loved, a life she loved. Kylie had done what she set out to do: she'd given her child happiness and stability.

She pushed the door open, and they entered. Her senses were assaulted by the smell of cleaning supplies and flowers. She stepped a little farther into the house. Everything gleamed. She dropped her keys, and Mark stooped to pick them up for her.

There were flowers. So many flowers. She started laughing, and she laughed until she cried. "What in the world?"

"We surprised you!" Junie jumped around, jostling the cat carrier. The feline inside gave a startled yowl.

"You definitely surprised me. I didn't expect this."

"It's okay?" Mark asked, looking unsure of himself.

"It's definitely okay. You did this?"

"I hired a cleaning crew that Parker recommended. I would have done it myself, but it wouldn't have been this clean."

"It doesn't matter," Kylie assured him. "I love it."

"Let's get you comfortable," he said as his hand went to the small of her back. "Living room?"

"My sitting room. That's where we spend most of our time. The room has magnificent windows." She'd picked furniture in pastel colors and wall hangings in floral prints. Everything in the room spoke of comfort. It was welcoming and warm.

"You've always loved this old house," Mark said as she led him through the house to the room in question.

"I had an unhealthy obsession with this house," she corrected.

"Because of who he was."

They didn't say his name or discuss it. They both knew what she'd thought about the family that lived in this house, the father that lived here, giving his children everything while she had nothing. That man was the reason her mother had dragged them to Sunset Ridge, probably hoping he'd do something more for them than buy the rundown trailer.

"Can I take my kitten upstairs to my room?" Junie asked.

"Yes, but don't forget that he has a litterbox and litter in the truck that need to be set up before he has an accident. You have to take care of him. Fill up his water bowl and give him food."

"I will, Mommy. I love you." Junie gave Kylie a quick hug, then she turned to Mark, and the hug she gave held on a little longer. Kylie feared for her daughter, for her tender heart that loved her daddy so much.

Her own heart had been trampled by him.

"I have a healthier attitude these days," she informed him as they entered the sitting room. "I went to him. It was two years ago. He and his wife live in Tulsa. I drove up there by myself, and I told him what I thought and how I felt about him."

"What did he say? How did he react?"

"He didn't deny that I'm his daughter. He simply doesn't want anything to do with me. I get that—he doesn't have a bond with me. I'm a stranger."

"He should have wanted to know you. You're remarkable, and he missed out."

"It's okay, really." As she said it, she realized that it had become the truth. She was over it. All of it. She'd given it to God. She'd found healing for her soul.

"Still, I'm sorry," Mark said as he sat on the ottoman.

"Don't be. I told him what I wanted to say and let him know that I bought this house. I told him I forgive him. Surprisingly, that was enough. I needed to tell him that he was my father, and I needed to forgive him."

"You've had to forgive the men in your life who should have been there for you."

"We're living in the present, Mark, not the past. The past holds us in chains and keeps us tied to memories. I need to move forward."

"I agree," he said. "Forward is my only option. Can I get you something before I leave? Or if it would help, I can stay here and sleep on the sofa. You look like this day has taken a lot out of you."

"That isn't a compliment." Her words brought a streak of red to his cheeks, and that amused her. She loved when he got flustered.

She loved it so much, the way she'd always loved him.

"You're always beautiful," he rushed to say, and then he closed his eyes, looking prayerful, thoughtful. When his eyes opened, he'd grown serious, and she knew that he wouldn't be stopped from whatever he planned to say.

"Can we start over?"

"Mark, we ended a long time ago. There's no going back."

He waved his hand around, shaking his head at the same time. "No, that isn't what I mean. I know that I'm not good relationship material. I'm barely able to trust myself."

"Then what do you mean?"

"I miss you. I miss our friendship, the way we used to be. We were there for each other. We had each other's backs. We were good as friends."

"I see." She did, but now that he'd said it, she felt let down, almost hurt. What she should feel, what she needed to feel was relief. He was right, they had been good as friends. Their marriage had destroyed them. His career had torn apart the remnants of their relationship.

"I'd like to be your friend. I want to be here for you. I want time with my daughter."

"Is that what this is all about, Junie? You have had years to be in her life, and you chose to only make brief visits."

"Sobriety has opened my eyes. Being sober literally took away the haze that I'd been living in. I want to be your friend and her father. I want to be a better man for the two of you."

"We can try. But don't hurt us. Don't let us down."

"I'm going to do my very best."

She wanted to believe him, believe in him. She didn't want him to pay for the sins of her mother, but she couldn't help it. Throughout her childhood, Mindy had promised to be better, to do better. During their marriage, Mark had also made the promises.

She would never give him complete trust. He'd had it once, and he'd tossed it away. *Fool me once, shame on you*, went the old saying. *Fool me twice, shame on me.* She wouldn't be his fool.

MARK FOUND HIS way upstairs and to his daughter's room. As he approached the door, he could hear her singing to the kitten. The song ended, and she began to tell the animal a story about bunny rabbits and insisted the cat understand that bunnies are nice and not to be chased.

As he drew up to her door, the story stopped. "Is that you, Daddy?"

"It's me." He peered inside.

He chuckled at the sight before him. She had managed to get the kitten in a dress, and it was curled up in a toy stroller, a tiny diaper visible beneath the pink outfit.

"What?" Junie asked, her brow furrowing in an imitation of her mother.

"I like the outfit. I think the kitten will prefer this litterbox." He lifted the bags of supplies he'd purchased for the kitten.

"I think I'd rather wear a diaper than put my paws in that," Junie insisted.

"Cats are different. They like to dig."

"Is the cat mends?" She asked the question with a little twist of her mouth and a pucker between her eyes.

"Mends?" He struggled to figure that one out.

"Yes, mends."

He must have looked very confused because she made a face and shook her head at his cluelessness.

"Like you're apologizing again." She picked the kitten up and held it close. "I already forgave you. I don't need mends."

"Amends," he corrected as gently as he could. He felt pummeled, truly knocked down by her words, by her expression. Would everything he did for her be something suspect, as if he could only do kind things as penance for the past?

"Is it?" She was persistent.

"No. The cat is for you because you wanted a kitten." He lowered the bags to the floor, and then he sat crossed-legged next to his daughter. "I did apologize to your mother for the kitten. I should have told her about the kitten and made sure it was okay with her."

"But you did it anyway."

"I did, and that was wrong."

Junie tilted her head to the side and gave him a long, careful look. "So, I should never do what you do."

"Never! You're a much better person than I am."

"I love you, Daddy."

"I love you, too, June Bug. I love you so much." Pieces of his heart seemed to fit back into place, pieces he hadn't realized were missing. This child and her love, she was like a healing balm.

"Will you come see me soon?"

"I will. Every chance I get, I'll be here."

"I'm glad. I don't want to miss you."

He pulled her close. "I don't want to miss you, either."

Together, they assembled the cat tower. They found a place for the litterbox and filled it. Next, they filled the water and food dishes. The kitten, gray and fluffy, followed them, watching with curious blue eyes.

"I named him Smoky." She picked the kitten up and sat him on the carpet-covered tower. "He's a king, and this is his castle."

Fifteen minutes earlier, the king had been dressed and diapered and riding in a stroller. His daughter had imagination. She was a wonder to him.

"Are you going back to my grandpa's house tonight?" Junie asked as they walked back downstairs.

"I am. Your mom is ready for peace and quiet."

"And you're not peace and quiet," she said with a sage nod of her head.

"I'm definitely neither of those things."

They found Kylie in the sitting room, curled up beneath the blanket he'd draped over her and sound asleep. They stood for a moment, watching the rise and fall of her steady breathing. Mark looked down at his daughter and saw the pucker between her brows, a sign that she had deep thoughts or worries.

"I'll be fine," Junie said out of nowhere. Was she convincing him or herself?

"Are you hungry?" They'd eaten at Buck's, but he could use a snack, so he guessed she might need something.

"I'm a little hungry. You don't have to stay." She said it in her "I'm almost grown" voice.

"I'll stay. Let me get her to bed. Where's her room?"

"Should you?" Junie asked, still the mature adult version of a six-year-old.

"I should."

"I'll show you. First, I'll pull back the blankets."

She hurried down the hall and returned moments later. Mark scooped Kylie up in his arms, relishing the feel of her, the way her head easily nestled against his shoulder and her arms went around his neck. Her breath, soft and warm, brushed against his cheek.

"She's heavy," Junie said.

"Shhh, she isn't. Lead the way."

Junie trotted off, the kitten held loosely in

her arm, bouncing as she skipped her way down the hall, as if this might be the best game ever.

"What are you doing?" Kylie murmured as he put her in bed, pulling the blankets up to her chin.

"Tucking you in," he said. "Do you want me to sing to you?"

"You used to sing for me," she whispered. "Please don't sing."

"I won't."

"You can go. I'll be fine."

He glanced back, searching for their daughter. She'd disappeared. Smart girl, she knew to give them space.

"Junie doesn't want to be alone."

"I'm fine. I can get up."

"You've been up, and now you're exhausted. Go to sleep, Kylie. I've got this."

Her eyes closed, but not before he saw pain and memories reflected in her expression. *Go on. I've got this.* Junie had been a baby, and Kylie had left her with him. He'd said that exact same thing, and he'd let her down. She'd come home to a crying, hungry baby and a husband who didn't know where he was. He couldn't ask her to trust him, not when he'd been that man.

"I was a fool," he whispered now. "I can

apologize a million times, but I can't take back the things I've done. More than anything, I want you to be able to trust me. I'm sober. I'm going to stay sober."

They'd traveled to a new place, both of them, but separately. She'd found independence and her own life, a life of stability and peace. He'd found peace in sobriety. Parallel lives, not meeting, but side-by-side, going in their own directions together.

"I want you to stay sober." It took a few minutes for her to get the words out. He'd watched her try to find what it was she wanted to say. "But it's hard to trust."

She nodded. "I'm trying."

"I know you are. Go to sleep, and please try to trust me with this. I won't hurt her or you."

He bent to kiss her cheek, and then he brushed back the silvery tresses that fell forward, soft like silk. Cherished. She should always and forever feel cherished. Someone better would come along.

"You should go," she said. "We'll be fine."

"I know you will, but I'm here. I'll get Junie settled in for the night."

"And the cat."

He grinned at that. "Forgive me for the cat?"

"It's going to require penance."

If it made her smile, he'd do penance every day of his life. Instead, he'd do the night shift so she could rest knowing that their daughter was taken care of.

CHAPTER EIGHT

SINGING. JUNIE'S VOICE and Mark's blended together, his gravelly tones and hers sweet and young. The song had always been one of Kylie's favorites, a song about country roads and wildflowers and love that lasted forever.

She forced herself out of bed, and she gave herself grace because it had been a rough couple of weeks, including the time before the surgery, when she hadn't realized how sick she was. A person couldn't have surgery and, one week later, be back to life as usual.

She needed to get back to the coffee shop. She had to find someone who could work for her while she supervised and perhaps worked the register. She knew she didn't have to worry about money, not really, but Mindy was her mother and her problem, not Mark's. She wouldn't ask him to foot the bill for the assisted living apartment where her mother lived and received daily help from an aide. It was a beautiful place, nicer than anything Mindy had ever lived in.

Drugs had taken their toll, and her mother wasn't mentally healthy. She wasn't physically healthy.

A few minutes later, she followed the singing, now a silly childhood song, to the kitchen. They were cooking together. Junie perched on a stool and Mark next to her, telling her to whip that batter up.

"You're going to make a mess of my kitchen." Kylie immediately regretted the words. Junie looked so happy, standing next to her daddy, the whisk ready to "whip that batter." Now her look changed to crestfallen, and Kylie knew that she'd taken something special from her daughter.

She looked at her normally immaculate kitchen, now cluttered with dishes and spills. She liked neat and tidy. The mess nearly made her skin crawl.

But Junie.

Why didn't she bake with her daughter? She used to, before the coffee shop had gotten so busy. It used to be a thing they did together.

"We're making breakfast." Mark used a calm, "step quietly and it won't bite" voice.

Kylie took a few deep breaths and found a smile, for her daughter and for Mark. "Carry on."

"You mean it?" Junie asked.

"I mean it. Clean up when you're finished and don't forget to touch the center of your pancake, just lightly, to make sure it's cooked all the way through."

"If it pushes in, it's mushy." Junie remembered what Kylie had taught her. It made her feel lighter on the inside, to know she could do this. She could let them make their mess. Her world wouldn't fall apart. Later, if the cleaning job didn't meet her standards, she could tidy up.

A dirty kitchen didn't equal her life falling apart.

"We're going to church together," Junie called out as Kylie poured herself a cup of coffee.

"I know. Do you have clothes picked out?"

Junie nodded, and then she licked batter off her hand. Kylie cringed, and Mark caught her eye and winked. They used to make breakfast together, the two of them in their tiny apartment. When had they stopped?

When the apartment became a part of their struggling past? She thought that had to be the case. They moved from that apartment to a pretty house in a gated community on the outskirts of Nashville.

She remembered the kitchen in that big house. It had been a modern wonder with all the bells and whistles of a customized home. She'd loved that kitchen, and she'd kept it spotless. They'd stopped cooking together, and then they'd stopped eating together.

They'd stopped going to church together.

"Go sit down with your coffee." Mark said it cheerfully, but she heard the worry in his tone.

"Thank you." She wandered to her sitting room, still lost in thought. For several minutes, she stood at the windows, looking out at her lawn and wishing for spring, for green grass and flowers. A movement caught her attention. She froze, her coffee cup lifted to her lips, and she watched deer, three of them, wander through her yard. They were nervous, ears twitching, occasionally reaching for a bite of grass.

They were beautiful.

"Mommy, the pancakes are finished. We'll bring you a plate," Junie's chipper voice called out. The deer darted away.

"We'll eat together in the dining room."

The room, furnished with a beautiful white table that gleamed beneath the chandelier, rarely got used. She and Junie typically sat at the bar in the kitchen.

They should eat together.

"Can we really?" Junie called out.

The joy in her tone brought a smile to Kylie's face. Eating together, such a simple thing, and yet it brought so much happiness.

"Yes, of course we can."

She joined them in the kitchen. The pancakes were a little on the brown side. The bacon had been microwaved. The syrup had been poured into a tiny pitcher and heated, drips running down the sides. One of the vases of flowers had been moved to the center of the dining-room table. The flowers were a riot of colors, a mixture of roses and other cut flowers. Daisies, zinnias and lilies.

"This is really nice." She surveyed their hard work, and then she gave her daughter a hug, holding her close for a long moment. "I love you so much."

"I love you, too, Mommy. Do you like our breakfast?"

"I think it might be the best breakfast ever." She hugged her again and let her go.

Junie hurried to a seat. Mark pulled out the

chair at the head of the table and motioned for her to sit. "We made orange juice."

"Wow, that's wonderful."

He winked. "I'm sure it's the best."

The wink might have been a warning. It didn't matter. The few seeds in the orange juice didn't matter. The crispy edges of the pancakes didn't matter. What mattered was the three of them sitting down together, Mark bowing his head to pray over their meal, Junie glowing with happiness. Those things mattered.

For that reason, it might have been the best breakfast ever.

"We should do this every Sunday." Junie made the announcement after breakfast, as they cleared the table.

"That isn't possible. We live here. Your daddy lives in Nashville. He has a job there."

Mark picked Junie up and sat her on the countertop. "I will do everything in my power to be here as many Sundays as possible. If your mom approves, we can share Sunday breakfast responsibilities. We can have breakfast at Grandpa Buck's or here. We'll cook together and clean up together."

"And go to church together?" Junie wanted

to know. Her nose scrunched as she gave his plan serious consideration.

"Your mom and I will work out the details."

She wished he'd thought about that before he made his plan, but Mark had always been impulsive. Not that his plan didn't have merit; it did. They could have separate lives but co-parent in a way that made Junie feel safe and loved.

How it made her feel, that was another matter altogether.

Junie looked from her father to her mother, and then she hopped down from the counter, a mighty jump for a little girl. Her eyes widened as she landed, and she looked proud of her accomplishment.

"I'm going to get ready for church. You two should hurry."

"We'll hurry," Mark promised. "I have to run to the ranch to change, but I'll be back in time to get you for church."

"Promise?" Junie asked, sticking out her pinky for him to hook his through.

"Promise."

Junie hugged his waist, and then she skipped away, singing her silly song from earlier.

"I shouldn't have done that." Mark sighed. "I

get so caught up in being here, in being in her life, and I forget that we're not…"

"We're a family, Mark. We're not a couple."

"I have to go back to Nashville. I have meetings. I really don't want to leave you without help."

"I'll ask at church. I'm sure someone can help. When will you be back?"

"Probably the first week of February. I promised to help your committee, and I'm not going to leave them high and dry. I have a fantastic idea that I'm going to discuss with them today."

She couldn't help but laugh. "I'd like to see you in a committee meeting with those ladies."

"Hey, I'm a good idea man."

"Oh, no doubt. It's just you and the committee— you're you, they're them. It's amusing."

"A little amusing," he agreed before going all serious. "I hate leaving you. I know you're still recovering."

"I'm fine. I really can take care of myself. I can also take care of Junie."

"I know you can, but you're not allowed to drive for another week."

"I have friends here."

Something she hadn't really had in Nashville.

Not real friends. Here, she had people she could count on. People she trusted.

"I'm glad." He took a step closer. "I really want to hug you."

"Hug me?" It seemed a strange request.

He gave a casual shrug. "Yeah, a hug. Just a hug."

She could really use a hug. She took a step closer, giving permission without saying the words. His arms, strong and always comforting, wrapped around her and pulled her close. She could feel his warmth, smell his woodsy scent. She leaned against his shoulder, wishing they could go back and do things right, better. If only they'd gotten help before it was too late.

If they hadn't done things and said things that couldn't be taken back, maybe they would have a chance at fixing their marriage. The things that had happened had ended them. Relationships didn't have a rewind, only a forward. And going forward was all Kylie had in her. She had to live each day in the present, for herself and for Junie. Mark being back in their lives changed everything. She had to learn to let him in without letting him break her heart again.

THE PARKING LOT of Sunset Ridge Community Church now had an overflow section. Matthew would say that God had brought the people. Maybe it had something to do with the gift God had given Matthew. He knew how to bring a message that changed lives.

Mark parked and got out to open the passenger door for Kylie. She hurried to remove herself from the truck, giving him a cheeky grin in the process.

"I'm very accomplished at door opening," she informed him.

"Buck didn't teach us much, but he did teach us that a man opens doors for women."

"Is this an argument?" Junie hurried between them, grabbing up Mark's hand and Kylie's and skipping between them. He'd come to realize his daughter didn't have a slow speed. Junie always seemed to be on the move.

He had also realized back at the house that she'd shoved the kitten in her backpack purse. He'd almost let her get away with it, but then realized that might not be a parenting "do." So he'd told her that Smoky might not appreciate church, especially if she escaped and got lost. She'd carried the kitten back upstairs and returned moments later with her backpack empty except for a coloring book and crayons.

"Good catch," Kylie had whispered.

"This is not an argument," Kylie informed their daughter now. "We just have different opinions."

"So I should open my own doors?" Junie asked.

Mark gave Kylie a look, feeling a bit smug as he did.

"You are fully capable of opening your own doors. You may also like to let men or boys open doors for you. It isn't at all bad for a young man to be a gentleman and to show a woman or girl that she is special."

"Thank you, Mommy." Junie slipped free from their hands. "I like to be special, and I like when Daddy opens the doors. Sometimes doors are heavy. I'm going to find Aunt Parker."

"Make sure you don't interrupt her if she's busy," Kylie warned. And then to him. "She's not wrong—doors can be heavy."

Man, she was beautiful. Her eyes were luminous and tilted just a bit at the corners, and she always knew how to wear her makeup without covering up her natural beauty. She was taller than average, and he only had a few inches on her, so she always seemed to be looking right at him when she talked to him. The moment made him want to reach for her hand, but he knew now wasn't the time or place.

"Mark?" She sounded a bit concerned.

"Just thinking."

"About Junie?" she asked.

He chuckled. "Nah, about you and how beautiful you are."

"Stop."

He did, but he caught the quick tilt of her lips. She might say to stop, but she still loved a compliment. They entered the church together, causing multiple heads to turn in their direction. Mark understood how small-town life worked. By evening, everyone would have a different version of their story, speculation would roam free. Were they together? Were they not? Would he stay or go?

A few would question how long he'd stay sober. After all, everyone knew Buck, and the apple didn't fall far from the tree.

He knew he should think better of people, but he was a product of Sunset Ridge, and he knew how the gossip chain went and the things people said. Not that Buck, and even the four brothers, hadn't given people reason to talk.

They sat next to Buck, Parker and, of course, Junie. She had cuddled up between her grandfather and her aunt Parker. Envy sprouted again, like a noxious weed that insisted on coming up. Due to his absence—and he had no one to blame but himself—Junie had a bond with her grandfather that she didn't have with him. Buck had changed, and he'd proven himself to Junie and even to Kylie.

Buck had managed real change. That gave Mark hope.

In the absence of a music minister, the worship service that morning was led by the youth-group choir. The church pianist did her best to keep up with the guitar and drums brought in by the teens, and she smiled as the trio, two teen girls and a teen boy, led the singing. Mark couldn't be sorry that he'd said no to his brother. The teens did a terrific job, and the congregation—although a few looked skeptical or even disapproving at first—rallied and took part.

Matthew came forward after the song service. Mark had listened to his brother's sermons but rarely sat in church as he preached. The sermon, probably not written with Mark in mind, still seemed directed his way. The verses were intended for husbands. Mark read and reread the Scripture. He'd heard the verses, but he'd never really thought about them. Even now, he wondered how he could ever possibly live up to what Matthew said was the love of God for His church.

"Husbands, love your wives, even as Christ also loved the church, and gave Himself for it."

The verses went on: "He that loveth his wife loveth himself."

He closed his eyes, wondering how often he'd put himself first. His wants. His needs. His career. Everything in their marriage had been about her supporting his dreams, and Mark had taken everything she'd offered and then kept taking.

He'd failed her. He'd failed Junie.

He had failed to be the man God called him to be.

There is forgiveness, a still, small voice whispered to his heart. *It's there for the asking.* As the thoughts came at him, the teen choir began to sing a song about surrender and forgiveness. The two came hand in hand, he realized. Surrender his will, his mistakes, his wants. Find forgiveness. At the cross.

He'd asked his wife to forgive him. He'd

come here to make things right. He'd never done as the old hymn said and surrendered all. He stood as the choir sang. Closing his eyes, he sang the words of the song, and he surrendered. To whatever God might have for him, whatever direction God might take him in. He even surrendered his relationship with Kylie because God had a plan that would far surpass his own.

The song ended, and he still stood there, in awe of the presence of peace that had settled over him. Whatever happened, he knew that God had a plan.

People drifted away as he stood lost in thought. They probably thought he'd gone crazy, again. Matthew appeared at his side.

"What does it mean? To love your wife as Christ loves the church?" he asked his brother.

Matthew sat down, and Mark sat next to him. They were alone now.

"I'm not perfect," Mark said. "I'm going to fail. I'm going to struggle. I'll sometimes be selfish. How can I love Kylie as well as God loves His people?"

"You always have taken everything to heart and found yourself lacking," Matthew said, his hands folded in his lap as if he were praying for wisdom. He'd need it for this conversation, Mark could assure him of that.

"I let the chickens out."

"You what?" Matthew shook his head, unable to wrap his mind around the statement.

"Mom's chickens. I let them out, and she left."

"Whoa, wait, are you telling me that you've blamed yourself? You were what? Nine years old? She made her own decisions, Mark. She and Buck were a train wreck, probably from the day they said their I do's."

"Maybe Kylie and I are a similar train wreck."

"Or maybe the two of you didn't have a clue how to be a married couple?"

"How, then? How does a husband love his wife in the same way Christ loves the church?"

"Well, first, you're not perfect, and I don't think that verse expects perfection. It expects selflessness. It requires sacrifice and putting someone else's needs ahead of your own. It requires listening because God listens to us when we come to Him. When we're happy, sad, elated over an achievement or just needing to unburden ourselves, He listens. A good husband is an active listener. Sometimes a fixer, but often just a listener. A Godly husband meets needs, takes the burdens that are too heavy, tends to his spouse when she's unwell, dries her tears when she cries. He sacrifices his own wants to make sure she feels loved and cherished."

"I'm pretty selfish because I hear what you're saying, but then I'm thinking, so I get nothing?"

Matthew guffawed at that. The loud burst echoed in the sanctuary.

"Nah, you're not God, so you're not expected to be entirely selfless. Wives can be very supportive. They nurture. They care for and tend to their families. Whether they work in the house or outside the home, they're nurturers. We all have dreams and ambitions, Mark. It's just finding a way to be intentional in our relationships."

"Intentional." He ruminated on the word for a minute. Had they ever been intentional? Maybe in the beginning. Or maybe they'd been obsessed with each other, who knew. He picked up his phone and searched the word because he needed more. *Intentional* meant deliberate, purposeful. He got it. Maybe he got it.

"What are you going to do?" Matthew asked as he looked at the phone and the word definition. They both knew what he meant by that.

"I have no idea. I'm supposed to leave tomorrow. I hurt her, and she forgives me, but she'd be right in thinking that she can't trust me again. Our marriage ended when she told me she'd spent a lifetime as Mindy Waters's daughter, lost in her mother's abuse, neglect and addiction. She wasn't going to spend her marriage repeating the cycle, and she wasn't going to allow Junie to grow up repeating the cycle."

"End the cycles, Mark. For her and for yourself. Prove to her that you can be the man she thought she was marrying, the man God called you to be."

"Who is that man?"

Matthew put an arm around him, the way they'd done as boys. "I guess that's for you to figure out."

"Where do I even begin? I love her, Matthew. I got lost for a while and forgot how important loving her is to me. I don't know, maybe I don't trust myself any more than she trusts me. What if I can't stay sober? What if I get lost in addiction and hurt them worse than I already have? Maybe it's better to be here for them when I can."

"Sounds to me like you have some praying to do."

"Thanks a lot."

Matthew stood, and Mark followed.

"Mark, I can't give you answers. I can't direct your paths."

"Of course not. Truthfully, I know that, but it would make my life a lot easier if you would."

"Even if you're no longer married, be the husband, the man, that you're called to be. You have a lot of decisions to make. Start by putting your wife and daughter first. Someday Junie will fall in love. She'll more than likely get married and have children. What type of man do you want in her life?"

"Not one like me, that's for sure."

"Be the dad she deserves." Matthew smacked him on the back, a little harder than was necessary. "Let's go have lunch."

Mark followed his brother out of the church. People were still gathered outside, small groups in conversation, children playing tag. The weather had turned mild, just above fifty degrees. A warm day for January.

A lady with short gray hair and a determined expression headed his way. He thought about pretending he hadn't seen her, but he'd committed himself to this Valentine's project. He didn't want to back out on them.

"Mrs. Pratt." He said it as if he knew and wasn't guessing.

She preened a bit. "Mr. Rivers. I thought I'd check with you about Valentine's Day."

"I'm glad you mentioned it. If this event is large, do you have thoughts about parking? The square will have to be blocked off for the event."

"Oh, now how did that skip our attention? I hope, judging from that smile on your face, that you have an idea."

"I actually do have an idea." He spread his arm out, indicating the church parking lot. "We can use the church, or churches, if necessary. What I'd really like to do is arrange several carriages to drive people from the parking lot to the event. I'd also like to recommend that we have an area for children. A prince and princess ballroom where they can go with their parents, dance, wear crowns and feel special. Also, if we have children in town who would like to attend but don't have a parent to bring them, what if we have assorted costumes and find out if the churches could bring those children as a church activity?"

"Why, Mr. Rivers, I do love that idea. It's

just weeks away, do you think we can find the costumes and the carriages in time?"

"Let me talk to Matthew about the carriages, and I'll take care of costumes. If you could talk to the churches about the use of their parking lots for parking and the carriage rides, that would be helpful. I'd even propose a small dining area with free appetizers, nothing to take away from local restaurants. Perhaps cakes, cookies and chocolate-covered strawberries. Don't you believe that Valentine's Day would be more special if it was about showing love to everyone?"

"Now that's a lovely idea. I'll get back to you in the next day or two. Will you be at the coffee shop?"

"No, I won't. Kylie is on the mend and ready to be back in her shop. But I'll be in touch with you."

What he should have said was that he had to leave. He had a career and meetings. He had a flight to catch the next day. The words failed him because at that moment he saw Junie and Kylie heading his way.

He knew one thing. He couldn't leave. Not yet.

CHAPTER NINE

THE CONVERTIBLE PULLED up to the barn, where Mark had just been contemplating putting his foot in the stirrup of the rangy quarter horse. The gelding, a buckskin with a scarred-up face and whites in his eyes that showed his complete distrust and disdain, hadn't stood still the entire time Mark had been saddling him up. He hadn't kicked, but he'd made the threat that he would.

He hadn't left on Monday. He hadn't left Tuesday. He'd stayed at the ranch with Buck, praying and trying to figure things out. Now it was Wednesday, and he hadn't bought another plane ticket. He hadn't rescheduled his meetings, he'd just promised that he would be back in town as soon as possible. He'd given Kylie's illness as an excuse.

"You're not really getting on that animal, are you?" The woman exiting the car had long dark hair, dark sunglasses and a posture that spoke of elegance and attitude.

Jael Rivers, the youngest and most privileged of the five Rivers offspring, rarely visited the ranch. She had a comfy life in Tulsa, the spoiled, almost only child of their mother. She'd taken the charitable job of advocating for children in foster care, probably as a way to pay back the brothers who had almost landed there a time or two. Buck had always managed to get his act together long enough to convince the state workers that he could handle parenting and his boys weren't abused.

"I'm thinking about it." He gave her a sideways glance and shook his head as she picked her way across the bumpy ground in her spikey high heels. City gals. "I'm surprised to see you."

Rather than swinging into the saddle, he planted both feet on the ground and waited for her to speak.

"You asked me for a favor. Since you rarely call and I'm sure you weren't going to visit, I decided to hand deliver rather than send it through the mail."

She was correct in her assumption that he wouldn't have visited. He had no relationship with Izzy, their mother. His relationship with

Jael had never been a close one, not that he could blame her for that. She was a little sister he barely knew.

"I remember when they unloaded that horse last year. Matthew bought him as a charity case. He felt sorry for him. Twelve years old and a hard life. He hates people."

"Right now, so do I." The words slipped out and he couldn't take them back, nor did he really understand why he'd said them.

"What cat climbed in your litterbox?" she asked, clearly amused by his bad mood.

The saying did pull a smile from him. It reminded him of Junie when he'd dropped his ex-wife and daughter at their house on Sunday, which was the last time he'd seen them. Junie had immediately gone upstairs to her kitten. Now that he thought about it, she'd barely even hugged him goodbye.

Kylie definitely hadn't hugged him goodbye. She'd smiled, thanked him for his help and then followed Junie inside.

"At least you still have a sense of humor." Jael teased as she approached the fence, pushing the sunglasses to the top of her head so she could watch. She had their mother's eyes, hazel. More green than hazel. She had Izzy's refined looks, like she just walked off a model's runway.

"I do have a sense of humor. I'm named after a disciple, not a woman who put a stake through a man's head."

"I can't even imagine why she named me Jael," his sister said with an exaggerated shudder.

Mark shrugged. "Jael saved God's people."

"I'm not a Jael." She said it with a hint of anger that surprised him.

A better brother, maybe Matthew, would have asked her what was wrong. Even if he asked, he wouldn't know what advice to give a troubled little sister that he didn't know all that well.

"I'm not much of a disciple," he said, hoping to move the conversation forward.

"You're still here. Are you staying?" she asked.

"I'm just hanging out for a few weeks," he answered. "Eventually I'll have to head back. I'm hiring a new agent."

"The old one got sick of your shenanigans?"

"Something like that." What he didn't want to admit, hadn't told anyone, was that unless he could prove his sobriety and his willingness to present a more wholesome image, he was out.

His agent had left him, his label wanted his act cleaned up. They wanted proof that he'd show up and perform. He got it. And he would add the public to the list of people he needed to convince. No one wanted to pay all that money for a concert, just to see him stagger around on stage. His band also deserved better. Everyone in his life deserved more from him than they'd been getting.

"How's Kylie and Junie?"

"They're good. Kylie is healing from the appendectomy."

"Which is why you stayed a little longer than you planned."

"Something like that," he answered again. He pulled the cinch a little tighter. The last thing he wanted was for the saddle to come loose and roll, putting him on the hard Oklahoma ground.

She sighed. "Go ahead, ride that old nag."

He didn't tell her that he'd been buttering this horse up for days. He'd been feeding him treats, brushing him, getting him used to the saddle and showing the horse all the kindness he'd never had before coming to this ranch. It had been good for him, handling the angry horse.

He'd been doing a lot that people weren't aware of. Except Buck.

"That horse seems to almost like you." Jael gave the animal a questioning look. "That's strange."

"We have a lot in common."

"Oh, the horse blew his career and his wife left him?" She said it with a typical "little sister" smirk.

"That's harsh," he pointed out, even though she didn't need to be told.

"Sorry, I should be kinder."

"You could be." He moved the horse in a circle and then brought him to a stop, patted his neck and put a foot in the stirrup. The process made the horse shudder, and he reached back to nip at Mark's boot.

"None of that." He pushed the velvety muzzle back, and the horse snorted. Mark grabbed the saddle horn and swung himself onto the horse's back.

The gelding twisted a bit and hopped, giving not the best attempt at unseating him. From the fence, where she still watched, Jael laughed and mumbled something about extra grain if the horse would take him for a ride.

"Thanks for the support," he tossed back

at her as he held the reins and began to talk sweetly to the old nag. Not a nag, just a horse who'd had some rough times and didn't trust.

He rode the horse around the corral, talking to him the entire time, occasionally giving his neck a firm pat. "Doing good, my friend."

"This is boring," Jael said. "So why did you ask me to make this delivery if you're not going to talk to me?"

"I will. I just want to finish what I started."

He loosened the reins and allowed the horse to trot. Buck had joined Jael at the fence. The two spoke quietly, but Mark's father continued to watch, probably wanting a rodeo the same as his youngest child.

"Your cupcakes are cool and ready to frost," Buck said as Mark and the horse made a third trip around the corral, this time at an easy lope.

"Cupcakes?" Jael asked, her nose scrunching. He didn't have time for her. He kept riding, easing into the jolting rhythm of the horse and trying to find a trot that wouldn't rattle his spine.

"He's a baker now." Buck said it with a sly grin that Mark ignored.

"Is he?" Jael cocked her head to the side and then shrugged. "Whatever floats your boat, big brother."

Mark ignored them and rode the horse across the corral, tying him opposite the two hecklers. He unsaddled the animal and carried the tack into the barn. When he returned, his sister had made her way inside the corral, obviously not caring about those fancy shoes of hers. In that moment, she looked at home, as if she'd grown up on this aging old place, rather than the gated property in Tulsa, the house with a pool, a stable and vinyl fencing.

She hadn't grown up dirt poor like her brothers. She didn't know about fried bologna sandwiches, making do with hand-me-downs and feeling embarrassed because Buck didn't always make it home at night.

He knew that Izzy had offered Buck Rivers money to help care for her sons, and Buck had tossed it back in her face and told her he'd take poverty over her money. Mark had resented that decision. He'd gotten past it, though.

"Why this horse?" she asked, her voice softer, her eyes questioning.

He glanced toward the fence where Buck had remained, not crossing and not getting involved in the conversation.

"He kind of reminds me of myself."

She gave a casual shrug and slid the sunglasses

back to her nose. Not before he saw the flash of sympathy and understanding.

"Cupcakes and boxes of costumes that had to be delivered today?"

"For this Valentine's Day thing they're planning in town. I wanted to help." He needed to be a part of this community, a part of his family.

"I'll do whatever I can to help out." Jael picked up the brush and started to help groom the horse.

"I'd rather do the grooming. We're building trust. But if you want to join me at the bakery, I'm going to head that way. I have a lot to figure out and a lot to do in the next few weeks."

"Sure, why not since you've already got me here."

"I do appreciate it." He gave her a careful look, the little sister he didn't know all that well.

She looked tired and maybe a little sad. He did something he had rarely done, he put an arm around her and gave her a quick hug. She leaned in for a brief moment and then pulled away, her armor back in place.

"Don't get sappy," she said as she headed for the gate. "I'll meet you at the house.

"Jael," he called out after her. "I do appreciate you being here."

She nodded and kept walking.

He had a lot to accomplish in the coming days. He now realized he also had a sister he needed to spend more time with. First things first, Valentine's Day. He wanted to make it special for his daughter, and for Kylie. It wouldn't make up for the times they'd lost, but it would be a memory his daughter would have, a good memory. A memory with him.

And Kylie, maybe she'd think a little more fondly of him if he could be more the man she deserved. He might doubt himself. He didn't doubt God. So maybe if he and God were working together, he'd be a better person.

THE CALL ABOUT Mindy had happened an hour earlier, right as Kylie started to think about cooking dinner for herself and Junie. She needed to go check on her mother. She couldn't drive. She'd had no choice but to call Parker and ask for a ride.

They'd called in an order to Chuck's and were going to pick it up and eat on the road.

"Wait, can you take me to my shop?" Kylie

pointed across the square. "Why are there lights on in my shop?"

At Kylie's question, Parker gave a little shrug, as if she didn't have a clue. Something in her expression said she did know.

Kylie spotted the old red-and-white truck. "What's he doing here?"

"Umm," Parker said.

From the back seat, Faith grew fussy, and Junie said something to her about having a special toy that would make her feel better. A rustle of bags and then a twisting sound. The car filled with the sound of "Wildwood Flower." It was a tinny dulcimer sound and Loretta's voice singing of her lost love.

The song had been based on a poem that she'd memorized as a child. "I'll Twine 'Mid the Ringlets." It was melancholy but beautiful, telling of a love that had gone sadly wrong.

He taught me to love him, he called me his flower…

She started to tell Junie to put the music box away, but Faith giggled and cooed, no longer sad. The song didn't usually bring cheer. Years ago, Mark had found an old dulcimer in the attic of his home, and he'd learned to play just that one song on the instrument. She'd learned to sing, just to accompany him.

Years later, he'd taken her to the Opry, and Loretta had been there. She'd signed the old dulcimer for them. She didn't know where the instrument had gone to, but she'd cherished it until it had seemed like a part of their demise.

My visions of love had all flown away...

She needed a new song. A song that brought memories that cheered her, not took her down a dark path of the past.

"I don't have time for this, but I need to talk to him."

"I thought you might." Parker pulled into a space and killed the engine of her car. "Want me to wait?"

"I don't know. Yes. Maybe. Why is he here? Is that man ever going to leave?"

"My guess is he doesn't even know why he's still here." Parker nodded toward the coffee shop. "Go. Junie and I will run over and get our orders from Chuck's."

"That works for me." Kylie sighed, too tired to deal with whatever Mark might be up to.

Since the surgery, she'd felt as if she couldn't overcome the constant exhaustion. She just wanted to be better and to get back to her life. Her very uncomplicated, un-Mark life.

"Here's a twenty for our dinner." She pulled the money from her pocket and got out of the car.

Her shop was unlocked. She pushed the door open and went inside. From the kitchen, she could hear him singing a Kenny Chesney song. He'd always loved Kenny. Someone else spoke, a woman.

"Hello," Kylie called out as she entered the kitchen.

Mark dropped a tube filled with pink icing, and the pink went everywhere. The woman standing next to him, a brunette with pretty green eyes, had the grace to flush a deep red.

"Oh, you weren't supposed to be here." Mark swiped his finger through the icing and tasted it.

"Was I not? As far as I know, it's still my coffee shop. If memory serves, you're the one who shouldn't be here. I thought you were flying out. You had meetings."

"And you didn't have anyone to help you so I stayed. I've been at the ranch, working on perfecting these cupcakes." He said it gently, as if she might be on the verge of a breakdown. She wasn't. She was absolutely in control of her emotions. "I wanted to help."

"And it appears you found help." She gave the woman a pointed look.

"Oh, you don't recognize me." The woman spoke, flashing white teeth and dimples. Those Rivers dimples. She didn't have the silvery gray eyes.

"Jael." Kylie felt like a fool. "You've done something with your hair."

"I let it go back to its natural color, and I stopped perming."

"Oh, I see." She'd been upset to think he had a woman here. She shouldn't have let it bother her. They'd been over for years. Divorced for three.

"I wanted to surprise you." Mark moved, giving her a clear view of the cupcakes. She stepped closer, inspecting the cakes with their swirled pink icing. "Ta-da!"

"Goodness." She wouldn't classify herself as speechless, but nearly speechless might describe it.

"They taste as good as they look." Jael picked one up and handed it to her. "Buck and Mark make a pretty decent baking team."

"I never thought about having cupcakes, I mean, other than the ones you burned last week."

"Cupcakes are always well received," Jael said

with a wink. "Go ahead, take a bite. I had one, and I feel fine."

Kylie licked the icing, ignoring the wide-eyed look on Mark's face. Ignoring, but enjoying. She took a little bite, closing her eyes at the sweetness and the flavor. "This is amazing. The flavor is very unique."

"You'd be surprised." Mark gave a little chuckle as he picked up the tube and began to ice the rest of the cupcakes.

"What is it?"

His brow arched, and he flashed those dimples.

"Strawberry and lime with strawberry icing."

"I never would have thought to put those flavors together."

"It's what Buck had in the kitchen, so I used it. It turned out really good."

"It's very good."

She looked at her watch. "I have to go."

"Where are you going?" he asked as he frosted another cupcake.

"My mom is a mess, and they're transporting her to the hospital for an evaluation. I'm not sure what they're going to do with her."

"Let me take you." He carried the icing tube

to the sink and ran hot water through it. "I can have this cleaned up in a jiffy."

"You didn't make a mess of my kitchen."

"I baked these at Buck's. His kitchen didn't fare so well. I might be able to bake—a talent I didn't realize I had—but I'm not doing a great job of being a neat chef."

"Parker would probably appreciate it if you could take me. Faith is teething and fussy. But do we have to take that old truck? The exhaust fumes…"

"Take my car," Jael offered as she pulled keys out of her pocket. "I'll drive the truck back to the ranch. I can also take Junie with me. We haven't spent a lot of time together, but I know we could have fun."

The offer took Kylie by surprise, and it also caused a little apprehension. She didn't know Jael, not really. Junie didn't know her that well. What she did know about Jael was that she worked for the state as an advocate for children in state's custody. She was young for a job that carried so much responsibility. Parker had told her that Jael had gone back to school and was getting a degree in psychology in order to better help the children.

"Let's see how Junie feels about that," Mark

suggested, and she nodded, hoping he understood how much she appreciated his insight.

When Parker returned, they asked Junie, and she loved the idea of going with her very fun and very cool aunt. As she got out of the car, she leaned in to kiss Faith, and then she pulled the music box out of the bag and started telling her aunt Jael the story of how her daddy bought her this music box and how her mommy had actually met Loretta at the Grand Ole Opry.

"You're sure you don't want me to take you?" Parker asked, even as Faith began to whimper.

"Go home and take care of your daughter. I'll be fine." She would be fine.

It made sense that Mark would take her. He knew her mother, knew the childhood and teen years that Kylie had survived with her parent. It made sense, and yet it created a thread between them, binding them. They had their past, not just their marriage, but a childhood of being friends, of him being there for her, caring for her. All of that past had a way of getting tangled up. The childhood trauma, the love they'd shared, the pain he'd caused.

Yet there he stood, that best friend again, making sure she had someone on her side.

He was on her side.

“Stop frowning.” He had backed Jael’s car out of the parking space, and now he was reaching for Kylie’s hand.

“Why can’t life be simple?”

“Because it’s life. Because it’s messy and unpredictable and full of surprises.”

“Like you not leaving town,” she said, half accusing and half thankful that he hadn’t left. For Junie’s sake, she told herself. Junie had been distraught over his departure.

“Where are we heading?” Mark asked as they drove out of town.

“I’ll put the address in the GPS.” She leaned in and gave the screen on the dash a careful look. “If I can figure it out.”

She fiddled with the navigation system and finally got the address entered. “Thirty minutes. They haven’t transported her to the hospital just yet. I want to make sure the right decision is being made.”

“I know this is tough, but you’re tougher than any situation you’ve encountered. You survived her, and you survived me. Honestly, no one should have to be this strong, Kylie. You deserve better.”

Tears stung her eyes, but she wouldn’t let them fall. She would not cry at the sweetness of his words, the way he said them making her wish they could have been better together. Would a stronger person have stayed with him, seeing him through the hard times?

Would a stronger person have put her mom in a home or brought Mindy to live in her house? A strong person held on to the people they loved and carried them when they were at their weakest.

"Stop!" Mark gave her hand a squeeze.

"Stop what?"

"Overthinking," he said, still holding her hand. "Don't doubt that you're one of the most loving, amazing people on this planet."

"How can you say that?"

"Because I've known your love, and I miss it every single day."

She blinked, but she couldn't stop the tears that trickled down her cheeks. She brushed them away, but more took their place. He always knew the right words, the words that went straight to her heart.

"I can't have this conversation right now," she told him. "I'm too emotional, too tired."

"Take a nap. The GPS will get us where we need to go. And Kylie, I want you to know, I'm praying that I can be a better man, for you and for Junie. I'm still here because I need to find a way to do that for you."

She shook her head, trying to cut off his words. "No. That isn't the direction we're going. I can't go back, not to that life, not to Nashville and not to the fear of losing you again."

"I know that." He said it so calmly. "I'm going to be the best version of myself for the two of you because that's what I'm called to do. This has nothing to do with going back. It doesn't have anything to do with uprooting you from your life."

Words, she reminded herself. He'd always been so good with words. Actions were what mattered.

Actions mattered, and she couldn't deny that he'd been there for her. In the past two weeks, he'd taken care of her, taken care of Junie. The man had even taught himself to bake and to make lattes. She couldn't help but smile as she dozed off.

Thirty minutes later, she roused herself from a short nap as the GPS announced their destination. They were pulling into the parking space in front of the apartment her mother had called home for the past two years. From inside came shouting and then laughter.

Kylie froze on the front step. She didn't want to go inside, to face her mother in this condition. Mark reached past her and opened the door. He stepped inside, holding her hand, tethering her to him and to his strength.

"What are you doing here?" Mindy Waters spoke with harsh tones, her expression wild as she faced her daughter. "I thought you dropped off the face of the earth again. Always a disappointment."

"I've been sick." She held tight to Mark, but she took deep breaths, calming herself. She reminded herself that her mother couldn't help it. Mindy had never been mentally healthy. She had a disease. As clearly as a physical illness, Mindy's illness mattered.

"Mom, they can't allow you to stay in this apartment if you're going to sneak out and use."

"I'm not using. They're lying to you. They say that stuff because they know that I know what they're doing here. They're stealing my money."

"Mom..." Kylie sighed her frustration.

"You could take me to your house. To his big fancy house." By "his," they both knew that Mindy meant the man who was her father.

Kylie couldn't take her mother to that house.

She wasn't a bad daughter or unfeeling, but she knew how Mindy's presence would change things, how it would affect Junie. She wouldn't subject her daughter to this behavior.

Every decision she made, no matter how difficult, had to be about her daughter. Their daughter. She leaned a little in Mark's direction, finding strength in his presence.

"Mom, I think you have to go to the hospital. You're going to need to be evaluated."

"I'm not going."

"You are, Ms. Waters. We've called an ambulance and the police." The nurse moved toward the door, as if she knew Mindy's next move. Fortunately, Mark also moved in that direction. "Ms. Waters, you can't leave."

Mindy began to pick things up and throw them, smashing her knickknacks on the floor. Her puppy dog collection, her Christmas ornaments that she insisted on keeping out year-round and an ashtray she'd had forever because it had been her mother's. She screamed, demanding to be set free.

Kylie felt the exhaustion again, so heavy and so hard to fight. This battle with her mother had been lifelong. It had humiliated her, enraged her, made her run away as soon as she graduated high school.

Now it made her want to weep with compassion because Mindy Waters would never be healthy. She would never know true happiness or contentment.

But God…

She closed her eyes for a few seconds, letting that thought wash over her and give her peace.

She needed that peace as the police came and then the ambulance. Mindy didn't go willingly. She ranted and raved that her daughter should stop them from taking her. Then she started a new tactic, blaming Kylie, yelling that this had been Kylie's plan all along.

They closed the ambulance doors. The police spoke to Kylie for a few minutes, and then they left. The nurse apologized for how difficult the situation had been, and she too left.

Mark remained.

He encircled her in his arms, the way he'd done on so many similar occasions in her life. He held her as she sobbed, finally letting go and letting the tears come. His hand on her back felt firm and strong. He had been and could still be her anchor.

She needed his strength. Today.

"Let's take the back roads home," he suggested after a few minutes of her just leaning against him, breathing.

"Why?"

"Because it's what we used to do when we needed time away from them. We'll take the back roads and open the windows to let the breeze blow in. I'll buy you a burger at Chuck's, and we'll share an order of fries and a milkshake."

"I don't want to share," she whispered against his shoulder. "You're not that poor Rivers boy anymore. I want my own fries and my own strawberry shake."

"I thought you liked chocolate."

She sniffled and then giggled. "No, you like chocolate. I never told you that I prefer strawberry."

He pressed his lips against the side of her head, his cheek then resting there. "Silly girl. You should have told me."

There were a lot of things she'd never told him. She'd never told him that she had always feared she would become like her mother. Her need for a clean, tidy house with no pets went far beyond simply being a clean person. She feared chaos and messiness because what if she let go of her strict and orderly life and everything crumbled and she became Mindy?

On the car ride home, he did indeed take the back roads. And even though it was cold, he rolled the windows down to let the cool breeze blow through the car. For a long time, he remained silent, giving her space and a chance to process everything that had happened.

After a while, she told him her fears and why she needed her home to be in order, why his messes and chaos disturbed her. She explained about the cat because what if one cat became two, then three or four?

He pulled off the paved road onto a dirt road and told her she would never be Mindy. She was strong and good, and even if her life got messy and a cat roamed her house, she would still be Kylie.

He stopped the car, pulling to the grassy shoulder.

"I can't do this," she told him as tears trickled down her cheeks. "I can't be strong for everyone."

"Let me be strong for you. Let me hold you."

She nodded and he pulled her close, holding her as his hands caressed her back. She looked up to tell him how glad she was that he'd driven her.

He kissed her then, and she kissed him back, and she wished they could have been different together.

CHAPTER TEN

MARK PICKED KYLIE UP Thursday morning. They were going to the coffee shop together. Junie climbed in the seat between them, still groggy and complaining that the sun hadn't come up. He ruffled her hair and told her she could sleep on the cot in the back room of the coffee shop. It was a new addition, something he'd bought for her. After all, little girls needed their sleep.

The drive took only a few minutes, but Junie dozed against him. Kylie sat quietly, watching out the window, not looking at him. Because yesterday he'd parked on a back road and kissed her. Not one of his best moments, not when he had made a decision to prove himself to be a trustworthy friend. She hadn't called him out, not really, but she'd grown distant on the drive back to the ranch, where she'd collected Junie and asked for a ride home.

He parked down the block from the coffee shop, saving spaces out front for the customers.

"It's dark," Junie grumbled as they got out and started in the direction of the coffee shop. "And cold."

"It is cold," Kylie agreed, and she pulled their daughter a little closer to her side. "It'll be warm inside the shop."

"I hope so," Junie said, teeth chattering.

Kylie unlocked the door, and they rushed inside, where it was indeed warmer than outside, but not the kind of warm they needed. Mark headed for the thermostat, while Kylie started the morning routine of preparing the coffeemaker before she began the baking process.

"It's good to be back," Kylie said as she started the coffee. "I've missed my customers and my days here."

"I'm sure they've missed your cooking." Mark entered her space behind the counter and saw her physically tense up. He'd done that. The kiss had been impulsive and careless, he realized. She'd been vulnerable and in need of comfort. He should have given his actions more thought.

After checking on Junie, he came back and

shared those thoughts with her. "I should have been a better friend to you yesterday."

"What does that mean?"

"I thought the back roads, some fresh air, that it would help you to relax. And then I let the memories swoop in. Kissing you has always been second nature, it seems."

"Mark, I let you kiss me. You're not guilty here, unless we're both guilty. I feel like I need to apologize because I don't want to mislead you."

"I'm not misled. We should both let it go and stop worrying."

She seemed to agree with him. The expression on her face brightened, and her eyes reflected humor rather than the troubled look she'd worn since yesterday.

"Thank you, for being with me yesterday. And for the drive down memory lane."

"Anytime," he assured her. "I'm your huckleberry."

"I'm not even sure what that means."

The moment lightened their moods and eased the tension between them. They'd always been good together, until they hadn't been. They'd shared their silly jokes and found ways to get through the difficult times.

Until they hadn't.

"Same. We'll have to do some research. What if it means something like I'm going to eat your cookie or take the last piece of cake?"

She already had her phone out, and she shook her head, disagreeing with his nonsense ideas. "It might have come from King Arthur's court, something about how a huckleberry scarf on a sword meant the knight swore allegiance." Her voice had trailed off as she read. Slowly, her gaze lifted to meet him.

"I'm your huckleberry," he repeated.

She shook her head and walked away. He had a bad habit of going too far, he realized, and it hinted at desperation.

"Stop trying so hard," she told him from the kitchen, where she'd pulled out a couple of cartons of eggs. "I'm going to make quiche. You should watch and learn."

"That's probably a good idea. Someday I might want to make you breakfast."

"Stop." She cracked an egg and emptied it into a bowl. The next egg followed. And the next.

"Can I help?"

She slid the bowl between them and then passed him a dozen eggs.

"Try not to get shells in the bowl." She watched as he cracked an egg and opened it above the bowl. No shells. He couldn't help but feel a little proud of the accomplishment. He didn't want to tell her that there might be tiny pieces of eggshell in the cupcakes.

"I don't know what to do about my mom." She'd been silent as she added eggs to the bowl. Now she leaned against the counter and watched as he finished up. "I should go see her. Why does the idea of visiting cause me to be so anxious? And then anxiety turns to guilt."

"Trauma does that to us." He finished his eggs and wiped his hands on a wet towel she'd placed on the counter. "The brain of a child who has suffered trauma is not the same as the brain of a child who had a fairly functional and happy childhood. I'm guessing the idea of seeing Mindy sends your brain into fight-or-flight mode. Growing up, you never knew what Mindy you were waking up to, or what you'd find when you came home from school. Or who you'd find. That kept you stressed out and in a constant state of coping with your life."

"You didn't have it much better."

"I had my brothers, and I always knew I'd have a home."

She slipped her hand into his. "And I always knew that I had you."

He gave her hand a light squeeze. "I let you down. I'm going to do everything in my power to make sure that never happens again."

She didn't respond, and he shouldn't have expected anything from her. Maybe she had the same response to him that she had to her mother.

"If you want me to go with you to see her, I will."

"Maybe," she said. She had slipped her hand free from his and now stood at the fridge with the door open. "What did I want from here?"

"One of my amazing cupcakes?"

She shook her head. "Not this early in the morning. Oh, ingredients for the quiche."

He glanced at the clock on the wall. "Should I turn on the lights and open up?"

"That would be good. If we have customers, the quiche will be ready in thirty minutes. I have French toast, too."

She'd mixed the ingredients at her house before they'd left. Eggs, cream, vanilla, a little sugar and a dash of salt. He had always loved watching her cook and eating her creations. It made sense that she would have this place with her name on it.

The first customers were already at the door, waiting to be let in. He ushered them inside to the warmth of the coffee shop. Kylie came out of the kitchen, drying her hands on a towel. Her welcoming look for the customers almost brought him to his knees. The way her face lit up when she saw her people, her customers, it made him a little envious.

He wanted that look for himself.

"Diana and Cora, it's so good to see you all." She moved around the counter to give the two ladies a quick embrace. "What can I get for you today?"

"We're so glad to see you open again. We were on our way to work and thought we'd make a turn around the square, just in case." This from the lady with a very immaculate shoulder-length hairdo.

He guessed from Kylie's greeting that she was Diana and the other woman was Cora.

The woman, Diana, gave him a sharp look. That brought a moment of discomfort. He could hurry to the back, pretending to help cook, or he could smile and move past what was probably well-deserved censure. Truth be told, he'd been deserving of more than those caustic looks.

Kylie grabbed an order pad.

Watching her, he saw what others probably did not. She put on a good front, but she still needed time to recover. Time that she wouldn't take because she knew that he would be leaving and because this coffee shop meant freedom from him.

After taking the order, she hurried to the kitchen and proceeded to make the French toast and bacon that her customers had ordered.

"Let me help." He moved in close. "If I can grill a PB and J, I can make French toast. Tell me what to do."

He thought she'd tell him that she could do it herself. Instead, she stepped aside and motioned toward the loaf of bread and the dish containing the dipping ingredients.

"Soak the bread, but not too long or it will fall apart. The key is just enough."

"What is just enough?" he asked, amused because no one could describe "just enough." He'd grown up with Buck telling him, "Do it until it's finished. You'll be able to tell."

Maybe Buck, who'd become quite a cook, should be the one helping.

"You'll know."

He chuckled at the answer.

"What's so funny?"

"I just knew that's what you'd say. Okay, I'll know. And then?"

"Put it on the griddle, not too hot. It needs to cook all the way through, not just get toasty on the outside."

"I can do this. You make the coffee, and I'll play chef. I wish I had a chef's hat."

"Is that a dream of yours?" she asked as she turned to go. She stopped and opened an overhead cabinet. For a moment, she rummaged and he ignored her because French toast seemed to be finicky and he didn't want to mess up.

She touched his head, and he realized she was putting a hairnet over his hair. And then she giggled and slid a hat on top. He moved his head sideways and felt the sway.

"Is it a real chef's hat?"

"It is. A friend bought it for me, but it seemed a little out of place in Sunset Ridge. But on you, perfection."

"Now I'm legit," he said as he went back to the French toast. "The hat is going to make everything I cook taste better."

"Of course it is." She kissed his cheek and hurried off to make coffee.

He made perfect French toast. He couldn't help but be a little proud of himself. And then a customer came in and ordered his special grilled PB and J. He heard the order and then heard Kylie groan. As someone else ordered the same, he heard her say, "You've got to be kidding me."

"Put it on the menu, Kylie." The customer sounded amused as he made the suggestion.

"You're killing me." She didn't look mad, but she managed a frown as she put in the order. "For real, I'm a classy coffee shop with a small but tasty menu. That's what the *Wagoner* newspaper reported when they did an article on local eating establishments. I have amazing coffee and tasty fare."

"Now you have something no one else has." He winked as he said it.

From the doorway of the inner office, he heard Junie say that she liked his sandwiches a lot. Earlier, he'd put her to work on math and reading, subjects that she breezed through with very little help. She was smart, like her mom. He guessed homeschooling wasn't for everyone, but for his daughter, it seemed to be the right choice.

"I'll make you one," he called out to his daughter.

"It's a mutiny," Kylie laughed as she walked away.

"But you like it," he retaliated.

She stopped at the door to give him a look, one that he couldn't decipher. Maybe because she couldn't decide what she felt about him?

He hoped, no, he prayed, that somewhere in her heart, she was beginning to trust again. If nothing developed between them, if they remained just friends, he wanted to know that her heart had healed and that he could prove himself trustworthy.

THEY CLOSED AT TWO. Kylie turned off the lights and worked on the dining area, with Junie's help. Mark insisted on doing the dishes and cleaning the kitchen. He wanted to prove himself. She knew that he needed to do this, for himself and probably for her, because he wanted to make her life a little easier.

Her phone rang, and she sat down to answer it. She truly needed to get off her feet. The caller ID showed the name of the hospital. She closed her eyes, waiting for whatever bad news would come. Mindy and bad news were synonymous.

"This is Kylie Rivers," she answered.

"Mrs. Rivers," the person on the other end said. *Mrs.* The title hadn't been hers for several years. "My name is Bailey Jones. I'm calling in regard to your mother, Mindy Waters."

"Yes."

"We have her in our psychiatric unit, and she's sedated but very agitated. She's asking to see you."

"Oh, I see." She must be the worst daughter in the world, but the announcement turned her inside out, making her feel anxious all over again. It had been such a good day, and now this.

A good daughter would tell them she'd be there soon to see her mother. After all, mothers and daughters had bonds. She and Junie had a bond. She prayed they would always be close. She prayed she would never be her mother.

She wasn't her mother. She'd never been Mindy or anything like Mindy.

"Mrs. Rivers?" The woman on the other end questioned, her voice hesitant. "I know this isn't easy. It's never easy to deal with a sick parent."

"No, it isn't easy." She cleared her throat. She tried to find her better self. "Could you tell her that I'll be there tomorrow?"

A hand touched her shoulder, strong and comforting. He massaged the muscles at the back of her neck, and she let her head fall forward. He had a way of releasing the stress. She breathed in, relaxing in his presence.

"I will tell her," Bailey Jones said with a sweet voice of understanding. "Thank you."

"Yes, thank you."

She set her phone down on the counter.

"Let's go to Chuck's for an early dinner," Mark suggested.

"I like that idea. "Thank you, for today and for being here."

"You're welcome. And I'm assuming that call was about visiting Mindy?"

She nodded, resting her head on her arm as she leaned over the table. Exhaustion swamped her, dragging her down, making her entire body feel so heavy. The doctor had warned her that recovery after such a vicious infection would take time. She didn't want it to take time.

"Chuck's special tonight is chicken-fried

steak and mashed potatoes." He tempted in a soft voice, "And I bet he has cherry pie."

"You know how to say all the things a woman wants to hear."

"I'm a romantic." He took hold of her hand, and she should have told him no. She needed to say that they shouldn't because Junie would get the wrong idea. What little girl didn't want her daddy to be the hero? What little girl didn't want a whole family?

Kylie had wanted those things, but her father had been a man who wouldn't claim her. He'd given her mother money that she used for drugs and for her friends who crowded into their tiny trailer.

A trailer that Kylie had spent her childhood trying to clean, always trying to make everything neat and tidy. As if an orderly home meant an orderly life. She'd learned better, and yet she kept trying—was still trying.

She pulled her hand free. "An early dinner sounds good."

"You need to stop feeling guilty." His words jerked her gaze up to meet his, his eyes so light gray, filled with compassion. "She isn't this way because of something you did or didn't do. She's just unwell."

"I know. I really do."

The tap of footsteps, Junie in her boots, meant the conversation needed to end. They parted just as their daughter hurried around the corner of the counter. "Guess what, I checked my spelling, and I got an A."

"Way to go!" Mark swooped her up in his arms. "To celebrate, we're going to Chuck's for dinner. That spelling test deserves a piece of cherry pie."

Kylie couldn't help but make a face. "I'm starting to think you're the one wanting cherry pie, and we're just your excuse. Since it's too early for dinner, maybe we could get pie and ice cream?"

He pulled her close. "You could be right about the pie, but I'm willing to share. Dessert before dinner sounds like a great idea."

"I want a sundae," Junie informed him as she yanked the hat off his head and put it on her own. "Why are you still wearing this silly chef hat?"

"I forgot that I had it on." He pulled off the hairnet that he'd worn under it. "You would have let me go to Chuck's with that on my head."

Kylie smirked at the accusation. "I absolutely would have let you."

Kylie pulled the white hat off her daughter's head and tossed it on a back counter. She grabbed her purse, checked the thermostat and then joined Mark and Junie as they headed out the front door. As she locked the door, she gave the front window a hard look.

"I need more decorations for the Valentine's event. And what is it you're up to for that night? Because I know you're up to something."

He pretended to lock his lips. "Not going to tell, but it's going to be fantastic."

"You'll be here?" She sounded too hopeful and wished she could take back the question.

"I'll be here."

"Can we walk to Chuck's?" Junie asked, wiggling free from her father's arms. He settled her on her feet and she moved between them to take hold of their hands.

She grinned and started to hop forward to swing between their arms, the way she'd done as a toddler.

"No swinging," Kylie warned. "I'm too tired."

Junie sighed her disappointment, but she walked. Or half walked and half skipped.

Chuck's didn't have a big "early dinner" crowd. There were several tables with customers. Of course, in a town like Sunset Ridge, everyone knew everyone else, greeting them as they entered the café with its downhome appeal. Chuck's wife, Jenni Stringer, came out of the kitchen as they entered. She called out to them, telling them to sit wherever they wanted.

Buck, Jael, Matthew and Parker, along with baby Faith, were seated at a large table near the back of the café. Mark led them to the table with his family. The last thing Kylie wanted was for people to assume they were together, but she couldn't shift gears now and ask him to take her home. Junie had already claimed the seat next to Faith. The little girl, now a toddler, banged her cup on the tray of the highchair and reached for Junie. Family. God had indeed made a family for Parker, Matthew and the baby girl that had been abandoned in his truck. They were Junie's family, too. And Kylie knew they considered her a Rivers, still.

She was surprised to see Jael. The younger woman sat next to Buck. She smiled and gave a cheerful greeting to Junie.

Mark pulled out a chair for her, and she accepted, sitting next to Parker. "How are you feeling?" Parker asked.

"Exhausted," Kylie admitted. "I'm obviously

better, but the first full day back at work just about knocked me down."

"Take it easy," Parker warned. "You have Mark there to help, so take a seat and order him around."

"And let him cook?" she teased, knowing he would hear, even as he moved to the seat next to his brother.

"I can cook."

"You are improving," she admitted. "And we sold out of the cupcakes he baked."

"Which is why we needed dessert at Chuck's," Mark said. "Now that I'm here, I'm starting to think I'd like more than dessert."

"Mark, did that Realtor get hold of you today?" Buck asked. "She called the house looking for you."

Mark gave a quick shake of his head and cut Buck off. Buck started to speak again, but Mark gave him another pointed look. If he'd just answered, she might not have been so curious. After all, she knew that he planned to find a home in Sunset Ridge, a place of his own for when he came back to visit his daughter.

Matthew asked her a question about the Valentine's Day event and if they had lined up the music and the special menus for each of the local restaurants. Jenni and Chuck's son, Brody, joined him. He didn't ask, but took a seat next to Matthew. Brody had Down syndrome and remained at home with his parents. Everyone in town knew Brody, and Brody knew everyone in town.

"My dad is making heart-shaped cakes for Valentine's Day." Brody played peek-a-boo with Faith as he made the announcement. She giggled, and he chuckled, the sound growly and endearing. "I told him to make steaks and pasta, but he said he wanted steak and shrimp. I don't like shrimp unless it's fried. Do you like shrimp Junie?"

She shook her head. "And I don't like steak."

"What do you like?" Brody asked. "Oh, my mom said to take your order."

"I like chicken strips and fries," Junie answered. "That's what I want today. And chocolate milk. Oh, and a sundae."

"I'll tell my mom," Brody assured her. He scooted back his chair and got up. "Miss Kylie, what can I get you?"

"Are we eating now?" she asked Mark. He shrugged and reached for the menu.

"I guess we are. Those salads at lunch didn't stick with me."

"I'll have the chicken-fried steak, Brody."

"Okay, Miss Kylie." Brody closed his eyes and repeated their orders. Mark started to speak, but Brody gave him a look and walked off.

"Ouch." Matthew sounded amused rather than sorry for his brother. "I think Brody might be mad at you."

"He'll have to get in line, won't he?" Mark answered.

Brody came back a moment later, his features set in contrition. He sighed big when he stopped in front of Mark.

"Mr. Mark, I am sorry for being rude. My mom said I had to say that. She told me to take your order."

"It's okay, Brody. I understand. And I'll have the chicken-fried steak, too."

"Okay. Do you want gravy?"

"I do."

"Chiken-fried steak and gravy." Brody gave him another narrow-eyed look, and then he walked away.

"Sorry, but not." Matthew still sounded amused. "You used to be his favorite."

"His real loyalty is to Kylie, and I don't blame him." Matthew grinned at her, and she flushed.

"What all are you planning for this big Valentine's event?" Buck asked.

Kylie answered. "It will have vendors, lots of twinkling lights, special menus at our restaurants and live music."

"I heard something 'bout..." Buck gave Mark a quick look, winked and closed his mouth on whatever he'd planned to say. "'Bout good cupcakes."

She laughed at the obvious cover up. "Oh, definitely we will have the best cupcakes."

Chuck joined them. He wasn't all that tall, but he was broad shouldered and still wore his hair buzzed as he had in the military. He liked to joke that there was less hair and less color, but he could still pull off the look. Each time he made the statement, Jenni would put an arm around him and kiss his cheek.

She didn't want to envy them, but Kylie could admit that watching Jenni and Chuck grow older and more in love was inspiring. Everyone should want a marriage with that much love and laughter.

Her gaze drifted to the man who sat across the table and down just a few chairs. Mark. He glanced her way, and they shared a look. In moments such as this one, she wanted her marriage back. Her heart wanted to give in and let him back into her life.

Her brain knew better. She knew how this story went. She'd traveled the road with her mother. She'd heard the apologies, lived through brief attempts at making things better, gotten her hopes up. Gotten her heart broken.

Mark had been the one constant in her life. The dependable constant. That was why his decisions had hurt more. She'd relied on him. She'd believed in them as a couple. He'd shown her that the love they shared didn't matter. He'd spent more and more time drinking and less and less time with his family. And then he'd cheated on her with someone she considered a friend.

She could forgive a lot, had forgiven, but now she wasn't sure if she'd forgiven him for that transgression.

CHAPTER ELEVEN

FRIDAY AFTERNOON, THEY left the hospital where Kylie had visited with her mother. Junie had stayed in Sunset Ridge with a friend. Mark had remained in the waiting room. The last thing he'd wanted was to rile Mindy up even more than she already seemed to be.

As they walked across the parking lot to his truck, he could feel the tension between them. Kylie had been reserved, pulling away from him. He knew better than to reach for her. If she needed space, he could give it.

For the moment, it couldn't be about what he wanted or about them. This time was for Kylie to process the situation with her mother.

"How was she?" he asked as he opened the truck door for her.

"Not well." She brushed a hand over her face. "I'm sorry, that answer isn't even close to correct. She's lost. Her memories are fading. She's angry. She's only fifty-eight. She should be living a nice life in a small house, baking cookies with her granddaughter, meeting friends for lunch. Instead, she's being transferred to a facility where they can care for her as her health declines. I hate this for her. I hate it for myself and for Junie."

"It isn't fair," he agreed. "I want to help—I just don't know what to do to make this easier for you."

She climbed in the truck, reaching to close the door. "There's nothing you can do. My mother is a ward of the state. It's a legal decision that I pushed for and got. It is what it is, and we'll get through this."

He climbed in the driver's side and started the truck. As he started to back out of the parking space, she reached for his hand to stop him.

"Today was difficult. It would have been more so without you here. Thank you."

"You're welcome. I just wish I could make it easier."

She shrugged her slim shoulders. "You don't have to. I'm trying to live with a faith like Paul. He said he'd learned to be content no matter his situation. It's crazy to think it, but I am content with my life. I've hit a rough patch, but

I'm moving forward with Christ, who strengthens me."

He backed out of the parking space and put them on the road to home. After driving a few minutes, he said, "You're my hero."

He glanced her way, and the sweetness of the expression on her face nearly undid his resolve to remain platonic. She'd had a rough day, but she did manage to look at peace. She looked like everything he'd ever wanted in his life.

"Mark, I have to say something, and it isn't going to be easy."

With those words, she jerked him back to their present situation.

"Okay, whatever you need to say, I'm listening."

"Hmmm," she said. Her expression serene, she spoke. "I forgive you for what you did to me. Not the drinking, the anger, but for cheating on me. I thought I'd forgiven you, but I realized I'd held on to that one. I wanted a reason to stay angry, but staying angry made me bitter, it kept me from having joy. I was only hurting myself."

"I'm sorry." The words were wrenched from him as he tumbled over all the old emotions, the guilt. "I'm not going to blame drinking or say I was in a bad place. I take full responsibility for my actions. They were reprehensible and unforgivable."

"There is no such thing as unforgiveable." She blew out a breath and looked away from him. "That doesn't make it easy to let go of the pain. I've let this be a weight that I've carried for years. I need to surrender my anger and my unforgiveness so I can move on. I'm sorry, but I have to do this for me, not for you."

"I know." He admired her so much. He loved her. He looked up to her for her strength and her faith. She had always been too good for him.

"We have to move forward," she told him as they drove down the back road to Sunset Ridge. No stopping on side roads this time.

"Yes, we do."

"Not together, but as friends."

"I agree." He didn't, not completely, but if he didn't agree, she'd pull away from him. The longer he stayed in Sunset Ridge, the more time he spent with Kylie and Junie, the more he wanted to be a better man and have a future with them.

"Do you want to go by and look at the old bank?" he suggested as they drove into Sunset

Ridge. The little town had settled into twilight, and the sun fading over the western horizon turned the trees into dark silhouettes and created a lavender and orange glow over the buildings.

Small towns had their own kind of beauty. Maybe that was the small-town boy in him talking, but he couldn't think of much that would be prettier or better than riding through this little place with her at his side and the view of the countryside and old buildings.

"The bank?" She looked perplexed. "I've seen it my whole life."

"I know, but I thought we could look at it through the lens of the Valentine's event—what needs to be done or purchased for decorations."

"I guess we could take a peek inside."

He turned onto the street that led to the town square. Her little shop sat in darkness with just the night lights twinkling from inside. Chuck's looked to be packed with cars lined up and down the street and customers coming and going. He turned right and pulled down the street to the bank, a building that had been built in the early 1900s. It had a brick exterior, large plate-glass windows and wide steps leading to the front door.

The Realtor stood out front, waiting for them to arrive.

"Why is she here?" Kylie asked as he parked.

"I asked her to meet us. We can't get the real feel of the place without going inside."

"This seems like a lot of trouble. But I do love going inside and poking around."

"I thought you'd like that."

"Thank you." She hopped out of the truck, and he hurried to catch up.

"Kylie, it's good to see you." The real estate agent held up the key. "Mark said the two of you wanted to take a look at the building. This is such a great place. I've had several people look in the last month."

Of course she would say that. He almost chuckled at the sales pitch. When Kylie gave him a sharp look, he managed to put on a straight face and followed the two women inside.

The building had potential. It had the high ceilings of its generation, polished wood floors, brick walls and large rooms. It also had an upstairs that had been recently used for apartments. That brought his plan together in a way he hadn't expected.

"Is this zoned residential?" he asked.

"It's a commercial property, and yes, the apartments can be rented. It's a multiple family dwelling. Sunset Ridge doesn't have a lot of zoning laws, as you know. They only ask that a commercial building be used as a business and only the upstairs be used for housing."

"Interesting." They walked upstairs, and he wandered through a large, two-bedroom apartment with black cabinets, tall, narrow windows and the same hardwood flooring as the downstairs.

"Why is this interesting?" Kylie asked as they walked into the second apartment, which was smaller than the first, but followed the same design.

"I want a place in Sunset Ridge, for when I'm in town."

He let it go at that and led them out of the apartment and back downstairs. The downstairs happened to be the original reason for their viewing of the property.

"This place has so much potential," Laura the Realtor said as she led them through the open main room. "This room is large enough for most types of gatherings. There are two large restrooms that were installed about ten years ago. Back here, you have a kitchen."

She led them through the building to the kitchen, then to a meeting room, next the promised bathrooms.

"What are you thinking, for Valentine's Day?" he asked Kylie.

"I mean, I never really thought we could do this, but definitely music and dancing."

"I'm thinking white tulle, twinkling lights, kind of a fairy-tale event."

"Really, that's where your mind goes?" Her eyes twinkled with amusement.

"I mean, yeah, really."

"I see," she said with narrowed eyes. "There's something you're not telling me."

"You know me too well. What if I said I want it to be a surprise?"

"I'd be suspicious, but I guess there's no way to force you to tell me."

"Nope."

They asked Laura for a few minutes to wander the building alone. She had a few calls to make, so she stepped away, and they walked back to the kitchen.

"I wanted this building." Kylie ran her hand down the stainless-steel countertop. "I pictured a place where couples could have a romantic dinner on Friday night, or maybe use it for showers and birthday parties."

"What stopped you from buying it?"

"The price. I didn't want to spend all of my money on a building."

"Why didn't you ask?"

She stepped close, facing him. "Because I didn't want anything else from you, Mark."

"What about now?" He needed to do this in the right way, or she'd walk out and never listen to him. "What if I want this building as an investment? I want it because it's a place where I can come and have time with my daughter. I want to spend more time with Junie. She shouldn't feel abandoned by her father, and I need a relationship with her."

"Okay and..."

"I'll buy it and give you a budget for renovations. Turn it into whatever you want. A restaurant, a venue, catering, whatever you can dream up."

"I can dream big, Mark."

He touched her face, tracing his fingers down her cheek. "I want you to have your dream."

He could give her this. Maybe to make amends for the dreams he'd taken, maybe because he wanted to see just what she'd do with her skills. He didn't believe in himself enough to try and be a part of this dream, but he wanted to make it happen for her.

ALL OF HIS plans overwhelmed her. He'd obviously been thinking about this for a while. Everything would change, but change was a part of life. Nothing ever stayed the same.

She needed a minute to process.

She walked out the back door of the bank to the grassy area that had once been parking. She loved this little courtyard area. She turned around, imagining it as it could be. She imagined the events that could take place here. She hadn't wanted to love this building and this idea of his so much.

"What do you think?" he asked, coming to stand next to her.

"Oh, Mark, I see it. I see this as an outside courtyard, reception area. Tables, walkways, a water feature, twinkling lights."

His shoulder bumped hers. "You didn't want to love the idea. I knew you wouldn't be able to help yourself."

"I do love it." The admission came easier than she would have imagined. "It's a brilliant idea."

"But it needs the right person to oversee the adventure. That person is you."

"You can't buy me."

She felt his shoulder move. He was laughing.

"I mean it," she said a little more firmly.

"I know you do. I'm not trying to buy you. I'm making a sound business decision."

She looked up at him, at his strong jaw, his firm mouth, twinkling gray eyes. She noticed the spot where he'd nicked his jaw while shaving and the scar from a fall when he was eleven. The Rivers boys had been a rough bunch, prone to fighting, but just each other. They'd ridden bulls, ridden broncs and played hard.

"It could work," she admitted.

"But you're not completely sure of doing this with me."

"I'm afraid, and I'm trying to 'fear not.'"

"Let's make a deal." He spoke softly, his fingers touching hers, but he didn't hold her hand. "Talk to me."

"We are talking."

"I mean, tell me what you think and feel. When you're worried, angry, even happy, tell me. If we can talk about it, we can be more intentional in this relationship. Even our friendship needs to be intentional."

He looked so determined, as if this might be the most important moment in their lives. A turning point. Or maybe a new beginning. They'd been children together and teenagers together. They'd set out on a grand adventure, intent on having fun and not thinking beyond the moment. They hadn't worked on becoming better together.

"This mature, grounded you is frightening. I like this person a lot, and I'm afraid he'll leave and not return."

"Believe me, that's my fear, too. I'm doing my best to hold onto this guy."

She felt her lips tug upward, but then seriousness grabbed her again. He was right; they had to talk. "Mark, I'm worried about Junie. I'm worried about my heart because I know that you want to have a place here so you can share our daughter. I feel sick to my stomach at the thought of splitting her up, a weekend with you, a holiday with me, summer vacations torn between the two of us. I'm her mom and..."

He pulled her into his arms and held her tight. She didn't cry, but she leaned in, needing to feel comforted, and he knew how to comfort.

"Shhh, stop worrying. Tearing our daughter

apart, pulling her back and forth, that's the last thing I want for her, or for you. I'm not buying this place with that in mind. Yes, I want to spend time with her, but we'll do it in a way that works for all of us and that makes the two of you feel comfortable."

"Thank you." She sniffled and pulled back from his embrace. "Okay, the other fear."

"There's more?" He said it with a brief flash of dimples, but she also saw a look of hurt. She didn't want to hurt him.

That thought surprised her. At one time, she would have liked to hurt him. Now, things had changed; she'd changed. She wanted him to be happy, to be well. For his sake and for Junie.

"There's more. I don't want you to breeze in and out of her life at your convenience, because she loves you and you'll hurt her. She needs to know when you'll be here and when you're spending time with her. Not here for weeks and nothing for months."

Junie had been a toddler when Kylie left Nashville. She'd barely known her daddy, and she'd adjusted to his being gone. The few times she'd seen him in the following years, she'd liked him, had fun with him, but they hadn't bonded. Now there was a bond. Junie loved her daddy.

"I will also be intentional in my relationship with my daughter."

"You like that word a lot." She studied his face, wondering where all of this intentionality came from.

"I do. I learned it in therapy and might have ignored it, somewhat. But in the past couple of weeks, it really hit home that *intentional* means deliberate. I need to keep that in mind in my relationships, to be deliberate in the time I devote to the two of you and to bettering our relationship."

"This isn't about me," she insisted, knowing he would ignore the statement.

"It is." He brushed a strand of hair from her face, pushing it behind her ear. "Have I told you how much I like this silvery hair of yours?"

"Thank you, but you're changing the subject."

"I am. Just accept that I need to do this, not just for you and Junie, but for myself."

"I can accept that." She pulled at a strand of her silvery lavender hair. "The truth about this. My hair is going gray, and it made me feel old to be gray in my early thirties, so I dyed it the color of gray that I chose."

"It's beautiful, and so are you." He touched his forehead to hers. "I really want to kiss you."

"I'd rather you didn't." The words didn't come easily. "That isn't true. I would actually like it very much, but I know it isn't wise."

"Now that's honesty." He didn't move away. "I guess that means the answer is no?"

What answer did she give to his humor-laced question? She wanted to say yes. She also knew they couldn't blur the lines, not when they were becoming friends again. Grown-up friends.

"The answer is still no. We shouldn't kiss."

"I won't kiss you."

"That's good."

Slowly, he moved away, and she instantly missed his presence. After so many years of being angry, resentful and hurt, somewhere in these past two weeks she'd started to enjoy the journey of friendship. Even stranger to want his touch, to want his lips on hers. She shivered and pulled her coat around herself, feeling a sudden chill.

"We should go in," Mark said, noticing her awkward gesture. "It's getting colder all the time."

"And dark." She glanced at her watch. "Junie will wonder where we've gone."

"She is having fun and not even thinking about how long we've been gone."

Laura found them still standing in the backyard. "What do you think? We could write up an offer if you're interested."

"We want to pray about it," Mark told the agent. He looked at Kylie, and she felt that shiver again. Not the cold, then, but his presence.

She nodded, agreeing with him. In the years they'd been together, they'd never prayed about the decisions they made. They'd rushed through life, taking their chances, making mistakes and laughing when things worked out.

"Oh, of course. So, I'll contact you tomorrow?" Laura looked confused. Kylie felt for her, but she didn't want to back down on praying, on taking their time and getting this right. It wouldn't be her money paying for the building, but she'd have an investment of time and energy.

"Make it Monday," Mark answered decisively. He looked at Kylie, and she nodded. Monday it was. That meant he'd still be here, in Sunset Ridge and in their lives. At least until Monday.

It wasn't his coming and going that worried her, it was his personal decisions. What if he couldn't stay sober? What if he couldn't continue to put them first, to be intentional in this new relationship they were building?

He'd always been her best friend. When their marriage fell apart, she'd missed that friendship. Now that she had it back, she didn't want to lose that part of him again.

CHAPTER TWELVE

MARK STOOD ON the front porch of the house, waiting for Buck so they could head to church. A cat circled his legs, a mangy yellow cat with one ear torn and a scratch on his face.

"You're a mess," Mark said as he reached to pet the cat. A loud meow thanked him for the attention, and the cat purred and rubbed against his pant leg.

"Pet that thing and he'll think he lives here," Buck grumbled as he came out the front door.

"As fat as that cat is, I'm sure someone has already made him feel like this is his home. I'm guessing that someone is you."

"I'm not soft," Buck growled, but he leaned over to pet the cat. "I just kind of like animals that are as worn out and scarred as I am."

"I can see the attraction," Mark observed. "You ready to head to church?"

"Depends on what we're driving. Do we have

to take that truck of yours? That thing rides rougher than an old buckboard wagon."

"What do you think we should take?"

"I think the Cadillac since it's Sunday."

"Is that really any better than my truck?"

The Cadillac lived in the detached garage at the back of the house. It had been bought new the year before Izzy left, and it had remained in the garage for most of his childhood and teen years. He and Matthew had snuck it out a time or two, when Buck hadn't been clear-headed enough to realize what they were up to. They'd driven it to the drive-in movies and, once, to Tulsa to see Izzy.

"It's got less than fifty thousand miles on it."

"Because you wouldn't take it out of the garage for a decade or two."

"It's a classic." Buck tossed him the keys. "Take it for a spin, you'll see."

"Oh, I've driven it once or twice."

"How's that?" Buck asked as they raised the garage door and entered the dark confines of the metal structure. "I kept the keys hidden."

"Matthew found them. We took this car out a time or two. The girls loved the Caddy."

"I guess it's too late to ground you." Buck

shook his head as he went to the passenger door of the car. "You boys raised yourselves."

They got in, buckled up and, a few minutes later, were cruising toward town. "We did okay, Buck." Mark glanced at his dad. "None of us have been to jail. At least not for any real length of time. We're fairly honest, and we know how to support ourselves."

"I worry about Jonah."

"I know you do. I worry, too, but I know he has to find his own way." The youngest of the Rivers brothers had always been the wildest, most likely to rebel of the group. He rode bulls and lived a hard, dangerous life on the road.

"I'm really sorry for letting you boys down. I wish I'd gotten sober a lot sooner, when it mattered."

"I feel the same way about myself." He pulled into the church parking lot and found a space for the car. "I forgive you."

"I know," Buck said. He patted Mark's shoulder in an awkwardly affectionate gesture. "I guess we make our mistakes and learn by them. I'm praying for you and Kylie."

"Me, too."

Matthew greeted them at the doors of the

church. He had a look on his face that immediately set off warning bells.

"Whatever it is, the answer is no." Mark tried to scoot around his brother. He spotted Junie and Kylie and intended to head their way.

"I really need your help." Matthew reached for his arm. "Mark, you know I can't lead the worship."

Mark laughed at the image of his brother trying to lead the singing. "Well, at least that's the truth."

"I'm begging for your help."

"Begging?" He shook his head, hoping to dissuade his brother. "Matthew, there has to be someone in this congregation who can do this better than I could, and someone more qualified."

"No, today you're the one." Matthew put an arm around his shoulder and drew him into the church. "Mark, I want you to do this."

"What am I supposed to sing?"

"Take a look at the old hymnal. You know the songs. We have a guitar. Give it a try."

"For you. I'm only doing this for you."

"Sure, okay." Matthew grinned as he walked away. "Thank you."

As Mark headed down the aisle in the direction of Kylie and Junie, he pulled off his cowboy hat and gave his ex-wife a wink. Her mouth hitched at the corners, and then her eyes widened.

"You cut your hair!" She put a hand to her mouth, and then she laughed a little. "Oh my. You look like fifteen-year-old Mark after Buck took the clippers to you all."

"Thanks, I think. Buck did take the clippers to me last night. This time with permission."

He sat down next to her, and she touched his shorter locks. He'd done it for her because it mattered.

"I love it," she said. "You look like my…"

"Your?"

"Friend. You look like the boy I grew up with."

"I am." He cleared his throat a little. "Matthew asked me to lead worship."

"Go you!" she said cheerfully.

"I'm not qualified."

"Mark, stop doubting yourself. If God leads you to this moment, then He is going to be with you."

"I have to pick the songs," he lamented.

She handed him the hymnal. "You know these, and you know other songs, songs that mean something to you. Pick the music that ministers to you, and I know you'll minister to this church."

He took the book from her hands and spotted several songs that he knew he could do, but then he thought of one that wouldn't be in this book. A song about God being the one who breaks chains and makes a way when there doesn't seem to be a way. He found it on his phone.

When he went forward, he felt a hitch of doubt, but he also felt a heavy dose of God. He wasn't alone as he walked to the front of the church and picked up the guitar that Matthew had left there for him. He smiled at the instrument and then at the congregation.

"When Matthew asked me to do this, I told him I'm not qualified. Then I realized there have been a lot of men before me, much stronger than I am, who also thought they weren't qualified. The Bible is full of men who made mistakes, who doubted themselves, doubted their faith, and then were used by God to do great things. I'm still finding my way. I'm not a Paul or David or a Joseph, but I'm a man who has struggled, who has failed, who has found his way back. I guess most of you remember the last time I sang in this church. It was a Garth song, and it wasn't one of my finer moments."

Laughter greeted that comment, and he smiled. "Hopefully, today I can do a little better."

He started with a few of the standard hymns. When he got to "I Surrender All," he felt the tears stinging his eyes as the words truly hit home. Had he surrendered? He felt in his heart that a surrender had happened. The congregation sang along, but he barely heard their voices. As the song ended, he swiped at the tears that had fallen free. He started the last song, the worship song that wasn't in the book.

The congregation knew the song and joined him. The chains had been broken, and he'd been set free. God had made a way. He sang the chorus twice, and then he set the guitar down and walked off the stage. Matthew met him. The two looked at each other, and then Matthew hugged him tight.

"And you thought you weren't called."

Mark shook his head. "Not now, big brother. Let me have a minute."

Matthew patted his back as Mark walked back to his family. His wife, his daughter. He sat next to Kylie, and she reached for his hand.

"That was beautiful."

He couldn't speak, so he nodded. She gave his hand a squeeze.

Matthew had stepped to the stage and stood behind the pulpit.

"I'm going to read a few verses," Matthew said. "And then we'll pray and be dismissed. There are moments when God says the work is done. This morning, after that worship service, the work is done. Now is time for prayer. It's time for God to change lives."

Mark felt an overwhelming need to cry. He shook it off.

"What are you going to do with that?" Kylie asked as the service ended and they left the sanctuary together.

"With what?"

"The music, Mark. That worship service was special. What you did up there..." She gave him a serious look. "Do not tell me you didn't notice."

"I noticed how it felt for me, and I hoped others felt it, too."

"You'll pray about it."

He nodded in agreement. What else could he do? He couldn't tell her that he had a career and it had nothing to do with leading a song service at his brother's church. God had opened this door, this once, for him to see that he could lead, but it wasn't his job.

Sometimes God's people are called to make tough choices. The random thought came to him, but he dismissed it. He knew his path.

Kylie let his hand drop, which meant something. Maybe she'd grown tired of him, or disappointed? He could understand that. He'd often been disappointed in himself. He'd often disappointed her.

THE CHURCH HAD planned a potluck that day, not merely for the congregation to spend time together, but also for the Valentine's Day planning committee to work on tying up loose ends. In less than two weeks, they would bring together all of their ideas, and hopefully, the night would be a success. Their town desperately needed this to be a success.

"How are you feeling?" Mark asked as they made their way through the food line.

"Better today," she answered. She hadn't thought much about it, but yes, she was definitely feeling better. She'd gotten more sleep the past few nights. The medication the doctor had given her seemed to be making a change in her body.

"You seem surprised," he said.

"Not really, just relieved."

"Relieved?"

She shrugged. "I felt like I should have felt better sooner and I wanted to make sure—my doctor wanted to make sure—the infection was taken care of."

"I wish you would have told me. You matter to me. I want to help if I can."

She had so many things she could say to that. She should have mattered more when they were married. She was no longer his problem, his responsibility. She didn't want to say those things because she didn't want to hurt him or the progress they'd made in their relationship. It felt good to be friends again.

"I agree," she finally said. "I should have said something sooner."

"What can I do?" he asked. "I could take you to a specialist. I know there are decent doctors here, but maybe we should go to the Mayo or somewhere. Isn't that where people go when they need real answers?"

"Mark, I'm fine. The blood tests show that I'm on the mend."

He brushed a hand through his now much shorter hair. "We need to hire someone to help you. And we shouldn't take on the bank if it's going to cause you to be stressed."

"Stop," she told him. "Mark, you have to let me handle this. It's my health, and I'm being proactive."

"I know you are, but I also know that resting is going to be important. The last thing you need is more work. I'll be around for a while, but we need to make sure you have someone to help at the coffee shop."

"Mark, I'll take care of it."

A small, silly part of her had wanted him to stay and help, to be the one who took part of the load. She knew that wouldn't be their relationship. He had his career. Her life was here.

"I know you will. I just want to make it easier for you."

"Everything okay here?" Parker came up behind them. She put an arm around Kylie, but she gave Mark a questioning look.

"I just told him about the tests."

"Ah, I see. He's going into the 'I'm the man and I need to fix this' mode?"

"Something like that." Kylie winked at him, hoping he would relax.

"I think she needs to hire someone at the coffee shop."

"I would agree with that," Parker said. "Even though she is healing and getting stronger, help is always good."

"Traitor." Kylie pushed Mark forward. "Fill your plate."

He did, piling on fried chicken, mashed potatoes, salad, a roll, a pasta dish. She shook her head as she watched him scoop out potato salad.

"Did Ora Sutters make this?" he asked Parker.

"I think so."

"I've always loved her potato salad." He moved on to the desserts.

"He's a mess," Kylie said, more to herself than to Parker.

"I think he's a mess because he loves you and doesn't know what to do to fix the situation."

"Love?" Kylie shook her head. "I'm not even sure what that means. I always loved him and felt pretty sure he loved me."

"Love is a strange, intangible thing." Parker looked at her plate. A salad, roasted chicken and green beans. Parker had always struggled with her weight. "I'm not doing this. I'm having cheesecake."

"Same," Kylie said. "Intangible. That's a good

description for love. It isn't the physical thing we feel. Love is putting others first. It's sacrifice. It's caring."

"It's commitment in the worst of times." Parker helped herself to the cheesecake. "The committee is at the back table. They're discussing the bank and the best way to use the building. Matthew said Mark made an appointment with Laura to look at the building."

"He did. It's a fantastic place and has so much potential."

"The two of you looked at it?" Parker said this with a smirk.

"Don't read anything into this. He wants to buy it and let me run it."

"I think you'd make something special of that place."

"Except that now he thinks I'm sick and I'm not."

They joined the ladies and two men who were on the committee for planning the Valentine's Day in Sunset Ridge event. Mark moved so she could sit next to him.

"What are we discussing?" Parker asked as she sat down next to Kylie.

"We're just discussing the way we plan to decorate the square," Mark told them. "The tent will be set up in the center of the lawn. The lights will be strung and music will play. The restaurants have special menus that will be posted. I think they're going to have a punch card. As people go from vendor to vendor and to the stores that are open, they can get the card punched and be entered in a draw to win a gift card package for businesses in town."

"I love that idea," Parker said. "What about advertising?"

Lena spoke up. "I've taken care of that. We have advertising in three area papers. I have fifteen vendors signed up to be in town. If it is too cold, we're going to move them into local businesses. Kylie, would you be willing to let a vendor move into the coffee shop? The nice thing is, heat for the vendor and extra traffic for you. We have to look at this as long term. These are potential customers for years to come."

"I'd gladly give space to a vendor." Kylie smiled at Lena. "As long as it isn't a food vendor. That would make things awkward."

"Oh, definitely. We'll make sure it's a craft or jewelry."

"What about the bank?" Parker asked.

"That's going to be a special surprise," Mark told her.

Kylie gave him a look, wondering what he meant. He wouldn't tell her. She could tell by the shuttered look on his face. He had something in mind, and he planned on keeping it secret. At least from her.

"I think this is all coming together quite well," Lena said at the end of the meeting. "Mark has given us great ideas. I'm really looking forward to seeing how the public reacts."

They dispersed. Parker hurried off to find her husband. The others left in search of more food or their families. Kylie pushed to her feet.

"I have to find Junie. She was going to the playground with friends."

"I'm sure she's fine," Mark assured her.

"Mark, what are you going to do in the bank? For Valentine's Day."

"It wouldn't be a surprise if I told you." He gave her a cheeky grin. "I know you're curious, but trust me, this will be fantastic."

"You'll definitely be here? I don't want Junie disappointed."

"I'll be here. Kylie, I wouldn't be anywhere other than here with you and Junie."

What did she say to that?

He leaned in close. "Kylie, we're going to be okay."

"We? You and me, Junie? I don't know what you want."

"I want us." He kissed her quickly, taking her breath in the process.

"No. Us doesn't work," she told him. "We want different things."

"We can work." He seemed so sure. She was anything but sure.

"We're working on being friends," she reminded him.

"And we'll keep working on being friends. In the meantime, I'm working on being the man God called me to be. The man who cares for his wife to the best of his ability."

"But I'm not your wife."

"I know you're not. If you decide you can't be more than my friend, then I'll be the best friend you need me to be."

"We're in two separate places," she reminded him. "I'll never go back to Nashville. I won't put Junie through that."

"I know." His hand held hers. "I get it. Kylie, I know the statistics for alcoholics. I might struggle. I might fall. The last thing I want is to hurt you."

"Mommy, Daddy, there you are." Junie ran down the hall to greet them. "Are we going to Aunt Parker's for dinner tonight? She said we could."

Saved by the tiny human who loved them both and didn't understand the incredible conflict between them. Kylie pulled away from Mark because she couldn't think with him standing next to her, his hand touching hers.

He answered Junie, telling her they would go to Parker and Matthew's. She wanted to tell him they couldn't. She needed to go home and clean house. She needed to do laundry. She needed to do anything other than spend more time with Mark.

CHAPTER THIRTEEN

THE COOKIES WERE sprawled out in order, each heart frosted in pale pink with darker pink for the words Mark had spelled out. He found a strange sense of accomplishment in each creation. Buck had baked the cookies, but Mark decorated. They weren't too shabby as a team.

He didn't even feel silly, standing in the kitchen of Kylie's coffee shop, an apron around his waist and the chef hat she'd jokingly given him scrunched on top of his now short hair. He glanced at the clock. He'd been here since five in the morning. She should be showing up at any moment.

They'd had this routine for the past week. He showed up early. She arrived with Junie in tow an hour later. She already looked healthier. Their relationship felt healthier.

He found it hard to think about leaving. He couldn't ignore his responsibilities in Nashville forever, but this felt right—this place, his wife and daughter. His phone calls from Nashville, from the new agent, had been insistent that time was of the essence. At the moment, Kylie and Junie had to come first. This time together mattered.

More than anything in life, he wanted to fix what he'd broken. He didn't know what that meant for his career, but he knew the future with Kylie and Junie mattered. No matter how it looked, together or just co-parenting as friends, he had to fix their relationship.

He wanted more than friendship. He wasn't going to lie to her or to himself about that, but he knew that friendship and trust needed to come first.

The ding of the front doorbell alerted him to her arrival. Mark stepped back, wanting his creation to be the first thing she saw as she walked into the kitchen. He smiled, listening to Junie's excited chatter. The kitten had slept with her, and it never missed its litterbox, she informed her mother.

Kylie sounded thrilled.

"Daddy, are you in here?" Junie's sing-song voice called out. Today she wore slippers; he could tell by the shuffle of the soft sole on the tile floor.

"I'm here," he answered. As she came around the corner, he put a finger to his lips to keep her from ruining the surprise. Her eyes widened when she saw the cookies, but she nodded and remained silent.

Kylie was shuffling around in the front, putting away her purse and preparing the coffeemaker. He peeked around the corner, not exactly patient as she fiddled and kept him waiting.

Not that she knew that she was keeping him waiting. Junie grinned up at him.

"Mommy, I think there's a mouse." And then she put her hand to her mouth and whispered, "She hates mice."

"Thank you," he leaned in to whisper. He wanted to hug his daughter and spin her in circles. She was precious and funny, and he'd missed out on knowing her the way he should have known her. He'd let alcohol rob him of her earliest years.

Never again.

His goal was to always put his wife and daughter first. First. Ahead of self, ambition and temptation.

Kylie hurried into the room, obviously worried about a mouse infestation. She looked around, saw him, spotted Junie and then noticed the cookies.

"You've been baking." She approached.

"Actually, Buck has been baking, and I decorated. What do you think?" He wanted her to love the cookies. More than that, he wanted her to love him.

"They're very pretty. Are we serving these for Valentine's Day?"

"That's my plan, but this batch is for you."

That was when she noticed the message on the cookies, and she shook her head at him. Be. My. Valentine. Each cookie had one word, and they were lined up in order. Junie began to clap and giggle.

"Mommy, say yes. Say yes."

He'd left two cookies to the side. A YES cookie and a NO cookie. Like his daughter, he wanted to prod her to pick YES. He didn't know what he'd do if she didn't. He'd never really asked her on a date. All of their lives, they'd just been with each other.

Her hand hovered over the wrong cookie. He wanted to push the other in front of her. A slow, sly smile slid onto her face, and she gave him a sideways look. Junie edged in closer, as if she, too, wanted to push the correct cookie into place. The suspense made his heart race as he waited, praying she'd pick YES.

Slowly, her hand moved, and she pushed the YES cookie forward.

"Yes, Mark, I'll be your Valentine." And then she picked the cookie up and took a bite. "Oh, this is really very good."

"Can I have one?" Junie reached for a cookie.

"Only if you promise to also be my date," Mark told his daughter.

"Daddy, Valentine's Day is for big kids, not little kids."

"But this Valentine's Day is for families," he said as he gave her a hug and then reached to pull Kylie to his side.

Kylie set the remainder of the cookie on the counter. Her smile disappeared, and she became serious again. "We should get to work. Junie, remember that today is history day. You have a project that I'll help you with after you read."

"Okay, Mommy. I love history. We're learning about women who helped during the Revolutionary War. There was a lady who pretended to be crazy so she could take ammunition to soldiers."

"Mad Anne Bailey," Kylie supplied.

"That's the one." Junie skipped away with her bag of books.

Kylie watched their daughter disappear into the little office before she spoke again.

"We have to talk."

He gave a quick nod. "Okay."

"About us."

"Us?"

"I'm serious Mark. This is serious."

He knew it was. He looked at the cookies, the YES cookie now half eaten. Junie had taken the NO cookie. This had been for fun. He'd considered cookie message boxes for the Valentine's Day event.

He told her that and explained. "I thought we could leave them plain and people could buy them as message cookies. We could frost the cookies with the messages the customers ask for."

"That's a great idea," she conceded. "But us, that's where we're at."

"I know. And I'm being serious. This is about the two of us doing what we should have done fifteen years ago. We should have dated. I should have asked you out, rather than assuming we would naturally be together. I didn't put effort into our relationship. I took us—took you—for granted."

She brought her gaze up to meet his, and he saw the troubled look in her dark eyes. "How does this end?"

"Or begin? Maybe continue." He liked those words better than "end." "I'm not sure, Kylie. I wish that I could say I trust myself completely. I don't, so how can I expect you to trust me? I came here determined to seek your forgiveness and leave. I stayed, and the longer I stay, the more I miss you in my life."

"I think maybe this is a bad idea, Mark. It's going to give Junie the wrong idea. It's going to make things more complicated between us. I'm just not sure about putting Junie in this relationship. She's a little girl who is learning to adore her daddy, and you could break her heart. My heart can handle it, but I have to protect hers."

"Hurting the two of you is the last thing I want to do."

"Then maybe we should back up a step. Let's not make this a date. We'll be together on Valentine's Day, but I'll be working, and you'll be around town helping with the event. At the end of the day, that's probably the best plan."

"I can respect your decision," he said. His

phone dinged, and he picked it up, read the text and set it back on the counter.

"Important?"

"Nope." Just troubling. "Just work stuff."

"You've neglected your own career to help with mine. I understand that you need to get back to your life."

"I'm committed to this event and to helping you get some rest."

"You don't have to worry about us." She reached for her cookie and popped the last bite into her mouth. After chewing it up, she gave him a cheeky grin. "Those are really good."

"Thank you. I think you just ate your answer."

"I did." she asked as she went to the fridge for a bottle of water.

"So is that your answer for me?" he asked.

She nodded and then gave a pointed look at the office, where Junie watched a TV show, pretending not to listen.

"You came here to make amends and you've done that. I think dating is a complication neither of us need right now."

"You're right," he agreed. The look on his face remained hopeful.

The door chime dinged.

"Customer." Kylie hurried off, leaving him with his thoughts and the messages from his agent.

Several weeks ago, he'd started on this journey, believing it would be simple. He'd been delusional, thinking he could separate himself from what he felt for Kylie, for Junie. He'd planned on protecting them from him. He should have known it wouldn't be as simple as coming to town, making a few apologies and going back to Nashville to his career.

He still didn't completely trust himself, trust that he was what they needed. He didn't trust that he could keep them safe—from himself.

AFTER THE MORNING RUSH, Kylie left the front counter in Mark's care and went to check on Junie and her schoolwork. She found her daughter in the kitchen, Mark's phone in her hand. Junie quickly put both hands behind her back; her mouth tightened, and her eyes grew large.

"What are you doing?"

"Nothing," Junie said a little too quickly.

Kylie sighed. "Junie, please tell the truth, not a story. Stories are what we tell that aren't real. They're not the truth. I want to know what you are really doing, the true story."

"I peeked at Daddy's text. I heard the sound and thought he'd want to know that someone sent him a message."

"It isn't your message to read, Junie."

Tears welled up in her daughter's eyes. She scrubbed at them with her fist, but more fell. The phone dropped to the floor, and Junie rushed into her arms.

"Daddy's leaving because now people will like him again."

"What?" Kylie shook her head, lost in that statement. "That doesn't make sense, Junie."

It wasn't her message, either. She knew that, but she couldn't stop herself from asking.

"Junie, what did the message say?"

"It said he's done a good job of fixing things." And then she cried big tears and buried her face in Kylie's shoulder.

"Hey, what's up?" He had entered the room, and he sounded far too cheerful. This moment didn't call for happiness. Couldn't he see that their daughter was upset? His focus went from Junie to the phone on the floor. "What happened?"

"She read a text," Kylie explained, holding Junie close.

"Text?" He reached for his phone.

Junie sniffled as she made the accusation. "It said you've kept your end of the bargain and—I think it was *bargain*." She closed her eyes and drew in a breath. "You cleaned up your image and made up with your family. Some of the words were big, but I sounded them out. I'm a good reader."

"Oh, Junie." Mark had the good sense to look sorry. He covered his eyes with his hands and shook his head. "That text..."

"It said you're leaving." Junie swiped at her tears.

Kylie wanted to grab her daughter up and hug her tight. She wanted to run again, to leave behind the pain this man caused them.

"I know." He shook his head, and Kylie really wanted him to deny the text, to undo the pain he'd caused them. "I have to take care of my career. People depend on me."

People depended on him. It couldn't just be them, she realized. It would always be the band, the agent, the fans. Kylie moved her daughter in the direction of the office. "Go watch a cartoon."

"With headphones?" Junie sniffled again, and another tear streaked down her cheek.

"Yes, with headphones."

Kylie watched as Junie did as she asked, and then she returned to Mark. She couldn't even begin to describe the anger she felt. She wanted to lash out, to tell him to leave and to never come back. She wanted to hurt him the way he'd hurt them.

"It isn't what it seems."

She laughed at that. "Oh please, you always say that. Usually when you're caught red-handed that's your defense. I used to give you the benefit of the doubt, but no more. So what was the deal, Mark? Did they tell you they'd take you back if you could use us to polish up your image?"

"No," he started. "Well, yes. But that isn't why I stayed. It isn't why I've been helping you and spending time with you."

"Of course it isn't."

"I love you." He spoke it so softly, so sincerely. Her heart almost melted, almost gave in.

"No, don't say those words." Her heart couldn't take those words. "I can't do this again. I can't take the constant fear of the floor falling out from under me."

"I'm coming back," he told her, his voice still calm, still so sincere that she wanted to believe him.

"I'm sure you are." She studied his face, wanting to see something in his expression, in his eyes, that told the truth. "Mark, did you come here knowing about this deal? What is it—to make yourself look like a family man?"

"My agent called me a couple of weeks ago."

"I see, so all of this has been about you, not about us. The intentional living, building our friendship."

"That wasn't part of the deal," he told her. "I came here to see you, to ask you to forgive me. I stayed because I wanted to stay. I stayed to help you and to spend time with you and with my daughter."

"I wish I could trust you. I don't want to go back to that life. I don't want to go back to never knowing what will happen next."

"I'm asking you to trust me."

Trust. The word meant so much, or for him, so little. All of the talk about being intentional. She'd believed him. She'd fallen for every single word because he'd seemed sincere. He still seemed sincere. That made it even more upsetting.

Maybe if he'd told her about the deal, been honest from the start. He hadn't, and that meant everything to her. She didn't need his kind of chaos. She needed a peaceful home, a peaceful life.

"You have to go." She closed her eyes against the tide of emotion that took her breath. "You should tell Junie goodbye. Tell her you'll visit next week, and you'll see her on Valentine's Day."

"Kylie, please..." His voice sounded ravaged, but she didn't care. She felt ravaged, as if he'd wrecked her, wrecked her heart.

She shook her head, unwilling to have a conversation that meant he would try to convince her to change her mind. She'd been down this road too many times to fall for that trick. Apologize, promise to never do it again, smooth sailing for a bit, and then it would come again, and they'd repeat the cycle.

For Junie, she would put an end to the cycle.

CHAPTER FOURTEEN

THE DOOR CHIMED. Kylie ignored it. She needed to find someone to help in the coffee shop. She'd resisted the idea for years, but now, having had Mark here to help, she couldn't deny that she needed someone to fill in and give her time off. If she could find someone she clicked with, someone who would love her shop and her customers, she would hire them.

"You look serious." Parker shifted Faith from her left side to her right, and then she wrinkled a brow and set the little girl down. "I am not sure why I keep carrying you. You have two perfectly adorable feet."

"She'll let you carry her until she's ten." Kylie looked up from the paper in front of her. "Do you know Dodie Calder?"

"Not that I know of. Might know the face." Parker held her daughter's tiny hand but stepped closer to look at the filled-out application.

"You're hiring someone? I thought you had Mark trained to be your second in command."

"He's gone." Kylie managed a smile and she felt a little bit of pride in the fact that her eyes remained dry. "It's not as if Mark Rivers was going to trade in his life for the life of a barista."

"That would be a big change for him, but you never know. Wait and ask when he gets back."

Kylie shook her head. "No, he's going to be in and out, but not permanent. Don't get me wrong, I'm glad that he will be here for Junie. She needs him."

"Wait, something happened?" Parker came around the counter and helped herself to a cup of coffee. "Do you have chicken salad? And cheesecake. I think this looks like a cheesecake moment."

"I've eaten my weight in cheesecake," Kylie admitted. "I'm just done, Parker."

There, she'd said it. She was done. And the feelings that had been growing, the ones she'd thought were genuine, possibly forever, those were gone, just a mirage.

"I kind of thought the two of you were working things out." Leave it to Parker to keep digging.

Kylie closed her eyes briefly, just long enough to get her emotions under control.

"We were working on being friends. He had this thing about being intentional in his relationships. More like intentional in not telling me why he had really come here. I'm so angry and…"

"Hurt."

She slipped a finger under her eye to stop the tears that she'd proudly kept in check but were now threatening to break free. "Yes, I'm hurt. He came here to fix his image. This is why we're not good together, because he does these things. He comes in like the hero, rescues me, makes me love him and then hurts me all over again. Actually, this hurts worse, because I thought that maybe we were fixing our marriage. That's silly, because our marriage ended years ago."

Parker grabbed a tissue from a box on the counter and handed it to her. "Men."

For some reason, that made her giggle. "Yes, men. And this man, I've always loved him. I still love him. I just wanted him to love us just as much."

Parker started to say something, but then seemed to change her mind.

"How's Junie?" she asked.

"Missing him, of course. When I left Mark,

she was too young to understand and to realize he was no longer with us. Now, she knows. I've made the best of it. I told her he's coming back and she will have visits with him."

A few more tears trickled down her cheeks.

"What are you going to do?" Parker asked, pouring a second cup of coffee and handing it to Kylie.

"I'm going to keep cleaning my house and organizing drawers, as if that will fix my life. It's such a ridiculous habit."

"It's a coping mechanism."

"That's a nice way to put it." Kylie grabbed a cloth and wiped up the coffee drips. "And there I go again."

"Let me take Junie for the day. She can come out to the house and play with Faith. Faith loves having someone to boss around."

At the mention of her name, the toddler gave a toothy grin. She was perfect, the sweetest with her round cheeks, bright eyes and curly dark hair.

The door opened, and Laura the real estate agent stepped in, her business smile firmly in place.

"Kylie, it's good to see you." Laura approached the counter, where she placed her leather briefcase.

"I'm sorry, didn't Mark tell you he's leaving

the state?" Kylie asked. She'd forgotten about the bank, about the dream, about sharing that moment with Mark as they'd planned what all could be done with the building.

"Oh, he called me. Actually, we met last week." She pulled papers out of the briefcase and pretended to look for a clean spot on the counter, which was spotless. "I don't want these to get wet."

Kylie forced a smile. The last thing she wanted to do was deal with Mark's business. Parker put a hand on her arm and stepped forward, moving her to the side.

"Maybe this should wait for Mark's return. I think his plan is to return Thursday morning. We can have him call you."

Laura slid a pair of reading glasses into place, and she looked over the top, giving Parker a hard stare. "And you are?"

"Mrs. Matthew Rivers. Mark is my brother-in-law. Whatever dealings you have with him would probably be best done in person with Mark."

"I'm not here to see Mr. Rivers." Laura pulled off the glasses, and her business persona melted away. She offered Kylie a real smile. "Kylie, I'm here to see you."

She pushed the papers across the counter. "Mr. Rivers purchased the bank. He arranged it all before he left. The building is yours."

"No." The word came out on a sob. She couldn't focus as tears ran down her cheeks. "Why does he have to do things like this?"

"Because he's Mark. He's a little wild, a little bit chaotic, but he wanted you to have that building." Parker gave her a side hug, holding her tight for a few seconds.

"It's too much. I can't take that building. I don't have the ability to manage both."

"Maybe move this business to the bank?"

"I love my little coffee shop."

Professional Laura returned, sliding the glasses back in place. "I don't know what you'll do with it, but it's yours. If you could sign this document for me?"

The agent handed her a pen. Kylie's hand trembled as she put her signature on the line. Another useless tear streaked down her cheek, this one from being humbled by this gesture.

"A few more signatures and we'll be finished." Laura moved through the papers, explaining what each meant and why it had to be signed, acting like she didn't see the tears. "I'm sorry this is so much, but there are serious legal ramifications if I don't explain and if you don't sign."

"I understand," Kylie said, feeling a little lost in this process and a myriad of emotions, both good and not so good.

Laura put some of the papers back in a folder and handed over a manilla envelope with the most important ones.

"There you go, Kylie. The building is yours. I can't wait to see what you do with it."

"Thank you."

"You're welcome, but the one you should be thanking is Mark. And before I go, could I get a latte and one of those cupcakes?"

"Of course." Kylie grabbed a cup and made the drink, not spilling a drop, even with hands that continued to shake. She handed it to the Realtor and pointed to the stand with sugars and creamers. "You can add whatever you'd like. I'll get your cupcake."

"Smells wonderful. Thank you."

A few minutes later, Laura left with a little wave and a "catch you later."

"Wow." Parker shook her head and then said it again. "Just wow."

"He bought the bank." Kylie stared down at the documents in her hands. "I can't stop crying. Why does he have to do such kind things? Or is this another way to make amends? Will I always question his motives?" The questions rolled out.

"I think in time, if he proves himself, you'll trust him or question him less. The bank building is a grand gesture."

"It is."

"What will you do with it?" Parker asked.

"Laura showed us the place. It's fantastic with high ceilings, big windows and beautiful wood floors. There are apartments upstairs. Oh, and outside, a perfect area for a courtyard. I think it would make a lovely venue."

"Do you have the keys? I want to see inside!"

"Oh, I hadn't thought about that. I own it!" She dumped the envelope Laura had handed her, and the keys fell onto the counter. "I can't do this. It feels like strings."

"Maybe you should talk to him and ask him why," Parker said in her very logical way.

"Talk." Kylie closed her eyes and breathed deeply, feeling the calm that came. "We had discussed that, the need for communication, for being more intentional in our conversations rather than letting misunderstandings grow."

Parker gave a little chuckle as she lifted her

daughter, snuggling her close. "Mark is becoming his brother."

"Maybe he read Matthew's book?"

"Highly possible," Parker said. "Talk to him. Don't make rash decisions or judgements without knowing his intentions."

"I'll talk to him. I just have to work up the energy and the strength."

"Good. And I'll take Junie. Do you care if she spends the night with us?"

"That would be great. I need to go see my mom."

"How is she doing?" Parker asked after blowing raspberries on Faith's pudgy little hands.

"She's angry, and it's my fault. I imprisoned her in a horrible, abusive detention center."

"Nice place, huh?"

"It's a beautiful place. They have lovely grounds, a fountain, the food is decent. But in her mind, I had her locked in jail."

"You know you're going to have to find a way to listen to her without taking it to heart, which is easy for me to say, and I'm sure hard to do."

"I know. It's just tough because I already feel guilty for putting her there. She simply can't be left on her own, unsupervised."

"No, she can't. You're doing the right thing."

"It doesn't feel that way. And then I feel bad because I don't want to visit her."

"Also understandable. Give yourself a break, maybe don't go see her tonight. Instead, go home and take a bubble bath, play with the kitten, take a walk."

"I could use a night off," Kylie admitted. "I need to breathe, to pray and to figure out what I need to do next. Mark is going to want time with his daughter. She needs time with him."

"It's going to be a change for you all."

"It is, and I have to tell him to stop buying things. He is paying for my mom's new facility. He said that's one less thing I have to worry about. Now he's bought the bank for me. I am angry with him, and I want him to just let me have a little time to process these feelings, but he keeps doing all of these kind things that really touch my heart."

He'd said he wanted her to trust him. If only he hadn't hidden his real reason for being in Sunset Ridge. To her heart, that had been a deal-breaker.

MARK LEFT THE meeting with his agent and the record label executives feeling freer than he'd ever felt, except maybe when he left the treatment facility last spring. That had been a good day. A day of second chances. Today had been a day of big changes and unexpected decisions.

He guessed, in a sense, this day had brought second chances as well.

He decided to walk for a bit, just to clear his head and adjust to the decisions he'd made. The weather had turned pretty, nearly seventy degrees. For a February in Nashville, that was a bonus day, the kind of weather a person looked forward to all winter. He decided to take a walk downtown. It had been a while.

He passed old haunts and a few new places that he hadn't been to, places that had opened since he got sober. These days, he avoided those places because they were a temptation. He avoided old friends, too. He'd let them all know that it wasn't anything personal, just a choice he'd had to make.

The sounds and smells were familiar, though. Country music, some good and some bad, the occasional argument, the smell of booze and fried foods. He drew in a breath and smiled. The smells of home. He hesitated outside a place he used to love. He'd started singing in that dive bar. He'd been "discovered" in that bar. The owner had pushed for him, showcased him whenever possible and told everyone who would listen that he'd found a star.

He should go inside and say hello to Bub. He started to. He took a step, and then he hesitated. Bub just happened to peek out the door and saw him standing there.

"Well, I'll be. If it isn't Mark Rivers. Son, I haven't seen you in nearly two years."

"I've been keeping a low profile." That was an understatement if ever there had been one, but they both knew the truth.

"I'd invite you in, but that might not be..."

"Bub, I'd love to be able to come in, but I'm going to give you a hug and move on down the road."

They stepped close and gave a good, solid man-hug and then they stood there on the sidewalk with familiarity and past friendship between them.

"So tell me what you're doing down here. Are you back to work?" Bub asked, his gray hair thinning and his middle a little more paunchy than it had been all of those years ago.

"I came here to meet with the label and my agent. I did meet with them."

"Well good for you. You're sober and getting back to work."

"I'm not," Mark said, needing to say it out loud to someone. "It's hard to say it, but I think there are more important things in my life than music."

Far more important. So important he didn't know how to breathe without them. He missed them, his wife and daughter. And if he had a chance to make things right, that's what he wanted, more than anything.

Bub gave him a long and almost fatherly look. "Son, you've got the right of it. You lost yourself, but it appears you are on the right track. As much as I like to pat myself on the back for discovering new talent, I also want the best for you personally. Maybe music isn't it."

"Maybe it isn't." Just saying the words brought a lightness he hadn't expected. He grinned at the bar owners. "I think I'm on my way."

They both laughed, because he'd said that when Bub introduced him to his first agent. Now the way was a different direction, but one that he thought would lead to more joy. Real joy, not the artificial, made up of stuff, kind of joy. "I'm definitely on my way," he said again, a little easier.

"That you are," Bub repeated from that day so long ago.

"Thanks for everything, Bub. I'll be back around to see you."

"You take care of yourself," Bub told him with a slap on the back.

"That's what I'm trying to do. See you soon, my friend."

"I hope so."

As he said it, he realized he wasn't sure. Maybe this would be his last day in Nashville. The first day in a future that looked, or felt, more promising. As if maybe he'd overcome a dark place in his past and he could trust himself to be the person that Kylie and Junie deserved, the person they could trust.

He walked on, but this time, he headed back to the parking lot where he'd left his car. After tossing his phone on the passenger seat, he picked it up and opened his camera roll. The images picked him up. Junie had taken a few selfies without him knowing. He'd never delete those photos. As a matter of fact, he planned on getting them printed and framing them. Photos of his daughter doing homework, but taking the occasional photo of her feet, her face, her work. And there were pictures of Kylie.

Junie had snapped pictures without her mother knowing. Kylie at work. Kylie smiling at a customer. Those picture filled his heart.

Right there, that was his reason for being, for making the decisions he'd made, for working hard to earn money that would provide a living. Man, he missed them.

He missed them, and now they were the reason for walking away from the career that had provided the living that had moved them out of poverty.

He hit a button on his steering wheel. "Call Jake."

He hadn't talked to Jake in a month. He shouldn't have neglected the relationship.

"Hey, big Mark, how you doing, buddy?" Jake, always up, always cheerful.

"I'm in town," Mark told his friend. "Would you mind getting together?"

"Anything for you." Jake hesitated. "You okay?"

"I will be. I just need a minute."

"You going to your place?" Jake asked.

His place. The house he'd lived in with his wife and daughter. It wasn't his place; it was Kylie's. There were rooms where he thought he could still smell her perfume. There were still diapers on the shelf in the nursery. The house held so many memories, so much of their lives together.

"Yeah, I'm going to my place." He hadn't slept there in months. He'd stayed in hotels. He'd stayed with friends.

"I'll meet you there," Jake said.

Jake actually beat him to the house. Mark had stopped at the store.

Mark eased through the gate and up the driveway of the brick French country–style home that had been their dream. Not too big, Kylie had insisted when they purchased the place. She didn't want to hire someone to clean or to help with the baby. She wanted a home that they could grow into, fill up with children, invite friends and family to visit.

Today it felt hollow, more hollow than when he'd come home after rehab. More hollow than the day she'd left. Their footsteps echoed. As he led Jake through the house, he realized it was time to put the place on the market. He didn't need this house, not here, in Nashville.

He smiled at the thought of the loft above the bank. Laura had delivered the papers to Kylie. He wondered how she'd taken the surprise. Had she been excited or angry? Maybe a little of both. He grinned, imagining her put out by his taking such a step without telling her.

"How was Oklahoma?" Jake asked as he watched Mark put away the groceries he'd picked up on his way to the house.

"Dry and flat." He laughed at the description. "Actually good, and not flat, not in the northeast where I live."

Mark pulled eggs out of a bag, along with milk and butter.

"What are you doing?" Jake asked.

Mark looked at the ingredients. He hadn't really thought about it, but now he knew.

"Making cupcakes. In rehab, they told me to find a new hobby, and I wasn't sure what that would be, until I started baking. Funny story, my dad also bakes."

"Funny," Jake said with a hint of sarcasm.

"Maybe not funny," Mark said. "Ironic."

"You struggling?" Jake asked as he cut to the chase.

"A little." He started with the eggs, then melted butter, added the milk and sugar. Vanilla. He couldn't forget vanilla. "I messed up and didn't tell her about the conditions of my new contract."

"Better public image, right?" Jake had taken

a seat on a barstool. "I'm guessing that didn't go over too well."

"It definitely didn't go over. We were building a relationship, working on trust. I had this grand scheme that if I could be intentional in my relationships, and although we're no longer married, if I could love her the way Christ loves the church, maybe we could be us again."

Us, but better, he thought. More grounded. More mature.

"But you didn't tell her the most important piece of the puzzle."

"Right." He turned on the beaters and let them do their work on the batter. "I'm an idiot."

"It happens to the best of us. Trust is fragile, you know that. She trusted you with her teenage heart, with your daughter and then..."

"No need to remind me. I messed up. I know that, and I won't begrudge her the anger she feels for me. I thought we could be friends." He pulled out the cupcake pan and used cupcake liners before filling each with the vanilla batter.

"That smells pretty good, and it isn't even in the oven yet."

"I have skills."

"And talent." Jake leaned back in the seat. "Do you have coffee?"

"I do. I can even make you a latte if you'd like."

"I'll stick with plain old coffee." Jake scratched his cheek. "Oh, I remember, the ex-wife opened a coffee shop and bakery."

"Yes, she did." Mark set a timer on the oven. "And I've been helping her. She had an appendectomy. Happened my first night in town."

"That must have been rough."

"Stop sounding like my therapist. You're a basketball player."

They both laughed. "You are correct. I'm also your sponsor, so it makes sense that I want to get a feel for what's going on in your life."

"I broke her heart, and she told me to leave."

"I'm assuming you don't have anything in this house that will ruin over a year of sobriety?"

Mark put his hands on the marble counters and stood there for a moment, finding peace, praying for strength. After a few minutes, he opened a cabinet door. Jake joined him, pulling out the bottle he'd kept. Now he realized he didn't want the bottle.

He watched as Jake poured it down the sink. "I told you, don't keep stuff in the house."

"I know. At least I didn't open it. Jake, how

long have you been sober? Like continuously, without relapse."

"Relapsed once, four years ago. It was a week that I truly regret. I've been sober for four years." He tossed the bottles in the trash. "The first year is the hardest. You've made it through that year, Mark. Every day you stay sober, your odds of defeating this monster grow."

"I want my family back, but right now, she thinks I was using her to get my career back."

"Country folks do love a little romance and a happy ending," Jake added, unhelpfully.

"This isn't a country song, it's my life. It's my family." Mark stepped away from the cabinets, from the smell of the alcohol. "When I walked away from that meeting a couple of hours ago, I wondered if I'd made the right decision. I even wondered if I'd get a few miles down the road and change my mind. I made the right decision."

"I guess the one you need to be talking to next is Kylie."

"I'll be going back for Valentine's Day. I hope she'll talk to me. I need to introduce her to the new me."

"I don't envy you. Being a single guy, I've

never had to worry about hurting a family, just my team and my mom."

"Wouldn't it be nice if life had road maps?"

At that, Jake laughed and tossed his pocket Bible on the counter. "In case you've lost yours."

Mark touched the Bible, then he raised his gaze to meet that of his friend. "Thank you for coming over today."

"That's what I'm for, to be here and be strong for you when you can't. Someday, you can be that person for someone else."

"I also like to call you a friend," Mark said as he palmed the Bible, one of many that Jake always had in a pocket, just in case someone needed it. "I have one of these."

"That's okay, keep that one. I have good notes in there."

Mark thumbed through the text and found the notes. One of his favorite verses was circled. "Resist the devil and he will flee." Resist. Don't give in. Don't fall for the temptations.

He flipped to the front cover, knowing the verse that would be there. Psalm 34:14. "'Depart from evil, and do good; seek peace, and pursue it.' Is it that easy?"

"It doesn't say it's easy. It's just a path forward. You know what you're supposed to do, Mark."

"I do," Mark admitted. "The last thing I'd ever ask Kylie is that she give up her new life, a life that makes her happy."

Her life made her happy. His life without them left him empty and alone. That pointed to only one right choice. He glanced back at the words, to see and pursue peace. He knew in Whom to seek for peace. He also knew the direction the giver of peace was taking him. Home.

CHAPTER FIFTEEN

On Valentine's Day, Mark parked his truck several blocks from the square. Jael had joined him. Buck had decided he didn't need to be "traipsing all over town in the cold. Valentine's Day is for the young." They weren't used to spending time together, so the ride had been quiet, with Jael looking out the window and Mark thinking about this night and all the reasons it mattered.

It mattered because, for better or worse, he'd put their Nashville house on the market. For better or worse, he'd told his agent he was positive he wouldn't be signing a new contract. Some things were more important than having his name in lights. Kylie and Junie were more important.

He and Jael exited his truck and started the walk toward the square, still cloaked in uncomfortable silence.

"You know you can't just waltz into this town and pretend you didn't break your wife's heart, your daughter's heart."

"I understand that." The idea that he'd broken their hearts broke his, undid him in a way that nothing else ever had.

As they walked the few blocks to the square, Mark had to agree with Buck; it was cold. His sister didn't seem to mind a bit. Youth, he thought, and then he chuckled because he sounded like Buck. It felt good, to laugh a little.

"What are you laughing about?" she asked, pushing her knit cap up just a bit and giving him a censuring look.

"I was laughing at myself. I'm thirty-three, almost thirty-four, and I just realized that I've started saying things our dad would say. Like you're not aware of the cold because you're young. When did I become Buck Rivers?"

"When you crawled in that bottle and didn't climb back out for ten years of your life. Did you ever stop to think that you missed out on memories that you can't get back?"

"Thanks, I needed something to drag me down just as I started to feel optimistic."

At that, it was her turn to laugh. "You're welcome. Negativity is my gift."

"You should work on that." He found he meant it. He wanted his little sister to find some joy. Everything about her was serious. "Find what gives you joy."

"I'll take your advice into consideration." She gave a little shrug. "So, back to you, because my life isn't that interesting. What's your big plan tonight?"

"Big plan?"

"I mean, there is one or you wouldn't have arranged so many little surprises for this night without telling Kylie. Obviously, you couldn't hide the details, like the carriages or the princess ball. That's pretty touching, by the way."

"This event is for the community, and it shouldn't be just for the ones who can afford dinner out or the vendors. It will be a beautiful night for families who otherwise can't do something like this."

"All in the name of love and convincing Kylie to give you a second chance."

"Cynical." He bumped his shoulder against hers. "It's for the children. That is separate from my relationship with Kylie. Did you know that there are several stories about Saint Valentine? One is that he was martyred for ministering to persecuted Christians."

"You're not persecuted."

"Yeah, that was a sidenote that has nothing to do with anything. I just wanted to teach you something today, other than to mind your own business. I thought you'd only planned to stay a few days?"

"I needed a break from work and Dad seems to enjoy having me here."

He guessed there was more to the story, but it wasn't his story, and he wasn't going to push for details she didn't want to give.

"I think Buck would like it if you moved in permanently. I'm sure he does get lonely. You can be his farm hand."

"I can't see that happening." She took several steps and then stopped, looking up at him. "I really do hope you fix things with your family. Junie deserves to grow up knowing you're there and she can depend on you."

The statement gave him a glimpse into her brokenness. She'd had more, but maybe she'd had less. In time, he hoped they could talk about what caused the dark shadows in her eyes.

While they'd talked, they'd reached the square. Although the actual event didn't start for thirty minutes, people were already milling about, perusing the vendors who had chosen to set up in the outdoors with tents and small heaters. He appreciated their fortitude, but he would have picked one of the heated buildings that had been offered.

The entire square had been transformed into a Valentine's Day winter wonderland.

The tent, a large white fixture, lit inside and out with Christmas lights, was situated at the far end of the lawn. There were tables set up inside and there would be dancing for adults who didn't want to participate in the princess ball held inside the bank. He could hear the band, a local country group, tuning their instruments and doing sound checks.

Chuck and Jenni Stringer had spiffed up their café, putting white tablecloths on the tables, adding bouquets of flowers and piped-in piano music. Chuck had changed out of the George Strait T-shirt that he typically wore on Saturday nights, and Brody had decided to wear a suit because that was what he'd seen in movies.

Mark glanced in the direction of Kylie's. She'd hired a young woman to help in the coffee shop. The new hire meant that Kylie and their daughter could enjoy the festivities, at least for a bit.

His phone dinged, and he pulled it from his pocket to read the text and then hit reply.

"Who was that?" his nosey sister asked.

"Matthew, letting me know that Kylie and Junie are in a carriage. If you don't mind waiting for me, I'll be back."

"Are you going to hijack their carriage?"

He grinned, winking at his sister. "Something like that."

"I like you a lot better than I used to. Are you going to also drag her back to Nashville? You know she hates the city, right?"

He did know that. "I'm not dragging her back, I'm hoping she'll listen to what I have to say. Say a prayer."

"I'll leave that to you."

His little sister was a broken person. He'd never noticed before. Of course, they hadn't spent much time together. As kids, they'd had the occasional visits, but as adults, they'd rarely crossed paths. He really needed to work on being better for her, too.

But right at this moment, he had a carriage to catch. He hurried down the street, finding it hard to jog in boots. He should have worn his running shoes. Two blocks from the square, he spotted them. The carriage was a pretty white affair, pulled by a couple of deep red Missouri mules. He liked the contrast between the carriage with its pretty lights and the plodding mules who would tire less quickly than most horses.

The driver came to a stop, and Mark hopped in, drawing a shriek from Kylie and a "Daddy, you're back!" from Junie as she leapt into his lap.

"Surprise," he said to his ex-wife and his daughter. "I hope you're enjoying the carriage." He hugged Junie tight as he sat down next to Kylie.

Personally, he'd never seen the romance of a carriage. It was rough, jolting and not really very comfortable. For some reason, people thought it romantic to take a ride around the block in one. He doubted the settlers who traveled across the country in wagons thought they were too romantic.

"I love the carriage," Junie said as she snuggled between her parents. "Did you know they have princess dresses at the church and silly costumes for boys?"

"And here I thought I'd jumped into the carriage of real princesses. I didn't realize it was just a costume."

"Daddy," she said with a roll of her eyes. "You're being silly."

"I am silly, but I do think you are both princesses."

"Mommy is the queen," Junie told him.

Mommy still hadn't spoken.

"Happy Valentine's Day, Kylie." He said it softly, hoping to break down the walls she'd put up. He'd messed up. He'd more than messed up.

"I'm glad you could make it," she said, her gaze dropping to Junie in a pointed way. No conversations with little ones aboard. He got it.

He desperately wanted to tell her everything. He wanted her advice. He wanted her for a partner again. He prayed, had been praying, for healing for their marriage, for her heart.

The carriage took them around the block and then to the square. They drove past Chuck's, and Kylie commented on the crowd inside. There were also quite a few customers in her coffee shop.

"I should…" she started.

"Later," he said. "I'll help you. Parker and your new assistant can handle this for a bit."

Her head craned in the direction of her business, and she exhaled, letting go. Her hand reached for Junie's. The carriage circled to the side of the square where the bank stood like a centurion of the past, guarding its corner with elegance. Lights illuminated the facade and sparkled from inside.

"Thank you for this building," she said as the carriage came to a halt. "I mean that."

"It's going to be something special." He believed that wholeheartedly.

"Let's go in." Junie had lost her struggle with patience.

Mark didn't blame her; it all looked very enchanting. Princesses, princes, court jesters and parents were entering through the double doors that were being opened by doormen he'd hired to give it all a very exclusive feel. Inside, he'd hired a caterer from the city to serve appetizers and desserts. A trio played instrumental music.

He helped first his daughter and then Kylie from the carriage. Her hand slipped into his. He hesitated, wanting to look his fill before handing her down to the sidewalk. Her gorgeous hair had been pulled up in a pretty style that framed her face. Her eyes were wide, her lips parted slightly. She smelled of tropical islands and summer gardens. The top she wore was a deep red and hung past her waist, flowing and silky over black leggings.

Her hand trembled in his, and he held it a little tighter, drawing her down from the carriage so she stood next to him.

"Mark," she started.

He winked. "Call me Prince Charming."

"You've always been charming," she said in a dry tone.

"May I?" He gave her the crook of his right arm. With his left hand, he took hold of Junie. Together, the three walked through the doors of the bank into a room that had been transformed into a ballroom.

"This is..." Kylie gave him an astonished look. "You did all of this?"

"I've never taken Junie to a father and daughter dance. I thought about it and thought there might be other parents who wanted this special moment with their children. Ta-da, welcome to the first annual Sunset Ridge Prince and Princess Ball. Happy Valentine's Day to you both."

Kylie didn't speak, but her dark eyes were luminous with unshed tears. "Mark, sometimes you steal my breath."

He wanted to steal her heart.

He bowed before his daughter, holding her hand as he did. "Princess Junie, could I have this dance?"

She curtsied and then giggled. "Yes, you may. And then you have to dance with Mommy because she's the queen."

"Gladly."

He led his daughter in a slow dance with Kylie just at the edge of his vision, watching. He had so much to say to her. Their future depended on this night.

KYLIE WATCHED AS Junie and Mark circled the dance floor, talking and laughing. Days ago, she'd been so angry with him. Tonight, she wanted to stay angry, just to protect her heart. She also wanted to hug him for his thoughtfulness, not just to Junie, but to all of the families who were being gifted such a wonderful experience. It wasn't about the money he'd spent, it was about his kindness in thinking of others.

This man who arranged such wonderful things was the man she'd loved, the man she'd married and had a daughter with. She'd taken vows with him to love him forever. She'd taken vows that spoke of love that had no end, that didn't faint and fall apart in a crisis, that didn't give up. She hadn't given up. He had. He'd given up on them.

That was her greatest hurt. He hadn't put his

wife and daughter first. He'd put his own wants and needs ahead of his family.

Tonight, she didn't want to think on those things, on the past. She wanted to let go of that burden and live a life free from those hurts. She'd become an expert at letting go. She'd been letting go her entire life. Letting go of dreams, of the hope she'd have a happy home, even in childhood, wanting her mom to be like other moms. She was done with letting go.

She'd always been a determined person. Determined to have better and be better. With or without Mark, she would continue to reach for better.

Mark circled back around with Junie, and the music ended. He bowed again, and their daughter did another excellent curtsy. This time, he bowed in front of Kylie. He extended his hand, an invitation to dance. Kylie closed her eyes briefly, thinking of ways to reject the offer. And then she nodded and took his hand, allowing him to lead her onto the dance floor.

The band began to play a Norah Jones song. Surprisingly, the violinist sang, and she did it well. The sweet words of "Come Away with Me" filled the lofty building, echoing sweetly.

"Did you ask for this song?" Kylie asked as Mark pulled her close.

He nodded, pulling her closer.

They danced well together. In their young and broke days in Nashville, they'd taken ballroom dance classes. They'd tripped over their feet, laughed until they cried, and then they'd found their rhythm and learned to dance.

"I've always loved her voice," Kylie said as she drew close, allowing him to lead her in the waltz.

"I've always loved you."

"Mark, please don't do this. Not right now."

"I have to," he said. She wished he wouldn't. The night was perfect. It was beautiful.

"Can we finish the dance?" she asked.

"We can." They circled the dance floor in each other's arms. On the sideline, Jael had found Junie and was keeping her entertained.

Kylie watched as his sister led his daughter to the buffet and they began to fill their plates. She didn't have to worry about Junie. She relaxed into the rhythm of the dance.

In that moment, in Mark's arms, Kylie felt whole. She felt loved. She felt all the things she'd longed for from him and none of the things that hurt. As the song ended, he led her away, away from the crowds and their daughter.

They went out the back door, and she gasped. There were candles everywhere, and as they left the bank behind, floating lanterns began to fill the sky. He'd planned this. She didn't even have to ask. Somehow, someway, he'd planned this.

Her heart wavered, wanting to be his. Her brain said to back away, to keep the boundaries that were necessary for safety.

"Why?" she asked, needing answers. They couldn't go back. She didn't know how to go forward.

"Because you're the most amazing person I know, and this night is for you, for you to feel cherished and loved."

Love? She shook her head at the word.

"Kylie, I messed up." He must have seen her roll her eyes. "Okay, a lot. I've messed up so many times. The young me was a stupid fool who got caught up in his own imagined self-importance. Kylie, before I came here last month, it was mentioned that a healthy relationship with my family would fix my public image. But that is not why I came. When Junie saw the text, and you didn't even hesitate to believe the worst in me, I didn't feel a need to try and explain."

"We keep going back to the issue of honesty and communicating," she said.

"Yes, we do. I wasn't joking when I told you I want to be more intentional in our relationship. Kylie, I asked my brother what the Scripture means when it tells a husband to love his wife the way Jesus loves the church. I've spent weeks journaling and praying about this. I'm to treat you as if you're the most important person in my life. I'm to care for you, to uplift you, to sacrifice for you, and I am to put your needs ahead of my own. Our marriage was broken, our family broken, because I put what I wanted ahead of what my family needed. I came back to Sunset Ridge to seek your forgiveness, and then I planned to go on my way because I don't want to put you through that again. I don't want to let you down."

"I think we both have trust issues, Mark."

"I know we do. Neither of us trust me." He said it with that smile of his that touched her heart. "I have come to realize that I was keeping God out of the equation. I, on my own, am a mess of a man. But I'm seeking the man God wants me to be. And that man is your husband.

That man is the person who loves you more than he loves himself. He loves his daughter. He loves you more than a career."

"More than a career?" she couldn't help but tease.

"I met with the record label, fully intending to sign the contract. I went back to the house and prayed, and then I put that house on the market, and I called and told my agent that I'd be coming back to Sunset Ridge."

"Okay, you came back. Now what? Do you go back to Nashville to sign the contract?" She felt her heart beat hard against her ribs. She wanted him to give an answer that told her they mattered. She feared he wouldn't.

"I put our house on the market, Kylie. I hope you're okay with that. I hired a moving company to pack everything and bring it here to storage, so you can decide what to keep."

"You haven't answered my question." And it was starting to hurt, to make her feel afraid.

"I'm not going back to Nashville. I told them there will be no contract, no new album. I had to come back to Sunset Ridge. I left something important here. I left the most important part of me. I left you."

She felt the walls around her heart crumbling.

A sudden wave of hope washed over her, hope that this Mark, the man standing before her, was the one that God had brought into her life, and the hope that he was seeking God in a way that would change their lives.

"Did you find it?" she asked. He looked a little confused. "What you left behind."

"I hope so. What I left behind was my wife and daughter. I want you back, Kylie. I want to be the man you can count on, the man who will keep you close and cherish you."

"I'm afraid," she admitted. She drew in a breath, held onto resolve that was quickly slipping away. "I can't rush into this Mark. There is so much at stake—not just our relationship, but Junie, her heart, her feelings."

"I know and I understand. I know you don't want to rush things and you shouldn't. I just want to know if there is a chance that you might love me and give us the opportunity to begin again."

"I do love you. That doesn't take away the fear."

"I get that. I have a whole lot of baggage, but I've given that baggage to God, and I'm going to be relying on Him to help me live each day for Him and for my family. For whatever He calls me to. I want to spend time growing in my walk with Him. I want to prove to you and to myself that I can be the man you deserve, that you can trust."

"Mark, is there a question in all of this?"

He pulled her close and kissed her, keeping her near, drawing her heart to his. He ended the kiss, but he remained close, his forehead touching hers.

"There is a question, but I'm afraid to ask, because I'm afraid you'll say no."

"I'm not going to say no," she said, surprising herself. "I'm also not going to say yes."

He pulled back a step and she saw the glimmer of gold and diamonds in the box he held in his hand. He chuckled nervously. "Now I'm not sure what to say."

"Promise me that you're going to be honest with me and that we're going to continue to work on being the couple, the family we were meant to be. It isn't going to happen in a month. It might not happen in a year, but in time, when we are ready."

"I can make that promise. This is a new ring for a new beginning. It's a promise for our future. That future is in your hands, if you'll take it."

Kylie held out her hand and he placed the ring on her finger. He held her hand for a moment and then he kissed her palm.

"Once upon a time, I put a ring on this finger and I didn't keep the promises I made to you. That ring was purchased by a younger, dumber version of myself, a man who didn't know how to be a husband and a father. I hope that I've grown and learned from my mistakes. I can't promise I'll be perfect, but I promise to be my very best self for you, for our daughter and even for myself."

She closed her eyes, holding those words tight and praying for them both, for their family and their future. "I'm going to give us a chance, Mark. I want a better version of us, too."

Fireworks rocketed through the night sky, and a lone violinist joined them to play a song about a marriage renewed, two people broken but finding a way to put the pieces back together.

As lanterns floated away on the night sky and cold air touched her cheeks, she felt the warmth of Mark's lips on hers and hope filled up the dark and empty places.

EPILOGUE

KYLIE LOOKED IN the mirror, again, worrying that her dress was too much for such a simple ceremony. Jael settled the veil on her head and smiled from behind her, their gazes meeting in the mirror.

"Why are you worrying?" Jael asked. Mark's little sister had become a friend of sorts, even though she still kept mostly to herself and kept her secrets.

"I'm not worrying, not about Mark, not about our relationship." For the past six months, he'd worked hard in the community, helping his brother in ministry, leading worship in church, being the father Junie had needed and deserved. He went to weekly meetings to maintain his sobriety. They talked, no, they communicated. Each night after Junie went to bed, they discussed their day, what was good and what went wrong, if anything. They shared their worries and their joys. They prayed together.

He put them first. At night, after their prayers, he went back to his loft apartment above the bank. After today, he would move back in with his family. He'd courted her for six months. It had been the dating period they'd skipped as teens.

"What is it?" Parker asked as she came forward with the bouquet of lilies and baby's breath.

"I'm walking down the aisle like it's my first wedding, and it isn't. I'm thirty-three, and Mark and I were already married. This all seems a bit silly."

"You were married, but you didn't have a real wedding." Jael stated the obvious. "You got married at the courthouse in Nashville."

"Yes, we did."

"Today, you're going to get married in your home church. You'll have a beautiful reception in the bank to celebrate the occasion." Parker gave her a big smile. The bank had been turned into a lovely venue.

"Yes, it's going to be beautiful." Kylie smiled at the two women who would be her sisters. "I'm so glad you're both my family."

Jael gave her a quick hug. Parker's hug held a little longer.

"Mommy, you're beautiful." Junie slipped into the room. She wore a pretty pink dress, and her hair was curled in ringlets thanks to her aunt Jael.

"You're a princess," Kylie told her daughter. "We should hurry. Let's get this over with."

Parker shook her head. "No, let's enjoy this moment. Celebrate it. Make it a beautiful memory."

"Yes, celebrate. Memories. Blah, blah, blah." Kylie reached for her bouquet. "Is he out there?" she asked Junie.

"He's at the front of the church, and he's sweating bullets." Junie gave a strong nod, her lips pursed.

"Sweating bullets. You've been eavesdropping again." Kylie leaned to give her daughter a kiss on the cheek. "Let's put him out of his misery."

"That's what he said." Junie giggled.

Buck waited for her, and he led her out the door of the church and to the front door of the sanctuary. The double doors were open. Her groomsmen, Matthew and Luke, were waiting. They walked down the aisle with Parker and

Jael. Junie came next, tossing silk flower petals as she walked.

Buck held tight to Kylie's arm, and he leaned a little closer.

"I'm real glad to see you all working this out. God planned the two of you. I never doubted that. It's just that things went a little off course."

"We're back on course," Kylie agreed. "Thank you for walking me down the aisle. It means so much."

"You mean a lot to me. I'm glad you gave that son of mine a second chance."

"Same."

As they walked, the song played that the two of them had claimed as their own. The lyrics to "Broken Together" filled the church. A song of being broken and being made whole again.

Broken together.

Mark reached for her hand as his dad nodded and walked away. She wanted to kiss him, to tell him how much she wanted them to always be this way, together. Whole.

Matthew cleared his throat and told them to let go of each other's hands until he gave them permission to take each other by the hand. Mark didn't let go. Matthew didn't argue. Instead, he spoke the words that would make them man and wife, make them a family. And then he told Mark he could kiss his bride.

Mark pulled her close. His eyes were intense; the look on his face brought a shiver down her spine.

"This time, Kylie, it's forever. I will cherish you, sacrifice for you, make you the most important thing I have on this earth. Trust me."

"I do trust you." God had made it possible to trust, to be healed of their past. "And I love you. I've always loved you."

They kissed and the crowd that had gathered, the people who loved them and supported them, cheered. As they left the church, Brody hurried forward to sing the song they'd given him to sing. "Fly Me to the Moon."

Brody, it turned out, had a very decent singing voice.

★ ★ ★ ★ ★

Their Inseparable Bond

Jill Weatherholt

MILLS & BOON

Weekdays, **Jill Weatherholt** works for the City of Charlotte. On the weekend, she writes contemporary stories about love, faith and forgiveness. Raised in the suburbs of Washington, DC, she now resides in North Carolina. She holds a degree in psychology from George Mason University and a paralegal studies certification from Duke University. She shares her life with her real-life hero and number one supporter. Jill loves connecting with readers at jillweatherholt.com.

Visit the Author Profile page
at millsandboon.com.au.

But Jesus beheld them, and said unto them,
With men this is impossible;
but with God all things are possible.
—*Matthew* 19:26

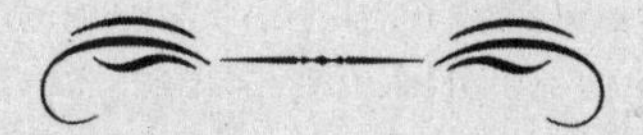

DEDICATION

For Derek.
Thank you for your enduring patience
during my perpetual meltdowns.

CHAPTER ONE

CANINE TRAINER JAKE BECKETT peered at his twins in the rearview mirror. Being a single father at the age of fifty had never been part of the plan. Then again, neither had losing his wife and their unborn child.

"Do you think Miss Myrna will bake her yummy snickerdoodle cookies for the class picnic?" Six-year-old Kyle called out from the back seat of Jake's cherry-red extended-cab pickup truck.

Myrna Hart's cookies were famous in the small town of Bluebell Canyon, Colorado. Without Myrna, the most beloved resident in town, Jake would have never survived that first year after his wife passed away.

"I don't see why not, but you can ask her yourself when we get to her house."

Jake stole a glance at his son. With his dark brown eyes and sun-kissed brown hair, Kyle was the spitting image of his late mother. His twin sister, Kayla, had many of his wife's features, like her thick, wavy brown hair and rust-colored freckles that dotted the bridge of her nose, but Kyle favored their mother more.

Jake brought the vehicle to a stop at the intersection. Cumulus clouds drifted over the Rocky Mountains. He glanced over his shoulder and noticed Kayla gazing out the window, lost in thought. "Are you okay, Kayla? You haven't said a word since we left the school."

"She's upset about the mother-daughter fashion show." Kyle nudged his sister's arm.

"Stop it." Kayla pushed back and stuck out her tongue.

The family dog, Tank, a three-year-old Border collie nestled between the children, raised his head and released a snort.

"Settle down, kids. What's this about a fashion show, Kayla?"

The sudden silence was ominous. As time passed, Jake was coming to realize that as Kayla got older, not having a mother would bring challenges he might not be prepared to handle.

"Nothing... It's stupid." She choked back tears.

"Yeah, who cares about seeing a bunch of

girls walking around wearing different clothes?" Kyle said. "It's silly, Kay. Forget about it. We can go fishing or something instead."

Jake was proud of his son. Kyle always tried to protect his sister. It was best to drop the subject for now. The event obviously upset her.

Moments later, Jake pulled into the circular driveway in front of Myrna's house. Rocking chairs lined the large wraparound porch, tempting a person to settle down with a glass of icy lemonade. For the past two years, Myrna's door was always open. After Laura died while giving birth to what would have been their third child, Myrna's home had become a refuge for Jake and his children.

Jake raked a hand through his cropped salt-and-pepper hair, unbuckled his seat belt and opened the cab door. Tank sprang from the truck.

"I'll race you!" Kyle called out to his sister before sprinting toward the front porch.

Kayla zipped off with Tank on her heels.

The children thundered up the steps, ran across the wide-plank flooring and jerked open the squeaky screen door. Myrna had told them long ago they didn't need to call ahead or knock—they were family.

Jake's long, muscular legs circled to the rear of the truck to retrieve the replacement stairway railing. Myrna's diagnosis of macular degeneration had propelled him on a mission to make her house more accommodating and safer. Jake and others in the community looked after Myrna following the death of her husband, Jeb, five years ago.

He walked across the driveway carrying the railing and ascended the stairs. Tank circled the porch twice, exploring the wood with his wet nose. Then he headed to the oversize dog bed Myrna had bought specially for him.

"Lie down, Tank."

The dog spun around three times before flopping on the pillow and releasing a sigh.

"Good boy." Jake opened the door and stepped into the foyer. The toe of his leather work boot caught on the runner that covered the hardwood floor. Jake made a mental note to inspect the entire house for throw rugs. They were a tripping hazard. To ensure Myrna's safety, they would have to go.

Voices echoed from the kitchen. Jake moved past the baby grand piano to the back of the house. He inhaled the aroma of sweet cinnamon. He stepped inside the kitchen and Myrna's face brightened. Measuring in at barely five feet tall, Myrna kept fit by her constant motion. Her seventy-year-old skin showed no sign of the hours she spent outdoors in her garden.

"Jake, I just told the children your timing is perfect. Not only are there fresh snickerdoodles, but you finally get to meet my beautiful granddaughter and brilliant doctor, Olivia." Myrna winked and ran a finger through her short silver hair. "She flew into town last night for an overdue visit. It was a delightful surprise."

Jake's pulse ticked up when he spotted a striking young woman sitting on one of the stools surrounding the granite-topped island in the kitchen. Kyle was chatting up a storm with her like she was an old friend. Olivia's auburn, wavy hair cascaded over the tops of her shoulders.

Jake placed the railing against the laundry room door. He approached Olivia and extended his hand. He swallowed hard against the knot in his throat. "I've heard a lot about you. It's nice to meet you in person. I'm Jake Beckett."

Olivia smiled. She stood, revealing her long limbs and slender stature, and accepted Jake's hand. "Hello. Olivia Hart. It's a pleasure to meet you."

According to Myrna, Olivia worked long

hours as an ER doctor in Miami, Florida. She was married, but he didn't remember Myrna ever mentioning children. Jake released her hand. At six foot one, it wasn't often he met a lady almost equal in height. "I didn't mean to interrupt your reunion. I thought I'd stop by and install the railing. I picked it up at the hardware store this morning since I'll be taking the kids to the car show tomorrow."

Myrna set the pitcher of sweet tea on the counter, then removed glasses from the cabinet. She glanced in her granddaughter's direction. "He has a mile-long list of improvements he'd like to make on the house. Jake is the most thoughtful young man you'll ever meet. He's always doing for others."

Jake's face warmed. "I'm not exactly young, but that's kind of you to say. I've added something to the list. We need to get rid of that runner in the foyer, along with the other throw rugs. They're a hazard."

"See, Gammy? Jake agrees with me. It's not safe for you to be living alone." Olivia addressed Myrna with a pointed look.

Jake shook his head. "I wouldn't say that. With some improvements and the help of a service dog, I think your grandmother will be fine."

"You're getting a dog?" Olivia glanced at her grandmother.

"Yes, and she's just the sweetest thing. Her name is Callie. Jake is training her." Myrna smiled and took a seat at the island.

Jake removed his wallet from his back pocket. He pulled out a business card and passed it to Olivia. "My brothers and I run a business together. They're out of town on a hunting trip, otherwise they'd be here devouring your grandmother's cookies."

Olivia examined the card. "Beckett's Canine Training. So you train service dogs?"

He nodded and straightened his shoulders. "Yes, ma'am, along with herding dogs. We train and place service dogs across the state. I also host a camp four times a year for Puppy Raisers."

"Why don't you bring Callie with you for Sunday dinner so Olivia can get to know her?" Myrna suggested to Jake.

He'd thought about bringing Callie along today, but she wasn't behaving well this morning. Jake left her at his brother's house. Callie had proved to be a slow learner. She would never make it as an official service dog, but Jake was confident she could meet Myrna's needs if her vision deteriorated. "I'll do that." He grabbed two glasses Myrna had left next to the pitcher. "Do you want some tea, kids?"

"Yes, yes!" Kyle bounced on his toes.

Kayla remained silent while sneaking looks at Olivia.

"Kayla, what about you?"

"I'm not thirsty," she whispered.

"Don't forget the cookies." Myrna pointed to the large porcelain Cheshire cat. "I had forgotten all about the car show tomorrow."

"We haven't," Kyle chirped. "Daddy said we could even stay until dark to watch the fireworks. It'll be so cool!"

Myrna looked at Jake. "Maybe you can take Olivia. I want her to experience everything that small-town life offers."

Olivia released a sigh and addressed Jake. "She's trying to convince me to give up my job and uproot my life in Miami." Olivia rolled her eyes. "Small-town life isn't for me."

"So, quaint and hospitable isn't your thing?" He laughed.

"I don't mean to be disrespectful. It's fine for some people." She drew her shoulders back.

"If you stick around long enough, you might change your mind." Jake couldn't imagine living anywhere else. He'd enjoyed growing up in Virginia, but after he and his brothers inherited the land in Bluebell nearly twenty years ago from their aunt who passed, the entire family had moved out West.

Olivia trailed her finger along the top of her glass of sweet tea. "I don't see that happening. But I will stay long enough to convince my grandmother to move back to Miami with me. So, the safety improvements and the dog training probably aren't necessary."

Jake's mouth dropped open. Wait. What? Was she serious? There was no way Jake could allow that to happen. Sure, he wasn't blood, but Myrna was family to him and his children.

Kyle moved closer to his father. Anguish filled his eyes. "Is Miss Myrna moving?"

Myrna sprang from her stool with the agility of a teenager. She opened the oak cabinet, removed a serving platter and scooped the cookies from the jar. Carefully, she placed them in a semicircle on the dish. "I'm not going anywhere. My home is here. It's where I plan to stay until I go home to be with the Lord." Myrna hurried to the island with the baked goods. "Let's change the subject and enjoy these cookies."

Kayla gave Olivia a callous once-over. After losing her mother, Kayla clung to Myrna. Two years had passed and their bond was stronger than ever. Kyle loved the older woman too, but Kayla and Myrna had a special connection that the little girl wasn't about to allow this interloper to destroy.

"Now, about the car show. You should go with Jake and the kids, Olivia." Myrna sat, broke off a piece of cookie and popped it into her mouth. "I think you'd have a good time. I won't be able to take you since I'll be baking cupcakes tomorrow morning and preparing for Bible study."

Jake considered Myrna's suggestion. It might be a good idea for Olivia to go to the show. She'd hear firsthand how much the people in the community loved her grandmother. There wasn't a person in Bluebell who wouldn't help Myrna in a time of need. Maybe then Olivia would drop this outlandish idea to move her. "If you're interested, you're welcome to join the kids and me," Jake offered.

"Yes!" Kyle jumped off his stool and circled to Olivia. "Please come with us, Dr. Olivia. It'll be so much fun. We're going to have a picnic. Daddy's going to make us his special triple-decker club sandwiches. We even get to have soda, too!"

Olivia looked at Jake. Her brow arched. "What about your wife? Shouldn't you check with her?"

Silence covered the room like mist drifting across a pond.

Jake's stomach twisted. His eyes darted between the twins. Kayla's face turned to stone. Kyle's lower lip quivered.

"Our mommy is dead." Kayla's abrupt response shattered the silence.

Kyle ran to Jake and buried his face in his father's hip.

Embarrassed, Jake addressed his daughter. "Kayla, I think you should apologize to Dr. Olivia."

Kayla eyed her father. "It's true. I don't have a mommy anymore."

"That may be, but I didn't like your tone."

The adults exchanged glances. Kayla remained silent, crossed her arms and rolled her lower lip.

Olivia cleared her throat. "I'm so sorry."

Olivia turned to her grandmother. "I guess I didn't remember."

The refrigerator's motor hummed. Outside, a car door slammed, and Tank barked twice.

"It sounds like I have more company." Myrna clapped her hands and rose from her seat. "So it's settled. Jake, you and the kids can swing by tomorrow morning and pick up Olivia on your way to the car show. I'll have a batch of cupcakes ready for the picnic."

Jake nodded. There was no point in arguing with Myrna.

Myrna headed to the door. Kayla remained quiet, and Olivia kept her eyes glued to the floor. Kyle inched toward Olivia's stool. "So, you'll go with us to the car show?"

"That's sweet of you, Kyle, but your father might want to keep this a family outing." Olivia looked up at Jake as though asking for permission.

"We would be happy for you to join us," Jake said.

"Please, will you come?" Kyle asked.

Olivia turned her attention back to Kyle and smiled. "I've always loved triple-decker sandwiches. Of course I'll go."

Kyle pumped his fist and whispered a *yes*,

perhaps not wanting to upset his sister, but it was too late. Kayla frowned at Jake before racing out the kitchen door and into the backyard to take refuge in the tree house. After his wife died, Jake had built the house for the kids on Myrna's property since the family spent so much of their time with Myrna.

"Please come and have some tea and cookies, Larry." Myrna returned to the kitchen with her guest.

For as long as Jake could remember, Larry Walker had been the branch manager of the only bank in town. He sometimes overlooked late payments when someone in the community experienced tough times. Larry was a good man. Jake extended his hand. "It's nice to see you. What brings you out this way?"

Larry placed his briefcase on the island and reached inside. "I need a couple of signatures from Myrna."

"For the home improvements. Don't you remember?" Myrna directed her question at Jake. "I took out a home equity line of credit to cover the cost. I know I mentioned it to you."

"You did. But I told you a loan wasn't necessary. I can do all the work for you."

Myrna smiled. "That's generous of you, but

I can't let you work for free. Besides, I have to pay for the materials."

Jake wouldn't be working for free. He couldn't count the number of meals and counseling sessions Myrna had provided him since his wife died. He'd never be able to repay her in his lifetime. "You can pay for the material, but I won't accept a dime from you for the labor."

Myrna rolled her eyes and looked down at the papers Larry had placed in front of her. "Where do I sign?"

Larry flipped the pages and pointed to the signature block at the bottom of page three. "Right here."

Myrna blinked her eyes before rubbing her fingers over her eyelids.

"Where? Let me put on my reading glasses." Myrna removed the eyewear from the top of her head and slid them on her face.

The three adults watched as Myrna squinted to see the signature line. Her glasses didn't appear to help.

"Gammy, when was the last time you saw the eye doctor?" Olivia moved closer.

"I had a follow-up appointment a month ago, but I had to cancel."

"Why?" Olivia asked.

"Elizabeth from my prayer group needed a ride to Denver for her cataract surgery."

Myrna always put others ahead of herself.

Olivia shook her head. "This is exactly why you should come to Miami. It's not safe for you to drive a car if you can't see to sign your name. I can't allow you to put yourself in danger. You have macular degeneration. If you don't stay on top of this disease, you could lose your eyesight."

Jake agreed about the seriousness of Myrna's condition. Since her diagnosis, he'd researched the disease. He was aware of what could happen if Myrna didn't receive proper treatment. Jake had found a well-regarded specialist in Denver and put Myrna's name on the waiting list for an appointment. But if Olivia had her way, Myrna would never have that appointment. Jake couldn't allow that to happen. Completing the safety improvements on Myrna's home and training Callie would be his top priorities. Jake had every intention of proving to Olivia that Myrna belonged in Bluebell, surrounded by the people who loved her.

"GOOD MORNING, SLEEPYHEAD." Myrna stood at the six-burner gas stove. A white-and-yellow apron hugged her waist.

A heavy sensation filled Olivia's chest. Her father used to call her "sleepyhead." Olivia often reflected on how different her life would have been if her father hadn't died when she was young. Her bare feet padded across the pinewood floor leading to her grandmother's kitchen. "Good morning." She hugged the woman and held on a little longer than usual. The tension she hadn't known she'd been carrying eased. "It's nice to be here with you, Gammy. I've missed you."

Myrna smiled. "I've missed you, too."

"I'm sorry I let so much time pass."

"There's no need to apologize. I still carry fond memories of the cruise you took me on several years ago. And remember, you visited a couple times when you attended medical conferences in Denver."

"Those were brief evening visits before I had to get back to Miami." Olivia lowered her gaze. "I should have spent more time with you."

"You're a busy doctor. And with the divorce, I'm sure it's been difficult. I only wish you would have told me about your marital issues before you arrived in Bluebell. Maybe I could have helped you."

Olivia hadn't shared the details of the breakup

with Gammy or anyone. She'd been in shock when her ex-husband told her he no longer wanted to have children. Her world went into a tailspin when Mark filed for divorce. Olivia wanted to work on their differences, but Mark believed it was best to end the marriage since he no longer shared her dream of having a family. "I'm not sure anyone could have helped, but there's no excuse for me not to have called you more frequently."

"You're here now. That's what's important. Breakfast is almost ready. I'm sure you're starving."

The aroma of bacon with a hint of sweetness caused her stomach to rumble. "I am. Why didn't you wake me up last night?" Olivia headed to the coffeepot. She removed a cup from the mug tree and poured. A baking sheet lined with a dozen cupcakes cooled on the countertop.

"After Liz dropped me off from my caring cards meeting, you were sleeping so sound, I didn't have the heart." Myrna speared a strip of bacon with a fork and turned it over. She reduced the flame. Hot grease hissed inside the skillet.

Olivia couldn't remember when she'd slept

so soundly. During the separation and following the divorce, with no one waiting for her at home, Olivia often covered for her colleagues who had families. "I don't think I've slept that long since I was in high school." She laughed and took a sip of the hot brew.

Myrna slid four slices of whole wheat bread into the toaster. "Between the time difference and the stress of traveling, you needed your rest. Since you slept through dinner, I've cooked you a big breakfast."

"That's so thoughtful. Thank you." Olivia took notice of the farmhouse table with five place settings. "Are you expecting company?"

"Since Jake was so sweet with his offer to take you to the car show today, I thought inviting him and the children over for breakfast was the least I could do." Myrna removed the second batch of cupcakes from the oven.

"Here, let me help you." Olivia grabbed a pot holder from the counter and took the baked goods from her grandmother. "It's only nine o'clock. I can't believe how much cooking and baking you've done. Do you ever slow down?"

"I could ask you the same. I worry about you working such long hours at the hospital."

Myrna opened the refrigerator and removed a plate of cupcakes.

Olivia wanted to cut back her hours now, but when her marriage was crumbling, she'd used her job to escape the truth. The man she'd vowed to spend the rest of her life with had decided he no longer wanted to have children. "If you move to Miami, we can look after each other. I can reduce my hours. Or maybe I can leave the hospital and start a small family practice of my own that could offer more flexibility." Olivia bit her lower lip. "What if something happened to you? You're all alone in this big house."

Myrna placed the dessert on the counter and rested her hand on Olivia's arm. "You're thinking about your father, aren't you?"

Since Olivia had learned about her grandmother's diagnosis, reliving the day her father died had become an everyday occurrence. If only she'd come straight home from school instead of disobeying her mother and going to the playground with her friends. The thought of her grandmother dying alone in her home, like her father, had consumed her mind. "I don't want to leave you here by yourself."

"I appreciate that, but my life is here. The

people in this town have been my family for almost twenty years. I couldn't imagine ever leaving Bluebell." Myrna pulled her hand away and pushed herself from the table. "Jake will be here soon. I better get the icing on these so you can take them with you."

The mention of Jake reminded her of the struggle she had earlier deciding what to wear. She looked down at her black jeans and pink blouse. "Is this outfit okay? I didn't know what to wear. I've never been to a car show." Since Olivia first woke up, she'd had reservations about spending the day with Jake and his children. "Are you sure you can't come with us to the car show? Jake is your friend. I feel uncomfortable going with him and his kids."

"Your outfit is perfect." Myrna glanced at the clock on the wall. She carried the plate of cupcakes and the bowl of icing to the table. "Come and sit with me, dear."

Olivia followed her grandmother and pulled out a chair from the table for each of them. She sat down and took a sip of her coffee.

"Why are you so apprehensive about going to the show with Jake and his children?" Myrna asked as she ran the knife with a glob of vanilla icing over the chocolate cupcake.

"I should have never asked about his wife. I feel terrible. To be honest with you, I didn't remember you mentioning that Jake had lost his wife. I guess I wasn't paying attention. I'm sorry." The coffee soured in Olivia's stomach.

"Don't be so hard on yourself. I never shared the details of what that family has endured with you." Myrna pulled in a slow breath and released it. "It should have been a happy time for Jake's family. His wife, Laura, was seven months pregnant when she went into labor. She had issues with her blood pressure and had a heart attack." Myrna wiped a tear.

"And the baby?"

Her grandmother shook her head. "It devastated Jake. He lost his wife and baby boy in a matter of minutes. If it weren't for his strong faith, I don't think he would have survived."

"That's so sad." Olivia placed her hand over her mouth and shook her head.

"Laura was a wonderful wife and mother. She kept the Beckett house running. Poor Kyle and Kayla, they didn't understand what had happened to their mother. Kyle had terrible nightmares, and Kayla wouldn't talk."

"How did Jake handle it by himself?"

"Oh, he wasn't alone. His brothers were here

to support him. Plus, the entire town rallied around him."

Myrna brushed a tear from her cheek.

"After Laura was gone, it paralyzed Jake. The poor guy couldn't operate the washing machine. He didn't know that Kyle liked sliced bananas on his peanut butter sandwich. Or that Kayla won't drink orange juice that has pulp. That was Laura's department. Jake's brothers were there to support him, but the kids needed a mother figure, so I stayed at their house for the first month."

"Why?"

"That's what family does. We support one another. We give our time and effort to someone other than ourselves."

"But you're not family." Olivia couldn't deny feeling a twinge of jealousy. Since the day she'd come home from school and discovered her father nonresponsive on the kitchen floor, all she'd wanted was to be part of a family again.

Myrna reached for Olivia's hand. "It's not blood that makes you family, dear. Love and loyalty bind people together. It's what makes Bluebell Canyon so special. Give it time. You'll see."

Olivia considered her grandmother's words.

Olivia's mother had been blood, yet after losing her husband, the only thing her mother seemed to care about was getting her next drink. Had her mother ever considered the effect that finding her father had had on Olivia?

"For weeks, Kyle couldn't fall asleep unless I was in bed with him. Jake and Kyle have come a long way, but Kayla is still in a lot of pain. I think it might be a good thing for her to spend time with you."

"Why would you think that?"

"Let's just say I have a good feeling about the positive effect you could have on her."

Olivia didn't plan to stay in Bluebell Canyon long enough to affect anyone, much less a child who had lost her mother. She still had unresolved issues after losing her father and later being abandoned by her mother. How could she help Kayla? It was clear to her that Jake's circumstances were going to make it more challenging to convince Gammy to come back to Miami.

Outside, car doors slammed. Children's laughter filled the air. Olivia's stomach tightened. It was too late to back out. She'd have to go to the car show with Jake and his kids. It was what Gammy wanted. But after today, Olivia would have to keep her distance from the Beckett family. Getting involved with a grieving widower and his two children wasn't part of her plan. And she certainly didn't want to develop ties to the other townspeople, either. She needed to focus on getting Myrna out of Bluebell Canyon.

CHAPTER TWO

"EVERY TIME YOUR grandmother feeds us breakfast, I feel like I've gained ten pounds," Jake joked, to lighten the mood inside his truck. Kyle had been a chatterbox since they'd left Myrna's house. Kayla had barely said a word at breakfast and remained quiet. Olivia sat in the passenger seat with her back ramrod straight, twisting the ends of her hair around her index finger. She stared out the window. The sunlight showcased her creamy complexion. Jake quickly shifted his eyes back to the road as he approached the four-way stop.

"Have you ever attended an antique car show?" Jake raised an eyebrow in Olivia's direction.

"No, I can't say that I have. What exactly happens? Do we drive the cars or go for a ride?"

Kyle's giggles carried from the back seat to the front of the truck's cab. Jake peered in the rearview mirror and saw Kayla rolling her brown eyes.

"Kayla, would you like to explain some car-show etiquette to Dr. Olivia?"

"No."

"I will! I will!" Kyle called out. "Ouch! Stop it, Kay."

"Kids, settle down."

"But, Daddy, Kayla is pinching me."

"Kayla, leave your brother alone. We'll let him explain the protocol to Dr. Olivia."

"There's a certain way to behave?" Olivia questioned.

"Yeah, but it's still fun. You can't touch the cars or lean against them. Stuff like that," Kyle explained. "You need to be respectful of the cars and the owners. They spend a lot of money—" his eyes grew wide "—like a humongous amount to make their cars nice again."

Jake listened to his son with pride. Kyle's mother had grown up going to car shows. Her father had been an enthusiast. Jake and his wife started taking the twins to shows when they were only a year old. Laura made sure as the children got older that they learned the proper etiquette. It was important to her to carry on the tradition she'd shared with her father. Jake couldn't blame Kayla for getting upset that Olivia had joined them. It was difficult for him to have another woman in his wife's seat on a family outing. If Myrna hadn't insisted Olivia join them, he would have never extended the invitation on his own. It didn't feel right.

Olivia looked over her shoulder. "Thank you for educating me." She turned to Kayla. "Is there anything else?"

Kayla stayed quiet while Kyle nodded his head. "Ask a lot of questions. The owners like that."

Olivia smiled. "Okay, I'll remember that. You seem to know a lot about car shows. Where did you learn all of this?"

"Our mommy taught us," Kayla responded curtly. "My family went to shows." She crossed her arms. "You're not in our family."

"Kay!"

"What?" Kayla shot a look at her brother. "She's not."

"You don't have to be so mean," Kyle said.

"Your brother is right. I don't like your attitude, young lady." Jake looked at Olivia. "I'm sorry."

Olivia simply nodded.

Jake turned on the radio to extinguish the

silence inside the vehicle. The plan to have a nice outing with his children wasn't going as expected. Kayla made it clear she didn't want Olivia to spend the day with them, yet Kyle seemed thrilled. It would be a long day if he didn't turn things around soon.

Thirty minutes later, they arrived at the fairgrounds. A cloud of dust swirled behind the truck as Jake searched for a parking space in the field. "We've got some time before the show starts. Do you want to go on a couple of rides?"

"Yay!" Kyle cheered and pumped his fist. "Kayla and I are tall enough to go on some by ourselves."

The group exited the vehicle. Food trailers lined the trampled path that led to the rides. The smell of popcorn and sugary-sweet funnel cake filled the air. The children took off running and headed toward the merry-go-round.

"Are they okay going by themselves?" Olivia's eyebrow arched.

Jake stuck his hands into the back pockets of his jeans and laughed. "This isn't Miami. We know practically everyone here. That's what makes living in a small town so great."

The twins took their place in line behind two girls who looked to be in their early teens.

"Do you want to have a seat over there?" Jake pointed to a wooden bench underneath an oak tree where he could see the kids and get to know Olivia. He had to try. It might be the only way to convince her how much everyone in Bluebell loved her grandmother.

They sat, and Olivia fingered her necklace and looked toward the children. "I feel like I'm spoiling Kayla's day. I don't think she wants me around."

"Give her time. She's not as comfortable around strangers as Kyle is." Jake wasn't so sure Kayla would soften up to Olivia. He knew his little girl. She was strong-willed when she set her mind to—or against—something. He planned to talk with Kayla tonight at bedtime about being more respectful toward Olivia.

"We didn't exactly get off on the right foot. I shouldn't have made that comment about asking your wife for permission. I'm sorry."

Jake adjusted his cowboy hat to shield the sun from his eyes. "Like I mentioned yesterday, there's no need to apologize. You didn't know."

Olivia resumed twisting her hair around her finger. "I know now. This morning, Gammy told me about Laura and the baby." She dropped her hands and folded them in her lap. "I'm sorry for your loss."

Jake noticed Olivia brushing a tear from her cheek. "Thanks. It's been a rough couple of years." When his wife had gone into distress, they had rushed him out of the delivery room. The staff raced in and out of the room. Jake stood by the door, feeling as if he were floating outside of his body. He'd been unable to escape the beeping machines. He knew something wasn't right, yet no one offered to tell him what was happening. When the doctor finally stepped into the hallway, his worst fear became a reality. Laura and the baby hadn't survived. His knees had buckled. He had dropped to the tiled floor. Thoughts of his children coloring in the waiting room with Myrna swirled in his mind. They weren't aware their mother was gone. He thought that taking the children home that night without their mother would be the hardest thing he'd ever do, but telling them what had happened nearly broke him. Jake's eyes scanned over to the children. "Kyle has handled it a little better than Kayla. I think he's trying to be the tough guy."

"Growing up without a mother isn't easy for a young girl," Olivia said.

"Are you speaking from experience?"

"Kind of. I had a wonderful and caring mother, until I lost my father when I was eight." Olivia looked up at the sky.

"I'm sorry." Jake knew Myrna's only son had passed years ago. He didn't recall anything about her son's wife.

Olivia nodded. "After he died, my mother kind of checked out."

"What do you mean?"

Olivia rubbed her palms down her thighs. "She started drinking…a lot. I was too young to realize she abused alcohol to mask the pain of losing her husband. About a year after he died, my mother left. That's when Gammy and Pops rented out their home down the road from ours in Denver and moved in with me. They stayed until I went off to college. Gammy didn't want me to lose the only home I'd known. For years, no one knew where my mother had gone. There was a part of me that was happy she had left. She wasn't the same person after she started to drink. Once I finished college and moved to Miami, Gammy and Pops sold my childhood home and moved to Bluebell."

"Do you ever hear from your mother?"

Olivia shook her head. "While I was in medical school, my mother died in a car accident."

"Even though she'd been absent from your life, that had to have been tough for you," Jake said.

Olivia paused and turned to Jake. "Really, the day my father died, I lost both parents. If it weren't for Gammy, I don't know what would have happened to me."

"She's a special lady. When my wife passed, your grandmother put her life on hold to help the children and me. She stepped in to help my brothers and took over, starting with the funeral arrangements. I couldn't think straight. I tried to stay strong for Kyle and Kayla, but my heart had shattered." Myrna never pretended to have all the answers. She was simply there during the darkest and most isolating time of his life. Jake had kept sinking further into a depressed state. "Myrna helped put the pieces of our lives back together again. She reminded me to lean on my faith, to look for the light through the darkness." Jake rubbed his eye. "She's an important part of our family."

"I'm glad she was there to help you and the children, but she's my only family and she's an important part of my life, too. That's why I want to help her. I can hire a full-time nurse until I work things out with my job." Olivia turned to Jake. "You saw her yesterday. She couldn't even see the signature line on the papers Larry brought her to sign."

Jake nodded. "I think we can both agree that Myrna's eyes are deteriorating. Over time, she'll need more help."

"So we agree? She shouldn't be living on her own." Olivia straightened her shoulders.

"Hold on a minute. I never said that." Jake didn't like the direction of this conversation.

"Daddy!" Kyle called out. The twins smiled and waved as the merry-go-round powered up. Jake was relieved to see Kayla smiling. His heart squeezed for his little girl, who smiled exactly like her mother.

Jake focused his attention back on the discussion at hand. "I hope you'll hear me out before you decide about moving your grandmother."

"I'll listen, but I can't make any promises."

"Since Myrna's diagnosis, I've been making modifications around the house to make it safer if her eyes worsen."

"I understand and appreciate that, but from what I saw yesterday, it's not a matter of if her eyes get worse. They already are. I don't think she should live alone." Olivia's eyes filled with sadness.

"That's the reason I wanted Myrna to get a service dog." Jake had known it wouldn't take much to convince Myrna. She'd always loved dogs and often had Tank over for sleepovers. Myrna even periodically volunteered with his business when things got too busy with him and his brothers. "At first, she didn't want to admit that she might need help, but she came around. She agreed having a service dog was the best solution to maintain her independence. Remaining independent is very important to her."

Olivia nodded. "I've seen many people come into the ER with service dogs, but I think a nurse would provide better companionship."

"Service animals are excellent companions and much more." The animals provided their handler with the confidence to get out and continue to live their lives to the fullest. Seeing these dogs change people's lives for the better made his work rewarding.

"Training dogs to assist people with disabilities is an admirable business."

Jake couldn't imagine doing any other type of work. "Thank you. It's wonderful to see the hard work pay off when the dog graduates and meets their new handler."

"Yesterday, you mentioned a camp for Puppy Raisers. What's that?"

"Puppy Raisers are individuals who commit to fostering a potential guide or service dog puppy in their home for the first year of the dog's life before formal training can begin."

"Interesting. I'd like to hear more."

Olivia was showing interest. This was good.

"My goal with Camp Bow Wow is to socialize and educate the puppy about everyday life and outdoor experiences while training the animals to work and perform tasks for people with disabilities. I expose the puppy to things they'd encounter working as a service dog, so they become comfortable and confident in any situation. For example, they visit grocery stores and restaurants, and learn how to behave and help their owners in all potential real-life scenarios. We meet Monday through Friday from three thirty to five thirty for three weeks. These hours allow the twins to help. I want them to see how blessed they are and to have compassion toward the disabled. After camp is over, I do follow-ups by video and make myself available to answer questions."

"Do all the puppies enrolled in your camp advance to train as service animals?"

"Usually, but now and then, we have a dog owner interested in training their own dog. The current group is all volunteer Puppy Raisers who will give up their dog after a year. Our business usually works with breeders who have ancestry lines that have proved to be successful in the past with specific disabilities. It's important to keep in mind that not every puppy is cut out to work as a service animal. That doesn't mean they'll make a bad pet. They just don't have what it takes to provide the critical support required of a service dog."

"Is Callie enrolled in your camp?"

Jake smiled. "Yes, but Callie is what you might call a work in progress. She's been a slow learner, but your grandmother fell in love with her the first time they met. I'll admit, I haven't had a lot of time to work with Callie, but I think she'll be a great help to Myrna."

"Did you get her through one of your breeders?"

"No, a local veteran named George Waters rescued Callie from a shelter in Denver when Callie was two months old. He planned to be her Puppy Raiser, but then he got sick and passed away. When he was diagnosed with cancer, he asked that I go forward with training Callie. I mentioned Myrna might need help in the future because of her recent diagnosis of macular degeneration. Since he and Myrna were good friends, he insisted I train Callie to help Myrna. I promised George I would carry out his request."

"So, you're training Callie to be Gammy's eyes?"

Jake nodded. "Myrna could live independently for years to come." Maintaining Myrna's independence—and keeping her and her friendship close—was Jake's goal.

"What if I take over as Callie's Puppy Raiser? Then she could get used to living with Gammy. I could help you train Callie. You said yourself that you've been busy."

Jake hadn't expected this from Olivia. With a hectic schedule at the hospital, he figured she'd be more likely to own a cat since they could be less maintenance. "Do you like dogs? I don't require my Raisers to have experience training, but they must have a love for dogs."

"Who doesn't love puppies?" Olivia smiled.

"Callie won't stay a puppy forever. A fully grown golden retriever can be quite large."

"I'm familiar with the breed. I think Callie and I will get along fine."

"It takes an enormous commitment. It would be your responsibility to oversee the care of Callie, like feeding, grooming, socialization and exercising. Do you think you'd have the time?"

"I've taken a sabbatical from my job with no set return date, so I can stay as long as it takes to get Callie trained. By then, I'll be able to better assess whether it's in my grandmother's best interest to stay in Bluebell or move to Miami and live with me."

Didn't Myrna get a say in the matter? Of course, that was between Olivia and her grandmother, so he held his peace on the subject. "Okay then." He extended his hand and gave a single nod. "It's a deal. We'll work together to get Callie trained if you agree to hold off on any decision about moving Myrna."

Olivia accepted Jake's hand. "All right, but Callie must prove to me that Gammy will be safe living independently."

Jake glanced up at the sun and released a slow and steady breath. Maybe having Olivia along today hadn't been such a bad idea. "I'll bring Callie over after church tomorrow so you can meet her." Once Olivia got firsthand experience with the service a trained dog could provide, she'd feel much more at ease with Myrna staying in Bluebell. At least, that was what he was hoping for. But not just for himself—for Kyle and Kayla. It would devastate them if Myrna moved away.

"Daddy, Daddy! Come quick!"

Jake's eyes shot toward the sound of Kyle's frantic cry. He sprang from the bench and bolted toward Kayla. Arms and legs flailed in all directions as Kayla rolled on the ground with a girl he'd seen in the line earlier.

"Ouch! My hair!" Kayla yelled.

"Kayla! Stop!" Jake reached down to pull his daughter off the other girl, who appeared older and bigger than Kayla.

"Let me go!" Kayla squirmed in Jake's arms.

Another girl who'd been in the line ran to the scene. "Come on, Lisa. Just say you're sorry. We have to go meet Aunt Jane at the concession stand."

"Would either of you care to explain what this is about?" Jake asked as Olivia joined the group.

Neither child said a word.

"I was talking to Jeremy, so I don't know what happened. I came back, and they were rolling around on the ground, pulling hair and stuff." Kyle spoke up.

Jake glanced at his son before addressing the girls. "Lisa, I think I know everyone in town, but I can't say I recall ever seeing you before."

"We're visiting our aunt Jane." Lisa's voice shook.

"Jane McWilliams?"

Lisa nodded and brushed her hair from her face.

"Okay, so do you want to tell me your side of the story?" Jake asked.

Lisa nodded. "We were waiting in line to go on the merry-go-round again. I said her mother was pretty. When I turned around, she jumped on me and punched me."

"Stop saying that!" Kayla lunged toward Lisa. "She's not my mother! She's not my mother!" Kayla wailed and pointed.

"Whoa, hold on." Jake reached for Kayla's arm before she could tackle Lisa once again. Kayla's body was stiff. Jake had never seen her this way. "Kayla, you need to calm down."

Jake turned in the direction Kayla was pointing. Olivia. He should have known. Lisa thought Olivia was Kayla's mother. A lump formed in his throat. He scooped up Kayla. Her torso went limp as she surrendered her tears.

"It's okay, sweetie." Jake stroked the back of Kayla's head.

"It's never going to be okay without my mommy."

"I'm sorry." Lisa looked up at Jake. "I didn't mean to make her cry."

Jake gave an understanding nod. "I know you didn't. Kayla shouldn't have lashed out at you. I'm sorry. I hope you and your sister can forgive her."

Lisa nodded.

"Let's go." Lisa's sister took her sibling's hand, and they walked away.

"I miss my mommy." Kayla's lip quivered as she buried her face into Jake's shoulder. His knees nearly buckled.

Olivia kept her distance to give Kayla space.

Jake hated to disappoint Kyle, but he had to take Kayla home. "I think we better forget the car show."

"But, Daddy!" Kyle whimpered. "You promised."

"I'm sorry, buddy, but your sister is upset. I think it's best if we go home."

"I want to see Miss Myrna." Kayla whimpered.

Kyle kicked his boot into the ground, stirring up a puff of dirt. "It's not fair."

Tension grew in Jake's neck, but he knew what he had to do. Myrna was the only one capable of calming Kayla down.

"Maybe I can stay here and take Kyle to the show," Olivia offered.

Kyle's eyes brightened. "Yes! Please, Daddy!"

Jake considered Olivia's offer.

"Let her stay. I don't want to ride in the car with her," Kayla whispered. Jake looked at Olivia, hoping she hadn't heard Kayla's request. It wasn't Olivia's fault, just like it wasn't Lisa's fault, either. Both were innocent victims of Kayla's grief.

"Are you sure you want to do that? You didn't seem too thrilled about the car show from the start." Jake tried to give Olivia an easy out.

Olivia looked at Kyle and smiled. "Actually, after listening to Kyle, I think we'll have a great time."

Kyle flew toward Olivia and wrapped his arms around her waist. "We'll have fun, Dr. Olivia! I promise!" Kyle turned back to his father. "Can me and Dr. Olivia still have a picnic and see the fireworks?"

How could he disappoint Kyle? Jake glanced at his watch. "It's not quite lunchtime."

"Maybe Kyle and I can walk back to the truck with you. I saw some picnic tables close to where you parked. We can take our sandwiches and hang out for a little while," Olivia suggested.

Kyle grinned. "Don't forget Miss Myrna's cupcakes."

Jake laughed. "I won't, but you might need to skip the fireworks this year, buddy." Having lunch and taking Kyle to the car show for a couple of hours were one thing, but staying for the fireworks would make a long day for Olivia.

"But we always stay and watch. Why do we always have to do what Kayla wants?" Kyle rolled his lower lip and crossed his arms across his chest.

"We can stay for the fireworks. I'd love to see them." Olivia placed her hand on Kyle's shoulder. "Kyle and I will have a great time."

Kayla buried her head deeper into Jake's shoulder.

"Can we, Daddy?" Kyle pleaded.

The thought of having both of his children upset was more than he could handle. "Okay, I'll come back to pick you up later. Maybe by then Kayla will change her mind and want to watch the fireworks."

"No! I want to stay with Miss Myrna." Kayla stiffened.

"If it's all right with Myrna, I'll come back

to catch the fireworks with you two." Watching the incredible light show had always been his wife's favorite way to close a perfect day. Of course, today had been anything but perfect. Given Kayla's feelings toward Olivia, Jake wondered if working with the doctor to train Callie was asking for more trouble.

"ARE YOU SURE the pressure cooker is okay, Gammy? Look at it shake. I think it's going to blow its top." Olivia covered her eyes and retreated from the pot. When she was a little girl, her mother had tried to cook in one of these. After her father arrived home from work, the pot blew its lid. Black beans exploded all over the room. A few even stuck to the ceiling. Olivia never saw her father laugh that hard again. A few weeks later, he passed away. She brushed off the reminder that the only two men she'd ever loved had left her with a broken heart.

"The green beans are fine, dear. That's what it's supposed to do." Myrna wiped her hands down the front of her apron. "Did you and Kyle have fun yesterday?"

Spending the day with Kyle had filled her heart with joy. "I don't remember when I've had a better day."

Gammy's eyes shifted to Olivia.

"That makes me happy. You work too much. Life's short. You need to slow down and enjoy the moment. Trust me. It goes fast. I don't want you to have any regrets when you're my age."

Olivia considered her grandmother's words. When she and Mark were first married, Olivia thought they'd have at least two children. In the early years, she couldn't put all the blame on her husband. Olivia was beginning her career. She thought there'd be time for children. But at thirty-six and single again, it felt like time was running out. The one thing she wanted more than anything was to have a family. But how could she trust another man after Mark had revealed he didn't want children after all? "I'll be fine."

"I know Mark changed his mind about having children, but that doesn't mean you don't have other options. Have you considered adoption?"

Olivia had plenty of friends who had adopted children, but they were married. Olivia wanted a family like she'd had before her father died and her mother turned to alcohol. "Unless I changed my schedule, raising a child on my own would be difficult."

"Keep your options open, dear. You could always marry a man who already has children."

Olivia couldn't ignore the twinkle in Gammy's eyes.

"Speaking of, did you enjoy the fireworks? I'm happy Jake joined you and Kyle for the show."

Her grandmother's motives were becoming questionable. "Yes, we had a wonderful time." Olivia had only wished Kayla had been with them.

The timer on the oven beeped. Olivia was thankful for the interruption.

"Can you get the biscuits?"

Olivia grabbed the pot holders and opened the door. She removed the cookie sheet and placed the tray on the trivet. "Since you were asleep when I got home from the car show, I wasn't able to tell you what Jake and I discussed."

"Jake phoned this morning and filled me in on your plans to work together to train Callie. I'm excited to have the dog here full-time. You're going to love her. Over the years, I've met many of the Puppy Raisers. I think this might be what you need."

"What do you mean?"

Myrna removed the lid from the slow cooker. The savory aroma of succulent beef and vegetables mixed in a spicy broth filled the air. "Between working long hours and the stress you were under during the divorce, maybe it's time to reevaluate your life."

"And you think training a puppy is the answer?" Olivia laughed.

"I'll let you come to your own conclusion over the coming weeks." Myrna replaced the lid. "The pot roast is nearly ready." She glanced at her watch. "Jake and the kids should be here any minute."

Olivia's suspicions mounted. "Did you invite Jake and the kids to dinner because of me? If you're trying to play matchmaker with the car show and dinners, it won't work." Olivia needed to put a stop to this. Sure, Jake was gorgeous, and he seemed nice enough, but putting her trust in another man wasn't in her plans right now, or perhaps ever. Her heart couldn't handle more pain. Besides, one of his two children probably wouldn't mind if she dropped off the face of the earth.

"I'm doing no such thing. I've had Jake

and the children over for Sunday supper since Laura died."

Olivia's cheeks warmed. "I'm sorry. I didn't mean to be disrespectful. I just need time to myself."

"Don't take too much time alone, dear. Like I said earlier, you have options. You don't want to put it off too long. Raising children takes a lot of energy."

"I can't jump and marry a man because I want children."

"No, but you could keep your heart open to the possibility. My grandmother always said there's a lid for every kettle. You'll find your lid."

"We're here!" Kyle's voice carried through the house.

Olivia turned to the sound of the front door opening. Dogs barked, and toenails skittered on the hardwood floor, rapidly approaching the kitchen.

A loud crash sounded.

"Oops! Sorry, Miss Myrna," Kyle called out. "Callie knocked over your plant stand."

Gammy didn't seem fazed by all the commotion. Olivia questioned if she could handle the dog. She raised her eyebrow at her grandmother. "This is okay with you?"

Myrna turned the setting on the slow cooker to warm and wiped her hands with the dishcloth. "I wouldn't have it any other way. Go grab the dustpan and broom from the pantry. Let's get it cleaned up so we can eat dinner."

Myrna pivoted on her heels and exited the kitchen.

Olivia sprinted from the pantry at the sound of more breaking glass.

Once in the living room, Olivia noticed the toppled plant stand had sent shards of broken porcelain and dirt all over the floor. The Oriental rug was a mess.

"Kids, grab the dogs and take them outside until we get this cleaned up. And put Callie on a leash so she doesn't run off," Jake instructed. "I'll get the other broom from the garage."

Olivia directed her attention to Jake. "Is she always like this?"

"Tank gets her riled up. Like I mentioned yesterday, Callie has a lot to learn."

"Obviously," Olivia mumbled.

"If Callie is going to live here full-time, we'll need to doggy proof the house. That will involve removing easily accessible items from dressers, tables and countertops. You don't want to leave things like shoes, socks, clothing, medications, chemicals, electrical cords or food lying around. If there are rooms where you'd rather Callie didn't enter, then I'd recommend you close the door or put up a baby gate. It's better to be safe than sorry." Jake spun around and headed toward the garage.

Olivia scanned the area. There was potting soil strewn over the floor and a second plant knocked over. "How did that one fall? It's on top of the end table."

Myrna laughed. "When puppies get excited, they like to jump. Like Jake said, if Callie can reach it, then move it."

"Look at this mess." Olivia went to work with the broom.

"You need to loosen up a bit, dear. Real life is messy. Everything doesn't have to be neat and organized," Myrna stated.

Olivia bit her lower lip. Gammy was right. She'd lost her joy when she discovered her father unconscious on the kitchen floor. In the years that followed, she'd buried her grief and replaced it with a determination to carry out her father's legacy to become a prominent doctor. Did her ex-husband believe she'd never make time for children? Was she the reason he'd changed his mind about having kids?

CHAPTER THREE

"OKAY, I THINK we're all done here. Everything seems to be back in its place." Jake swept the last pile of dirt and broken glass onto the dustpan.

Olivia placed her hands on her hips. "What about Gammy's plants? The dogs destroyed them."

"I'll replace them. It's not like this hasn't happened before." Jake chuckled and looked at Myrna. "Right?"

Myrna nodded. "Remember the first time you brought Tank over to the house? He snatched the rib-eye steak from the countertop and ran all over the house. It took us twenty minutes to get our hands on him."

"I remember. He'd hidden under the guest room bed, and by the time we found him, all that was left was bone," Jake recalled. It was the first time since losing his wife that he'd laughed.

"Well, nothing like that will happen to Callie. I'll have her house-trained in no time," Olivia said.

"Yeah, right," Kayla mumbled from the corner of the living room.

Jake focused his attention on his daughter. Her tears from yesterday had faded, but her attitude toward Olivia remained. "Didn't I tell you last night if you don't have something nice to say, hold your peace?"

"But, Daddy, you said Callie was difficult and training dogs is your job." Kayla frowned at Olivia. "She's probably never been around one. You always say to be a Puppy Raiser, you have to love dogs."

Jake watched Olivia's face flush. When he'd told the kids Olivia would help train Callie, Kyle had been ecstatic. Kayla had run out of the room in tears.

Myrna moved toward Kayla and placed her hand on her shoulder. "You've helped your father with other Puppy Raisers. Maybe you can help Dr. Olivia, Kayla. She doesn't have a dog of her own, but I know she's always loved animals."

"I can help, too!" Kyle raced toward the two women and bounced up and down. "I'm pretty responsible. I put Callie and Tank in the fenced area before we came inside."

Jake smiled. "Good thinking, son."

Kyle straightened his shoulders.

"She doesn't want my help. I don't think she likes kids, either." Kayla shrugged Myrna's hand away.

"Stop being so mean." Kyle frowned at his sister.

Jake approached his daughter. "That's enough, young lady."

"But she's old, and she doesn't even have any kids." Kayla's words rolled quickly off her tongue.

"I don't know where you left your manners today, but I believe you owe Dr. Olivia an apology."

"Sorry." Kayla kept her eyes focused on the floor and crossed her arms.

Olivia nodded.

An awkward silence hung in the air. Outside, the only train that crossed through the town sounded its whistle.

"Let's all take a deep breath and go have our dinner. I've made your favorite, Kayla, pot roast with baby carrots." Myrna motioned her arms toward the kitchen.

"Can we go outside after we eat?" Kyle asked. "I can show Dr. Olivia some stuff that might help her with Callie. Kayla can help, too."

Jake glanced in Olivia's direction. Sadness filled her eyes. Yesterday, Jake could excuse Kayla's actions toward Olivia, since the car show was her mother's favorite family activity. The day had stirred memories for Kayla, but today was a new day and her behavior was inexcusable. He'd discuss her punishment once they got home. Jake was proud of his son for trying to be the peacemaker. "I think that's a great idea."

Myrna stooped in front of Kayla. "You're good with Tank. Maybe you can show Dr. Olivia a few things."

A tiny smile parted Kayla's lips. "Okay."

Jake's shoulders relaxed. He would never have been able to convince Kayla to help Olivia. Myrna had a special touch with his daughter.

"I'll race you to the kitchen, Kay!" Kyle yelled. Kayla accepted his challenge and took off running. Myrna followed the children.

Olivia kept her feet firmly planted.

"Are you ready to eat?" Jake stepped closer and noticed the scent of lavender surrounding Olivia.

"I do like children. I guess I'm just not comfortable around them." Olivia twirled a strand of her hair. "I don't have experience with kids, except in the ER."

"Kayla's behavior toward you is unacceptable. I'll be sure and speak with her when we get home later."

"Don't be too hard on her."

Jake ran his hand across his chin. "Sometimes I feel like I can't do anything right as far as Kayla is concerned. Your grandmother is so good with her. Myrna always knows exactly what to say to make her feel better."

"Is that your subtle way of saying Gammy should remain in Bluebell Canyon?"

"I'd like that, but it wasn't what I meant. Besides, you agreed to postpone any decision until we get Callie trained and I finish more of the home modifications. I have some great ideas that I'd like to run by you."

"I'm sorry. You're right." Olivia nodded. "Thank you for offering to share the improvements you'd like to do on Gammy's home. I appreciate it. Maybe I could help you with them."

"I can always use an extra hand." Jake smiled. "I'm starving. What do you say we head back to the kitchen and get something to eat before the kids devour everything?"

"I'll be there in a minute." Olivia slid her hands into the back pockets of her jeans.

Jake walked away, leaving Olivia alone in the living room. He sent up a silent prayer that going forward everyone would work together for the shared goal of helping Myrna.

LATER, WITH THEIR stomachs full, Jake and Olivia headed outside with the children. Olivia offered to help Myrna, but she insisted cleaning the kitchen was relaxing and something she preferred to do alone.

The late-afternoon sun peeked through the large oak trees lining Myrna's property.

"Come over here." Kyle reached for Olivia's hand and led her toward the fenced area where Tank relaxed in the shade. Callie circled the property, looking for a way to escape.

Kyle looked up at Olivia and squinted. "The most important thing you need to remember is that puppies are hyper."

Olivia laughed. "Is that so?"

"Tell her, Daddy."

"Kyle's right, but she'll grow out of that stage. Eventually you won't have to worry about her running through the house destroying things like you saw earlier. But for now, we need to keep things out of her reach."

"Has she been potty trained?" Olivia asked.

"She is now. When George rescued Callie, he learned that was the reason she'd ended up in the shelter." Jake never understood people who purchased puppies but didn't have the patience to put in the time required to train them properly. "It's one of the main reasons dogs end up in shelters. People don't want to come home from a long day at work to find their flooring or rugs destroyed, but they won't train their pet."

Olivia glanced between Jake and Kyle. "Isn't having accidents a given for a new puppy?"

"It doesn't have to be if the owner puts in the effort. But it doesn't end after the animal is potty trained. Dogs need exercise, especially service dogs," Jake explained.

"That's not a problem." Olivia shrugged her shoulders. "If Gammy and Callie end up coming home with me, there are several dog parks near my condo in Miami."

Jake laughed.

Olivia directed her gaze at Jake. "What's so funny?"

"Taking Callie out once a day for a walk in

the dog park won't cut it. Puppies can go all day long. By nightfall, they'll still have the same energy they had from the start of the day. In addition, pups must have exposure to a variety of indoor and outdoor sounds, especially if they are to become a service animal."

"Why is that necessary?"

"This is something we cover in camp, but have you ever tried running a vacuum cleaner near a puppy?"

Olivia shook her head.

"Whether a vacuum, a lawn mower or a leaf blower, motorized tools can terrify a puppy and result in a fight-or-flight reaction. It's important they have repeated exposure in order to become accustomed to the noises. In time, the puppy will learn it is safe as long as it has a history of being safe around it."

"I never realized there was so much involved with training a dog."

Jake nodded. "Most people don't." He looked across the yard. "Come here, boy!"

Immediately, Tank was up and running toward Jake. Once at his feet, Jake reached down and scratched the dog behind his ear. "Tank might not be a puppy, but he benefits from outdoor activities like most dogs." Jake pushed his hands into his back pockets.

"I'm fairly active, so I'm sure I won't have any trouble keeping up with Callie," Olivia explained.

Kyle looked up at his father. "I don't think she understands."

Jake shrugged his shoulders. He couldn't say he hadn't warned Olivia. He hoped in time, she'd realize the effort and patience that were necessary to train a puppy. "I'm going to run inside and get their food. It's time for the dogs to have their dinner. Keep your eyes on her, kids."

"Dr. Olivia or Callie?" Kayla questioned.

"Both." Jake winked and jogged inside the house.

"How's it going out there?" Myrna called out over her shoulder as she rinsed the dinner plates.

"I'm afraid Olivia doesn't realize training Callie won't be easy. I know she's a doctor, but I'm not sure she understands the time and energy required to be a Puppy Raiser."

Myrna turned off the faucet and dried her hands on the dish towel. "I think she got a little taste of it earlier," she said with a smile.

"Believe it or not, Callie has settled down

a bit since I've gotten her into a routine. She's rowdy when she's first let out of the car, but at least she hasn't gotten her teeth into my wallet again." After Callie had chewed up a one-hundred-dollar bill, Jake learned quickly to keep his wallet in his nightstand drawer.

"I'm happy Olivia wants to be a Puppy Raiser and help with Callie's training at Camp Bow Wow." Myrna smiled.

Jake hoped that after Callie completed her training, Olivia would see firsthand how much Callie could help her grandmother. "So am I, but best of all, she said she will put off deciding on moving you until I have time to finish the modifications to your home and see how things progress with Callie."

"That sounds promising, but don't worry about me leaving Bluebell." Myrna swatted her hand in the air. "That will never happen."

"Daddy!" Kyle raced through the kitchen door.

"What is it? Is Kayla hurt?" Jake's pulse quickened.

Kyle blinked rapidly. "No! It's Callie. Dr. Olivia accidentally put her outside the fence without her leash. Callie took off like a rocket ship."

"Oh, dear." Myrna placed her hand against the side of her face.

"Hurry, Daddy!" Kyle cried out.

"You and your sister stay here and feed Tank. I'll go after Callie. Don't worry. I'll find her." Jake sprinted out the door and right past Olivia.

"Jake, I'm sorry!" Olivia yelled. "Let me help!"

Jake ignored the apology and her offer to help. He had to find Callie. He increased his pace as he neared the steep hill. On the other side were deep woods, and with the cloud cover that had moved in, it would be dark soon. Jake pumped his arms as he neared the top of the hill. If Callie continued into the wooded area, finding her would be impossible.

"Dear, please sit down and have some tea. Jake will find Callie. He knows those woods inside and out."

Olivia continued to pace the wraparound porch. The moment Callie had taken off, guilt had consumed her mind. Jake had warned her about removing Callie's leash. Her eyes scanned the property. The wildflowers covering the fields were quickly fading into the shadows. Olivia shuddered to think what could happen if it got too dark to keep searching for the puppy. "What if he doesn't? I'll never forgive myself if something happens to her."

"Relax. You worry too much. Jake will find her."

Myrna stood up from the rocking chair and picked up the teakettle from the side table. She filled a cup and placed it on a saucer. "Here, drink this. It's chamomile. It will calm your nerves."

Olivia accepted the beverage and sat on the edge of the rocker. A brisk breeze whooshed up the porch steps and caused a shiver to move down her spine. *Callie is too small to be off on her own. What if there are coyotes in the area? Why in the world did I remove the leash knowing Callie isn't trained?*

"Miss Myrna!" Kyle called out as he and Kayla raced through the yard and scaled the steps. Tank trailed behind, secured on a leash. "It's almost dark. Do you think we should take Daddy's truck and look for Callie? He keeps the key under the floor mat." Kyle sank into the empty rocking chair. Tank plopped on the floor beside him.

Olivia didn't have to look in Kayla's direction. She could feel the child's eyes burning into the side of her face. This was all her fault. "That sounds like a good idea. I could drive."

Kayla crossed her arms. "You'll make it worse."

"Kayla! Didn't your father tell you to hold your peace if you don't have something nice to say?" Myrna asked.

"Yeah, Kay. Dr. Olivia can't help it if she doesn't know anything about puppies. She's not a dog doctor. Besides, maybe Daddy should have used the crate from his truck to keep Callie from running loose."

"Isn't that cruel to lock a dog up in a cage?" Olivia asked.

Kayla rolled her eyes.

Myrna motioned for the child. "Come over here and sit with me. I think we all need to relax and take a deep breath. There's no point in us rushing off to help with the search. Your father will be back with Callie any minute. We just have to be patient."

Kayla's shoulders slumped and her lower lip rolled as she crossed the porch. "What if Callie is gone forever?" Kayla climbed on Myrna's lap and nuzzled her face against the woman's shoulder.

Myrna's phone rang. Olivia hoped it was good news.

Following a brief exchange, her grandmother ended the call and slid the phone into the pocket of her apron. "That was Jake."

"Did he find Callie?" the twins asked in unison.

"Yes, and she's fine. So you can stop worrying. Why don't you two run inside and start working on that jigsaw puzzle you dumped on the dining room table? I'll be along to help you in a minute."

All smiles, the children hurried into the house. The screen door closed with a bang.

Olivia released a slow and steady breath. "I'm glad Jake found Callie safe." Despite the good news, her grandmother looked concerned. "What is it? Did you say Callie was okay for the children's sake?"

"No, it's Jake I'm worried about."

"What's wrong?"

Myrna stepped toward the screen door. "I don't want the children to hear. After losing their mother, they're so afraid something will happen to their father—especially Kayla."

Olivia understood. After her father died, she raced home from school each day to ensure her mother was okay, especially after her mother started abusing alcohol. Olivia's heart would pound in her chest as she got closer to the kitchen. Flashes of her father on the floor would replay in her mind. For months leading up to her mother leaving, Olivia refused to go out and play with her friends, afraid that something would happen to her mother.

Myrna pulled the door closed, silencing the laughter echoing through the foyer. "I need you to drive to the Pearsons' ranch and pick up Jake and Callie."

"Of course. I can do that." With the sun setting soon, Olivia assumed it might be too far to walk.

"Jake twisted his ankle. He says it's no big deal, but I think you should check for broken bones. Ronnie can't drive him and Callie back here because the truck he uses to putter around the ranch has a dead battery and his wife took their SUV to visit her ill sister."

"Don't worry. I'll pick them up." Olivia ran inside to grab her car keys.

Ten minutes after Olivia left her grandmother's house, the sun had set as she navigated the vehicle down the winding road. With assistance from the high beam headlights, she spotted a two-story farmhouse with a large wraparound porch up ahead. She often dreamed of a home like this. With children chasing each other around the property while a dog nipped at their heels. Her shoulders slumped at her current reality. Her home in Miami was empty.

Olivia arrived at the end of the driveway and two porch lights turned on. She placed the vehicle into Park. A door slammed while she fumbled with her seat belt. Olivia looked up and spotted Jake.

She exited the car and released a sigh of relief when Jake approached with the puppy nestled in his muscular arms. Her heart pumped a little faster. What was it about a man with a puppy?

"Your grandmother sure is stubborn. I told her I could walk back. I'm sorry to trouble you." Jake lifted his foot and gave it a shake. "It feels fine now."

"You know Gammy. She never takes no for an answer." Olivia looked down. "Are you sure your ankle is okay?"

"Not even a limp." Jake gave a reassuring nod.

"That's good to hear, but you still might want to ice it once you're home."

"Okay, Doc." Jake saluted.

"How's Callie?" Olivia moved toward the animal and scratched her head.

"She's fine, but she'll sleep well tonight. For being so young, she covered a lot of ground." Jake secured the leash around Callie's collar before placing her back on the ground.

"I'm sorry I took Callie off the leash." Olivia gazed at the animal. "If anything had happened to her, I would have never forgiven myself. Please, I hope you'll accept my apology."

Jake nodded. "There's no need to apologize. I should have crated her, so let's forget about it. The important thing is that we work together to get Callie trained, so that she can assist Myrna." Jake looked down at Callie. "Are you ready to go home?"

Callie jumped to her feet and barked.

Jake turned to Olivia. "I think she's hungry. Let's head home."

Olivia took quick, shallow breaths as they headed toward the SUV. Why did the thought of being alone in the car with Jake suddenly make her nervous?

Once inside, they both secured their seat belts. A spicy, masculine scent filled the air.

Whatever their disagreements were about moving her grandmother, she couldn't deny the man was easy on the eyes. Way too easy.

CHAPTER FOUR

TUESDAY AFTERNOON, OLIVIA squinted against the sun's light as her SUV crested the top of the hill. With the window cracked, she inhaled the crisp air while taking in the picturesque scenery of the Rocky Mountain range, the complete opposite of the views in Miami. The sight of the palm trees that lined the Florida streets had always calmed her nerves, but there was no disputing that the Sunshine State was almost shockingly flat compared to Colorado.

From the back of the car, Callie whined three times and then started to bark nonstop. She obviously wasn't happy to be inside the crate.

"Settle down, Callie," Olivia called out over her shoulder. She pushed away a strand of hair that had escaped her ponytail. The dog wasn't the only one who was nervous. Thinking about spending the afternoon with Jake at Camp Bow Wow had Olivia's nerves rattled all morning.

At least there would be other Puppy Raisers in attendance to keep her from being distracted by Jake's rugged good looks. She needed to focus on Callie.

Cruising down the winding dirt road, Olivia slowed the vehicle to steal a glance at the handwritten map lying on the passenger seat. She chuckled at the map Gammy had drawn for her. It triggered childhood memories of the maps she and her friends drew when they played treasure hunt.

About a mile and a half back, Olivia had made a turn off the main road, but she hadn't yet spotted any houses. According to Gammy, Jake's two younger brothers and business partners, Cody and Logan, lived on the massive plot of land they'd inherited years ago. It was divided into several parcels with five homes. A third brother, Luke, a retired professional bull rider, lived in Virginia with his family, but he maintained a residence on the farm. Jake's father also had a house on the land, but he resided in Denver to be close to his wife, who was in late-stage Alzheimer's. The family had cared for Mrs. Beckett at home, even providing her with a trained companion service dog. But in the end, she needed the professional care of doctors and nurses not available in Bluebell. Their father believed moving her to a nursing home was best for his wife. Jake had a close-knit family, something Olivia always dreamed of for her future. But was Gammy right? Had she allowed her job to consume her to where it may become the only future she could have?

Callie barked twice and released a whimper.

"I know. You're ready to get some exercise." On Sunday, Jake had given Olivia a flight kennel to transport Callie in the car. It was a plastic cage, but smaller than the crate he planned to give her today at Callie's first day at Camp Bow Wow. "We should be at Jake's any minute."

Callie's nails scraped incessantly against the plastic.

Olivia bit her lower lip. "I forgot to let you go to the bathroom before we left the house. Is that it?"

Callie barked.

"Was that a yes?" Olivia laughed.

Another bark echoed inside the vehicle. Olivia eased her foot off the accelerator and hit the brake. "All right, we'll make a quick pit stop, but you'll have to hurry. We don't want to be late for your first day of camp. I have a feeling the instructor doesn't appreciate tardiness."

Olivia stepped from the car and quickly rounded to the back passenger door. The tantalizing aroma of wildflowers decorating the open field along the road scented the air. She reached inside the car and gripped the plastic latch of the kennel. "What in the world?" Callie's wet tongue covered her hands, making it difficult for Olivia to unlock it. "Hang on. I'll have you out in a second."

Finally, the lock released. Olivia opened the sliding door and lifted Callie from the kennel. She squirmed and kicked her hind legs.

"Wait just a second. I need to get your leash," Olivia pleaded as Callie's head butted against her chin.

Callie continued to wiggle. Her sharp toenails pierced Olivia's arms. "Ouch! Settle down, Callie." With one powerful jolt, the animal escaped from Olivia's grasp. She hit the ground and took off running.

"Wait!" Olivia's heart hammered against her chest.

The thought of running after Callie crossed her mind, but the dog had already nearly covered an entire football field. Seizing her on foot would be impossible. Olivia pivoted on her heel and hurried back to the driver's side of the car. Once inside, she pushed the ignition button, fastened her seat belt and peered through the windshield. Between the glaring sunlight and the film on the glass, she struggled to see. Since the dirt road wasn't parallel to the field, the chances of finding Callie by car seemed as hopeless as traveling on foot. How could she face Jake? What would she tell him? In nearly forty-eight hours, she'd lost Callie for the second time. Perspiration peppered her forehead. Olivia jammed her foot on the accelerator, kicking up a cloud of dust. There was no way she could show up at the camp without Callie. What kind of Puppy Raiser lost her dog on the first training day?

"LOOK, DADDY!" KYLE ran from the inside of the barn and pointed. "It's Callie."

Jake pulled his attention from his iPad and shielded his eyes from the sun. He spotted Callie across the north pasture, racing toward the barn.

"Oh, man. Dr. Olivia let her off the leash again." Kayla rolled her eyes.

Jake wasn't sure what had happened. Olivia had agreed to bring Callie to the camp, but he'd expected they would arrive together.

As Callie approached, the four other puppies enrolled in the camp rose to their hind legs and barked. The Puppy Raisers held tight to their leashes.

Callie ran to Jake and jumped up and down before flopping on the ground at his feet. "How did you get here?" Jake bent over and scooped up the dog. He ran his fingers through Callie's coat. "Run and grab a leash, Kyle."

Kyle sprinted to the barn and returned with the leather strap.

Jake secured Callie's collar and glanced at his watch. "Kayla, why don't you handle Callie so we don't hold up the class?"

"Okay, Daddy." Kayla took the leash and joined the group.

Jake moved inside the center of the orange cones that formed a large circle. He scanned the group and sent up a silent prayer, giving thanks for these dedicated volunteers. "Since we have already been chatting online in the Puppy Raiser group, I won't waste your time with introductions. Thanks for being here. As a Puppy Raiser, your role is critical and the first step your puppy will need if he or she will advance to formal service dog training." Jake turned to the youngest in the group. "Rebecca, this is your third puppy, isn't it?"

Rebecca stepped forward with her golden retriever. "Yes, this is Honey. My other two puppies were Labradors. This is my first golden. Being a Puppy Raiser has been a rewarding experience. It's hard to say goodbye to your puppy once they are ready to train to become a service dog, but knowing I've helped to make a difference in someone's life makes it all worth it."

The group broke into applause. Jake smiled. He was proud of Rebecca. She took her role as a Puppy Raiser seriously, as did most of the volunteers.

"Thank you for sharing with us, Rebecca. That's exactly the reason my brothers and I started this academy. The goal of Camp Bow Wow is to teach each puppy about trust, bravery, basic obedience, socialization and love. These skills will give them the foundation to eventually, with further training, become service dogs if that's your goal. Many enroll in the camp to train their family pet."

Off in the distance, tires crunched along the gravel road. Before Jake saw the vehicle, he knew it was Olivia.

"There's Dr. Olivia's car!" Kyle pointed to the SUV cresting the hill.

"She's driving way too fast!" Kayla yelled.

Jake shot his daughter a look. "Remember what I told you about holding your tongue?"

"But she is!"

The SUV came to a screeching halt, stirring up a cloud of dust. Olivia haphazardly parked her vehicle in the lot next to the barn. She sprang from the car and raced toward the group. "Callie got away from me again." Olivia stopped long enough to catch her breath. "We have to find her!"

Jake moved closer and caught the faint scent of Olivia's perfume. The citrus aroma smelled like freshly cut oranges. He placed his hand gently on her shoulder. "Relax."

"I can't! I got out of the car to let her use the bathroom and she got away from me again. She sprang from my arms before I could put the leash on her." Olivia pushed her hair away from her face. "I've lost her again. Maybe I'm not cut out for this."

"Don't be so hard on yourself. Callie is safe." Jake knew he was wasting his breath. In Olivia's eyes, losing Callie for a second time was unacceptable.

Kyle stepped closer to the adults. "It's okay, Dr. Olivia. Look over there." Kyle grinned and pointed toward Callie, stretched out on the grass, enjoying the warmth of the sun. Kayla had a firm grip on the leash. "Callie is okay."

Olivia ran to the dog and dropped to the ground. She scooped up the animal and snuggled her close against her chest. "I was so worried about you." She kissed the top of Callie's head. "I'm glad you're safe."

Callie returned the affection, licking the side of Olivia's face. It was the first time Jake saw Olivia connect with Callie. This was a good sign. Progress was being made.

Olivia giggled as the dog continued to give her wet kisses. "This won't happen again. I promise." Olivia placed Callie on the ground and stood to address the class. "I'm sorry if I held everyone up today."

"No harm done." Jake looked out at the group. "Everyone, this is Olivia Hart. She hasn't been a part of our online group, but she'll be joining us. She's my good friend Myrna's granddaughter."

"Hello," the class responded in unison.

Jake clapped his hands. "Is everyone ready to get started?"

"Yes." The group cheered. The outburst caused the dogs to jump to their feet and bark.

"Okay. First, we'll touch a little on your puppy's socialization skills. We want to ensure they become a friendly and confident adult. At home, it's important to introduce your dog to different sounds and to teach them to be okay being alone."

Harry Dearwester, the oldest in the group, raised his hand.

"Yes, Harry. Did you have a question?" Jake asked as the class turned their attention to the portly, gray-haired man.

"Why would we want to teach them how to be alone if they're going to work with people who might have a disability? Shouldn't they learn how to be with other people?" He bent over and patted his eight-week-old retriever, Tex.

"Being comfortable around strangers is a brilliant point, and one I'll touch on in a moment." Jake strolled around the group and eyed each animal. "First, teaching your dog how to remain calm while home alone can help prevent the animal from developing separation anxiety. I can't tell you the number of stories I've heard of dogs becoming destructive when left home alone. Callie is a prime example. Two weeks ago, while the twins were at school, I ran out to the store. Callie appeared to be having a good day, so I let her have the run of the house, rather than crate her."

"Uh-oh," Harry remarked.

"Yes, it was a big mistake. I should have known better. I'll post a couple pictures of the aftermath of tornado Callie on the website."

The group laughed.

"It wasn't a pretty sight, but a prime example of the importance of using a crate early on. That's why purchasing one is at the top of the list of essentials I provided in your welcome packet. I know a couple of you probably already have one. The crate will create a safe place that the dog will want to keep clean. In addition, keeping them in the crate and allowing them out to use the bathroom will teach them that going outside is good."

Jake took notice of Olivia's furrowed brow.

"Is everything okay, Olivia?"

"This just seems so involved. Won't most of this come natural to the dog?"

Being an ER doctor, Olivia knew a lot about human behaviors. Dogs? Not so much. "Has that been your experience so far with Callie?"

Olivia's face reddened. "Not exactly, but I haven't had a lot of time with her."

"These foundational skills need to be taught early on. A good example is the leash."

"I know, I know. Keep it on. I have that rule memorized." Olivia rolled her eyes. "Trust me, I've learned my lesson."

"Do you know why it's so important to keep the animal leashed early in their training?" Jake waited for a response from Olivia, but only received a shrug of her shoulders. "Anyone?" He scanned the group.

A black crow called out overhead.

Jake continued. "It's imperative for your dog to know their limits. Trust me, they will constantly test you. The leash is one way to teach the animal to keep their focus on you, not on their surroundings."

"Like the squirrels running around in the yard," Rebecca called out.

"Exactly. When my dog Tank was a puppy, he tried to go after every squirrel and rabbit that crossed his path. I spent a lot of time chasing him around the ranch. That was a great point, Rebecca," Jake said. "We'll use the leash, along with a dog bed or mat, to teach your puppy the Place command."

George Thielhorn, a middle-aged man who'd recently inherited a nearby ranch from his father, cleared his throat. "What's that?"

By the blank expressions on the faces of the group, except for Rebecca, Jake realized no one was aware of the most essential command to teach your dog. "Some people say it's a magical cue." Jake laughed. "Seriously, though, most new owners think Sit, Stay and Down are the basic training commands to teach. They make the mistake of believing that's all the animal needs to know. But they couldn't be more wrong."

"Yeah, when I first became a Puppy Raiser, my friend told me I was wasting my money on this camp. She said dogs weren't able to learn a bunch of stuff," Rebecca told the group.

"Your friend must not have any experience with service dogs. I'd venture to guess that if she's a dog owner, her dog barks when you ring her doorbell." Jake had a lot of experience with dog owners who believed their animal needed little training.

"She has a Jack Russell. Every time I go to her house, the dog barks nonstop." Rebecca shook her head.

"That's exactly why the Place command is so

important. It will teach your dog, in any situation, to settle down onto a dog bed, a blanket or even the dog's favorite place in the house. It will give them a job to do instead of allowing them to choose one for themselves. They might choose jobs like barking at the doorbell, jumping up on people, begging for food at the dinner table, running wild through the house and destroying everything in their path, or jumping out of a car without permission." Jake glanced in Olivia's direction. "These are just a few of the undesirable behaviors of an untrained dog."

George cleared his throat. "If I can teach Maggie this command, I'll be confident with my investment. She's been shredding everything she can get her mouth on. My wife is close to shipping her off to her sister's ranch."

"I don't think that will be necessary, George. Once Maggie learns that Place simply means for her to go to the spot you tell her and stay there until you release her, your wife will be happy. I guarantee it. Maggie will have no choice but to stay. And she'll do it like it's her job, because it is."

"That's a relief," George stated while the rest of the group chatted among themselves.

Olivia remained quiet and attentive. After

the way Callie had acted out at Myrna's during Sunday dinner, Jake was reminded that the dog might need extra attention beyond the camp. At the end of the three-week program, he'd have to evaluate Callie's progress. Either way, he'd made a promise to his friend George. He'd train Callie to assist Myrna, and he planned to keep his word.

"Okay, I'd like for you to pair up and switch dogs with a partner so the animals can get used to being handled by a stranger. We'll circle the ring a few times before you take control of your dog, and then we'll practice a few commands. After that, we'll work a little on your dog's attentiveness by using dog treats to give them a lesson on eye contact. You'll find detailed instructions in the packet I provided. You can practice at home."

Two hours later, the animals and their owners were ready to wrap things up for the evening. While the group said their goodbyes and headed toward their cars, Olivia and Callie lingered behind.

Jake moved toward Olivia, where she sat in the grass, scratching behind Callie's ear. "Did you have a question?" Jake knelt and patted the dog.

Olivia lifted her head and fixed her eyes in his direction. Jake's pulse increased when their fingers brushed.

"I wanted to apologize if I sounded like a know-it-all in class. It's pretty obvious I don't know what I'm doing with Callie."

Olivia stood, and Jake followed her lead.

"There's no need to apologize. You're no different from any other first-time Puppy Raiser I've had in previous camps." Jake doubted his words. Olivia was different. He'd never had to teach someone as beautiful as Olivia, which he had to admit made it difficult to keep his attention on the class. "As I mentioned before, training a dog properly takes a great deal of patience, and trial and error. Keep in mind, Callie is adjusting to her new environment now that she's living at Myrna's house. It's also important to remember that every dog is different. Each will have their own strengths and weaknesses, just like humans."

Olivia nodded. "I see that now. I can't believe how naive I've been to think I could train Callie on my own."

"Well, to quote Myrna, you are a brilliant doctor. It's only natural for you to believe training a dog would come easy to you."

Olivia's face flushed, and she playfully swatted Jake's arm. "Oh, please. I'm far from brilliant." She paused and gazed out over the field. "In fact, lately I've wondered if I'm truly cut out to work in the ER."

"From what I've heard from your grandmother, I'd say you're probably just exhausted. She's mentioned your long hours."

"I didn't realize how tired I was until I boarded the plane from Miami. The flight attendant had to wake me when we landed." Olivia laughed.

"It sounds like this trip is exactly what you need. I'm sure your husband is missing you, though." Myrna had told Jake about Olivia's husband and his successful career. Maybe that was why he hadn't traveled with her.

"I don't think so. We're divorced." Olivia's face reddened and she avoided eye contact.

"I'm sorry." Jake reached his hand toward her shoulder, but quickly dropped it to his side. "I didn't realize. Myrna never mentioned it." Jake only remembered her talking highly about Olivia's husband. He couldn't deny he was curious as to the reason for their breakup, but it wasn't his place to ask.

"She only learned about it a couple of days

ago. I wanted to tell her in person. It's not something I'm proud of."

"I'm sure it's been difficult for you." Jake had a friend who'd gone through a divorce last year. It was tough, especially for his children.

"He didn't want kids." Olivia volunteered the information. She shook her head and looked up at the sky.

Unsure how to respond, Jake remained silent.

"I know what you're thinking. That's something we should have discussed before we got married."

"Didn't you?"

"Many times. In fact, we talked about it early in our relationship. He came from a large family. He told me he wanted a lot of children."

"What changed his mind?" After losing his wife, Jake's children were his world.

Olivia released a sigh and shrugged her shoulders. "He decided he didn't want the responsibility or expense."

Olivia wiped away a stray tear.

"After he told me, he filed for divorce. It all happened so fast, but in retrospect, I wonder if there were signs I had missed. I guess it doesn't matter now. Having kids has been a lifelong dream for me. Maybe he thought he was doing me a favor?"

"You should have children if it's what you want. I couldn't imagine my world without Kyle and Kayla."

A comfortable silence passed before Kyle approached. "Can we take Tank and Callie for a walk?"

Jake glanced at his watch. "I don't think so. You've got math homework to finish before dinner."

"Oh, man." Kyle kicked his tennis shoe into the ground. A cloud of dust erupted.

Jake looked at Olivia. "Math isn't his strongest subject."

"I'm pretty good with it. Maybe I can help," Olivia offered, twisting a strand of her hair.

"That would be awesome!" Kyle bounced on his toes.

"That's kind of you to offer, but I'm sure you have more important things to do."

Olivia shook her head. "Actually, Gammy is having dinner with a friend from church this evening, so I'm on my own."

"Maybe Dr. Olivia can stay and eat with us! Can she, Daddy?"

Jake couldn't help but notice the smile that

parted Olivia's lips. Was she open to an invitation to have dinner with his family? Perhaps if she got to know the children better, Olivia might have a more difficult time uprooting her grandmother and taking her away from people who loved her, too. It was worth a try. "We'd love for you to join us. We planned to make homemade pizza, so there will be plenty."

Kayla remained silent. She obviously wasn't as enthused as her brother.

Olivia tilted her head and tucked a strand of hair behind her ear. "I'd love to."

Jake fought to temper the thrill of spending an evening with Olivia and his children. Knowing now she was single, he had to take a deep breath to wrangle his emotions under control. It wouldn't be wise to go down that road with Olivia. She was only here temporarily. Besides, he was all too familiar with the pain of losing someone you loved. He couldn't take that risk a second time.

CHAPTER FIVE

"DO YOU WANT me to show you how to roll out the dough, Dr. Olivia?" Kyle offered with a smile. "I had to practice, but I'm pretty good at it now."

An hour after agreeing to come to dinner at Jake's house, Olivia wiped her flour-covered brow with the back of her hand. She always loved to bake, but her ex-husband did most of the cooking, including making pizza from scratch. He considered himself a master chef. Olivia had loved the conversations they shared while he cooked at the beginning of their marriage. She'd sit on the island stool and watch Mark slice and dice. He had the remarkable skill of turning simple ingredients into a mouthwatering meal. But when her schedule at the hospital consumed more of her time, he spent less time in the kitchen and more time at his office.

Olivia took in the spacious kitchen. Apart

from the ingredients and bowls strewn across the quartz countertop, the room was immaculate. Except for the kids' drawings on display, the stainless steel appliances sparkled. Olivia would give anything to one day be able to cover her own refrigerator with drawings her children created.

She returned her attention to the task at hand. "This is the most stubborn stuff I've ever seen. I push it forward and it pulls right back." She placed the rolling pin on the counter and kneaded her fingers into the cool dough while appreciating her local pizza shop back home.

Jake laughed and moved toward the roll of paper towels next to the sink. He turned on the faucet and ran the towel twice under the water. While Olivia continued to struggle, he reached across the island. "Here, let me get that." He brushed the dampened paper towel across her forehead. "You had a little flour up there." He pointed to her brow.

His gentle touch ignited warmth in Olivia's cheeks. A moment of awkward silence filled the room.

"Thank you. I guess my secret is out."

"What's that?" Jake asked.

"That I have the local pizza place back home on speed dial."

Jake grinned. "I didn't want to say anything, but that dough has had you tangled up for quite a while. Don't be so hard on yourself. I probably should have kept the dough at room temperature for a while longer. Would you like a hand?"

Olivia pulled away and rotated her palms face up. "Yours are probably cleaner than mine." Sticky clumps of dough clung to her fingertips.

Kyle clattered around in a nearby drawer and pulled out another sparkling rolling pin. "My mommy taught me and Daddy all the secrets to make a pizza. It's pretty easy once you get the hang of it."

Callie and Tank both barked in the backyard.

"I thought Kayla was going to feed the dogs?" Jake looked down at Kyle.

"She said she was." Kyle shrugged his shoulder.

The barking continued, but this time, it was only Callie. Olivia walked to the sink, rinsed her hands and peered out the window above the faucet. Tank was curled up underneath the weeping willow while Callie ran circles around the yard. Kayla was nowhere in sight. "Do you mind if I go check on Callie?" She reached for the hand towel and then turned to Jake.

"Do you want me to go with you?" Kyle volunteered. His eyelashes fluttered.

Olivia smiled. Kyle was such a thoughtful little boy. Thoughts swirled in her mind. He was exactly the type of child she dreamed of having one day. "Maybe you should stay here and help your daddy with the pizza. The two of you are much better at handling the dough than I am."

"Okay, but what toppings do you want? I hope not those fishy things." Kyle crinkled his nose.

Olivia knelt in front of Kyle. "No way. I love cheese. In fact, I've never met a cheese I didn't like."

The corners of Kyle's mouth tilted up into a smile. "Me too!" He jumped up and down.

"What about the pepperoni lovers over here?" Jake waved his arms.

Kyle rolled his eyes. "My daddy and Kayla love pepperoni."

Olivia stood and gazed down at Kyle. "Let me go outside and get Callie settled. I'll ask Kayla if she wants to help. The two pepperoni fans can make their pizza and we'll make ours. How does that sound?"

"Awesome! After dinner, can we do the jigsaw puzzle in the dining room? It's got tons of cool farm animals." Kyle's smile lit up his face.

Jake placed his hand on his son's shoulder. "That will have to wait. Remember, you have math homework to do."

Kyle's smile faded, but quickly returned when he looked up at Olivia. "But you're going to help me, right?"

"Of course. Earlier, I said I would help you. I always keep my word." Olivia understood the importance of keeping her word, especially to a child. After her father died and her mother began to abuse alcohol, broken promises were ubiquitous.

"Some grown-ups don't, so I was just checking." Kyle returned his focus back to the dough. "I won't touch it until you come back. Daddy told me that Mommy always said don't work the dough too much because it will fight back."

"I think she was right. I'll be back." Olivia headed to the back door.

Outside, Olivia's steps slowed. She admired the bright yellows and reds of the snapdragons lining the backside of the privacy fence. Their sweet fragrance drifted through the late-spring air. Unable to recall the last time she'd slowed long enough to notice flowers, she wondered when the season had changed. Living in Miami was a never-ending race from the moment her feet hit the floor each morning. As she studied the flower bed, she wondered if Jake's wife had created the garden or if the family had planted the flowers together. The latter was a beautiful image. Something she'd often dreamed of doing one day with her family.

Callie raced toward Olivia, pulling her mind back to the moment. She reached down and pulled the dog into her arms. "Hey, girl. What's got you so riled up?" Callie licked the side of her face. "You want some attention? Is that it?"

Olivia scanned the yard, but there was no sign of Kayla. A hint of a breeze cooled her face. On the opposite side of the grounds, she spied a small house with light pink shutters and a lime-green roof. It looked like the playhouse her best friend had when they were in grade school. Kayla had to be inside.

With Callie still in her arms, Olivia advanced across the grass, careful not to frighten the child if she was inside. The door to the house was ajar. Olivia peeked through the crack. White twinkle lights lined the ceiling. Her heart squeezed at the sight of Kayla sitting on the floor with a picture frame in her hands and tears racing down her cheeks.

Olivia's first instinct was to retreat. Go back into the house and pretend she hadn't seen Kayla. But how could she? Kayla was obviously upset. If Olivia entered the house uninvited, she could make matters worse. Kayla had made her feelings toward her apparent.

Olivia contemplated her next move. During her career, she'd treated plenty of children in the ER. What if she couldn't help Kayla? But what if she could? She straightened her shoulders, raised her hand and gently knocked on the pink wooden door. "Kayla, may I come inside?"

A bumblebee buzzed past while Olivia waited for an answer that never came. She took a deep breath, reached out and tightened her grip on the doorknob. She opened the door and stepped inside. To her surprise, despite the small outer appearance of the house, once inside Olivia didn't have to hunch or lower her head. It was spacious enough for two people. "Are you okay, sweetie?" Olivia froze. With closer proximity, she could see the picture of a strikingly beautiful pregnant woman contained inside the frame. The woman had brown hair that cascaded well past her shoulders.

Tears streamed down Kayla's face.

Olivia took a deep breath, trying to compose herself. Her first instinct was to drop to the ground and wrap her arms around Kayla. She'd tell her that the pain wouldn't last forever, but Olivia knew that wouldn't be the truth. The ache of losing her father still clung to her like a weighted vest. Losing a parent was something a child should never have to experience, but the stark reality was she and Kayla shared the same heartache. Olivia remained quiet, allowing Kayla time to respond to her uninvited guest.

Callie wiggled and whimpered in Olivia's arms. She placed her down and Callie's toenails scratched the wooden floor as she ran to Kayla. The dog pounced on her lap and licked her hands that were still clutching the frame.

Next, Callie slid her tongue along the child's face. A slight giggle erupted from Kayla's lips.

"Okay, Callie." Olivia patted her hand against her leg to get the dog's attention. "That's enough."

"She hasn't learned her place yet," Kayla whispered.

Olivia stared at Kayla for a moment before realizing what she was referring to. "You're right.

Once she learns her place, when I put her on the ground, she'll stay, right?"

Kayla nodded and wiped her cheek. "Yeah."

Olivia knelt to face Kayla. "Is it okay if I sit with you?"

Kayla gave a slight shoulder shrug. Olivia took it as a yes.

Positioned on the floor, Olivia pulled her knees against her chest, looked around the room and sighed. "When I was your age, my friend had a clubhouse just like this, except it didn't have electricity. I always wanted one of my own."

Callie finally settled down on the floor and rested her head against Kayla's leg.

"My daddy built it for me." Kayla scratched the top of Callie's head.

"That was nice of him." Olivia took in the space. She admired the pink lace curtains covering the two windows. A table with two chairs sat on top of a thick pink throw rug. Kayla was certainly daddy's little girl. "It feels so cozy."

Kayla looked down at the photograph and ran her fingers across the glass. "He made it after my mommy died."

At a loss for words, Olivia remained silent.

"He thought I might want it to get away from

the boys in the house." Kayla kept her eyes fixed on the photo. "But I think he didn't want to think about Mommy."

A lump formed in Olivia's throat. It was a wise observation for a six-year-old. Olivia could remember her mother responding the same way after losing her husband. The day after the funeral, Olivia's mother decided she wanted to repaint the interior walls of the entire house. Day after day, her mother went nonstop, never sleeping or taking time to eat, which meant she didn't prepare any meals. Olivia ate cereal for breakfast, lunch and dinner until the milk ran out. Then she ate the cereal dry. It wasn't until Gammy and Pops moved in that she finally had some normalcy.

"Do you mind?" Olivia reached for the photograph.

Kayla clung to the frame for a moment and then finally let go. She handed it to Olivia. Her eyes never left the photograph.

"Your mother was beautiful." Olivia studied the woman who looked so much like her children. Her brown eyes sparkled with glints of gold. Her skin was like that of a porcelain doll. "What's the best thing you remember about her?"

Kayla's eyes widened. She bit her lower lip and shook her head.

Olivia passed the picture back to Kayla. "You know, it's okay to talk about your mommy."

Her brow crinkled. "It is?"

"Yes, that's how we can hold tight to the memories. I know that's what your mommy would want."

"Every time I try to tell a story about her, my daddy and Kyle talk about something else. Kyle says it hurts Daddy too much. He says we shouldn't mention Mommy. But I'm afraid if I don't, I'm going to forget her."

Olivia gazed around the space before meeting Kayla's eyes. "Well, right now it's just me and you. I'd love to hear a story about your mommy."

"Really?"

Olivia nodded.

Kayla inched closer to Olivia and smiled. "My mommy loved snow. We used to make giant snowmen in front of the house and dress them in Daddy's clothes." She giggled.

Olivia pictured the scene in her mind and her heart warmed. "That sounds like fun."

"Yeah. She made everything fun. After, we'd come inside and have cocoa and warm brownies with strawberry Jell-O."

"Tell me more," Olivia encouraged Kayla.

"Before school, on days when it was cold, my mommy would put my coat, hat and gloves over the heat vent on the kitchen floor. Everything was warm and toasty when I got ready to catch the bus."

"I'm sure it felt nice." It sounded like something Olivia's father would have done for her. He was always doting on her.

Kayla looked up with tears in her eyes. "I really miss her."

For a second, Olivia hesitated, but when Kayla leaned into her arms, Olivia provided an embrace. She stroked the back of Kayla's head and held her tight. Her hair smelled like sweet honeysuckle. "I know you do, sweetie."

"It's not fair. All my friends have mommies. They get to do fun stuff together like me and my mommy used to do."

"I'm sure that's hard." Olivia kissed the top of her head.

Kayla pulled back and looked up. "I'm sorry I was mean to you when you lost Callie." Kayla blinked several times.

Olivia laughed. "You were just being protective."

"My daddy was right."

"About what?"

"He says sometimes my mouth speaks before my head has time to think."

"I used to do the same when I was your age." Olivia recalled many times that her mouth got her into trouble. "You know, you and I have a lot in common."

"Like what? I'm not as pretty as you. I'd like to be a doctor one day, but I'm not smart like you."

Kayla's lack of confidence was unsettling. "You're a beautiful young lady. Don't compare yourself to anyone else. God made you exactly how He wanted you to be. Did you know there is no other person in the world with the same fingerprints as you?"

Kayla looked down and examined her fingers. "Really? That's cool."

"I hope you'll always remember that you can do anything you put your mind to. If you want to be a doctor, then work hard in school and you'll reach your goal." Olivia placed her hand underneath Kayla's chin, tipping it upward. "Sweetie, don't let anyone steal your dreams."

Kayla nodded. "Okay. I promise." She bit her lower lip. "So, what do we have in common?"

Outside, a woodpecker drilled the side of the clubhouse as daylight faded.

"When I was a little older than you are right now, my daddy died."

"He did?" Her brow crinkled. "I'm really sorry."

"Thank you." The years had passed, but the pain was like a wound that kept getting bumped and never healed. If Olivia closed her eyes, she could picture her father lying on the kitchen floor. She had opened her mouth to scream, but there was no sound. Dropping to the floor, she'd rested her head against her father's chest and cried. "The kids at school never seemed to understand. Sure, they were nice and apologetic at first, but as time passed, they seemed to forget about it, but I never could."

Kayla's head quickly bobbed up and down. "That's exactly how I feel."

"It's important to remember that your friends aren't doing it on purpose. They've just never been in your shoes. It's like being in a private club. Only the members truly know what's going on."

Olivia wasn't sure if this made sense to Kayla. Even as an adult, it was difficult for her to understand why God would allow a child to lose a parent. She thought of Jake and his loss. How did anyone move past such a heartbreaking event?

Kayla pushed her hair away from her face. "I sure wish I wasn't a member of this club. I don't like to feel this way."

"Even though it doesn't seem like it, you can always talk to your daddy or Kyle." After Olivia's father passed, without siblings, it wasn't until Gammy came to live with them that Olivia had someone to reminisce with about her mother.

"But I don't want to make my daddy sad. I can see the look on his face when I mention Mommy. And Kyle seems like he's already forgotten about her."

"People grieve a loss in different ways, sweetie. It might be too painful for your father and brother to talk about her."

"But I'm afraid we're going to all forget. I always feel better after I talk about her. Sometimes I even tell my stuffed animals stories about her."

"I did the same thing." Olivia paused. "I have an idea. Maybe while I'm here, you can talk to me about your mommy and I'll talk to you about my father. Does that sound like a good idea?"

Kayla lunged forward and wrapped her arms around Olivia's neck. Warmth surged through Olivia's body. She'd never held a child in this way. It felt good—too good. Getting attached wasn't part of her plan. She was here to help her gammy and convince her she'd be better off in Florida. Olivia would never be happy living in a small town. Yet the feeling she had with Kayla in her arms seemed to bring her more happiness than she'd felt in years.

JAKE RUBBED HIS eyes and did a double take. Were his eyes playing tricks on him? He blinked three times and once again looked through the kitchen window. He wasn't mistaken. Olivia and Kayla were walking through the backyard holding hands. After Olivia's arrival, Kayla avoided interaction with her, but now they looked like best friends. Kayla and Olivia becoming buddies wasn't good. Kayla's heart could break if this new friendship continued to blossom. Olivia's time in Bluebell was temporary.

"Wash your hands, sweetie," Olivia instructed Kayla as they stepped into the kitchen.

"Okay." Without hesitation, Kayla skipped to the sink, humming a tune.

"Do you want to help me make our pizza?" Jake asked Kayla as he drizzled olive oil on the dough.

Kyle glanced up from the counter. "Yeah, Kay. You help Daddy. Me and Dr. Olivia are making this pizza." He motioned with his hand across the ingredients. "See all the extra cheese? This is ours."

"I want to work with Dr. Olivia," Kayla said. "After dinner, she's going to help me with my book report."

It wasn't his imagination. Something had occurred outside between Olivia and Kayla. But what?

"I thought Dr. Olivia was going to help me with my math after?" Kyle kicked his shoe against the wood floor.

Jake and Olivia looked at each other. Her brow arched while she appeared to wait for him to resolve the dispute.

"Dr. Olivia offered to help your brother with his math first. You know he's been struggling."

Olivia cleared her throat. "Maybe, if it's okay with you, I can help both of them."

"That's kind of you to offer to help Kayla too, but I'm sure you'll want to get home after we have our pizza." Jake assumed Olivia was being nice, so he offered a way out.

"I'd love to help. I'd just be going home to an empty house. Gammy said not to expect her until at least ten o'clock." Olivia pinched a mound of cheese and sprinkled it over the pizza. "I offered to drive her, but she said she'd be fine. With her poor vision, I worry about her being on the road after dark, so it might be best for me to stay and keep myself busy. I'll just sit up worrying otherwise."

Jake nodded. "She can be as stubborn as a rusty bolt."

Olivia chuckled. "I think you're right. She probably shouldn't be driving day or night. I need to find out when she last had her license renewed."

Jake agreed. He also worried about Myrna being out on the road, particularly at night. But taking away someone's driving privileges was a sensitive topic. It would be best for a medical professional or someone at the DMV to handle it. "I believe Myrna renewed last summer, but it appears her eyes have deteriorated since then."

"Quit touching the dough, Kyle. You're going to ruin it." Kayla interrupted the adults, bringing them back to the task at hand.

"All right, I think it's time to get these pizzas into the oven. Kyle, do you want to help me with the pepperoni? We don't want to keep Dr. Olivia out too late."

Kyle jumped off the step stool and sped to his father's side. He snatched a piece of pepperoni and popped it into his mouth.

"I said help, not eat." Jake ruffled the top of his son's hair.

Kyle giggled, and the oven beeped.

"Ours is ready to go in," Olivia announced.

"Great. The pot holders are in the top drawer to the right of the oven." Jake placed the last sprinkle of garlic powder over the pizza.

Olivia's eyes popped as she peered inside the oversize oven. "The oven is huge. We can put the pizzas side by side."

"Daddy bought the oven for Mommy. She loved to cook. He said one Thanksgiving she baked three turkeys at once for the homeless shelter in Denver." Kayla spoke with pride.

Kyle nudged his sister in the arm.

"What?" Kayla flinched.

"It makes Daddy sad when we talk about Mommy."

"But Dr. Olivia told me it's okay. She said it's good to remember. It's what Mommy would want." Kayla shot a look in Olivia's direction.

Olivia's eyes shifted to Jake.

Jake cleared his throat. He couldn't miss the

redness in Olivia's face. "Dr. Olivia is right. We should never forget your mommy."

"Then how come you don't like us to talk about her?" Kayla wrapped her arms around her stomach.

It was true. When his children or someone from town mentioned Laura, he did his best to change the subject. Despite the advice from Pastor Kidd, Jake struggled to keep her memory alive. It was too painful. It wasn't fair to Kayla and Kyle. He prayed about it every morning. "I believed not talking about your mommy protected you, but really, I wasn't giving you the opportunity to grieve the loss of your mother in your own way. It was easier for me not to talk about what had happened. I've been wrong. I'm sorry."

Kayla moved toward Jake and wrapped her arms around his waist. "It's okay, Daddy. I don't want you to be sad. When I was outside, I told Dr. Olivia stories about Mommy, and it made me feel good. Maybe you should try it, too."

Jake's heart warmed. "I think that's the best idea I've heard in a long time."

Kayla's smile lit up her face. "You do?"

"Yes. In fact, I think I have the perfect way to share your stories about your mother."

Kyle and Kayla moved closer to Jake. Their eyes grew wide. "How?" they both asked.

"Maybe each night before we say our bedtime prayers, you can take turns sharing something you remember about your mommy."

"We can talk about Mommy?" Kayla questioned as though she were asking for the impossible.

Jake nodded. "If you'd like, we can start tonight."

"Yes!" Kyle did a fist pump. "I can't wait to go to bed!"

The adults laughed.

"But what about you, Daddy?"

Jake looked down at Kayla.

"You knew Mommy a lot longer than we did. You must have tons of stories. Can you share, too?"

Jake's heart squeezed. *God, give me the strength.* "There's nothing I'd rather do more." He'd known Laura since college, so there'd be an endless amount of stories to share with Kyle and Kayla. He'd do his best to remember every detail about his wife. In his desire to protect his children, he'd actually done more harm than good. But thanks to Olivia, that was all about to change. He glanced in her direction and she smiled. A twinge of excitement coursed through him, but he quickly pushed it away. He had to remain loyal to Laura's memory.

CHAPTER SIX

LATE FRIDAY AFTERNOON the sun dipped behind the Rockies, prompting Olivia to check her watch for the third time in twenty minutes.

"Come, Callie." She clapped her hands three times, and the puppy obeyed the command. "Good girl. Let's head inside and get your dinner." Since returning from Camp Bow Wow, Olivia had worked on the homework Jake had assigned at the end of their session. Callie was making good progress, but according to Jake, she still had a lot to learn. Olivia couldn't deny the idea of spending more time with Jake was appealing. He was easy on the eyes, but she needed to remind herself this trip was for Gammy, not to fall for a handsome service dog trainer and his adorable children.

Noting the time, Olivia shivered. It would be dark soon, but Gammy was still out. When Olivia had arrived home from camp, a scribbled note was on the kitchen table. Gammy had taken Ruth Westerly for a medical procedure after her ride had fallen through. Olivia admired her grandmother's generous heart, but the idea of her driving home in the dark didn't sit well. She didn't have a phone number to call Ruth to check if Gammy had dropped her off. She'd have to try her grandmother's cell for the second time.

Olivia stepped inside the laundry room. Callie jumped up and pawed at Olivia's feet. "I know you're hungry. Just give me a minute." Callie released a bark, followed by a whimper.

Olivia removed the sealed canister of dry food from the shelf and poured it into Callie's dish. The ravenous pup pushed her face into the bowl and gulped the meal. "I guess Jake was right when he said puppies have enormous appetites. All that exercise at camp made you hungry. Didn't it, girl?" Olivia scratched the top of the animal's head. "Eat your dinner. I'm going to fix something for me and Gammy. I'm starving, too."

Outside, thunder rumbled in the distance. Olivia scanned the contents of the refrigerator as she rubbed the back of her neck. A flash of lightning filled the kitchen at the same time as her phone sounded an alarm. Olivia dropped the head of lettuce she'd pulled from the shelf.

A tornado watch has been issued in your area.

What? Living in Florida, Olivia was used to the occasional tornado warning, but even living in Colorado as a child, she'd never realized the state experienced these weather patterns, too. Or maybe she didn't pay much attention to the weather as a child. Her heart hammered against her chest. She snatched the phone off the countertop to check the radar. Two quick taps on the screen caused her hands to shake. A huge red blob covered the map. Severe weather was heading toward Denver and it appeared to be moving toward Bluebell Canyon.

Olivia quickly pulled up her contact list and smashed her finger on Gammy's name. Again, the call went straight to voice mail, but this time Olivia left a message. "Gammy, please call me as soon as you hear this. There's a severe storm coming. Wherever you are, wait for me. I can come pick you up. Please call me." She pressed End and slipped the device into her back pocket. An engine rumbled outside. Was Gammy finally home? She raced to the front window and peeked through the slats of the plantation shutters. A delivery truck was in the driveway. A man stepped from the vehicle and climbed the front steps carrying a large box. Before he rang the bell, Olivia flung open the door to greet him.

"I have a package for Mrs. Hart." He peeked around Olivia's shoulder. "Is she home?"

Olivia accepted the delivery. "Thank you." She turned and placed the box on the chair inside the foyer. "No, she's not here right now, but I'll be sure she gets the package."

"I wanted to thank her for the cookies she baked for me last week. They were the best I've ever had. She's okay, isn't she?"

The young man's genuine concern touched Olivia. This would only happen in a small town like Bluebell. "She's fine, thank you. She drove a friend to a medical appointment."

"It must be Mrs. Westerly. She had her colonoscopy scheduled for today. I would have driven her, but I couldn't get the time off from work." His brow knit. "I hope Mrs. Hart gets home before the storm hits. The radio says it could be a big one."

The pulse in Olivia's neck fluttered. "I hope so, too. I'll let her know you enjoyed the cookies." Olivia glanced at the name tag pinned to his company shirt.

"You be safe too, Jeff."

Olivia closed the door and considered her next move. Jake. He would have a phone number for Ruth. Actually, she should have asked Jeff. He probably had the entire town on his phone.

Olivia slipped her phone from her pocket and intently scrolled her contact list. When Jake's number appeared, she tapped to call. Her fingers tightened against the phone. He answered on the first ring.

"Hey, Olivia. What's up?"

"I'm sorry to bother you. It's Gammy." Her voice shook. "She's not home and there's a storm coming. I'm worried."

"I'll be right over."

The last thing Olivia wanted to do was disrupt his evening with the children, especially if it was a false alarm and her grandmother walked through the door any minute. "I don't want to trouble you. I wanted to know if you had a telephone number for Ruth Westerly?" Olivia explained the situation.

"I'll call Ruth and call you back." Jake quickly ended the call.

Olivia paced the floor and prayed her grandmother was safe. Maybe it was only a poor cell signal. But something gnawed at her, telling her otherwise.

Olivia's phone gave a half ring before she answered Jake's call. "Did you reach Ruth?"

"There was no answer. But I'm not surprised. Ruth lives alone. Her husband passed away a few years ago."

Olivia sensed the concerned tone in Jake's voice. "What should I do? I don't have a good feeling about this. Gammy should be home by now. The weather report mentioned tornadoes."

"Stay put. I'll be right over." Jake hung up.

Despite the situation, knowing Jake was coming over instilled a sense of comfort in Olivia. Something she hadn't felt since before the dissolution of her marriage.

Less than fifteen minutes later, she heard the crunching of tires on gravel out front.

Callie jumped to attention and raced to the door. Olivia followed.

Before Jake knocked, Olivia flung it open.

"It's raining," he announced as he wiped his feet on the welcome mat and stepped inside.

"Where are the children?" Olivia asked.

"I dropped them off at my brother's house.

I didn't want them to worry when it turns out to be nothing."

Olivia admired Jake. He always put his children first and would do whatever he could to protect them. "Good thinking."

"You mentioned a medical appointment. Do you know what time?"

Olivia nodded. "Her note said it was three o'clock."

Jake rubbed his hand across his chin. "Anything else?"

"No."

Jake walked across the floor, then pivoted. "I can try to call Dr. Dickerson. He's the town doctor. Most likely, he referred Ruth to a doctor in Denver, or perhaps he set up the medical procedure."

"That's a great idea."

"Don't get too excited. I'm not sure how much Dr. Dickerson can share, given the confidentiality laws." Jake pulled his phone from his back pocket and tapped the screen.

Olivia's shoulders sank. Jake was right. She should have asked Jeff the delivery boy since he knew about Ruth's appointment.

Jake looked up from his device. "I'm not getting a good signal in here—could be the storm.

Do you mind if I go out on the porch to make the call?"

Heavy rain pelted the roof. Water overflowed from the gutter.

"Of course not." Olivia appreciated Jake asking permission. She wondered if Jake realized how much she loved her grandmother. Her thoughts quickly returned to Gammy being out on the road in these treacherous conditions. Why didn't she push the issue more? Olivia should have tried harder to convince her grandmother that with her vision deteriorating, it was too dangerous to drive—particularly after dark.

Jake stepped back inside the house. His face was wet from the driving rain.

"Did you find out anything about the doctor? We need to find her!"

Jake approached and gently placed his hands on her upper arms. His stormy eyes connected with hers, creating another wave of nausea, along with a swarm of butterflies. "Please, try to calm down. Dr. Dickerson said he referred Ruth to a gastrointestinal doctor in Denver. Ruth had told him her appointment was at one. He's calling the doctor's office now to find out what time they left his office. He said he'd call right back."

Olivia inhaled a deep breath and released it.

"If Ruth's procedure was on time, they should have been on the road long before four o'clock." Jake glanced at his watch. "It's after six now. They should be home any minute."

Outside, a gust of wind rattled the shutters before tapping sounded against the windows.

Jake turned at the noise. "That sounds like hail." He walked toward the window and opened the plantation shutter. "I think small pellets are falling. It looks like the winds are picking up, too. Make sure you have a full charge on your phone in case we lose power."

Olivia hurried into the kitchen and retrieved her charger from her purse. She plugged the phone into the outlet, keeping the phone turned on so she wouldn't miss a call. A chill raced up her spine thinking about Gammy in the storm.

Jake stepped into the kitchen and his cell phone rang. He answered on the first ring. Olivia heard a voice on the other end. Thankfully the connection was better. She busied her hands by dumping the cold pot of coffee from earlier in the day into the sink and sent up a silent prayer for her grandmother.

Jake pocketed his cell and approached Olivia.

"What did Dr. Dickerson say?"

"It looks like we'll be making a road trip. Dr. Dickerson spoke with the physician who performed the colonoscopy. He'd had an earlier cancellation, so he actually finished up with Ruth around three fifteen."

The sudden turn of events was unsettling. She had hoped her grandmother's absence was because of the doctor running behind schedule, but Jake just confirmed that the opposite was true. Olivia ran her fingers through her hair. "Then why hasn't Gammy dropped off Ruth? Something isn't right." A sudden beeping from her phone made her jump.

A severe thunderstorm warning has been issued in your area.

Olivia read the message and shuddered.

"I'm going to put a call in to my friend. He's a state trooper in Denver. Maybe he can tell us of any accident reported." Jake drew his phone from his pocket.

Olivia could barely breathe. If anything happened to Gammy, she would be all alone in the world. "We have to go find her," Olivia pleaded with Jake while he searched his device for his friend's number.

She paced the kitchen floor. Callie nipped at her heels while Jake spoke on the phone.

Minutes later, he ended the call and approached Olivia.

"Has he heard of any accidents?" Olivia wrapped her arms tight around her waist.

Jake's expression was solemn. "My buddy Nick isn't on duty, but I spoke with Dispatch. They don't have any accident reported along the route Myrna would have been traveling."

Olivia dropped her arms to her sides and grabbed her purse off the counter. She unplugged her phone from the charger and tossed it inside her bag. "I need to go find her."

Callie barked twice.

"I can't sit here waiting." She bit her lower lip. The tears she'd fought to hold back broke free and streamed down her cheeks. "My grandmother is all I have."

Jake moved closer and pulled her into his arms. "Please don't cry. She'll be okay. We'll find her. I promise."

For a moment, Olivia found comfort in Jake's warm embrace, but that was a dangerous place to be. She quickly pulled away, turned toward the window and the pounding rain, and shivered. "Let's go find my gammy."

MINUTES LATER, THEY were on the road. Jake gripped the steering wheel and willed the windshield wipers to move faster. The heavy rain was blinding. The car's high beams did little to assist Jake with the poor visibility.

Despite his cautious speed, he suddenly lost control of the car.

With the treacherous weather, Jake would have preferred to make this trip alone, but he couldn't blame Olivia for wanting to help with the search. She loved her grandmother and was concerned for her safety.

Olivia leaned forward with a paper towel in hand, frantically wiping the fog that the defroster failed to eliminate. "Can you see?" Her voice shook as she leaned closer to him.

Their shoulders brushed, providing a moment of comfort despite the weather conditions. Jake shook off the feeling. He needed to keep his focus off Olivia and on the road. This was another reason he'd wanted to search for Myrna on his own. Lately, Olivia's presence made him feel like a nervous schoolboy.

"Do you think it would be better if we use the main interstate to get to Denver? These country roads have huge potholes. I don't think Gammy would go this way." Olivia continued her attempt to clear the windshield, which seemed to be a losing battle.

"You're right about the highway being a safer route, but Myrna won't travel on the interstate. She always avoids the highway and takes the back roads because she doesn't like to drive over forty miles per hour."

Olivia tore another towel from the roll. "I guess her eyes are worse than she wants any of us to know."

"Long before Myrna's diagnosis, she wouldn't get on the interstate. She said merging into fast-moving traffic caused her blood pressure to sky-rocket." Jake laughed.

Olivia leaned back against the leather seat. "It sounds like you know my grandmother better than I do. It's kind of sad, don't you think?"

"Don't be so hard on yourself. It happens. Things aren't like they used to be."

"How so?"

Jake eased his foot from the accelerator as the car rounded a sharp curve. A flash of lightning lit up the sky. "Families used to live closer to one another. They were there to help each other during times of need."

"From what I hear, you still honor that tradition. Gammy told me you and your family all live on the same plot of land. She also shared how you and your brothers worked together to help your father care for your mother before she went into the nursing home." Olivia paused and released a sigh. "It must be a comfort to know there's always someone around who has your back."

"Yeah, it's nice to have family nearby, but it doesn't take blood to make a family. Your grandmother is proof of that. Of course, my brothers always come through for me, but your grandmother was my rock after my wife died. She helped me and the kids so much in those first few months. I'm not sure I would have survived without her."

Olivia squirmed in her seat. She wrapped her arms around her stomach. "I'm glad she was there to help you. She did the same for me after my father died. Once my mother turned to drinking as a coping mechanism, I had no one to help me deal with the loss. I honestly can't fathom what would have become of my life if Gammy hadn't come to take care of me. I hope you can understand why it's important for me to bring her back to Miami. I want to help her like she helped me. With her eyes getting worse, she can't continue to live alone, with or without a guide dog. Tonight is a perfect example. Callie wouldn't have stopped Gammy from driving her friend to Denver, but I could have."

"I don't want to argue with you about moving Myrna. We both want what's best for her. I agree she shouldn't have made this long drive, but I think her heart overpowered her logic." Now wasn't the time to debate the moving issue. Jake knew plenty of disabled people who lived independently with the help of a service dog and upgrades to their home.

They rode in silence for the next few miles. Olivia continued with her attempts to reach Myrna, but the calls went straight to voice mail.

"Look! Do you see those lights flashing ahead?" Olivia pointed.

Jake slowed as the wipers continued at a rapid pace, trying desperately to keep up with the deluge. "That's the driveway to the Potters' farm. It's been empty since Sam died over a year ago. They have everything tied up in probate court."

"There was a car. I saw it. Pull over!"

Jake hit the turn signal and navigated his extended-cab truck off the road. The headlights hit the familiar white sedan and his pulse slowed. "That's Myrna's car."

"Thank You, God!" Olivia cried out. "I hope they're okay."

Jake placed the car into Park and turned off the engine. "You wait here. I'll go check on them." He unfastened his seat belt, pulled the hood of his jacket over his head and opened the door.

"Not on your life." Olivia repeated Jake's actions. "I'm going, too." She jumped from the car.

Jake jogged to Myrna's vehicle with Olivia close behind and tapped on the driver's-side window. He didn't want to frighten the women. With the rain coming down so hard, it was likely they couldn't see him and Olivia.

A second later, the window rolled down about half an inch. "I've been praying that you would come," Myrna said.

"Why didn't you call? Are you two okay?" Jake scanned Myrna's face. His shoulders relaxed when he saw no sign of distress.

"When the weather got bad, I pulled over at the first safe spot. I tried to call, but my cell phone battery went dead."

Olivia peered into the back seat. "Is Ruth okay?"

Jake looked through the glass. He spotted

Ruth stretched out across the back seat with a yellow afghan covering her.

"She fell asleep ten minutes outside of Denver. I guess the anesthesia is still working on her." Myrna glanced over her shoulder at her friend. "Poor thing. On our way out of the doctor's office, she said she was starving after fasting. She wanted a double cheeseburger. Then, within seconds of getting into the car, she was out."

"I wish you would have used Ruth's phone to call. I've been worried sick." Olivia sighed.

Myrna unbuckled her seat belt. "Ruth doesn't have a cell phone. I gave her one last year for Christmas, but she donated it to Penny, who runs the women's shelter in Smithville. She said Penny could use it more than her."

Olivia frowned. "With your eyes, you shouldn't drive without a fully charged phone. In fact, you shouldn't drive, period. What if we hadn't found you?"

Myrna pulled her hood over her head. "Maybe we should wait and discuss my driving privileges when we're all safely home."

"Okay, ladies, we'll talk about this later. Olivia, you can follow me. We'll swing by Ruth's house and drop her off first."

Olivia nodded.

Jake helped Myrna from the car and circled her around to the passenger side while Olivia took the driver's seat.

With the women safely inside the car, Jake trudged across the muddy driveway to his truck. Based on their earlier conversation, it was clear Olivia still believed Myrna would be better off in Florida. However, the more he learned about Olivia's past, he was gaining a better understanding of Olivia's position. She loved Myrna as much as he and his children did. Of course, protecting Kyle and Kayla from any additional pain and suffering was his number one priority. He'd have to continue with the upgrades on Myrna's home and pray Olivia would reconsider her plan. Bluebell would not be the same without Myrna Hart...or without the woman who was slowly stealing his heart.

CHAPTER SEVEN

Olivia used the back of her palm to wipe the moisture from her cheek. She tugged the cool satin sheet under her chin and squeezed her eyes closed. A soft whimper filled the guest room, followed by another round of wetness across her eyebrows. She slowly opened one eye and found herself face-to-face with a shiny brown nose.

"What are you doing up so early, Callie?"

The puppy dug her paws furiously into the fluffy down comforter and barked.

Olivia eyed the digital clock on the dresser and jerked her head off her pillow.

Eleven fifteen.

Kicking the covers tangled around her ankles, she sprang from the bed. When her bare feet hit the floor, she nearly tripped.

Callie barked and raced to the door.

Jake had stressed the importance of keeping Callie on a schedule. Last night, before going to bed, she'd double-checked the alarm on her phone. Had she been so tired that she slept through it?

Olivia sprinted to the closet and quickly dressed. The shower could wait until after she took Callie for a walk and fed her breakfast.

"Come on, girl." Olivia opened the bedroom door and raced for the staircase. Halfway down, her socked feet skidded to a stop.

"Whoa!"

Olivia stopped just short of running full force into Jake, who was hunched over on the landing.

"Where's the fire?" Clutching a piece of carpet in his right hand, Jake pushed himself up. His biceps bulged through his Beckett's Canine Training T-shirt.

Olivia's messy hair and flannel lounge pants were proof that the last person she had expected to see this morning was Jake. Had she known he was in the house, she would have at least run a comb through the tangled mane.

"I overslept." Olivia glanced down at Callie. Warmth filled her cheeks. "I never oversleep. The day is half-gone! I should have taken Callie out hours ago. I marked my calendar for a two-hour hike this morning."

"Relax. Not everything in life needs to be planned. You must have needed the sleep, and it's hard to resist the positive effects of the mountain air." Jake winked. "Don't worry. Myrna took Callie out before she left."

Guilt took hold. First, Callie ran off on her watch, not once, but twice. Now Olivia got caught slacking off on her puppy-raising duties.

She twisted a strand of hair. "I'm sorry. We'll get out of your way." Olivia called to Callie. "Come on, girl. Let's get your breakfast before it's lunchtime."

"Myrna fed her already. I think she got up with the chickens." Jake laughed.

If Olivia wanted to keep up with her grandmother, she'd have to get a louder alarm clock. "Where did Gammy go?" Getting her grandmother to sit still long enough to talk to her about relinquishing her driver's license and relying more on neighbors for transportation would be a challenge. Following yesterday's scare, Olivia was more convinced that driving was no longer safe for Gammy.

"She's working her volunteer shift at the library from eight until noon. Then she was meeting Hilde for lunch in Denver. They also planned to do some shopping for the twins' birthday party."

"Boy, I hope I have that kind of energy when I'm her age. Gammy has a way of making me look like a lazy bum."

Jake laughed. "She doesn't allow a blade of grass to grow under her feet. She loves to do for others."

Since arriving in Bluebell, Olivia kept witnessing the positive impact her grandmother had on her community. "When is the twins' party?"

"It's a week from today. I still can't believe they're going to be seven years old." Jake shook his head. "You're invited, of course."

"That's nice of you. It sounds like fun." Olivia admired Jake. Raising his children without their mother couldn't be easy, yet he seemed to handle things effortlessly.

"I'll add you to the guest list. The kids will be happy."

Olivia wasn't sure about Kayla. She had hoped they'd connected after she told Kayla about losing her father, but she still sensed the child didn't fully trust her. Olivia couldn't blame her. She understood how Kayla felt. "I'm sure you and Gammy have everything under control, but I'd love to help."

Jake smiled. "With ten kids currently on the guest list, we could use an extra set of hands."

As an adult, Olivia had never been to a child's birthday party. When her desire to have children started growing, she used to imagine throwing big birthday celebrations with pony rides, face painting and inflatable bouncy houses. "I'd be happy to help. Do you have anything special planned outside of the typical birthday festivities?"

"I do. I plan to take the children to the county fair. It just so happens that opening day is on their birthday."

"That sounds like perfect timing."

"I thought Kyle would burst with excitement when I told him. He's been marking the days off on our calendar hanging in the kitchen."

Olivia laughed. "What can I do to help get ready for the party?"

"Are you sure you'll have the time? Your plate seems pretty full with Myrna and Callie."

"I like to stay busy. Besides, I need to repay you for all that you've done for Gammy. Remember, I told you I'd like to help with the repairs you're doing around her house." Olivia paused and pointed to the floor. "Like this. If I had known you were coming over, I would have made a point of getting up in time to help you."

Jake slid the tape measure into the back pocket of his jeans. "No worries. You're up now. Are you ready for some coffee?"

"I work in the ER. I'm always ready for coffee." Olivia smiled.

"That's right." He palmed his forehead. "You probably live on the stuff."

"In moderation. I've seen the effects too much caffeine can have on the body."

"But a cup or two is good, right?"

Olivia nodded. "Absolutely."

"I made a fresh pot about ten minutes ago. Get yourself caffeinated and then we can go over my plans for the steps."

"Sounds like a plan." Olivia turned to head to the kitchen.

"You can let Callie out back. The kids are out there with Tank." Jake picked up his coffee from the foyer table and took a sip.

"Great. I'll be right back." Olivia continued down the hall.

The aroma of bacon lingered in the kitchen. Her stomach rumbled. Of course, Gammy had cooked breakfast for Jake and his kids. If only she'd woken up earlier, she might have enjoyed a hot meal. For now, coffee would have to do.

Radiant sunshine filled the room. It was a glorious day to be outdoors, but she'd already committed to helping Jake.

Outside, the children's laughter reminded Olivia of recess on the first warm day following a long, cold winter spent indoors. She moved to the open kitchen window. Callie followed and whimpered, longing to join in the fun. "I know, girl. I feel the same."

Olivia peered through the screen. Her heart squeezed. A backyard filled with children was her dream. Had she missed the warning signs during their marriage that her ex-husband had changed his mind about having children? Were those years with Mark wasted? Olivia shook off the thought and reminded herself of what Gammy believed. *Choices don't determine your future. God does.* Olivia released a steadying breath. Mark was only part of her story. She couldn't allow him to put an end to her dream.

Unable to pull herself away from the window, Olivia laughed as Kayla yanked Kyle's baseball cap from his head and raced through the yard, determined to win the game of keep-away. Kyle chased his sister while Tank barked and nipped at the boy's tennis shoes.

Callie barked and scratched at the door.

"Okay, just a minute."

Olivia opened the cupboard next to the window and grabbed a large mug. She filled the cup three-quarters full and contemplated letting Callie outside without going out to greet the children herself. The last thing she wanted to do was spoil Kayla's fun.

Callie continued to scratch at the door. Olivia's stomach fluttered. She placed her sweaty palm on the door handle, but quickly dropped it to her side. She wiped her hand down her leg, knowing the fear behind her hesitation. Olivia saw herself in Kayla—a little girl who had put up walls to protect her broken heart.

Kayla's giggles filled the kitchen. Olivia opened the door to let Callie outside to join the fun. She closed it slowly. It was probably best to keep her distance. The last thing she wanted to do was steal Kayla's joy.

A slow and steady breath parted her lips. Olivia couldn't deny the truth. She was thirty-six and alone. With each passing year, her desire to have a child grew stronger. Olivia brushed away a tear racing down her cheek and turned away from a glimpse at a future that she feared would never be.

JAKE PULLED UP the piece of carpet runner covering the last step of the staircase. Maybe the busy pattern was in style years ago, but with Myrna's eyes deteriorating, it was an accident waiting to happen. The solid carpeting he planned to place down the hardwood steps along with a colorful strip of tape on the edge of each step would provide additional contrast to ensure Myrna's safety.

The sound of dishes clattering in the kitchen surprised Jake. He assumed Olivia would have taken Callie outside to join the children and Tank. Of course, Kayla still wasn't exactly rolling out the welcome mat for Olivia.

"The coffee tastes fantastic."

Jake lifted his head from the task at hand. His pulse quickened at the sight of Olivia standing in the foyer. The sunlight streaming through the large window over the front door highlighted her delicate bone structure.

"I'm glad you like it. I brought it over this morning. It's one of my favorite blends. Myrna enjoys it, too. Are you ready to get to work?"

Olivia approached and tucked a strand of hair

behind her ear. "I'm all yours. You're doing so much for Gammy. It's not fair for you to do it all alone."

"I can't think of anything I'd rather do more after all Myrna does for me and the twins."

Jake tossed the piece of rug into the pile.

"I appreciate everything you've done for Gammy. You're a good man, Jake."

He stood and dusted his hands off on his jeans. "There's nothing I wouldn't do for your grandmother. She means the world to me, like she does to you, too."

"I'm pretty sure Gammy feels the same about you."

The back screen door closed with a bang. Feet padded against the hardwood.

"Hi, Dr. Olivia!" the twins called out.

"Hello." Olivia tossed up a hand.

"Daddy, we're hungry," Kayla announced.

Jake turned with a smile. "After the big breakfast Miss Myrna cooked for you? Your tummies must be bottomless pits. Between the two of you, I think you polished off at least a dozen silver-dollar pancakes."

"That was hours ago." Kayla rolled her eyes.

"Yeah, besides, those pancakes are little. Can

we go to Charlie's?" Kyle tugged on Jake's tool belt.

Jake glanced at his watch. "Well, I had planned to go into town to pick up some new light bulbs for Miss Myrna."

"Yay!" The children cheered.

Kyle stepped closer to Olivia. "Do you want to come with us?"

"Who's Charlie?" Olivia looked down at Kyle. "Is he a friend of yours?"

Kyle giggled. "No. It's a place to eat."

"Charlie's Chuck Wagon is a local diner in town. It's owned by Mary Simpson. Charlie was Mary's great-great-grandfather," Jake explained.

"They have the best cheeseburgers in the world!" Kyle looked at his father. "Not as good as yours, Daddy."

Jake ruffled the top of Kyle's head. "Thanks, son, but my burgers can't compete." He turned to Olivia. "You're welcome to come along. We can show you around town a little. If you're going to stay for a while, it might be a good idea to familiarize yourself with some of the local establishments."

Olivia chewed her lower lip. "Actually, I wanted to check out some of the local markets and also the bank."

Jake laughed. "It won't take long to check out the markets since we only have one here in Bluebell."

"I guess people shop at the big-box store instead?"

Jake had never been to Miami, but he'd read enough about it to know that it was a different world from Bluebell. It would take time for Olivia to become acclimated in a small town. "Most make do with what we have here locally. For the bigger stores, you need to travel to Denver."

"Well, since I won't be here permanently, I'm sure I'll be fine."

Jake hoped when Olivia returned home, she'd leave Myrna and Callie here in Bluebell, where they belonged. "Okay, let's feed the dogs and secure them before we hit the road."

Thirty minutes later, the foursome sat inside Charlie's Chuck Wagon. Dark wood paneling surrounded their corner booth. Peanut shells covered the hardwood flooring.

Olivia peeked over her menu. "I feel like I've stepped onto the set of a Western movie. I'm surprised there isn't one of those mechanical bulls."

"Oh, they got rid of that in the early '90s

after Seth Davis nearly broke his neck. He had one too many root beers minus the root and tried to ride the bull standing up." Jake laughed.

"Cool!" Kyle exclaimed. "Maybe I can try that on the merry-go-round at the park?"

Jake tossed his son a look and shook his head. "You'll ride sitting down, young man."

"Hi, Jake. It's nice to see you and the kids."

Evelyn Simpson, Mary Simpson's older sister, had worked at Charlie's for as long as Jake could remember. She greeted the customers with a warm smile, along with a side order of the latest gossip. If you wanted to know what was going on around town, you asked Evelyn.

"Well now, who is this pretty young thing?" She cast her eyes on Olivia. "Wait a minute. You must be Myrna's granddaughter."

"She's a doctor!" Kyle announced.

Evelyn nodded. "ER, from what I hear. That's quite impressive. Bluebell isn't as exciting as Miami, but I hope you enjoy your stay. Of course, I have a sneaking suspicion you'll fall in love with our town and never want to leave."

"It's nice to meet you. I'm Olivia Hart." She extended her hand to Evelyn. "I don't have plans to stay since my home is in Florida, but I'm enjoying my visit."

"You might have a change of heart." Evelyn winked. "Now, what can I get everyone?"

"Cheeseburgers?" Jake scanned the table.

"Don't forget the fries and chocolate shakes, Daddy." Kyle bounced up and down. "You'll love the fries, Dr. Olivia. They're curly!"

"Did you get that, Evelyn?" Jake winked at the server.

Evelyn scribbled on the pad and slid the pencil behind her ear. "I'll get your orders back to Henry, pronto." She pocketed the pad and scurried toward the kitchen.

"Daddy, can I have a quarter for the jukebox?" Kyle reached his hand across the walnut tabletop.

Jake reached into the pocket of his jeans and fished out a handful of change. He eyed Kayla. She hadn't spoken a word since they'd left the house. "Kayla, do you want to play your favorite song for Miss Olivia?"

The child shrugged her shoulders.

"Come on, Kay. You always love to hear that song about Jeremiah the bullfrog." Kyle tugged on his sister's arm and took off.

Without saying a word, Kayla jumped off the seat and ran across the restaurant, chasing her brother.

Olivia kept her eyes on the children. "Kyle is protective of his sister. That's so sweet."

Jake was thankful Kyle kept a watchful eye on Kayla. "After their mother died, he thought it was his responsibility to look after her. Sometimes I think he does a better job with her than I do."

"You shouldn't be so hard on yourself. You're doing an amazing job. It can't be easy. Kayla told me you built her the clubhouse after you lost your wife."

After Laura passed away, life went on for his brothers and they went back to living their normal lives. Jake no longer knew what normal was. How could he go on without his wife? She gave him the two greatest blessings he'd ever received—his children. Laura brought joy and inspiration to his life every day. "Kayla wouldn't talk for weeks. I took her to the doctor, but he said to give her time. The more time that passed, the more helpless I became, so I built the clubhouse. When I couldn't sleep at night, I'd work on it. Constructing that little house kept my hands busy and my mind occupied. Your grandmother was staying with us and she kept the coffee coming. On those really dark days, she'd share stories about Laura.

She stressed how important it was to talk about her, just like you taught Kayla, but that was so hard for me. I thought if I didn't bring her up, my pain would go away."

"And did it?"

"No, it stayed fresh. I caused a lot more pain for Kayla." Jake glanced over at the kids dancing near the jukebox. His heart warmed. "Thank you for opening my eyes to what I was doing wrong."

Olivia leaned back in the booth. "So, last night's story time must have ended well?"

Jake couldn't have asked for a more perfect night. With the children fresh out of a bubble bath, they'd cuddled up in their pajamas. The three snuggled into Jake's bed while he reminisced about their mother. "I slept better than I had in the last two years. I told the kids about the night I proposed to their mother." Jake remembered the evening as though it were yesterday.

"I'm sure they enjoyed hearing that story." Olivia's chin tilted and she tucked a stray piece of hair behind her ear. "I'd love to hear it, too."

"Really?"

Olivia nodded. "I would."

Jake smiled. "I picked up Laura at her house.

I still remember the feeling I had in the pit of my stomach as I drove to her house."

"Butterflies?"

Jake shook his head. "More like bats. Not just one or two, but a swarm. I had spoken with her father the day before, so he and Laura's mother had given us their blessing, but I wasn't sure if Laura would say yes."

"How long had you been dating?"

It was difficult to remember his life without Laura. "Since the seventh grade. That's when her family moved to Virginia, where I'm from. Two weeks before the first dance of that year, a friend told me Billy Parker was going to ask Laura to be his date. I couldn't let that happen, so that day in the cafeteria, I asked her if she wanted to be my girlfriend. Of course, at that age, neither one of us really knew what that meant."

Olivia laughed. "I remember."

"We were together until we graduated from high school. That's when I realized I wanted to marry her."

"That's sweet. You married your high school sweetheart."

Jake explained to Olivia that he had sat at his desk in his bedroom the night before, mapping out his plan to propose. He even checked the time the sun would set the next day. "I had everything planned out. First, we'd go to an afternoon movie. After, a sunset picnic at Sawyer's Canyon. That's where I wanted to propose to her. At the movie theater, I remember her asking me what was wrong. I was so nervous I spilled our jumbo bucket of popcorn. When she passed me the box of sour balls, I dropped it, and the candies flew all over the floor."

Olivia covered her mouth before a giggle escaped.

"Yeah, there I was, the star quarterback, and I was so nervous I couldn't even hold on to a little box of candy." Jake paused and looked up at Olivia. Her smile lit up her entire face. "Trust me, it gets worse."

"I have a feeling it has a happy ending, though." Olivia picked at the folded napkin on the table.

"After the movie, we went outside. The film had run a little longer than the guide had stated. I still needed to make the twenty-minute drive to the canyon, but the sun was setting fast."

Olivia moved toward the edge of her seat. "You made it, didn't you?"

"Well, I had to hurry. I opened the door for

Laura and then I raced around to the other side of the car. I stumbled on a rock in the street and dropped the car keys." Jake paused, picked up his glass of water and took a sip.

"And?"

"The keys bounced down inside of the sewer."

Olivia's brown eyes doubled in size. "Oh, no!"

"It gets worse." Jake shook his head. "Within seconds, the rain came. That was something my teenage brain didn't consider when making my plan. I forgot to check the weather."

Olivia stifled a laugh.

"Laura unlocked the driver's-side door so at least I could get inside. For the next half hour, it poured. Water gushed down the street and into the sewer."

"And the keys?" Olivia's brow arched.

"Never found them."

"But you still proposed, right?"

"Well, that's where the story takes another twist. Our geometry teacher, Mr. Preston, pulled up. After I told him what happened, he drove me and Laura home."

"I'm sorry your plan didn't work out that night. Did you surprise her another time?"

"Actually, her mother did." Jake laughed.

"What happened?"

"By the time we arrived at her parents' house, the rain had stopped. When we pulled into the driveway, Laura's mother came running from the house. You would have thought there was a fire. We got out of the car and her mother grabbed Laura in her arms and cried. She told her how happy she was that we were going to get married."

"No! Oh, Jake!" Olivia couldn't hold back her laughter. "I'm so sorry."

Jake burst out laughing. "It was like being in a sitcom. Her mother was grabbing her hand and looking for the ring. Of course, at first, Laura was clueless. Then her father came out and welcomed me into the family. In the end, we all had a good laugh about it. Her parents were ecstatic because they got to see the proposal live."

"So you asked her that night?"

"Yep, right there in the driveway."

Olivia sat back. "That's the best proposal story I've ever heard."

For a moment, Jake remained silent. In less than twenty-four hours, for the second time, talking about Laura had come easy for him.

Olivia reached across the table and rested her hand on top of Jake's. "Are you okay?"

He released a long breath and looked at their hands. "Life doesn't always go as we plan, does it?"

Olivia shook her head. "I know mine hasn't."

Jake watched the smile Olivia had worn while he'd shared the proposal story slip away. "Thank you for listening."

"I appreciate you sharing the story with me."

Silence hung in the air as the server approached with their orders.

"Okay, I've got two burgers with double cheese."

Olivia flinched and quickly pulled away her hand.

For a split second, Jake longed to feel her touch again, but out of respect for Laura, he forced the thought away.

CHAPTER EIGHT

"I've made a list of the things we need to pick up for Kayla and Kyle's birthday party." Myrna flipped through the pages of a brown leather journal.

Olivia approached the light signal and eased her foot off the accelerator. "I wish I had one-half of your organizational skills, Gammy."

"I just write everything down in here." She lifted the journal. "I have boxes of these at home filled with every store list, appointment, Bible study, recipe and thoughts from the day. You name it and it's recorded."

Olivia worried what Gammy would do when she could no longer see to write about her daily events. It was obviously an important ritual. Maybe she could use the recording feature on her cell phone. "So, what's first on the list?"

"Hank Garrison will drop off the tents tomorrow afternoon. There's only a slight chance of rain in the forecast for Saturday, but Jake thought it was best to play it safe. Hank and his crew will set up the tents in front of the house."

"I thought the party was going to be at the fairgrounds?" One year, Olivia and her father attended the Colorado State Fair and made some of her fondest memories. Her mother had planned to attend, but she'd come down with the flu. Olivia remembered her father had let her eat as much cotton candy as her stomach could hold. "I remember seeing the dog stunt show. It was hilarious. Daddy and I laughed so hard our stomachs hurt."

Gammy smiled. "It makes me happy when you recall the good times."

Olivia only wished she'd had more time to create memories with him.

"Make a left here, dear." Myrna pointed to Garrison's Mercantile Company.

Olivia hit the turn signal.

"I guess Jake didn't mention that the twins' party is an all-day event. Garrison's will have most of what we need." She closed her journal and slipped it inside her purse. "We celebrate big here in Bluebell. Once you get a taste of it, you won't want to leave." Myrna laughed. "We'll spend the morning and afternoon at the fair. After, we'll come back to Jake's place for a cookout, fireworks and other activities."

"Sounds like fun, but a lot of work for Jake."

Myrna swatted her hand. "He'd do anything for those kids. Besides, practically the entire town has volunteered to help. In fact, I put you in charge of baking the cakes. We'll pick up the ingredients today."

Olivia loved to bake, but once she went to work in the ER, she began purchasing her baked goods. She navigated the SUV into an open parking spot in front of the store. "Of course I will. What's their favorite?"

"They both love my recipe for German chocolate cake. It's been in the family for generations."

Olivia smiled. "I remember. You baked it when you and Pops came to stay with me and Mom."

"It was your father's favorite." Myrna unfastened her seat belt and patted Olivia's hand. "Let's only think good thoughts today."

"That sounds like a plan."

Olivia stepped inside the store and took in the rustic surroundings. The uneven floorboards and rough wood walls gave the mercantile a warm and welcoming feel. It was the complete opposite of the high-end boutiques with modern designs that lined the streets of Miami. The aroma of cedar sent a flood of memories through her. She pictured the chest that sat at the foot of her childhood bed. After her father died, she'd packed away pictures and special gifts he'd given her. Over the years, the chest had traveled with Olivia as she moved from one home to another.

"Look who's here."

Olivia spotted a petite, gray-haired woman coming from the back room and walking around the checkout counter at a swift pace. An oversize box in her arms didn't hinder her speed. Every strand of her short silver hair was in place, as though she'd just returned from the hairdresser.

"This is Nellie Garrison, Hank's wife and co-owner of the mercantile." Gammy made the introduction. "Nellie, this is my granddaughter, Olivia."

The woman set the box on the counter and approached her customers. "I'd recognize that beautiful face anywhere." Nellie placed her hands on Olivia's cheeks. "Your grandmother is so proud of you. She's shared many photographs of you. I knew who you were the moment you walked in. I'm glad you finally got away from that ER and made it to Bluebell. You'll never want to leave."

What was it about this place? It was like everyone who lived in town worked for the chamber of commerce. Was there something about Bluebell Olivia couldn't see? "My work is back in Miami, so I'll only be here long enough to convince Gammy it's time for someone to take care of her."

"Is she still on that silly idea?" Nellie tugged on Myrna's arm and laughed. "There's no one in this town who would think twice about helping your grandmother, so there's no need to worry about her. Of course, if you moved to Bluebell, you could keep a close eye on her yourself," Nellie said with a wink.

Olivia bit her tongue to keep the peace. Her stomach twisted as she realized it wasn't only Gammy she'd have to convince that moving would be in her best interest. The entire community might be an obstacle for her. But if she didn't feel confident in Callie's abilities, Olivia would have no option but to carry out her original plan.

The front door swooshed behind them.

"Look who's here." Nellie nodded her head toward the customer.

Olivia spun on her heel in time to see Jake strolling into the store. His boots scraped across the hardwood. His normally straight posture was gone and instead he appeared hunched. Underneath his dark brown cowboy hat, Olivia saw lines crinkling along his forehead.

"Jake, is everything okay?" Myrna asked.

She hadn't imagined it. Even Gammy noticed the weight Jake carried.

"Jake," Olivia asked, "is everything okay?"

"I don't want to interrupt..."

Nellie took advantage of his brief pause. "I'm just getting to know Myrna's gorgeous granddaughter. You should show her around Bluebell!"

Olivia's face warmed. She quickly changed the subject to the twins' birthday. "Gammy and I just stopped in to pick up some things for the party."

Jake's expression darkened further. "That's what I wanted to talk with Myrna about."

Nellie took Olivia's hand. "We'll leave you two alone to talk."

"No, I'd like to get all of your opinions." Jake

removed his hat and raked his hand through his hair.

"What is it, Jake? I'm worried," Myrna said.

"Kayla came home from school today and announced she wasn't going to her birthday party." Jake slipped his hands into the back pockets of his mud-splattered jeans.

"Oh, my stars, that's the silliest thing I've ever heard." Nellie pulled out a stool. "Here, dear, take a seat." She patted her hand against the larch wood stool next to the counter. "It sounds like you need a good cup of strong coffee." Nellie scurried to the back room, but Jake didn't sit. Instead, he paced the floor.

Myrna cleared her throat. "Does Kyle have any idea why his sister had this sudden change of heart? Just last week, Kayla was so excited about the party. She'd chattered endlessly about all the different animals she wanted to see at the fair."

Jake shook his head. "Kyle said during recess he saw a couple of Kayla's friends whispering and pointing at her while she was getting a drink from the water fountain. A couple of minutes later, Kayla ran to the far side of the playground and hid behind a tree. He went to check on her, but she wouldn't talk to him."

"Poor Kayla. Sometimes children can be cruel when they decide to gang up on one of their friends," Myrna said.

Olivia saw the pain in Jake's eyes.

"I suspect the teasing may have been about the mother-daughter fashion show. Kyle mentioned it recently, but I kind of brushed it off because I didn't hear more about it." Jake sighed.

Nellie crossed the room with a tray of cups, along with a carafe of coffee. "I got an email the other day from my women's club about volunteering for the fashion show. I signed up. It sounded like fun."

Jake dipped his chin. "Maybe not for a little girl who lost her mother. I'm afraid this event is triggering a lot of sad memories for Kayla."

Olivia's heart ached for Kayla. A few months after her father passed away, her elementary school hosted a father-daughter dance for all grades. Weeks before the event, her girlfriends talked nonstop about what they'd wear and how their dads were all taking them out to a fancy, grown-up dinner.

"You okay?" Gammy whispered to Olivia.

Olivia nodded and smiled. She found comfort in knowing that her grandmother remembered the dance as well. If it hadn't been for Gammy, that evening would have been the worst night of her life. Instead of the dance, they got dressed up and went to the movies. After, Gammy took her to the most expensive restaurant in town. It was the first time Olivia had eaten at a table draped with a linen tablecloth and with a candle as the centerpiece. For one night, thanks to her grandmother, the pain of losing her father waned.

"The kids raced out of the house so fast when the bus honked its horn for school this morning, I wasn't able to talk with Kayla. But after they left, I went up to their rooms to strip the sheets from their beds and I found this under Kayla's mattress. It's the flyer announcing the fashion show." Jake slipped a folded piece of paper from his back pocket and passed it to Myrna.

Olivia watched as Gammy opened the paper and nodded. "There's no doubt about it. It's the fashion show that has Kayla upset. We'll have to put our heads together to come up with an idea to help her."

"I can take her." The words spilled out of Olivia's mouth before her brain could process the offer. She was usually an overthinker, always weighing the pros and cons of her ideas before speaking or acting.

"That's a wonderful idea." Gammy wasted no time with her response. She rested her hand on Olivia's arm.

The touch brought her back into the moment. Was this the right thing to do? What made her think Kayla would even want to go with her? Although they had a moment of connection in Kayla's clubhouse, their relationship appeared to have regressed to its original state when they first met. It was obvious Kayla felt threatened by her presence. In her mind, Olivia was trying to replace her mother.

"I appreciate the offer, but I'm not sure if that's a good idea." Jake kept a close eye on Olivia.

Now was her opportunity to back out. But as much as Olivia wanted to run out of the store and take the offer with her, her heart had a different idea. Olivia had been in Kayla's situation. She knew the agony of losing a parent. How could she walk away?

"You've come a long way." Olivia scratched Callie underneath her collar and, with the other hand, fed her a treat.

After skipping lunch with Gammy on Friday, Olivia packed up Callie and headed to Jake's place. She wanted to work with the pup before camp started.

"Not quite."

Olivia looked up and squinted into the late-afternoon sun. Jake towered over her, twisting a piece of straw between his teeth. She wasn't sure if there were any magazines that featured cowboys, but if so, Jake could be on the cover.

"Why would you say that?"

Jake squatted and rubbed Callie's head. "I think we've got our hands full with this little one."

"Are you saying Callie can't help Gammy? I remember you said some dogs don't have what it takes to work as service animals."

"That's true, but I still have hope." He picked up Callie and rubbed his nose into her coat. "It's okay, girl. I believe in you."

Callie covered Jake's face with sloppy kisses.

"You certainly have a way with her." Olivia laughed.

"I wish I could say the same about Kayla."

Olivia hoped Kayla would change her mind about attending her birthday party, but according to Gammy, she hadn't mentioned it.

"It's obvious you mean the world to her. Losing a parent is a lot for a child to handle, but it's a blessing Kayla and Kyle have each other. After my dad died, I'd pretend my stuffed animals were my siblings, so I could have someone to talk to." Olivia stood.

Jake reached out and placed his hand on Olivia's arm. "Thanks for sharing that with me. I appreciate it."

A warm sensation traveled up her arm. She moved her eyes toward his hand. "You're welcome."

"Daddy! We're home!" Kyle called out from across the pasture.

Jake's hand pulled away and Olivia looked up. His eyes remained fixated on her as though neither wanted to be the first to look away. Warmth spread across her face. What exactly was happening? She'd missed lunch. Maybe it was her blood sugar dropping. That had to be the reason.

"I aced my spelling test!" Kyle smiled, revealing a missing front tooth.

"That's wonderful, son. Congratulations."

"Hey, when did that happen?" Olivia pointed at Kyle's mouth. She looked over and noticed Kayla walking slowly toward them with her head down.

"This morning! Isn't it cool? Daddy said if

I put it under my pillow tonight, I might get a surprise."

Kayla joined them but remained silent.

"Did you have a good day, sweetie?" Jake asked.

Kayla shrugged her shoulders.

Olivia noticed the redness around her eyes.

"Run inside and change. I need your help to set up the cones for camp."

"I'll be right back," Kyle called out over his shoulder as he sped toward the house.

"Daddy, do I have to help with camp today?"

"What's wrong? You're not sick, are you?" Jake brushed Kayla's hair away and placed his hand on her forehead. "Cool as a cucumber."

"I feel okay."

Jake's brow arched. "Did you do poorly on your spelling test?"

Kayla shook her head. "I didn't miss any words."

"That's great, sweetie. Then why so glum?"

Kayla glanced at Olivia before turning her attention back to the ground.

Olivia could see Kayla was upset, but her gut told her it had nothing to do with a spelling test. It was more. When Kayla's eyes met hers for a second time, Olivia sensed maybe Kayla wanted to talk, but not necessarily to her father.

"Sweetie?" Jake kept a close eye on his daughter. "Do you want to talk about what's bothering you?"

Olivia took a step back. "I'm going to take Callie and get her some water. You two talk."

"No!" Kayla snapped. Her face turned red.

Jake turned to Olivia, then back to Kayla. "I can't help you if you don't talk to me."

Kayla kicked her tennis shoe into the ground and bit her lip. "It's just— Forget it. You wouldn't understand." Kayla pivoted and ran across the yard to her clubhouse.

Jake slid his hands into his back pockets. "What am I missing here?"

"You're just being a guy."

Jake sighed. "That's the only thing I know how to be." He scratched his head and looked toward the clubhouse.

"Sometimes a girl needs—"

"Her mother. Is that what you think this is about? Girl talk?"

A look of understanding washed over Jake's face. He was a good father and sensitive to his daughter's needs. "Exactly. May I?" She pointed at the clubhouse.

"Would you?"

"Of course I will." Olivia handed Callie's leash to Jake.

Jake took the leather strap. "Thank you."

"Don't thank me yet." Olivia smiled and headed across the yard.

The closer she got to the little pink house, the more her stomach knotted. Olivia's steps slowed. What if it had all been a mistake and Kayla didn't want to talk with her? It was a chance she would have to take. Olivia had seen the pain in Kayla's eyes. She couldn't allow her to keep everything bottled up. It wasn't healthy.

Outside the door of the clubhouse, Olivia leaned close to the little building, but no sound came from the other side. She gently tapped her knuckles against the door. "Kayla. May I come in?"

Olivia waited in silence. She fought the urge to push the door open, take Kayla into her arms and tell her everything would be okay. She had to remain patient. The last thing Olivia wanted to do was push Kayla even further away.

The second she raised her hand to knock again, the door slowly opened.

"I was hoping you'd come." Kayla peered around the door.

Olivia's breath hitched. Kayla wanted her there? The child's eyes looked redder than earlier. Clutched in her left hand was the photograph of her mother.

Olivia's heart broke as memories of her father and how she'd felt after he died flooded her mind. "Do you want some company?"

Kayla pulled the door open wider. Olivia stepped inside.

A music box played. Kayla moved toward the table with two chairs. Olivia followed behind, recognizing the song. "Bridge Over Troubled Water."

Frozen, Olivia stared at the music box in the middle of the table. She closed her eyes and saw her mother and father dancing in the kitchen. It was the only time Olivia had ever seen her parents holding each other. Olivia could still picture the joyful smiles on their faces. Her mother had giggled softly when her father whispered something in her ear. After her father died, Olivia never heard her mother giggle again.

"Dr. Olivia, are you okay?"

Kayla's voice startled her back into the moment. "Yes. I'm sorry."

"It's okay." Kayla looked at the music box. "Do you know that song?"

Olivia nodded. "Yes. I remember my parents dancing to it."

Kayla turned her attention to the picture frame. "It was my mommy's favorite song. She gave me this music box the day after she told me I was going to have another brother."

"That's a very special gift."

Kayla put the picture frame on the table and picked up the music box. "She shouldn't have given it to me."

"Why would you say that? I'm sure your mommy bought it special just for you."

She ran her tiny fingers around the gold-plated casing. "I was mean to her."

"Why, sweetie?"

Kayla bit her lower lip. "I didn't want another brother, or another sibling." She tipped her head down. "Kyle was born first. If Mommy had another kid, I wouldn't be her baby anymore."

"And you were afraid she might not love you as much anymore?"

Kayla nodded. "But I did something bad."

Olivia couldn't imagine Kayla doing anything bad outside of the ordinary things that children did. "Maybe it's not as bad as you think." Olivia pulled out a chair for Kayla and then took the other seat. Outside the clubhouse, dogs barked.

Olivia glanced at her watch. They had twenty minutes before camp began. "Do you want to tell me what happened?" She reached across the table and took Kayla's hand.

"I prayed." Kayla spoke barely above a whisper.

"Well, that doesn't sound too bad."

"I asked God to make me Mommy's baby forever."

Olivia's stomach twisted. Kayla blamed herself for the death of her mother and baby brother.

"It was my fault they died."

"Sweetie, you can't blame yourself for that. Your mommy had a medical emergency. What happened to her and your brother had nothing to do with your prayers."

Kayla's brow crinkled. "Really?"

"I promise." She gave Kayla's hand a squeeze.

"Last week, I told Cindy, my best friend, about my prayer, and she told Missy, the mean girl in my class. Yesterday, on the playground, Missy told me it was my fault."

That was why Kayla didn't want to go to her party. It wasn't only because of the fashion show.

"I never told my daddy. I thought he'd get mad at me."

Olivia offered a small smile and leaned in. "You can always tell your daddy anything. He might get upset or disappointed, but he'll never stop loving you."

Kayla wiped at the tear racing down her cheek. She looked up. "Kind of like God?" Her eyebrows drew together. "I learned in Bible school that God will love me no matter how much I mess up. Is that true?"

Olivia nodded. "Yes, thankfully it is the truth. And your daddy will always love you too, no matter what you do."

A tiny smile parted Kayla's mouth. She sprang from the chair and wrapped her arms tight around Olivia's waist. "Thank you for making me feel better. I think I'll tell my daddy about my mean prayer tonight when we say our prayers together."

Olivia embraced Kayla and closed her eyes, savoring the connection. "I think that would be the perfect time."

Kayla pulled back. "You know what else I'm going to tell him?"

"What's that?" Olivia gently brushed a strand of hair away from Kayla's face.

"I'm going to tell Daddy that I'm going to my party tomorrow." She grinned.

"That will make him very happy." Olivia checked her watch. "Maybe you should go help your daddy get ready for camp?"

"Okay." Kayla gave Olivia another quick hug.

"I'll be there in a minute," Olivia added.

Kayla skipped out the door, taking a piece of Olivia's heart with her. Olivia wrapped her arms around her body. If only she could forget the past so easily. A painful lump formed in her throat. She picked up the music box, turned it over and wound the key. Thoughts flooded her mind as the familiar song played. She recalled her father's death, her failed marriage, and thought about a possible future without children. Alone in the clubhouse, she rested her head on the table and wept.

"Wow! This is so cool!" Kyle squeezed Jake's right hand and bounced on his toes.

Jake couldn't have asked for better weather. The prediction of rain earlier in the week had failed to materialize. The tents Hank Garrison set up at the house weren't necessary unless people wanted to escape the bright sunshine.

"Where are we going to meet everyone, Daddy?" Kayla held tight on to Jake's left hand.

Jake still didn't know what Olivia had said

yesterday in the clubhouse, but he was thankful she had somehow convinced Kayla to attend her seventh birthday party.

"We have some tables set up near the concession area." He and Myrna had concluded being close to the food would be the best place for the party guests to gather. The kids and their parents could come and go while having a home base to rest or grab something to eat.

"That's good because I'm hungry," said Kyle.

"You're always hungry." Kayla rolled her eyes at her brother.

Jake smiled at his children's banter. Although today was a day to celebrate, he couldn't help but think about Laura and the baby. Early this morning, before the kids were out of bed, Jake had gone for a long walk on his property. He thanked God for all his blessings and prayed for the strength to remain present for this special day for his children. Over breakfast, the children shared memories of their mother.

"Look over there at the big sign, Kayla. That's for us!"

"Wow! Cool!" Kayla ran toward the sign. Kyle pulled his hand free from Jake's grip and followed his sister.

Jake had ordered a personalized "Happy

Birthday" banner designed by a Denver company he'd found on the internet. It showcased his children's names in large block-style lettering. It thrilled Jake to see the children so happy.

A group of people swarmed below the banner. Judging by the size of the crowd, it looked like everyone had already arrived. His shoulders slouched when he didn't see any sign of Olivia.

"Daddy!" Kyle raced to his father's side. "Uncle Logan said he and Uncle Cody want to take us to the rodeo. Can we go?"

"Of course you can, but what about the stunt dogs? That's going to start at the same time." Jake had carefully studied the schedule of events. He wanted to make sure Kyle and Kayla didn't miss a thing.

"I'd rather see the bull riders. I see dogs all the time." He giggled.

Jake recalled growing up in Whispering Slopes in the Shenandoah Valley of Virginia. His parents took him and his brothers to the state fair, where seeing everything was impossible. Kyle was smart to choose something new. "Today is your day, so you get to decide, but first it's important for us to greet your guests. They're here to celebrate with you and your sister."

Kyle pulled his father toward the group. The

aroma of sugary funnel cake teased his sweet tooth. Jake spotted Olivia. He narrowed his eyes and watched her talking with his younger brother Logan. He was taken aback by how beautiful she looked with her hair pulled back in a ponytail and a cowboy hat on her head. It appeared the city doctor was fitting right in with the locals.

Logan noticed Jake's arrival first. "Hey, bud, I thought you were going to miss your own kids' party," Logan joked.

Jake smiled. "Welcome back. How was the trip?"

"Alaska was amazing. Cody is already talking about going back. Our flight was late getting in last night, so we're both a little worn out."

"I'm sure you are. I appreciate you both coming to celebrate today," Jake said.

"We wouldn't have missed it." Logan palmed Jake's shoulder. "I was just getting to know Myrna's granddaughter. We could use a doctor like her in town. I've heard some chatter that Dr. Dickerson might be retiring."

Jake shook his head. "Those beauty shop women gossip too much. Doc Dickerson will keep practicing medicine as long as he's upright."

"You're probably right." Logan tipped his hat

to Olivia. "It was a pleasure talking to you. I better start rounding up the kids who want to go to the rodeo. Are you interested in going?"

Olivia glanced in Jake's direction. "Is everyone going as a group?"

"No. While we're here, everyone is kind of doing their own thing. There's too much to see to please everyone. Later at the ranch, we'll have more organized events." Jake placed his hand on his brother's shoulder. "I had a little surprise planned for Olivia, which is scheduled to begin in fifteen minutes. So, if she's game, we'll pass. Thanks for taking the twins, buddy."

"Sounds good. A couple of parents are going along, so don't worry about me losing any of the kids." Logan laughed, turned on his heel and moved to the group of parents congregated around one of the picnic tables.

Olivia cleared her throat. "You probably don't know this, but I'm not big on surprises. I'm more of a routine person."

"I never would have guessed." Jake nudged her arm. "Sometimes it's good to be spontaneous and not follow a schedule."

Olivia placed her hands on her hips. "You sound like Gammy. Just the other day, she said that exact thing to me."

"Well, you are on vacation, aren't you? Maybe now is a good time to start some new habits. Make some changes that might make you happier."

"What makes you think I'm not happy? Did Gammy say something to you?"

The last thing he wanted to do today was upset her. "I'm sorry. Maybe my advice was out of line. I know how precious life is, that's all. I have a habit of trying to make sure people I care about don't take life for granted. Putting things off until they fit into your schedule isn't the way to live. There's no guarantee for a tomorrow."

A look of understanding crossed Olivia's face. "You're right. I am on vacation, after all. What better time is there to do things a little spur of the moment?"

"There you go." Jake smiled. "By the way, nice hat." He winked.

She fingered the brim and her cheeks flushed. "Gammy bought it for me." She looked down at her feet. "She purchased the boots, too. Do I look silly?"

That was not how Jake would describe her. Between the hat, the faded jeans and the pair of cowboy boots, she was the prettiest cowgirl he'd seen in a long time. "You look great. No one would ever know you're a city girl."

Olivia's eyes widened. Her hand cupped her cheek. "I just realized this all plays into Gammy's grand plan to keep me here in Bluebell."

Jake laughed. "I wouldn't worry. It will take more than some Western clothing for you to uproot your life and move."

"You're right. Miami is my home. That will never change."

Olivia's words ignited a sinking feeling in his stomach. While they headed toward the arena to watch the dog stunt show, Jake struggled to brush off the disappointment Olivia's comment had sparked. Today was a day to celebrate the twins' birthday. This wasn't the time to lose his heart to a woman who lived a couple thousand miles away and wanted children of her own. Having more children wasn't part of his plan.

CHAPTER NINE

From the moment Olivia had arrived on the grounds with Gammy, a sense of nostalgia consumed her. She loved everything about the fair. And the best part was the day had just begun. The cheerful sounds of children enjoying themselves, the food trucks lining the trampled grass, the air filled with the sweet smells of treats, all brought back wonderful memories of the trip to the fair with her father. Jake's advice from earlier entered her mind. For most of her adult life, she'd allowed work to dominate both her schedule and her ability to enjoy the gift of life. She could never imagine the pain Jake had endured. If anyone understood the reason to live each day as if it were your last, it was Jake Beckett.

"I can't believe you're not asking where I'm taking you. I thought you'd want to pull out your cell phone and put it on your schedule."

Jake playfully nudged his arm against Olivia, making her keenly aware of his broad shoulders. "Stop it." She pushed back against him, giggling like a child. "I've decided my phone is off-limits today."

"Good for you. But I know from experience, sometimes old habits are hard to break."

"I'll keep that in mind." Olivia knew all too well about breaking habits. Lately, she'd been more guarded of her time off from the hospital. At first it was difficult to say no to colleagues who once relied on her to cover when she wasn't on the schedule. But now she looked forward to those days where she was able to do something for herself. Going to a coffee shop and reading for hours was her latest obsession. "So, are you going to tell me where we're headed?"

"You're worse than the twins." Jake laughed. "Are we there yet?" His voice mimicked the twins' higher voices.

Olivia rolled her eyes and laughed. A group of senior women approached from the other direction.

"Hello, Jake."

"Hi, Mrs. Hinton. I hope you ladies are enjoying yourselves."

"Yes, we are. It looks like you are, too." The elderly woman winked as she and the others moved toward the line at the cotton candy vendor.

Since their ten-minute walk to wherever they were going began, Olivia noted that everyone who passed seemed to stop and say something to Jake. "Is there anyone you don't know?"

"That's the best part about living in a small town. I couldn't imagine raising my children anywhere but Bluebell." Jake stopped at the metal gate that surrounded an enclosed building. "We're here."

Olivia's heart raced. She didn't know what was behind the gate, but the anticipation was exhilarating. "Can you tell me now?"

Jake turned, wearing a smile. "We're going to watch the stunt dogs perform."

For a second, Olivia had to remind herself to breathe. Her mouth was dry. She struggled to find the right words.

Jake gently placed his hand on her shoulder. "Are you okay?"

Olivia bit her lower lip. Tears peppered her eyelashes.

"What is it? I thought you'd enjoy this."

Olivia shook her head. "I haven't seen the

stunt dogs since I was a kid. They were my dad's favorite."

"Your grandmother mentioned it. That's why I thought you'd like to come to the show."

Jake's thoughtfulness was endearing. She'd forgotten she'd mentioned to Gammy about going to the dog show with her dad. She inhaled a deep breath. "I'd love to go with you."

"I'm happy to hear that. Shall we?" Jake gently clasped her hand, creating a reaction she couldn't quite identify. Whatever it was, she liked it.

Ten minutes later, Olivia sat alone in the stands while Jake was off getting popcorn. He said one of the best parts about seeing the show was the butter-laden popcorn. She couldn't argue with that. She even ordered a diet soda. After all, she was on vacation.

Her shoulders relaxed as she took in the crowd of mostly children with their parents. A longing tried to take hold, but she forced it aside. Today was a day to enjoy life. She refused to dwell on the past.

Olivia spotted Jake working his way through the crowd, carrying a cardboard tray with their snacks. Her pulse ticked up a few beats. Western-style clothing was never her thing, but Jake sure looked good in his long-sleeved denim shirt with silver buttons down the front, paired with khakis. As he moved toward their seats, she couldn't ignore the way the shirt brought out the blue in his eyes.

"Okay, I got buttered popcorn and your diet soda. I think we have a couple of minutes before the show starts." He settled in the seat next to her and passed the drink.

Olivia put the straw between her lips. She drank as though she'd been in the desert for days, while sneaking peeks at his freshly shaven face.

"You are hooked on that stuff. I think you'll need a refill before the show starts." He laughed.

She wasn't sure if it was the syrupy sweet taste or the carbonation of the soda, but whatever it was, the cool drink settled her nerves. Olivia didn't recall ever feeling nervous during their classes at camp. Today, something seemed different. She was relieved when the announcer came over the loudspeaker to say the show would start in a few minutes.

Jake settled the tub of popcorn on his right knee and helped himself. "The stuff is great." He crammed a handful into his mouth.

Olivia reached inside the bucket and grabbed

an equally large handful. "I better eat up because it looks like it will be gone before the show even gets started," she teased.

"Don't worry. They have free refills." Jake laughed.

"You better pace yourself." Olivia smiled, feeling more at ease with her one-on-one time with Jake as their conversation continued.

"Are you kidding? When I was little, I could eat this stuff all day." He raised the tub and took another handful.

Olivia scanned the program she'd picked up on the way inside. "This looks like a great lineup of stunts. I guess dogs have gotten smarter since I was a kid. I remember the juggling. It was hilarious, but also impressive. I never understood how they trained the dogs to do that."

"What about the dancing? Last year two Border collies did the tango. I tried to get Tank to do it, but he didn't want any part of it."

Jake's comment triggered a fond memory of her father. She closed her eyes for a moment. "Once, when I was little, my dad took me to a minor-league baseball game. Like my mother, I thought baseball was boring, but if I was with my dad, I was happy to go. Before they threw out the first pitch, a group of Jack Russell stunt dogs performed. I'll never forget it. I didn't know dogs could jump so high. They were even jumping rope. When we got home after the game, I remember my dad had convinced himself he could teach our dog, Tootie, to do the same."

"And did he?"

Olivia shook her head. "Tootie was a one-hundred-plus-pound Saint Bernard. What do you think?"

Jake laughed. "Excuse me for a second. My phone is vibrating." He reached into his back pocket and pulled out the device.

Olivia watched while Jake tapped the screen to open a text message.

He jumped to his feet. "I have to go. Logan said Kayla is upset."

Olivia stood.

"No, you stay and watch the show. I know how much it means to you."

That was true. Watching the stunt dogs was a trip down memory lane for Olivia, but Kayla's well-being meant more. "If you don't mind, I'd rather go with you."

"I don't mind at all. Lately, it seems like

you're able to handle Kayla's issues better than I am. Let's go."

Outside of the building, Olivia heard the announcer introducing the first stunt dog. The laughter grew distant as they moved at a brisk pace toward the rodeo venue.

Moments later, Olivia spotted Logan. He jogged in their direction. Kyle trailed behind.

"Where's Kayla?" Jake scanned the area.

"She's inside the women's bathroom." Logan pointed to a nearby toilet rental as Kyle caught up with the group.

"Is she sick?"

"No, Daddy. It was that mean ole Missy. She was teasing Kayla again about the fashion show," Kyle explained.

"Before the show started, the kids went outside to get a snow cone. Missy and some other girls were in line. Kyle came back inside to tell me Kayla had locked herself in the bathroom and that's when I texted you. I'm sorry, man. I should have gone with them to get the snack." Logan rubbed the side of his temple.

"It's not your fault. This fashion show has had Kayla upset for over a week. Maybe I need to speak with Missy's mother. I know kids tease each other, but this is a sensitive issue for Kayla."

Logan nodded his agreement.

Olivia's chest tightened. She glanced toward the bathroom. "Would you like for me to talk to her?"

"Yeah, if anyone can get her to come out, it's Dr. Olivia," Kyle added.

Jake agreed with his son. He turned to Olivia. "Like I said earlier, lately Kayla seems to respond better to you," Jake said.

Olivia rested her hand on Jake's arm. "Don't take offense. I'm sure you've tried your best. It may be easier for her to talk to another female. After my father died, the mean girls chased me into hiding many times."

Kyle moved closer to Olivia. "I'm sorry you got teased, Dr. Olivia."

Olivia's heart squeezed. "Thank you, Kyle." She patted his shoulder. "Let me get Kayla and maybe we can all watch the rodeo together."

"That sounds like a great idea. We'll just hang out here for a while," Jake said.

"But, Daddy, I never got my snow cone. Can we get one now? We can get one for Kayla when she comes out of the bathroom." Kyle tugged on Jake's hand.

"Sure." Jake looked at Olivia. "We'll meet back here?"

"Hopefully we won't be too long." Olivia turned and headed toward the restrooms. She sent up a silent prayer to be able to comfort Kayla and convince her to come out of the restroom and enjoy the fair.

Outside the door to the restroom, Olivia raised her hand and knocked. "Kayla, can you open the door, sweetie? It's Dr. Olivia." She scanned the area surrounding the two bathrooms for signs of Missy or any other children. "There's no one here except for me. I'd like to talk to you, but I'd rather see your face than talk to a door."

A soft giggle came through the vent at the top of the bathroom. This was promising. "Your daddy told me how word spreads in a small town. Can you imagine what people would think if they heard the lady from Florida talks to toilets?"

Another giggle sounded, but this time the door slowly opened. Kayla cautiously stepped outside. Her eyes were red and swollen. She hesitated for a moment before lunging into Olivia's arms.

The lump in Olivia's throat prevented any words from escaping her lips. Instead, she clung to the child like her life depended on it. At that moment, it did. Nothing else mattered but to protect Kayla and lessen the pain of losing her mother. Olivia had carried the same pain throughout her childhood and into her adult years. Yet the time spent with Kayla seemed to ease the heartache.

"Missy is so mean." Kayla sniffled and choked on her words. "She ruined my birthday."

"Let's go sit over there." Olivia pointed to a bench perched under an old weeping willow tree.

Kayla loosened her arms from around Olivia's waist but kept hold of her hand. They walked to the tree and took a seat.

"Do you want to tell me what happened earlier?"

Kayla inched closer to Olivia. "Missy said I wear boy clothes because I don't have a mommy to teach me."

Olivia's stomach clenched at the cruelty Kayla had experienced. "That wasn't nice of her to say that to you, sweetie. Sometimes words have more power than we realize. I'm not excusing Missy, but I don't think she's learned that lesson. We have to be careful when we choose our words. When I was a little girl, Gammy always told me sometimes it's best to say nothing." Olivia wasn't sure if Kayla understood. After Olivia's father died, a couple of kids at her school spoke horrible words to her. They said she should have done something when she'd come home from school and found her father on the floor. They told her his death was her fault.

"Like when Daddy says to hold my tongue?" Kayla nuzzled her head against Olivia's side.

Olivia smiled. "Exactly."

"Yeah, sometimes I probably say things I shouldn't, especially to Kyle." Kayla wiped her eyes and looked up. "I'm sorry, Dr. Olivia."

"For what, sweetie?"

"I said some mean things to you when you first got here."

Olivia ran her fingers through the back of Kayla's hair. "It's all forgotten." She kissed the top of her head, inhaling the sweet scent of her shampoo.

"I'm glad you came to get me. You made me feel better."

"Well, today is your special day. You shouldn't spend it hiding."

Kayla nodded. "It wasn't the best place to hide. It didn't smell too good in there."

Olivia laughed. "I'm sure it didn't. Are you ready to join the others and watch the rodeo?"

Kayla jumped off the bench. "Can I ask you something first?"

"What is it, sweetie?"

Kayla pushed the toe of her red tennis shoe into the grass. "Will you take me to the fashion show?"

"I didn't think you had any interest in watching the show."

"I don't want to watch. I want to be in it with you." Kayla twisted a strand of her hair.

Excitement coursed through Olivia's veins. Yesterday at Garrison's Mercantile, she'd eagerly volunteered to accompany Kayla to the fashion show. But then her heart sank when she recalled Jake's words. He didn't think it would be a good idea. How could she say no to Kayla? It would break her heart.

Kayla's eyes filled with hope as she waited for an answer. Olivia couldn't disappoint her. She wanted to put an end to Missy's teasing once and for all. But was that the real reason? Or was it because it would give Olivia an opportunity to be a mother? Even if it was only for one night. "There's nothing more that I'd rather do."

"I'M GOING TO run a few errands. Do you need anything?" Myrna tapped on the counter.

Jake peered from underneath Myrna's kitchen cabinet beside the sink. "I think I'm good, thanks. Are you sure it's nothing I can run out and get for you?"

Myrna snatched her purse off the island and flung it over her shoulder. "Not unless you're interested in getting your hair permed." Myrna scurried toward the door and turned around. "Olivia and I took Callie out earlier this morning to work with her, but she's still not back. Can you check on her? I know she didn't have breakfast. That girl doesn't eat enough. I don't know how she survives living alone in Miami."

"Sure, I'd be happy to check on them." Jake had hoped to see Olivia while he was working at Myrna's house. Lately, he couldn't stop thinking about her.

Myrna fumbled in her purse. Her keys dropped to the ground.

Jake approached as Myrna got on her knees and felt around on the floor.

"Here they are." Jake picked up the leather strap right in front of her. Myrna should have been able to see it. But maybe not. While researching online, he remembered reading about blind spots in the center of the vision of patients with macular degeneration. "Maybe I should take you to the hairdresser and whatever other errands you have to run? We can go out for lunch, too. I can finish installing these lights underneath the cabinets later."

Myrna stood and brushed her hands on her pants. "You sound like Olivia."

"What do you mean?" Jake asked.

Myrna released a heavy sigh. "Just because I didn't see my keys on the floor, you're ready to take away my driver's license and lock me up in the house."

Jake put his hands in the air. "Hey, wait a minute. Remember, I'm on your side to continue to live independently. That's why I'm trying to get Callie trained and doing all the upgrades around your house. I want you to maintain your freedom for as long as you can."

"I'm sorry. I didn't mean to sound so defensive. I appreciate everything you and Olivia are doing for me. Olivia cares about me and her motives come from her heart. Perhaps my actions don't reflect it, but I know my limitations and I don't plan on doing anything foolish. As difficult as it is for me to admit, I need help. I've reached out to my friends and I'll continue to do so."

Jake was coming to his own realization that Olivia's motives were coming from a place of love. Saturday night, after the twins' party, while Jake tucked Kayla into bed, he learned Kayla had asked Olivia to take her to the mother-daughter fashion show. Olivia had agreed, even though he had told her he didn't think it was a good idea. Initially, Jake had jumped to conclusions. Since Kayla had been so upset about the show, he believed she didn't really want to go. Perhaps Olivia had pressured his daughter. But after talking with Kayla, he learned his conclusions were way off base. Olivia knew how much the fashion show meant to Kayla. She understood what it felt like for a child to be left out because they'd lost a parent. "So what's got you upset?"

"Olivia's been struggling with Callie acting out. The pup basically goes bonkers when someone comes to the door or when a phone rings. I told her it takes time to train the animal, but being the perfectionist she is, she thinks if it hasn't happened yet, it won't."

Jake ran his hand through his hair. This wasn't good.

Myrna sighed. “Bless her heart. Even as a little girl, Olivia lacked patience. I remember one Christmas I took her to see Santa Claus at the local department store. When she saw the line snaking through the store, she told me she’d rather just write him a letter than wait. I can’t help but think Olivia’s patience is wearing thin with Callie because she’s eager to return to Miami. And of course, when she leaves, she wants to take me with her.” Myrna placed her hands over her stomach. “I know she believes she’s doing what’s best for me, but just the thought of moving makes my stomach sour.”

Jake couldn’t stand to see Myrna upset. He was upset, too. It would crush the twins if Myrna left. The town wouldn’t be the same.

Myrna glanced at her watch. “I need to get going. I don’t want to miss my hair appointment. Maybe when you go outside you can remind Olivia that training a dog doesn’t happen overnight. Otherwise, I’m afraid she’s going to pack my bags.” Myrna turned on her heel and scurried out the door.

Jake cleared his tools from the kitchen counter. He’d have plenty of time to finish the lighting installation before camp started this afternoon. He grabbed his insulated cup and unscrewed the lid to top off his coffee before going out in search of Olivia.

Outside, the midmorning sky was overcast. With a 70 percent chance of rain in the forecast for later today, he'd have to set up a few things inside the barn in case he needed to move the camp inside.

Jake scanned the open field, but Olivia was nowhere in sight. Off in the distance, he could hear Callie barking. Olivia must have taken her to the pond. He crested the hill and followed the grassy path that led to the benches Myrna's husband had built before he passed away. Jeb was handy with a hammer. He'd built the home where his wife still lived.

Jake squinted into the sunlight peeking through the clouds. He spotted Olivia sitting on the bench. She was leaning forward with her elbows resting on her thighs. Both hands covered her eyes.

Callie barked twice and came running toward him. Olivia didn't seem to notice the puppy was off her leash.

Jake scooped up the dog and moved closer to the bench. Olivia's shoulders quivered. She was crying.

He wasn't sure if she wanted to be alone to

deal with whatever had her so upset. He didn't want to pry into her personal business, but he couldn't just leave her there.

Cautiously, Jake continued in Olivia's direction. He didn't want to startle her.

A gentle breeze blew and swept a tissue from Olivia's hand. She reached to pick it up, but Jake beat her to it. "Are you okay?"

She startled and quickly wiped her eyes on the back of her hand before pushing herself off the bench. "I didn't know you were here." Her brows rose as she looked at Callie. "Oh, I'm sorry. I was working with her and I got a phone call. I should have put her back on the leash before I took the call." Her arms dropped to her sides. "You're right. I'm not cut out to be a Puppy Raiser. I don't know what I'm doing."

"Hold on." Jake reached up with the tissue and blotted away the tears running down Olivia's cheeks. "I never said that. This is all new to you. It takes time. You're doing a great job with her."

"But I don't have time. I'll be thirty-six next month." Olivia flopped back down on the wooden seat.

Jake considered Olivia's words along with her actions. Something told him this wasn't only about training Callie. He took a seat next to her and put the puppy at his feet. "What does your birthday have to do with training Callie?"

Olivia shook her head. "It doesn't. I'm not talking about Callie."

Jake didn't want to pressure her, but it seemed like she was open to talking about what was bothering her. "I know you don't know me very well, but people tell me I'm a good listener. Maybe if you feel like talking about what's got you upset, I can help you."

"That's sweet of you, but I don't think anyone can help me."

"You'll never know unless you talk about it. Come on. I can't stand to see you like this," Jake said.

Olivia sat up straighter and pushed her shoulders back. She slowly turned to Jake. "My college roommate Beth called me. Mark, my ex-husband, got remarried last week."

"I'm sorry. I would imagine that's hard news to hear." Since Jake hadn't experienced a divorce, he couldn't imagine how this kind of turn of events would affect him. He always believed marriage was for life, but from what Olivia had shared, Mark had wanted out. *How do you stay with someone who no longer wants you?*

"It's not the marriage that surprises me. It's the rest of the story that—"

Olivia burst into tears again.

Callie perked up and jumped to her feet, releasing a cheerful bark.

Jake reached down and picked up the dog. He gently scratched her under the collar. "It's okay, girl."

Olivia sniffled and then shook her head, as if she wanted to shake out the last of her tears. "They are expecting a child."

Jake's stomach twisted. Unsure how to respond, he waited.

"I'm such a fool. Why did I ever marry him?"

This was unfamiliar territory, but he knew it was wrong for Olivia to blame herself. "You loved him. That's why you married him. Look, I don't know what happened, but I can tell you that Mark is the fool, not you."

Olivia rubbed her eyes. "Since we split, I kept telling myself it was all for the best. I wanted to have children, and he didn't. But that was all a lie. He wanted kids."

Jake's heart broke for Olivia. He couldn't imagine experiencing that kind of betrayal.

"He just didn't want to have them with me," she sobbed.

Jake squeezed his fists together. He'd never been the violent type, but if Mark was here, it would take every ounce of restraint not to punch the guy's lights out. Look what he'd done to Olivia, a beautiful and vibrant woman. But his actions had filled her with self-doubt. He placed Callie back on the ground and reached his arm around Olivia, not sure how she would respond.

Olivia slowly rested her head on Jake's shoulder. "Why did he stop loving me?"

Jake didn't know what to say. Olivia was only trying to process this devastating news. A part of him was glad he was there for her, yet a bigger part felt this was way too personal. The last thing he wanted to do was become invested in Olivia's personal life. Eventually, she'd be leaving with or without Myrna.

"It's my fault. He didn't believe I could ever slow down long enough in my career to raise a family."

From what Myrna had told Jake, she didn't believe Olivia could, either. Although Myrna said she had prayed about it constantly, she thought Olivia believed giving up her career would disappoint her father. "Could you slow down? You invested a lot of time to become a doctor."

"If slowing down meant having a family, then yes, that's more important to me. After the divorce, I stopped taking extra shifts on my days off."

"That's a positive step in the right direction," Jake said. Maybe Mark and Myrna were too quick to judge Olivia.

"Having a family is something I've dreamed of since I was a little girl. It might sound silly to you."

Jake shook his head. "Dreams are never silly if they're what God has put into your heart. You should never give up on a dream."

A gust of wind blew, swirling the smell of honeysuckle in the air.

Jake glanced up at the sky. The clouds were thickening. "It looks like we might get some rain this afternoon."

"That's not good. I don't think Callie can afford to miss a class. I've been having a hard time with her."

"Myrna mentioned your recent challenges with Callie. I'll help you. She'll be fine. As for camp, it goes on—rain or shine."

Olivia flinched and pulled away. She'd been so upset maybe she hadn't realized how close they were sitting on the bench. "I'm sorry I dumped all this Mark stuff on you. That wasn't really fair."

"There's no need to apologize. I'm glad I was here to listen. I guess I'm returning the favor. You've been listening to Kayla a lot lately. I really appreciate it."

"Yeah, I've wanted to talk to you about that. I'm sorry if I was out of line when I accepted Kayla's invitation to the mother-daughter fashion show. I should have spoken with you first, but it broke my heart to see her so upset about Missy teasing her that when she asked, I couldn't say no." Olivia tucked her chin against her neck. "If you'd rather I didn't take her, I understand."

"Are you kidding? Ever since you agreed, she's been talking about it nonstop. If I told her she couldn't go, she'd never speak to me again." Jake smiled.

Olivia laughed. "I doubt that. She worships the ground you walk on."

"Well, my sources say you're high on her list of favorite people yourself," Jake stated.

Olivia smiled, and her face radiated. "I'd be dishonest if I said I didn't feel the same way about her—about both of your children. Getting to know them has been the greatest joy of my trip. I'm honored Kayla invited me to the show. I honestly can't think of anything I'd rather do—so thank you for allowing me to accompany your daughter."

Jake leaned in closer. "You know what?" He took both of her hands in his. "I think one day you're going to make a terrific mother."

Olivia took a deep breath. "Thank you, Jake."

Across the field, a black crow landed at the top of a pine tree and cawed.

"There is one thing I'm a little concerned about." Olivia squirmed on the seat. "Gammy has told me how people like to talk in Bluebell. I wouldn't want anyone in town to think—"

"What? That there's something going on between us?"

Olivia's cheeks blossomed into pink blotches. "Well, yes."

"It might shake things up a little around here." Jake wiggled his eyebrows. "Maybe a few people need to learn to keep their noses out of their neighbors' business."

Olivia poked her elbow into his arm. "Be nice. I think they all do it out of concern."

"Oh, look who's defending the small-town people now. I was joking, but you're right. We all take care of one another. That's the way it's always been."

Olivia gazed out into the open field and took a deep breath. "You know, the longer I'm here, I'm realizing that might not be such a bad thing."

Jake agreed. It was a great thing. Bluebell was the perfect place to settle down and raise a family. Once upon a time, his life had been proof of that. But he'd been there and done that. If Olivia changed her mind and stayed in Bluebell, could he take a chance on love for a second time? Or would his fears prevent any possibility of a future with Olivia?

CHAPTER TEN

"Good girl. You're doing great." Olivia dropped to her knees and kissed the top of Callie's head. She couldn't be prouder. The puppy's tail wagged back and forth as she devoured the attention.

All the credit went to Jake. He knew training Callie would require extra work and the skills Olivia didn't possess, but he went the extra mile. Despite his objection about her desire to move Gammy to Miami, he'd been generous with his time. Camp would end soon, but Jake planned to continue to work with Callie.

"It looks like she's finally got the Place command figured out," Jake said.

Olivia got to her feet and spun around in the open field. She spotted Jake approaching, dressed in faded jeans and a crisp white buttoned-up shirt. Despite the warm air temperature, goose bumps peppered her skin. His good looks were something she couldn't deny. Lately, they'd become more of a distraction. "I think you're right. Did you see her in camp today? Not only did she take her place on the mat without being told, but she stayed down, too. I felt like a proud mama."

Jake laughed. "You should be proud. You've worked hard with Callie."

"The extra time you've spent with us has helped. You're good at what you do."

"It helps when you love your work, but you probably know that."

Olivia believed practicing medicine was what she loved. She also believed it was what her father would have wanted. Had she been wrong? Honestly, she hadn't missed Miami and the stress of working long hours. She could never admit it to Gammy or to Jake, but Bluebell was part of the reason she had mixed feelings about returning home. "I don't think I love my work as much as you do. I used to, but sometimes seeing so much pain and death takes its toll."

Jake shook his head. "I don't know how you do it. I remember after Laura died, I wondered how the doctors dealt with death day in and day out."

"In our defense, sometimes we save lives or

bring new life into the world." Olivia tried to convince herself that the good outweighed the bad, but she had the battle scars to prove that wasn't always the case.

"Daddy!" Kayla yelled as she and Kyle skipped across the field. "We finished putting away all the cones. Are you ready to go over to Miss Myrna's?"

"What's going on over there?" Jake asked.

"The church bake sale is this Sunday. We're going to help Miss Myrna bake snickerdoodles. I told you the other day." Kayla rolled her eyes.

Olivia's ears perked up. "That's right. I'm supposed to pick up some ground cinnamon on my way home today. I totally forgot."

"I guess it slipped my mind, too." Jake looked at Olivia and shrugged his shoulders.

Olivia picked up Callie. "I better get to the store."

"I need to pick up a couple of things from the store, too. Why don't I grab the cinnamon and you go ahead to Myrna's house?" Jake suggested.

"Can I ride with Dr. Olivia to Miss Myrna's house?" Kayla tugged on her father's arm.

Olivia nodded to Jake.

"We'll have to get the car seat loaded into Olivia's car first."

"We should buy Dr. Olivia a car seat since we'll be together a lot," Kayla suggested.

Olivia's heart warmed at the thought of a car filled with child seats. She forced the thought away. This was only temporary. Once she got back home to Florida, there would be no need for a child restraint system.

"It's only a trip to the grocery store, sweetie," Jake answered.

"But we'll be doing a lot of shopping for the mother-daughter fashion show, right, Dr. Olivia?"

Olivia willed herself to stop thinking about the future and enjoy the moment. "You're right. We have a lot of shopping to do. In fact, we might need to take a trip to Denver, if it's okay with your father."

"Yay! Can I, Daddy? Please! Please!" Kayla pleaded.

"Are you sure about this?" Jake asked.

"Of course. We can make a day out of it. We'll have lunch out, maybe get our nails done." Olivia rested her hand on Kayla's shoulder. "How does that sound?"

"Great! Maybe we'll run into mean ole Missy!"

Olivia and Jake shared a laugh as they headed to their vehicles.

Jake opened the back door of his truck and unfastened the car seat. "I'll just slip this into your back seat and we'll hit the road."

Kayla and Kyle raced to the cars.

"I'm going with Daddy!" Kyle announced.

"It's just us girls in your car, right?" Kayla looked at Olivia.

"That's right. Girls only." She winked.

"Okay then, we'll all meet up at Miss Myrna's house," Jake suggested.

Jake fastened Kayla into her seat. Then he and Kyle got into the truck and drove away.

"Come on, Dr. Olivia. Let's go," Kayla called out.

Olivia crated Callie and then climbed behind the wheel of the SUV. She settled against the leather seat and peered in the rearview mirror at Kayla. Her body shivered. This was what it felt like to have a family.

For the first five minutes of their trip to Gammy's house, Kayla chattered nonstop about the fashion show.

"When do you think we'll go shopping, Dr. Olivia?"

"Maybe next weekend, if your father says it's okay."

"Why do we have to wait so long? I wish we could go today." Kayla giggled.

"You have school. That always comes first," Olivia said.

"School ruins everything."

"Also, Callie's camp graduation is this Saturday. I'll need your help to get her ready." Olivia was looking forward to spending the day with the twins.

"But you and Daddy are still going to train her since she's a slow learner."

"That's true. Callie needs more work if she's going to help Gammy, but she's coming along." Olivia admired Jake for keeping his promise to his friend George. Thanks to Jake's dedication and additional training, she was confident Callie would meet her grandmother's needs.

"I heard Daddy tell Miss Myrna if Callie can't help her, you were going to leave and take Miss Myrna. Is that true?" Kayla's voice trembled.

Olivia tightened her grip on the wheel. The twins loved her grandmother as much as she did. "Try not to worry about it."

"Okay," Kayla answered.

Olivia relaxed her hands. Kayla appeared to accept her response, so she changed the subject. "If we get up early, we can get in a lot of shopping time. We'll each need to pick out two different outfits. One casual wear and the other something we can wear to church." Olivia loved that the clothing they planned to purchase would go to charity after the fashion show.

"Next weekend is so far away. I don't know if I can wait that long," Kayla said.

Olivia laughed. She remembered feeling the same. Now she wished she could stop the clock. "My daddy used to tell me not to wish my life away."

"What did he mean?"

"He wanted me to enjoy each day as it comes. We never know what the future may hold. You'll realize when you get older the time goes quickly."

"Yeah, I guess he was right. Do you miss your daddy? I really miss my mommy. Even though Daddy tells us stories about her now, I feel like I'm forgetting her."

Olivia's biggest fear after her father passed was forgetting him. The sound of his voice, the touch of his hand, and how every night when he tucked her into bed he would tell her that tomorrow would be better than today. "Yes, I still miss him, but I learned the best way to keep him fresh in my memory was to talk to him."

"But how can I talk to my mommy when she's not here?" Kayla asked.

"You might not see her, but she's watching you. She knows everything you're doing. When you're upset, you can talk to her, just like you talk to God when you pray."

"Because Mommy is in Heaven?"

"Yes. And because of that, she'll always be with you. She's in your heart." Olivia spoke from experience. In times of difficulty, she often had chats with her dad.

"Can I ask you something else, Dr. Olivia?"

"I hope you know you can always ask me anything," Olivia answered.

"Is it bad for me to wish you were my new mommy?" Kayla's voice was barely a whisper.

Olivia was thankful for the stop sign because Kayla's question rocked her to her core, but it didn't come as a surprise. Two nights ago, she had dreamed the same, but it could never happen. It was wrong to give Kayla false hope. She took a deep breath and expelled. "Of course it's not. But it's important to remember I don't live in Bluebell. There will come a time when I have to return home."

Kayla remained silent. Olivia glanced in the

rearview mirror and saw her rub her eyes. This was exactly what she was afraid of.

"Sweetie, are you okay?"

"Yeah." She nodded.

"Can you tell me what you're thinking?"

"I don't want the time to pass fast if it means you go away sooner."

It crushed Olivia to see Kayla's upbeat mood extinguished. "Why don't we follow my daddy's advice and enjoy each moment of every day?"

"Okay, but I'm still going to pray that you change your mind and stay."

Ten minutes later, Olivia navigated the SUV down the long driveway leading to Gammy's house. She filled the silence with music from an oldies station. Olivia always enjoyed listening to music from the 1950s. It surprised her to learn Kayla enjoyed the same. She said it was the station her mommy liked. "Okay, let's get inside and see what Gammy is up to. Your daddy and Kyle will be here soon and we can get started baking for the sale."

Olivia turned off the ignition and exited the vehicle. She opened the back door and reached in to unfasten Kayla's car seat.

Kayla wiggled out of the chair and jumped

to the ground. "What's your favorite kind of cookie?" she asked as she took hold of Olivia's hand.

"Of course, Gammy always bakes the best snickerdoodles, but I've never told her that my favorite is oatmeal chocolate chip."

"Mine too! Do you think we can make those today?"

"I don't see why not. Gammy's pantry is well stocked, so I'm sure we can find some oats."

"Let's go inside and check," Kayla said.

They scaled the front steps. Olivia opened the screen door, and they moved inside.

"Miss Myrna! We're here," Kayla called out from the foyer.

The house was eerily silent. Olivia had seen Callie sniffing around in the side yard when they pulled into the driveway. "Gammy? Are you up there?" Olivia yelled from the bottom of the stairs.

"I'm in my bedroom," Gammy finally answered.

"Come on down so we can get started with the cookies. Jake and Kyle are on their way with the cinnamon."

"I need to wait a few minutes."

Something wasn't right. Her tone sounded

weak. Olivia looked at Kayla. "Let's go check on her."

At the top of the steps, Olivia paused and sent up a silent prayer that Gammy was okay. They headed toward her bedroom at the end of the hall.

Olivia stepped inside. Gammy sat in her reading chair. She had her left foot propped up with a pillow on top of her footstool. In her right hand, she held an ice pack. "What's wrong?" Olivia raced to her side and dropped to her knees.

"It's nothing, dear." She fanned her hand in the air. "Go on and get started on the cookies. I'll be down in a minute."

"You never sit during the day except at mealtime. And even then, you're jumping up to do one thing or another."

Her grandmother laughed. "I just tripped, that's all."

"Where? Do I need to take you to the emergency room?" Olivia asked.

"Should I call my daddy?" Kayla cried out.

"You both sure have a lot of questions." Myrna rested her hand on Kayla's arm. "I'm fine."

"How can you sit there and say that? Tell me exactly what happened," Olivia demanded.

"My cell phone rang, so I was rushing from the family room into the kitchen. I tripped on the step. I shouldn't have been walking around in my socks."

Olivia released a heavy breath. That step was nothing but trouble. Her grandmother had no business living in a house with a sunken family room. "So you didn't see the step? Your eyes are getting worse."

"I just missed the step. I've done it thousands of times over the years, even when I was a lot younger."

Olivia wet her lips. "How did you get up here?"

"I just took it slow and exhibited a little determination." Myrna gave a dismissive glance. "Exactly the way your grandfather used to handle difficulties in life."

Olivia's fists tightened. Sometimes, her grandmother was as stubborn as a coffee stain on a white shirt. She would never admit to being in pain, her failing eyesight, or that this house couldn't accommodate her needs. It didn't matter how many changes Jake made—her gammy couldn't stay in this house. She took the melted ice bag from Gammy. "Kayla, stay here with

Gammy while I go downstairs and get some fresh ice. Make sure she doesn't get up."

"I'm not a child, Olivia. I don't need someone watching me." Myrna attempted to stand, but winced in pain and dropped back into the chair.

Olivia stood and shook her head. "I'll be right back." She stormed from the room and rushed down the stairs, not sure who she was angrier with, Jake or herself. She shouldn't have made this agreement to train Callie. Obviously, the dog did not help prevent the fall. Olivia shuddered at the thought of how much worse it could have been.

Outside, car doors slammed. Jake and Kyle were home.

Olivia moved to the refrigerator and opened up the freezer. The icy blast of air did little to cool her temper. She needed to talk to Jake, but not in front of Kyle. The sooner she got her gammy moved to Miami, the safer she would be.

"CAN YOU TAKE this bag for me, son?"

Kyle reached for the grocery bag. Jake unloaded the other three bags from his truck.

Callie raced to the fence to greet them.

"Let's go inside and see what the girls are up to," Jake suggested.

Jake entered the kitchen and spotted Olivia wrestling with the ice maker. Her back was to the door. She murmured under her breath, but Jake couldn't quite make out what she was saying.

"I thought the place would smell of baked cookies by now," Jake announced.

Olivia jumped. "I didn't hear you come inside."

"Maybe it was because of the racket you were making with the ice maker. Is something wrong with it?" Jake moved a little closer and placed the grocery bags on the counter.

"Not the machine, but Gammy." Olivia slammed the freezer door closed.

Jake couldn't miss the anger washed across Olivia's face. He turned to Kyle. "Why don't you go find your sister?"

"She's upstairs in Gammy's bedroom," Olivia answered.

Kyle zipped out of the room.

Jake spotted the ice bag sitting on the counter. "What's going on?"

"Gammy fell and hurt her foot."

Jake's pulse ticked up. "You should have

called me. Do we need to take her to the emergency room?"

Olivia picked up the ice pack and screwed the lid tighter. "She said she's fine, but I think she's only saying that because she knows I'm upset. She tripped on that stupid step from the family room into the kitchen."

Jake knew of the step. He had it on his list of things to address. "I know that's an issue in this house."

Olivia placed her hands on her hips. "I don't see how it can be fixed without remodeling the entire family room area."

"Relax. We can install a ramp. It's not that big of a deal," Jake explained.

"Well, it sounds like another costly expense. You know my grandmother is on a fixed income."

"Myrna has been open with me about her finances. A couple of guys plan to do the job for free. This is a small town, remember? Your grandmother has done so much for this community, it's the least we could do for her. I know it's hard for you to understand, but we take care of each other in Bluebell."

"So you've said." Olivia shook her head. "I'm afraid that step is just one of many issues in this house. What about the fact that her bedroom is upstairs? Are you going to install an elevator or something?"

"Look, I don't have all the answers now. I'm doing the best I can to help your grandmother stay at her home. It's what she wants."

"I'm not sure Callie is the answer. She obviously wasn't there for Gammy today."

Jake raked his hand through his hair. "Of course she wasn't. She's a puppy who's not fully trained. It takes time. It's what we agreed."

"Daddy, why are you fighting with Dr. Olivia?"

Jake spun around at the sound of Kayla's voice. "We're not fighting, sweetie." He glanced at Olivia, who simply shook her head.

Kayla shrugged her shoulders. "It sounded like it." She walked over to Olivia. "Miss Myrna wanted me to get the ice." Kayla took the bag.

"Thank you, Kayla. Tell Gammy I'll be up in a minute."

"Okay." Kayla raced out of the kitchen.

"I'm sorry. I didn't mean to pounce on you. I was upset about Gammy."

Jake understood Olivia's concern. She loved her grandmother. "You don't have to apologize.

I know you're worried. Let's drop this for now. We agreed to help with the bake sale, so let's get the kids and have some fun."

"You're right. I'm going to run up and check on Gammy. I'll be right back with the kids." Olivia scurried out of the kitchen.

Jake slipped his cell phone from his back pocket and scrolled through his directory. He connected the call, but it went straight to voice mail. "George, hey, it's Jake. Remember that project I mentioned at Miss Myrna's house? Can you order the material this week? I'd like to get going on the ramp sooner rather than later. Call me when you have a chance."

Footsteps echoed down the front staircase. Jake moved to the cabinet that stocked all of Myrna's cookbooks.

"I don't know why you won't stay upstairs and keep the ice on your foot." Olivia guided her grandmother into the kitchen.

"I did ice it."

Olivia rolled her eyes. "For like two minutes."

"Ice, smice, I'm perfectly fine. I told you I just tripped. It was nothing. You worry too much, dear." Myrna walked toward Jake. "Hand me that cookbook. It's the one that has the biggest collection of cookie recipes."

Kayla moved close to Myrna. "Dr. Olivia said you probably have some oats in your pantry. She likes oatmeal chocolate chip cookies, too."

Just like Laura. Jake pulled the canister of oats from the bag and passed them to Olivia. "I bought these today."

"Thank you." She took the container and their fingers brushed. When their eyes connected, Jake noticed the pink hue that covered Olivia's cheeks before he pulled his eyes away.

Myrna slid a stool closer to the island and took a seat. "Okay, we've got a lot of baking to do. Olivia, did you pick up the cinnamon?"

"I got it," Jake answered and removed two bottles from the grocery sack.

"Perfect. We'll need at least eight dozen snickerdoodles to start. After we finish with those, you can bake the oatmeal chocolate chip. I also had a request for a few dozen peanut butter kiss cookies."

"We might be here all night." Jake rolled his eyes.

"That would be so cool!" Kyle cheered.

"Not when you have school in the morning, buddy. We better get cracking."

"Your father is right. Since I only have one oven, I think it's best that we each grab a mixing bowl and start making the batter." Myrna pointed to a stack of stainless steel bowls on the counter next to the sink. "Once the dough is ready, you can use these scoopers to make the balls." She passed a utensil to everyone. "I have more than enough cookie sheets, so we should be able to take one batch out and pop another into the oven. I've got the cooling racks lined up over there." She pointed to the counter on the other side of the kitchen.

"I feel like we just stepped inside Betty Crocker's kitchen," Jake joked.

"Who?" the twins asked in unison.

"Don't pay any attention to your father. He's just being silly." Myrna got up and scurried to the pantry. "Let me get everyone an apron so you don't mess up your clothes."

"Gammy, I wish you'd sit down and rest your foot."

"I've forgotten all about that. I wish you would too, Olivia. Really, I'm fine." Myrna passed a yellow apron to Olivia. "Here, put this on and get to work."

Olivia did as she was told. Jake locked eyes with her and smiled. Olivia moved to the empty counter space next to him. He leaned closer. "You better do as you're told or she might make you stay after class," he said with a laugh.

THREE HOURS LATER, Myrna's kitchen smelled of sweet cinnamon and chocolate. Racks of cookies lined the countertop. A dusting of flour covered the floor.

"My hand is getting tired from stirring." Kayla dropped the wooden spoon into the cookie batter.

"Here, Kay. We can switch. I'm getting bored scooping the cookies off the baking sheet." Kyle extended his hand, offering the spatula.

Kayla snatched the kitchen tool and ran toward the cookies fresh out of the oven. She reached for the first tray. "Ouch! My hand!"

Jake jumped off his stool and ran to Kayla. "Did you touch the hot cookie sheet?"

"Yes. It burns!" Kayla cried out.

Olivia sprang into action. "I'll get my medical bag." She ran from the kitchen.

Jake heard Olivia's feet hit the wooden steps. A door slammed overhead. She was back in the kitchen in less than thirty seconds.

"Let me see." Olivia reached for Kayla's hand.

"Ow, it hurts."

"Right here?" Olivia pointed to the red mark.

"Yeah, it burns."

"I know it does, sweetie. I've got some gel in my bag. It will make it feel better."

"Will it stop the burning?"

"Yes, but first let's put your arm under some tepid water."

"Okay."

Olivia guided Kayla to the sink, turned on the faucet and gently placed her arm under the running water.

"Ouch!" Kayla cried out.

"I'm sorry, but I've got to get the area clean before I can put on the cooling gel. Are you okay?"

Kayla nodded and her lower lip quivered.

"You're being very brave. This is going to feel much better once I get the medicine on it."

"Okay." Kayla chewed on her lower lip.

Olivia squirted a dollop of the gel onto the burn. "Does that hurt?"

Kayla shook her head. "No. It feels kind of cold."

"That's how it's supposed to feel. That means the medicine is helping." Olivia continued to rub the ointment into Kayla's skin.

Jake stood close as Kayla's tears subsided.

Olivia placed the tube of medicine back inside her bag. She pulled out a bandage and unwrapped the packaging. "I'm going to cover the burn loosely with this bandage, okay?"

Kayla nodded and kept her eye on the wound.

"Now, you let me know if it hurts."

"Okay."

Olivia wrapped and taped the burn. "I'll send the medicine and bandages home with your daddy, so he can do the same before you go to bed tonight."

"Can't you do it later?" Kayla pleaded with Olivia.

"You'll be at your house and I'll be here looking after Gammy. I'll show your daddy how to doctor the burn just the way I did, okay?"

Kayla lunged from her stool and wrapped her arms around Olivia's neck. "Can't you come to our house? I only want you to do it."

Jake watched as Kayla squeezed Olivia tight, with no sign of letting go. His daughter's affection toward Olivia was both endearing and worrisome. The last thing he wanted was for Kayla to get too attached to Olivia. Her heading back to Florida soon would only leave a void in Kayla's life.

"Sweetie, come on now." Jake attempted to

pry Kayla's arms from around Olivia, but she refused to let go.

Olivia looked up at Jake and shook her head, telling him it was okay. But was it?

"Thank you for taking care of me, Dr. Olivia. I wish you were my mommy." Kayla nuzzled her head into Olivia's shoulder.

Kyle sprang off his seat. "That would be so cool!"

Jake noticed Myrna's smile before she covered her mouth.

Kyle danced around the kitchen and glided toward Jake. "Why don't you marry Dr. Olivia? Then you won't be lonely anymore."

This was getting out of hand. Jake didn't doubt that Olivia was as uncomfortable with the direction of this conversation as he was.

Myrna clapped her hands. "Okay, now. Who's hungry?"

"We are!" the twins cried out.

"Who would like pizza?" Myrna called out to the group.

"We do, we do!" Kyle and Kayla cheered.

Myrna grabbed her purse off the counter. She removed her wallet and glanced at Jake. "Why don't you and Olivia run out to Mr. Pepperoni and pick up a couple pizzas for our dinner?" She passed her credit card across the island. "I'll call in the order."

"Pizza party!" Kyle jumped up and down doing a fist pump.

"You don't have to feed us dinner. I've got some leftovers from last night in the refrigerator."

"We don't want meat loaf again, Daddy. Pizza is much better," Kayla chimed in.

"Quit arguing with me. After all the help you all have given me, we're having pizza. Take my card. Olivia, you go along with Jake. The kids and I can finish the cookies."

Olivia grabbed her purse and looked at Jake. "You're wasting your breath."

"I know, I know. Shall we?" Jake motioned with his arm for Olivia to head out. He turned to Myrna. "Give them my cell number," he said.

Several minutes later, behind the wheel of his truck, Jake fiddled with the radio. "What kind of music do you like to listen to?"

Olivia pulled down the sun visor. "I like oldies music."

Jake's heart squeezed. "That's what my wife used to listen to. She loved it."

"Kayla told me that was why she liked it, too.

We were also talking more about our girls' trip to Denver. I'm sorry I didn't check with you first before I mentioned it in front of Kayla." Olivia tucked a piece of hair behind her ear. "I guess I got excited about the idea. It's been a long time since I had a day out with the girls."

"You don't need to apologize. I just hope Kayla didn't talk you into it. The fashion show might not be your thing."

Olivia ran her hands across the top of her jeans. "Actually, I'm excited about the show and spending time with Kayla."

"I know she's crazy about you." Jake hit the brake as the railroad crossing lights flashed.

"She certainly wasn't when I first got to town." Olivia laughed.

"True, but that's obviously changed. I hope she's not getting too used to having you around. I don't want her to get hurt when it's time for you to go home to Miami."

"I would never intentionally hurt Kayla. She's been through so much already."

"I'm sorry. I guess I worry too much."

"Kayla isn't the only one getting attached. Believe me, I've thought about how hard it will be for me to say goodbye."

"You could always stay in Bluebell." He

hadn't meant to say that out loud. Or had he? He looked over at Olivia.

She examined her fingernails and turned her head.

They held each other's gaze.

Did she want to stay? If she did, it wouldn't be because of him. He was too old for her. There was too much baggage from his past. Yet the sparkle in her eyes told him *maybe.*

Excitement coursed through him and he leaned in.

Olivia followed his lead until their lips almost brushed, but then she glanced away.

"I can't. I'm sorry," Olivia said, turning away.

Heat filled his face. "No, I'm sorry. I don't know what I was thinking." Jake leaned back against the seat.

"I'm not sure what either of us was thinking." She pushed the hair away from her face.

Olivia broke the silence with a sigh. "Gammy is dropping hints for me to stay every chance she gets. During dinner last night, she even mentioned me becoming the town doctor. Luckily, she got a phone call and dropped that topic."

"There's been chatter about Dr. Dickerson retiring." Jake wasn't sure what would happen. Most doctors probably weren't interested in working in a small town where they might get paid with homemade apple pies. "We're hoping Doc hangs around a little longer. It's a long trip to Denver."

"There's no doctor's office closer?"

Jake shook his head. The train passed, and the gate lifted. He eased his foot on the accelerator. "Unfortunately, no. Doc tried to retire over a year ago, but he couldn't find anyone to take his place. His son, David, is also a doctor. We had hoped that he'd fill his dad's shoes upon retirement, but David went for the big bucks at a research hospital in California."

"I guess for some, it's all about the money."

After Jake lost his wife, he realized having money helped, but family and friends mattered the most. "Not you?"

"I'll admit, the money was nice as far as paying off all my student loans was concerned, but a few years into my career, I went to work in the ER. That position was what I'd worked so hard for. It was a lifelong dream finally realized. I make a real difference every day in the ER, and I think my father would be proud of me."

"So now you have your dream job?" Jake asked.

Olivia remained quiet and gazed out the window. "Have you ever wanted something so bad, or looked forward to an event, but when it finally happens, you're left feeling…?"

When Olivia couldn't find the right word, he took the lead. "Empty?"

"Yes. That's exactly how I feel." Olivia sighed.

Jake hit the turn signal and pulled in front of the local pizza parlor, Mr. Pepperoni. He turned off the engine and unfastened his seat belt. "I don't want to sound like I'm getting into your business, but maybe you're one of those people who prefers the race over the finish. I think that's common in goal-driven people."

"You might be right. After I finished my residency, I became obsessed with reaching my next goal. People who took time off were slackers. I volunteered to speak at seminars and covered coworkers' shifts. I did anything to keep my mind occupied. I worked nonstop."

"What were you avoiding? Or what *are* you avoiding?" Jake asked.

Olivia turned to Jake and unbuckled her seat belt. "What makes you think there's something I'm avoiding?"

"It's been my experience that people who fill

every minute of their day with work are usually trying to avoid something or someone."

Olivia squirmed in the leather seat. "You're a wise man, Mr. Beckett. Are you speaking from experience?"

Jake laughed. "I think we all go through times where we bury ourselves in our work in order to cope with something we want to but can't control."

For a moment, silence filled the cab of the truck.

"Any advice on what to do when the person you're trying to avoid is yourself?" Olivia laughed half-heartedly.

"Maybe not advice, but like I said, I'm a good listener if you want to talk about anything on your mind."

Olivia looked at her watch. "What about the pizzas? I don't want to keep everyone waiting."

"Don't worry about that. Mario is always running behind on his orders. Besides, he'll send me a text when the order is ready for pickup. Tell me what's going on. Is this about your ex-husband and his expanding family?"

"I can't put all the blame on him. He spent years listening to my excuses about why I couldn't make it home for dinner. Or why I couldn't attend a function at his work. He put up with me for a lot longer than I would have."

"Why did you make excuses?" He hoped Olivia could trust him enough to share the burden she'd been carrying.

"After my father died, I blamed myself for his death."

Jake shook his head. "But why? You were only a little girl."

"I should have been there for him, but I wasn't. I know I can't change that, but I've lived my entire life trying to make up for my shortcomings. Trying to make sure that I lived a life he would be proud of. I've done everything for him, and in doing so, I've lost the opportunity to have the one thing I've always wanted—a family of my own."

Silence hung in the air. There was nothing more Olivia wanted to share.

Jake's phone signaled an incoming text message. He checked the device resting on his console. "The pizza's ready."

"Great. I'm starving." Olivia opened the truck door and stepped from the vehicle.

Jake considered Olivia's words, and something struck him in his heart. The feelings for her that were growing in him needed to be pushed away. He wouldn't be responsible for denying her of her only dream. Olivia wanted kids, and on the day he lost his wife and child, he vowed never to have more children. The risk was too great. That chapter of his life had come to a heartbreaking close.

CHAPTER ELEVEN

"THANK YOU ALL for coming out today." Jake scanned the crowd and smiled. "The last day of camp is always bittersweet for me, but it's time for you and your puppies to spread your wings."

The crowd broke into cheers and applause.

Olivia reached down and picked up Callie. "Today's your day," she whispered in the puppy's ear before turning her attention back to Jake. It was becoming more difficult to not notice him, especially after their almost kiss in the car the other day. As much as Olivia didn't want to admit it, she wished the pizza had taken a little longer to bake.

"Today is a special day. It represents not only the culmination of all your hard work, dedication and love over these past several weeks, but also the beginning of your puppy's journey toward the opportunity to change someone's life. There will be a lot of blood, sweat and tears ahead for each of you because raising a puppy isn't easy. It's downright hard sometimes, but trust me when I say the day you see your puppy helping its assigned handler, you'll forget those challenging times.

"Since Rebecca has the most experience with being a Puppy Raiser, she has volunteered to help with any concerns now that camp has concluded. If you have questions or problems, Rebecca and I will be available to support you either by phone, email or video conference. You'll never be alone, so don't forget that. After we eat, I want to get a photo of each of you with your puppy. Now Kayla and Kyle will pass out your certificate of completion while I go fire up the grill."

The class clapped and cheered, and shouts of "thank you" could be heard.

Jake handed Kyle and Kayla the folder with each participant's certification.

"My tummy doesn't feel good, Daddy," Kyle moaned.

"I can pass them out by myself." Kayla glanced at Kyle.

Olivia's ears perked up. Even though she wasn't working at the hospital, she was always on call. She moved closer to Kyle. "Does your tummy hurt or do you feel sick?"

"I don't know. It just feels funny."

"Can you show me where?" Olivia asked.

"Right here." Kyle held his belly button.

"Maybe you should go lie on the sofa for a while," Olivia suggested.

Jake felt his head. "He doesn't seem to have a fever. Maybe he's hungry. A piece of barbecue chicken or maybe a hamburger might make you feel better. He ate little at breakfast this morning."

Kyle wrinkled up his nose and shrugged his shoulders.

"Would you rather your sister take care of the certificates?"

"No, I want to." Kyle and Kayla left and headed toward the class.

Maybe Jake was right about Kyle just being hungry. She'd check on him later.

Jake packed his tablet inside his backpack and zipped it closed. "I guess I better get the grill started. Do you want to help me?"

"Of course. Just tell me what I can do," Olivia said.

"Myrna is up at the house getting some of

the side dishes together, so that's covered." Jake flung his bag over his shoulder.

Gammy had left the house this morning while Olivia was still having her coffee. She said she had a list of things a mile long she wanted to do before the cookout. "Do you think I should go give her a hand?"

"You know your grandmother likes to take total control of the kitchen. Besides, I thought if we worked together, we'd get the food out quicker. We have a hungry crew here." Jake laughed. A light breeze blew a few strands of hair from Olivia's ponytail as they strolled toward the patio area.

"Watch your step." Jake reached for her hand as they climbed up the steep hill that led to an oversize brick patio. Once at the top, Jake let go of her hand. Olivia looked down and missed the feel of his large, calloused hand.

"Wow! This is quite a barbecue. It almost looks like you have a full kitchen." Olivia strolled toward the large barbecue with a brick base. The impressive design had a six-burner grill, a stainless steel refrigerator, a side burner and an abundant amount of counter space.

"This is incredible. It almost makes me want to take up cooking." Olivia opened the steel doors below the countertop and noticed a supply of plates, serving dishes and skewers.

"I built this a few years ago. My brothers and I like to have family cookouts in the summer months, so I thought I'd make it big enough for all of us to enjoy. Hopefully, our hectic schedules will slow down so we can plan something."

"You did a fantastic job. It looks like something you'd see in a home-and-garden magazine. I can't even have a small grill at my condo."

"Thanks. Another perk to living in the country, I guess." Jake scanned the property. "I'd like to do a bit more landscaping."

Olivia put her hands on her hips and looked out across the land. "With that incredible view of the Rockies, I don't think you need to do anything." She spotted an oversize swing situated underneath a massive Douglas fir. "I'm sure that's a beautiful place to watch the sunset."

Jake nodded. "It's one of the best views on the property. Maybe you'd like to check it out sometime?" Jake held her gaze.

Once again, their almost kiss came to mind, igniting a warmth on her face.

"Are you okay?" Jake asked. "Your cheeks look a little flushed."

Olivia placed a hand on the side of her face. "It must be this warm sun."

"Jake, dear," Gammy called from the open back door. "Do you want me to wrap up the corn on the cob in some tinfoil to throw on the grill? I've got all the hamburger patties ready to go. I still have to put the sauce on the chicken."

This was the perfect opportunity to put some space between her and Jake. The reaction Olivia had in his presence was becoming more confusing. "I'll come inside and help you." She turned to Jake. "If you want to get the grill started, I'll go bring out the food."

"That sounds good. Maybe I can throw some hamburgers and hot dogs on first, since they'll cook faster."

"I'll get them." Olivia turned on her heel and hurried into the house, unable to get the thought of watching the sunset with Jake out of her mind.

Two hours later, with everyone's stomach filled, Olivia stood alone in Jake's kitchen. Gammy and Kayla had gone to help Nellie with the inventory at the mercantile, so Olivia had volunteered to clean up while the guests played a game of horseshoes outside.

She walked toward the kitchen sink. The

twins' drawings covering the refrigerator captured her attention. She'd seen them before, but a few more had been added. Her heart ached.

"Need some help?"

Olivia jumped, her fingers losing their grip on the top plate in the stack, and the porcelain dish crashed to the floor. "Oh, I'm sorry." She quickly set the other dishes on the counter so she could clean up the mess she'd created.

"No, it's totally my fault. I shouldn't have snuck up on you. It was obvious you were lost in thought." Jake moved toward the pantry, stepping over the broken dish. "Let me get the dustpan and broom. I'll have this cleaned up in no time."

Olivia picked up the remaining dishes from the counter and brought them to the sink. She turned on the water and began washing each by hand. Her thoughts stayed with the drawings on the refrigerator.

Jake swept up the remaining pieces, carried the dustpan out to the laundry room trash can and returned to the kitchen.

"What's on your mind?" Jake leaned in over her shoulder.

For the second time, Olivia flinched in surprise, but this time nothing shattered. She turned off the water and placed the plate into the drying rack. "What makes you ask?"

"When I walked in, you were a thousand miles away. Remember, I'm a good listener." Jake gently nudged his shoulder into hers.

Olivia took in a breath and moved to the refrigerator. "Can you tell me about some of these?" She pointed to the colorful drawings.

Jake followed her steps. He reached his hand toward the picture of a purple turkey. "I know the holiday is far off, but I found these when I was cleaning out my desk. They make me smile." Jake pointed to one of the drawings. "You're probably familiar with the traditional trace of your hand into a Thanksgiving turkey."

"I can take a wild guess who drew it—Kayla. She told me purple is her favorite color."

Jake nodded. "Even if it wasn't her favorite color, she would have picked something out of the ordinary. Kayla always likes to think outside the box, as noted by the red-and-yellow socks the turkey is wearing."

Olivia chuckled. "Unlike her brother." She pointed to the other turkey colored a rich brown.

"Kyle is exactly like his mother. She always followed the rules."

"What about this?" Olivia touched another drawing with a note written in the picture.

Jake rubbed his hand across his chin. "I remember that day like it was yesterday."

Olivia studied the attempt of a self-portrait created by Kyle. The boy in the drawing, dressed in a pair of denim overalls, stood with his hands behind his back and a tear streaming down his cheek. "What was he sorry for?"

"Kyle had gone fishing with his friend Zack and his father. They went to Mirror Lake, which is one of the largest in the area. Without my permission, Kyle took my pocket watch given to me by my father when I graduated from high school. It belonged to my grandfather. The watch didn't run, but my family had passed it down from many generations. My plan was to gift it to Kyle when he graduated. Unfortunately, it's somewhere at the bottom of the lake."

Olivia placed her hand to her mouth. "Poor Kyle. He must have felt so terrible."

"When Zack's father brought him home, Kyle was so upset he couldn't tell me what happened. He ran straight to his room and hid under the bed. I couldn't get him to come out. The bed didn't have enough clearance for me to go under after him, so I slept on top. Laura had passed a couple of months earlier. If she'd been alive, he would have gone straight to her. She always knew the right thing to say."

"So, when did he draw the picture for you?"

"I'm not exactly sure. When I got up the next morning, it was at my place on the kitchen table. He must have come out from underneath the bed in the middle of the night long enough to make the drawing, because when I woke up, he was still under the bed sleeping."

Olivia swallowed the lump in her throat. "That's the sweetest story I've ever heard." She tried to hold back the tears.

"Hey, don't cry." Jake reached for a napkin, tore it in half and gently blotted her eyes.

"You're blessed to have such wonderful children."

"I thank God every day for them. If it weren't for Kayla and Kyle, I don't think I'd have a purpose in this world."

Jake spoke the truth and didn't mean any harm, but his words were like acid on her open wound. Had she wasted her life believing her purpose was to follow in her father's footsteps and be a successful ER doctor?

"Daddy, I don't feel good." Kyle entered the room. His face looked drawn and colorless.

Olivia cast her feelings away and raced to his side. She placed her hand on his forehead. "He's burning up."

"I've got to call Doc Dickerson." Jake slapped his hands against the back pockets of his jeans. "I must have left my phone outside by the barbecue."

"Here, you can search the internet for his number and use mine." Olivia grabbed the device off the counter.

"After Kayla's reoccurring bouts of strep throat last winter, I've got Doc Dickerson's number embedded in my brain." Jake stepped aside to make the call.

"Do you want to go lie down?" Olivia dropped to her knees, holding Kyle's hands.

"I feel like I'm going to—"

Before Kyle could finish his sentence, vomit projected onto Olivia's shirt.

"I'm sorry," Kyle whispered.

"It's okay, sweetie. Let's get you to the bathroom while your daddy calls the doctor."

Minutes later, Jake ran into the bathroom. "Doc is out of town on a family emergency."

"He doesn't have an on-call doctor who covers for him?" With Kyle in her arms, sitting on the bathroom floor, Olivia held the cool washcloth across his head.

Jake shook his head. "Only you." He knelt beside Kyle. "Are you feeling any better now that you threw up?"

Kyle nuzzled his face against Olivia's torso.

"I'd like to get him into his bed. I don't think he has much left in his stomach. Are you ready to go rest, sweetie?" Olivia asked.

Kyle flinched in her arms. "Ow!"

"What is it, son?"

"My tummy hurts."

"Can you show me where you feel the pain?" Olivia flung the cloth onto the vanity.

"Here." Kyle placed his hand against the lower right side of his abdomen.

"We need to get him to the hospital." Olivia rose to her feet with Kyle in her arms, careful not to alarm him.

"I don't want to go!" Kyle cried out.

"What do you think is wrong?" Jake's eyes widened.

"It could be his appendix. Has he ever had it removed?"

"No, but how can you tell?"

"The pain he experienced earlier was around

his navel, but it's moved to his right side. Of course, I can't be sure without an ultrasound or CT scan."

"We'll have to take him to Denver. I'll go tell Logan what's going on. He can take over for me and wrap things up with the graduation festivities. I'll give Myrna a call, but I'd rather she not let Kayla know what's going on until we know anything for sure," Jake said.

"Good idea. Let me clean up my shirt a little and we'll get going." Olivia kissed the top of Kyle's forehead.

"I'll meet you outside in my truck." Jake sprinted out of the bathroom.

"I'm scared. I don't want to go," Kyle whimpered.

"There's nothing to be afraid of. You need to go to the hospital so the doctor can fix your tummy." Olivia brushed her hand across Kyle's cheek.

"But why can't you fix it?"

"Because the doctors at the hospital have everything they'll need to make you feel good again," Olivia reassured Kyle.

"But what if it hurts?"

"You'll be asleep, so you won't feel a thing.

Then, when you wake up, your tummy will feel better."

"Will you be there when I wake up?" Kyle asked.

"I promise." Olivia took Kyle's hand and gave it a gentle squeeze.

"Okay, I'll go." Kyle rested his head on Olivia's shoulder.

With Kyle held tightly in her arms, Olivia raced outside to Jake's truck. The sound of birds chirping filled the air. She looked up and prayed silently to God that if Kyle was experiencing appendicitis, they'd make it to the hospital before the organ ruptured.

"I THINK I'M going to be sick again," Kyle moaned from the back seat.

Jake gripped the steering wheel and glanced in the rearview mirror, easing his foot off the accelerator as he navigated the two-lane mountain road.

"It's okay. I have this pan for you." Olivia held it underneath Kyle's chin.

Since Kyle first got sick, Olivia had been tending to his every need. She'd climbed in the back seat and held him close.

Kyle heaved, but nothing came up. He slumped

against Olivia, and she reapplied the cloth to his forehead.

When Jake had explained to Logan they were taking Kyle to the hospital, his brother jumped into action. He'd taken the sodas from the cooler and loaded the icy water into Jake's truck, along with some washcloths. He'd thrown the pan into the back seat, which had come in handy three times since they'd left Jake's house.

Olivia continued to monitor Kyle's temperature.

"We should be at the hospital in about five minutes, buddy."

"I'm scared to go there, Daddy," Kyle whimpered from the back seat.

Jake's heart hurt for his son. What he wouldn't give to be the one in pain. "There's nothing to be frightened of. I'll be with you."

"But you were with Mommy and she never came home," Kyle cried.

This would be the first trip to the ER since he'd taken Laura that fateful night. Jake was afraid it would spark some memories for Kyle. It certainly had for him. He'd driven this route with the same sense of urgency. *Lord, please don't let it be the same outcome.*

"You're going to be just fine," Olivia reassured Kyle. "I promised you, remember?"

After what felt like an eternity, Jake spotted the entrance to the hospital and hit his turn signal. "We're here."

TWO HOURS LATER, Jake sat in the familiar chapel where he'd prayed for his wife and son. This time, he prayed for Kyle.

By the time they'd arrived at the hospital, Kyle was in serious condition. Following a scan, the doctor came into the waiting room and delivered the news. If they'd been a few minutes later, Kyle's appendix would likely have ruptured. But thanks to Olivia's expertise, Kyle would be okay.

He should have never brushed aside Kyle's initial complaints of not feeling well.

"Would you like some coffee?"

Jake looked up. Olivia's smile warmed his heart. He rose to his feet and took her into his arms, not caring if he spilled the beverage all over himself. "Thank you."

"It's only coffee." Olivia laughed. "If you're not careful, it's going to end up all over your nice shirt."

He pulled back and reached for the cup.

"Thank you for what you did for Kyle. If it wasn't for you—"

"Stop. It's nothing any trained doctor wouldn't have done."

Jake shook his head. "I brushed him off. He came to me because he didn't feel well and I told him it was only because he was hungry."

"You had no way of knowing at that point it could be something serious."

With their mother gone, Jake was his children's sole protector. It was his job, and he had failed. "But you knew. I don't want to even think what could have happened if you hadn't taken charge of the situation and realized what was going on with Kyle's stomach."

"Remember, I get paid to know when people are sick." Olivia rested her hand on Jake's arm. "Try not to be so hard on yourself."

Jake captured her gaze. "You were wonderful with Kyle. I know you're trained to treat people, but the way you were with him—the way he responded to you…"

"You're welcome." Olivia smiled, and they both took a seat.

Thoughts swirled in Jake's mind. Could he love again? Was he being unfair to his children by closing the door to the possibility of a relationship with another woman? With Olivia? It was obvious Kayla and Kyle adored her. Did she feel the same about them? About him?

For the next several minutes, they sat in silence.

Moments later, a sense of peace took hold. Jake hadn't felt like this in years. Was it because he knew Kyle would be okay? Or was Olivia opening his eyes to the opportunity of a new future?

CHAPTER TWELVE

Olivia took a sip of her coffee and unfastened her seat belt. It had been a wonderful week. Thankfully, Kyle had fully recovered from the appendicitis and was back in school on Tuesday. Jake and his friends had completed work on the ramp in Gammy's sunken living room, along with a few other improvements. Olivia couldn't deny that with all the improvements, Gammy's house was probably now safer than her condo in Miami.

"Dr. Olivia!"

Kyle raced across the front lawn, wearing a smile from ear to ear. "Why are you just sitting there? Come inside. Daddy made pancakes."

Olivia's stomach grumbled at the mention of food. She'd gotten up early to take Callie for a long walk. Easing herself into the day wasn't something she was used to, but she had to admit, it felt great. "I hope he puts chocolate chips in them." She exited the vehicle, opened the back door for Callie, and the dog jumped to the ground.

"Sit," Olivia commanded. The puppy sat at her feet and looked up.

"Hey, she's listening." Kyle smiled.

Olivia laughed. It had taken a lot of hard work and determination, but she and Jake had turned the corner with Callie. Jake definitely was a pro.

"Yes, she is. Thanks to your father." Olivia ruffled the top of Kyle's head. "Let's get some pancakes. I'm starved."

Kyle ran ahead with Callie chasing behind.

Olivia smiled as she moved through Jake's house toward the kitchen. Family photos filled the tabletops and the wall going up the staircase. It was exactly what she dreamed of having for herself one day.

Outside the kitchen, she paused. Kayla was chattering nonstop about the day ahead. Jake laughed when she asked if she could get her fingernails painted purple. The banter between father and daughter was endearing. Jake was the type of father a woman would handpick for her children. But he'd closed the door on more children. What if he hadn't? Would things be different for them?

"Dr. Olivia!" Kayla's attention turned to Olivia. She jumped from the chair at the kitchen table and ran across the room. "I'm so glad you're here!" She wrapped her arms around Olivia's waist.

"I'm glad I'm here, too. I heard there are pancakes." Olivia took Kayla's hand and strolled toward the stove, where Jake stood with a spatula in one hand and the handle of the skillet in the other.

"Good morning." Jake smiled.

"Good morning to you." Olivia moved her head closer to the pan. "Those smell delicious."

Jake picked up the open bag of chocolate chips and poured them into the bowl of batter. "There's a slight wait on special orders." He winked.

Olivia's heart fluttered. Was it her imagination, or was Jake even more handsome this morning? "Word travels fast."

"Before Kyle took off upstairs, he told me you like chocolate chips in your pancakes. That's a favorite of mine too, but I don't make them often. I don't want to get the kids hooked on them."

Olivia crinkled her nose. "You're no fun. That was one of the best memories of my childhood."

"Pancakes?"

Olivia playfully nudged Jake's shoulder. "On Saturday mornings my mother always got her hair done, so my father was in charge of breakfast. He'd make us chocolate chip pancakes. He loved them, too."

"That's a wonderful memory."

Olivia nodded. No matter how much time passed, she still missed her father.

"Kayla, run upstairs and tell your brother breakfast is ready."

"Okay, but we have to eat fast. I want to have Dr. Olivia to myself for the whole day."

Olivia melted. She longed for the same.

Kayla ran out of the room and thundered up the hardwood steps.

"You might need a little extra sugar this morning if you want to keep up with Kayla." Jake poured another handful of chips into the bowl. "From the second her feet hit the floor this morning, all she's talked about is the shopping trip. I can't remember when I've seen her so excited."

"I think we'll have a wonderful time. I found

a place to go for lunch where we can eat outside." Olivia had stayed up late last night scouring the internet for the perfect restaurant.

"She'll enjoy that. It's going to be a beautiful day. That's why I wanted you to bring Callie over. Kyle and I plan to take her out and about. It's good for her to continue to get more comfortable being around people in a public setting. She seems to enjoy the attention."

"I think you're right, but she has come a long way from our first solo outing." Olivia had taken Callie to the market, which turned out to be a disaster. After plowing into a few displays, she'd texted Jake for help. "I appreciate that. Some of the public spots in Florida might not be as welcoming to dogs as a small town like Bluebell."

Jake jerked his head toward Olivia. "So you've made your decision about moving Myrna? Does she know this?"

Her shoulders tensed. The last thing Olivia wanted to do was put a damper on her day out with Kayla. She hadn't decided. In fact, each day she spent in Bluebell made the thought of leaving more difficult. "I'm sorry. I shouldn't have brought it up. No definite plans. Let's not discuss that right now. Today is about Kayla… and pancakes."

Jake smiled and turned his attention back to the skillet. "I like the way you think."

"LOOK, DR. OLIVIA! This is my size, and it looks just like the dress you bought for the fashion show." Kayla snatched the garment from the rack and held it under her chin.

The department store buzzed with activity. Olivia scanned the store. She spotted several of what looked to be mothers and daughters spending a lazy Saturday afternoon shopping. Today was a dream come true, except Kayla wasn't her daughter. Was it fair to Kayla to pretend that she was?

"Maybe I should get this dress and we can be twins."

Joy welled up in Olivia's heart. She couldn't resist this vivacious little girl. "I think that's a wonderful idea. Let's go try it on."

A few minutes later, Kayla burst out of the dressing room door and twirled. "It fits me perfectly. Can I get it? Please! I want to look exactly like you and be exactly like you when I grow up."

The possibility of one day seeing Kayla all

grown up, walking down the aisle to the man she planned to marry, was a glorious thought. But the truth stared her in the face. She'd be returning to Miami and leaving Jake and his family behind. Reality had followed her like a dark cloud over the past couple of weeks. No. She couldn't ruin Kayla's big day out. "Yes, we should definitely get it. I can't think of anything I'd like more than to be your twin." Olivia winked.

A smile spread across Kayla's face. She raced to Olivia and wrapped her arms around her midsection. "I wish this day could last forever."

Olivia's heart skipped a beat. She bit hard on her lower lip to fight back the tears. She, too, longed to hold on to this day for eternity. "That would be nice, wouldn't it? But remember, the day has just started, so there's a lot more shopping. Then, after lunch, we still have to go to Winston's and get our manicures."

"Oh yeah, I forgot!" Kayla jumped up and down.

"Do another spin and I'll get it on video."

"Yeah! We can send it to Daddy!"

"That's a great idea." Olivia removed her phone from her bag and hit the record button. "Perfect."

Kayla giggled and spun in circles, causing the dress to fan outward. She nearly lost her balance.

Olivia laughed and stopped recording. "Okay, go get changed back into your jeans and sweater and we'll pay for your dress."

"Okay." Kayla skipped back to the dressing room.

Olivia wrapped her arms around her waist. How could she ever say goodbye to this sweet child?

Seconds later, her phone vibrated in her hand. Her eyes narrowed on the screen at the text message. A weight settled on her heart. It was her supervisor. Olivia's mind raced. She hadn't given Lisa an exact date of when she planned to return to work at the hospital. If she responded to the text now, she'd tell her boss she was never coming back. Bluebell was where she belonged. Of course, she couldn't do that. She had to go back. Working as an ER doctor was her life. It was what her father would have wanted.

Olivia tapped the screen. Call me was all it said.

She crammed the device into her bag. Today wasn't the day to think about the stress and long hours that filled her days and nights working in the ER. She was having too much fun pretending to be Kayla's mother. Whether it was right or wrong, Olivia didn't care. At this moment, she was the happiest she'd been in a long time. Correction—ever.

JAKE AND KYLE strolled along the brick sidewalk in downtown Bluebell. Flower baskets bursting with purple petunias hung from the lampposts lining the street.

"Maybe we should take Callie into the library, Daddy. Miss Myrna goes there a lot."

"You're right. She volunteers there at least once a week." Jake patted his son's shoulder. "Good thinking."

Kyle looked up and smiled. "Do you think Dr. Olivia will change her mind and stay here?"

Lately, that question had caused Jake some restless nights. A part of him couldn't imagine Olivia no longer being a part of Bluebell, but he wanted her to be happy. "I don't know. I guess we'll have to wait and see."

"Can I ask you something?" Kyle chewed his lower lip.

"You know you can always ask me anything. What is it?"

"Is it wrong for me to want Dr. Olivia to be my mommy?"

Kyle's question was a punch in the gut. Jake could no longer deny the fact that he wanted the same. Lately, he envisioned what it would be like to share the daily activities of life with Olivia by his side. Even the possibility of Olivia being the mother of his future children had swirled in his mind. Day by day, his desire was outweighing his fears. How could he fault Kyle for his feelings when he was experiencing the same longing? "Of course it's not wrong."

"That's good because I think about it a lot." Kyle grinned.

"What do you say we pop into The Hummingbird Café and grab a German chocolate doughnut before hitting the library?" Jake definitely needed to change the subject.

Kyle's eyes widened. "Even though I had chocolate chip pancakes for breakfast?"

"Why not? Who says your sister and Dr. Olivia get to have all the fun today? Besides, Callie needs to learn how to be inside a restaurant and not beg for food. Right, Callie?" Jake looked down at the dog.

Callie barked.

"Let's go." Jake tugged on the leash as they headed to the café.

Minutes later, the threesome stepped inside the establishment. Jake removed his cowboy hat. His eyes zeroed in on the chalkboard covering the wall behind the cash register. Cowboy Chili was the special of the day. He loved that stuff.

Sally Raphine, the owner, waved and stepped out from behind the counter. "I had a feeling my special would bring you in today."

"Hi, Miss Sally!" Kyle waved back.

"Hello, Kyle." She reached down and scratched the top of Callie's head. "This must be Myrna's dog, Callie. She told me the puppy is quite the handful, but she sure is cute."

Jake was proud of Callie's progress. "It was slow going at first, but Callie has come a long way."

"That's good to hear. I certainly don't want Myrna being uprooted and moved to Florida." Sally pressed her wrinkled hand to her cheek. "This town wouldn't be the same without her."

Jake couldn't agree more. Myrna was a pillar in Bluebell.

"Should I put in two orders of chili?" Sally asked.

"As much as I'd love a bowl, we just popped

in for a couple of to-go doughnuts. We're headed to the library," Jake said.

"Two German chocolates?"

"Thanks, Sally. Take your time." Jake scanned the tables and spotted Dr. Dickerson sitting alone with a cup of coffee. "We'll go say hi to Doc."

"Can I go outside to the ball pit?"

The side courtyard area had several picnic tables for outdoor dining, along with a play area. When they arrived at the café, they'd seen two of Kyle's friends romping among the balls. "Sure, but be careful."

"Thanks!" Kyle took off to the front entrance.

Jake led Callie across the floor. "Hey, Doc. Do you mind if we join you?"

"Please, have a seat, son." Deep crevices surrounded the doctor's eyes and mouth, evidence of a life filled with smiles.

"Sit, Callie." Jake tied the leash to the back of the chair before he took a seat.

The doctor tipped his head toward the dog. "It looks like you've done a good job with her."

"I can't take all the credit. Myrna's granddaughter and I have worked together to train Callie."

"I've seen you two together. You make a good team."

Jake smiled and his face warmed.

"Have you fallen in love with her?"

Jake froze. The doctor was never one to sugarcoat a situation. The chatter inside the café seemed muted, and Jake felt his face flush. He turned away from the doctor, but he couldn't escape the truth. He was in love with Olivia.

"Son, it's okay. I knew Laura all her life. I brought her into this world. She would want you to be happy."

Jake had been denying his feelings for weeks. A part of him felt invigorated to admit the truth to someone. "I know she would." He massaged the back of his neck. "But how do I move past feeling like I'm betraying her by falling in love with Olivia?"

"God wouldn't have brought Olivia into your life if He didn't know you were ready. He's shown you your future."

Jake brushed the tear that ran down his face.

Doc leaned across the table. "He created us to love. God doesn't want you to live the rest of your life grieving over a loss. He doesn't work like that."

The doctor pushed himself away from the table and rose to his feet. He moved behind Jake's chair and placed his hand on Jake's shoulder for a second. Jake expected the doctor to say something more, but he remained quiet before he turned and strolled out of the café.

Was Doc Dickerson right? Had God brought Olivia to Bluebell to become his wife instead of moving Myrna to Florida? Had those butterflies and feelings of excitement over the past few weeks when he spent time with Olivia been part of God's plan? Jake blinked away the tears and closed his eyes. *I trust You.*

CHAPTER THIRTEEN

OLIVIA TIPPED HER chin to the sun and relaxed her head against the back of the rocking chair. The curved legs slid her forward and backward while a soft breeze blew against her face. Gammy's front porch had become one of her favorite spots to share some quiet time with God. Something she could admit to neglecting back home. These daily moments of solitude had given her time to reflect and had provided her with clarity about what was best for Gammy.

The porch was also a perfect spot to relive every second of her shopping trip with Kayla. Four days had passed, yet she couldn't get the day out of her mind. She hadn't seen Kayla since dropping her off at the house on Saturday evening. Jake and his brother Logan had traveled south to pick up two Labrador puppies, so Kayla and Kyle were staying at Cody's house. Jake was due home today.

She traced her fingers over the top of her laptop. She'd brought it outside to read her work emails. Before last Saturday, she'd checked her emails regularly, but now they seemed like an intrusion—something that would only cause her stress and angst. By logging in to the hospital's secure site, she'd be transported from the idyllic world of Bluebell to a stark, clinical environment filled with fluorescent lighting and antiseptic smells that assaulted her senses. The constant beeping of the monitors served as a reminder of the high stakes involved in her work.

The screen door slammed behind her.

"There you are. I made a fresh pot of coffee. I thought you would like a cup." Gammy passed a steaming mug to Olivia.

The emails could wait. "Thank you. I had a cup of tea earlier, but the caffeine hasn't kicked in enough to motivate me to check my work emails."

Gammy swatted her hand. "You're still on vacation. You shouldn't be checking in with work."

Her time in Bluebell with Gammy, Jake and the twins had opened Olivia's eyes to how her struggle to separate work from her personal life had negatively impacted her marriage. She'd never quite put two and two together. Or perhaps she didn't want to admit it. But the reality was the reason she was single again and childless at thirty-six was because she put work first. "My supervisor texted me the other day and I haven't gotten back to her."

"You've been busy. Besides, like I said, you're on vacation. She shouldn't be bothering you."

Olivia turned off her laptop.

"Oh, I almost forgot to tell you. Jake phoned earlier. He'd picked up the kids from school and was out running errands."

Olivia's pulse quickened. Lately, Jake, like Gammy, was occupying a lot of space in her mind. As much as she wanted to deny it, she'd fallen in love with him. But they were at different stages in life. She wanted children, and he had closed that chapter after he lost his wife.

"Jake wanted to know if we want to meet him and the kids at Charlie's Chuck Wagon in about an hour for dinner. I told him we'd love to. I figured you'd want to see him and the kids since it's been a few days."

Olivia was aware her grandmother wanted nothing more than to see her and Jake become a couple. "I think I can go a couple of days without seeing the Beckett family. Besides, soon I'll be returning to Miami and I won't see them again until I come back to visit you."

Gammy smiled. "Does that mean you're not taking me back to Florida with you?"

How could she do that to Gammy? If there was one thing she'd learned during her time in Bluebell, it was that her grandmother belonged in this town. Everyone loved her. Jake had proved his love and devotion to Gammy. He'd made her house a safer place and continued to train Callie. Olivia was at peace knowing Jake and the people in this town would watch over Gammy. "No, I'm leaving it up to you if you want to come and live with me. But I hope you'll remember my door will always be open for you and for Callie, even if your vision doesn't deteriorate."

"I appreciate that, dear." Gammy took a seat in the rocking chair next to Olivia. "It sounds like you've been doing a lot of thinking lately."

Olivia reached for her grandmother's hand and gave it a squeeze. "That's an understatement."

"I've been praying that you'll reconsider staying in Bluebell, maybe pursue a relationship with Jake. Is that something you've been thinking about?"

"Every day."

"And?"

"You know I can't do that." Her grandmother knew her better than anyone. Gammy understood why becoming a doctor was important to her.

"I had hoped you'd realize that life isn't all about work. It's about sharing special moments with family and friends. I don't want you to continue to spend your life trying to make up for something that was out of your control. You were a child. You couldn't have saved your father. I know you want to honor his memory and you believe working in the ER will keep you closer to him, but he would want you to have a family of your own and to be happy. I'm worried you're not truly happy with your life right now."

"But if I stay in Bluebell, I'll never have children of my own," Olivia argued. "Jake doesn't want to have more kids. I can't fault him for that after what he went through losing his wife and child. I love Kayla and Kyle and I know I could love them as my own, but I can't give up my desire to have my own children with the man I marry."

Gammy shook her head. "Jake would never

ask you to give up your dream. I've seen you two together. I can tell you have feelings for each other, but unfortunately, you're both stubborn. You need to talk to him."

Olivia swallowed past the pain. "What's the point?"

"I've said my piece. If going back to Miami brings you happiness, that's what you should do. All I've ever wanted for you was to be happy. But remember, working in a job that no longer gives you joy won't lead you to the life God has planned for you." Gammy smiled, then stood and made her way back toward the screen door.

Olivia considered her grandmother's words. As a child, she remembered her father talking about "God's plan." But had finding him unconscious on the floor been part of His plan? "I guess I should get cleaned up so we're not late for dinner."

FORTY-FIVE MINUTES LATER, Olivia spotted Jake and the kids—despite the dim lighting in the restaurant—sitting at a corner table. The aroma of grilled sirloin teased her taste buds. She was starving after skipping lunch to take Callie on a long walk.

"Dr. Olivia!" Kayla jumped from her chair.

"That child adores you," Gammy whispered in Olivia's ear as Kayla ran across the room.

"It seems like it's been forever since I've seen you. I missed you." Kayla wrapped her arms around Olivia's waist.

"I've missed you, too. Did you have fun with your uncle?"

"Yeah, Uncle Cody is funny." Kayla pulled on Olivia's hand. "I saved a chair for you next to me."

Olivia moved toward the table. Jake smiled broadly as she approached. The sweater she'd carefully selected to wear this evening did nothing to prevent the chill of excitement that radiated through her body when she saw the twinkle in his eyes.

"It's good to see you both." Jake stood and helped Gammy into her chair before turning to Olivia. "Kayla saved a seat for you." He placed his hand on her lower back and guided her to the space beside his daughter. "I thought after dinner we could take a walk around the lake—just the two of us," he whispered in her ear before she sat down.

Olivia had noticed the lit path that circled the lake when she and Gammy arrived. The idea of walking it with Jake hadn't crossed her mind, but it sounded more appealing than that sirloin steak she'd been craving. "I'd like that," she whispered back.

After their meal, the server cleared away the plates. While they waited for dessert, the children went to the jukebox with a handful of quarters.

Gammy cleared her throat. "Well, if you don't tell him, I guess I will."

Olivia wasn't sure what Gammy was referring to, so she complied. "Go right ahead."

"My granddaughter has decided that after all of your renovations and dog training, I'm safe to stay in Bluebell on my own."

Olivia's heart plummeted to the bottom of her stomach. Although it had been her decision, hearing it spoken out loud made it permanent.

Jake clapped his hands. "That's the best news I've heard all week. So you'll be staying on as well?"

Was that a hint of hopefulness Olivia detected in Jake's voice? "No, but I'm sure I'll be back for visits." Would she? Or would she get pulled back into the endless cycle of late-night shifts that left her too exhausted to do anything but sleep? Her phone chimed inside her purse.

"I've been hearing that phone ring all evening, dear. Don't you think you better check?" Gammy suggested.

"I didn't want to be rude."

Jake shrugged his shoulders. "I don't mind. Go ahead."

Olivia grabbed her bag from where it was hanging on the back of her chair and fished out her phone. She tapped the device and opened the text message. Her eyes opened wide and her hand trembled. The room felt as if it were spinning.

"What is it, dear? What's wrong?" Gammy asked.

Jake leaned in closer. "You okay?"

For the second time, Olivia read the incoming text message from her supervisor to make sure she'd read it correctly. Her mind reeled. Since she'd first arrived in Bluebell, all she could think about was how to convince Gammy to move back to Miami. She wanted no attachments with anyone in the community, particularly Jake and his adorable children. Now the last thing she wanted to do was leave, but what choice did she have? She'd lose her job if she didn't return. But it wasn't just a job for Olivia. If she wasn't practicing medicine, she'd lose the only connection to her father she had left. Her chair screeched as she forced herself away from the table and ran toward the front door, ignoring the calls from Gammy and Jake.

Once outside, Olivia raced to the lake. She sprinted down the path until she was out of breath. She stumbled to a bench and collapsed. Why was this happening? Why was she being forced to choose? It wasn't fair. Again, she scanned the screen to triple check, but she hadn't been mistaken. Her supervisor had booked her on the first available flight late tomorrow evening, which meant she would miss the mother-daughter fashion show. Either she would be on that flight or she'd have no job to go home to.

JAKE NEARLY FELL on his face when his foot stumbled over a rock. He didn't care. Finding Olivia was all he cared about. The look on her face when she'd read the text message terrified him. Regaining his footing, he picked up his pace and headed farther down the path. Thoughts raced through his mind. Was the message from her ex-husband? Whoever it was from owed Olivia an apology.

Finally, he spotted her sitting on one of several benches circling the lake. It was a good thing because he wasn't sure he could run much farther. Slowing his steps, he approached with caution. "Are you okay?"

Olivia had her face buried in her hands.

Jake sat down and waited for her to speak. He'd wait all night if need be. Shoot, he'd wait forever. He loved her.

Olivia lifted her head and cleared her throat. "The text was from my supervisor. There's a major staff shortage at the hospital because of the flu. She's booked me on the next flight back to Miami."

His stomach dropped. "When?"

Tears streamed down her face. "Tomorrow evening."

"What about Kayla? The fashion show is on Friday. You promised her." He squeezed his fists tight. Every muscle in his body tensed. He'd known this would happen, yet he'd done nothing to prevent the relationship between Olivia and Kayla from growing. Now his baby would have her heart broken, exactly like he'd predicted.

"Don't you think I know that? I've been looking forward to it as much as Kayla."

Jake shook his head. "That doesn't matter.

She's a child. She won't understand why you have to go, only that you're leaving her."

"It's my job, Jake. I don't know what I can do."

"Can't you ask for your return to be delayed a couple more days?"

"I've ignored her emails, texts and phone calls for the past week. She's not cutting me any slack. It's tomorrow or I won't have a job."

Jake raked his fingers through his hair. How would he tell Kayla?

Olivia inched off the bench. "I'll talk to Kayla. Maybe Gammy can take her in my place."

"No!" Jake grabbed her hand. "I don't think you understand how much this means to Kayla."

"How can you say that? I've walked in her shoes. Growing up without a father, I missed out on countless special events. I know exactly what she's going through." Olivia wiped the tears from her face. "Please don't say I don't understand. That's not fair."

Jake forced his shoulders to relax. He was being too hard on Olivia. It wasn't all her fault. "I'm sorry. I know you understand. My protective instincts are getting the best of me, I suppose. I just hate to see her disappointed. She's been looking forward to the show since you agreed to go with her." Jake couldn't forget the look on her face when she'd come home from their shopping trip last weekend. Kayla had talked nonstop about their matching outfits. Olivia leaving before the fashion show would crush her.

"If there was any way I could stay until Friday, I would, but I can't risk losing my job."

Jake nodded. "Let's go back inside and have our dessert. But don't mention this to Kayla."

"Don't you think I should be the one to tell her?"

"No. I'll talk to her when we get home. It will be better if it comes from me."

Olivia rubbed her arms. "Can't I even say goodbye to her and Kyle?"

"No, I think it's best if you just leave. Let me handle everything." Jake pushed himself off the bench. "We better go back inside."

A couple of minutes later, Jake and Olivia rejoined Myrna at the table. Thankfully, the children were at the indoor play area.

"What's going on?" Myrna asked. She looked at Olivia. "Have you been crying?"

Jake leaned back in his chair while Olivia explained the situation to her grandmother.

"You can't leave!" Myrna's brows furrowed. "Kayla will be heartbroken."

"I explained everything to Jake, Gammy. I don't have a choice. If I don't go back on Thursday night, I won't have a job."

"Would that be the end of the world?"

Olivia looked over her shoulder. "We shouldn't be talking about this now. Jake wants to tell Kayla I'm leaving after they get home."

Myrna released a heavy breath and shook her head. "I don't agree with any of this, but for Kayla's sake, I'm going to stay out of it. I hope you both know what you're doing."

The table remained quiet for the next five minutes until Kyle and Kayla returned.

"What's for dessert?" Kyle asked, breaking the silence.

"I want a piece of chocolate cake," Kayla announced. "You should try it, Dr. Olivia. It's the best."

Jake waited for Olivia to respond, but she simply forced a smile. Myrna tossed him a look of concern.

"What's going on?" Kyle looked at the adults. "Why's everyone acting funny? Did you ask Dr. Olivia on the date?"

Jake flinched and Kyle's eyes widened.

"I'm sorry, Daddy. I forgot it was a secret." Kyle covered his mouth.

Kayla bounced in her seat. "What secret?"

Her brother dropped his hand away from his mouth. "Daddy likes Dr. Olivia. Last night when he tucked me in, he told me he was going to ask her on a date."

"Kyle!" Jake shouted loud enough for the neighboring table to glance their way. "Sorry." He waved a hand.

"Cool!" Kayla voiced her opinion.

Myrna laughed out loud. "I love it."

Olivia's face turned red.

Jake could do nothing but shake his head.

LATER THAT EVENING, Jake sat hunched at the kitchen table with a cup of coffee between his hands. The pitter-patter of feet vibrated overhead as the children scurried around getting ready for bed. The entire trip home from the restaurant, Kayla had talked about the fashion show. He dreaded telling her that Olivia wouldn't be taking her, but at least she could go with Myrna. After dessert, Myrna had pulled Jake aside and offered to accompany Kayla to the show. Jake appreciated her kind gesture, but he knew in his heart Kayla only wanted Olivia.

Since learning Olivia was leaving, Jake had wrestled with his emotions. Should he have made his feelings toward her known when he'd found her down by the lake? Would that have affected her decision to leave? It was too late now. She planned to leave.

"Daddy, we're ready to be tucked in," Kayla called from the top of the stairs.

Jake sent up a silent prayer, asking for the words to come before he headed upstairs.

After Kyle said his prayers, Jake moved down the hall to Kayla's room. Before entering, he could hear his daughter telling her stuffed bulldog, Rocky, all about her trip to Denver with Olivia and the upcoming fashion show.

"Hey, sweetie. Are you ready to say your prayers?"

Kayla nodded and tucked Rocky under the pink comforter. Midway through her prayers, she yawned before saying "Amen."

Jake kissed the top of her head. "I need to talk to you for a minute about the fashion show."

Kayla's sleepy eyes lit up. "I can't wait!"

"Well, there's been a slight change of plans."

Kayla's brow crinkled.

"You'll still be going, but Miss Myrna will take you instead of Dr. Olivia."

Kayla pushed the comforter aside and popped upright in the bed. “Why? Did something happen to Dr. Olivia? Did she go to Heaven like Mommy did?” Her face turned pale.

Jake placed his hands on her shoulders to settle her down. “No, don’t worry. She’s fine.”

“Then why isn’t she taking me? She promised.” Tears spilled down her face as she burrowed back under the comforter.

“She really wanted to, but she has to go back to work. Remember, she has a very important job. She helps sick people get well at the hospital, but right now, they don’t have enough doctors, so she has to go back to help.”

Kayla appeared lifeless in the bed.

Jake gently brushed her hair away from her face. “She’d stay if she could. I know she cares a lot for you.”

“Then how could she go? I thought she was going to be my new mommy.” She turned onto her side. “Leave me alone,” she said and buried her face in the pillow and cried.

Jake reached over and turned off the princess lamp on the nightstand. “Tomorrow will be better, sweetie,” he whispered. “I promise.”

CHAPTER FOURTEEN

Thursday morning, Olivia took a deep breath and tucked the last sweater into her suitcase. She'd been awake since three o'clock. Tossing and turning, she'd spent a restless night in bed, knowing it would be her last sleep in Bluebell.

At first light, she'd peeled herself out from under the down duvet and thrown on a pair of yoga pants, a sweatshirt and tennis shoes to take Callie for a long walk. Once home, Gammy made her applesauce pancakes with warm maple syrup. Olivia would miss her grandmother and Callie after she returned to Miami, but she was confident Gammy belonged in Bluebell.

One thing she wasn't confident about was leaving Jake and the twins. Olivia had picked up the phone to call Jake many times since last night. She wanted to share her heart and tell him she'd fallen in love with him—that she could sacrifice her desire to have children of her own, if it meant she could be with him and his children. But what was the point? After breaking his daughter's heart, he'd probably never want to speak with her again. She couldn't blame him.

"Lunch is ready," Gammy called from downstairs.

Olivia sighed. She placed the last pair of pants into the luggage and zipped it closed. Her time in Bluebell had come to a close. It was time to get back to reality.

Once downstairs, she placed her suitcase next to the front door. Moving to the kitchen, she stopped short just outside the entrance, taking in the sounds of Gammy busying herself as she made their last meal together for a while. The familiar sounds of clanking pots and pans were as soothing as a dollop of honey in a cup of freshly steeped tea.

Olivia's senses were aware of all that surrounded her. She wanted to remember everything about this place, hoping it would provide comfort once she was back home and alone in her condo. The aroma of Gammy's fried chicken caused her stomach to rumble and drew her into the kitchen.

"Are you hungry?" Gammy turned the burner

off and moved the skillet onto the trivet. Her normally cheerful smile was noticeably absent.

"I am now. The chicken smells delicious. You shouldn't have gone to all this trouble. I could grab something to eat at the airport."

Gammy swatted her hand. "This is no trouble. It's what I do."

It certainly was. Her grandmother was the most selfless person she'd ever known.

The doorbell rang. Callie took off running to greet the visitor.

"Grab a plate. I'll get the door." Gammy untied her apron and flung it on the counter.

Muted conversation carried through the foyer until Dr. Dickerson entered the kitchen.

"Hello, Olivia." The elderly gentleman nodded and rubbed his right knuckles with his left hand. "My arthritis is acting up. There must be rain in the forecast."

Olivia extended her hand. "I think I heard something about storms. It's good to see you, Doctor. Did you smell the chicken from town?"

He ran his palm in a circular motion over his stomach. "It's my favorite. I always told Myrna she should have opened a restaurant. She'd have customers from all over the state."

"Well, there's plenty for everyone, so please

sit down and I'll bring the food to the table." Gammy smiled, happy to be serving a meal.

With the plates filled, Gammy took her seat across from the doctor. "What brings you by, besides my fried chicken?"

Dr. Dickerson picked up his napkin and wiped his mouth. "Well, after months of going back and forth, I'm finally taking your advice, Myrna. I plan to retire next month."

Gammy's eyes lit up. "That's wonderful. I'm sure Doris is thrilled."

"She's already planning our first cruise. She reminded me we haven't taken a vacation in over twenty years."

Olivia admired his dedication to the town. "Congratulations. I'm happy for you and Doris. Did you find someone to take over your practice?" Olivia would hate to see the town without a doctor. When Kyle got ill, she experienced firsthand how stressful it was to travel a long distance when a loved one was sick.

"Actually, that's why I'm here." Dr. Dickerson took a deep breath and continued. "I hope I can convince you to take over the practice. Apart from the necessary licensing requirements, you could step in without missing a beat. I've spoken to many people around town and everyone is in full agreement. You are the best person for the job."

Gammy clapped her hands together. "Wonderful!"

Stunned by the offer, Olivia was tongue-tied. The idea of staying in Bluebell and being a part of such a wonderful community was appealing, but the reality was she belonged in Miami. It was what her father would have wanted for her. Besides, given her feelings toward Jake, living in the same town with him and the twins would be too painful. "I'm flattered by the offer. Truly, I am."

"I detect some reservation." The doctor's smile slipped from his face.

"I'm grateful for my time in Bluebell, but Miami is my home. The ER needs me, especially now with the doctor shortage." Olivia glanced at Gammy, who discreetly wiped a tear from her cheek.

"I can't say that I'm not disappointed, but I respect your commitment to your position and your colleagues," Dr. Dickerson said. "I'm sure the hospital appreciates your dedication."

A casual conversation carried them through the rest of their meal. The excitement over the upcoming retirement that earlier filled the air had faded.

Thirty minutes later, Dr. Dickerson left and Olivia and Gammy cleaned up the kitchen in silence.

"I think I'll head out to pick up my outfits for the fashion show." Myrna approached Olivia with open arms. "It's probably best if I'm not here when you leave. It's too sad."

Olivia moved forward and the women embraced.

"I'm going to miss you bossing me around. You know that, don't you?" Olivia joked.

"It's only because I love you so much."

Olivia took a deep breath. "I love you, too."

"I know you have to do what's best for you. I admire your strength, dear. You're so much like your father." Myrna drew back and narrowed her eyes at Olivia. "I hope you realize how proud he would be of you."

Olivia buried her face in Gammy's shoulder and hugged her tighter. A part of her didn't want to let go or decline the doctor's offer. But she had to face the reality. There was no future for her and Jake.

Following a few seconds of silence, Myrna pulled away and wiped her eyes. "I better go."

Olivia was grateful when Gammy volunteered to take Kayla to the mother-daughter fashion show. Hopefully, her presence would ease Kayla's disappointment. "I don't like the idea of you driving to Denver alone."

"I won't be going by myself, dear. I'm heading over to Ruth's house. She will be driving, so you don't have to worry." She moved across the kitchen to the sink.

Olivia stepped closer to the kitchen sink. "Will you email me photos of the show?"

"Of course."

Olivia hugged her grandmother one more time. "Please drive safe."

"I always do." Gammy grabbed her purse from the pantry and headed out the door.

Moments later, Olivia heard Gammy's car start and drive away.

A chill caused Olivia to shiver as she stood alone in the kitchen. Her eyes scanned the room, taking in every sight and smell to carry back to Florida. She inhaled one last deep breath before heading out to the airport. It was time for Olivia to go home.

"MAYBE YOU SHOULD call her?" Logan opened the crate, and Buddy, the German shepherd puppy, cut loose across the field as if chasing a rabbit.

"Who?" Jake glanced in his brother's direction.

"You're kidding, right? Come on. You've been moping around all day." Logan shook his head and mumbled as he headed toward the barn. "You better go after her, man. God has given you a second chance—don't blow it."

His brother knew him well. Despite his best efforts, Jake hadn't been able to stop thinking about Olivia. Last night, he'd searched her flight information multiple times. Her plane left on time and landed safely. In between checking her flight status, he'd been consoling the kids and trying to explain why Olivia had to go back to Miami. The rest of the evening, he'd questioned whether he'd made the biggest mistake of his life by not telling her he was in love with her and wanted nothing more than to raise a family together.

Jake glanced at his watch as he headed toward the house. A sky of restless clouds drifted overhead. Myrna had phoned this morning to let him know she planned to meet the kids' school bus and help them with their homework, but he wanted to be there when they walked in the door.

Myrna was doing everything in her power to keep their minds occupied and off Olivia. Jake had tried his best to stay upbeat, but he missed Olivia, too. There was a giant hole inside him he couldn't seem to fill. Even working to train his latest service dogs couldn't fill the emptiness. Hopefully, once the mother-daughter fashion show was behind them, Kayla would get past the void left in her life by Olivia's departure. But the question was, would he?

He reached the back patio and his eyes focused on the swing between the Douglas firs. *I'm sure that's a beautiful place to watch the sunset.* Olivia's words played in his head and he kicked his boot into the ground. Because of his stubborn ways, they wouldn't share a sunset together.

He scanned the property and listened to a song sparrow trill in the distance. Olivia was right—there was nothing more the land needed. Except, in Jake's opinion, it needed her presence.

"Daddy! Kayla locked herself in her bedroom and she won't come out," Kyle shouted from somewhere in the house. Jake wiped his boots on the laundry room rug and took a deep breath. *Lord, give me strength.*

He scaled the stairs and found Myrna and Kyle outside Kayla's bedroom door. "What's going on?"

Myrna spoke first. "It seems Missy is at it again." She rolled her eyes.

Jake's busy schedule hadn't given him time to call Missy's parents. Now he wished he'd made it a priority. "Do you know what happened?"

"She's so mean!" Kyle wasted no time in reporting the story. "We were in the lunchroom and she came to our table. She started teasing Kayla about the fashion show."

Of course. That seemed to be the hot topic lately. Jake just wanted the show to be over. "What did she say?"

"She said it wasn't a grandmother-and-granddaughter fashion show, so Kayla and Miss Myrna shouldn't be in it. She said..." Kyle paused and looked down at the floor.

"What is it, son? You can say it." Jake glanced at Myrna.

"She said Miss Myrna was too old to be a model." Kyle turned to Myrna. "Sorry."

Myrna straightened her shoulders. "It's not your fault, Kyle."

Jake didn't have a good feeling about this evening. His instincts told him to keep Kayla home. Why subject her to more ridicule by Missy? But what would that teach his daughter? Jake's father always taught him to never give the power to a bully. The best way for Kayla to handle someone like Missy was to stand up to her. Easy for him to say. "I'll talk to her." He knocked on her door and waited for a response. When she didn't answer, he knocked again. "Kayla, can you open the door?"

"Go away!"

Myrna's and Kyle's eyes darted in Jake's direction.

"Why don't you and Kyle go down to the kitchen? Kyle is probably ready for his snack."

Myrna nodded to Jake. "Let's go, hon. I brought over some fresh chocolate chip brownies."

Jake waited until they were downstairs. He reached up over the door frame and grabbed the key to Kayla's room. Slipping the key into the hole, he slowly turned the knob. "I'm coming in." He paused before entering.

Jake's heart sank when he spotted his daughter sitting at her desk. Kayla gazed at the portrait of her mother he'd had professionally matted and framed for Kayla's birthday last year, after she'd told him it was her favorite photograph of her mother.

He slowly approached the desk and placed his hand on Kayla's shoulder. "Can you tell me what happened, sweetie?"

Kayla sprang from the chair and threw her arms around Jake's waist. Without hesitation, he scooped her up. He couldn't recall when she'd ever held on so tight. She buried her face in his shoulder and cried.

"Oh, baby, I'm so sorry." He carried her across the room and sat down on the edge of her bed. When would it ever get easier? Jake had always considered himself a problem solver. There was nothing he couldn't fix when he put his mind to it. But raising a little girl on his own was more than he could handle. Even with Myrna's help, he felt like he was failing his daughter.

Finally, Kayla's body stopped quivering, and her tears subsided. She lifted her head off his shoulder and looked him in the eye. "I'm sorry I locked my door. I know I'm not supposed to."

"It's okay. I understand you wanted to be alone, but sometimes it's good to talk to someone when you're upset."

Kayla nodded. "That's what Dr. Olivia told me. She said keeping stuff inside makes you feel worse."

Jake missed Olivia's words of wisdom. He missed a lot of things about her. "She was right. So, are you ready to talk?"

Kayla pushed her hair off her face and wiped her eyes. "Do I have to go to the fashion show?"

Jake studied his daughter. "Not if you don't want to."

Frowning, she chewed her lower lip. "Does that make me a scaredy-cat?"

Jake flinched. "Who called you that?"

"Kyle said if I didn't go, Missy would start calling me a scaredy-cat."

"What do you think?"

Kayla's forehead crinkled. "Well, if I go, she can't call me that."

"That's true." Jake nodded.

"What do you think Dr. Olivia would do?" Kayla studied his face.

"I think Dr. Olivia would probably go with Miss Myrna and have the best time that she could. She wouldn't allow Missy or anyone else to steal her joy."

Downstairs, the doorbell chimed.

Kayla hugged Jake and jumped off his lap.

"Thanks, Daddy. I think I'll go. I won't let mean ole Missy steal my joy, either!"

"That's my girl. Let's go downstairs and see who's at the door."

Kayla held Jake's hand tightly as they walked down the steps. Halfway down, he looked up and froze.

"Dr. Olivia!" Kayla yelled.

Jake blinked his eyes several times to make sure he wasn't seeing things. He wasn't imagining it. Olivia stood in his foyer wearing a dress exactly like the one hanging in Kayla's closet.

Kayla dropped his hand and raced to Olivia. "I knew you'd come. Daddy said you left, but I knew you'd come back."

Jake wasn't sure what to think. His first instinct was to protect his little girl. He couldn't bear the thought of her being hurt again.

Olivia opened her arms and picked Kayla off the ground. They twirled in a circle, both giggling.

When Olivia placed Kayla on her feet again, her eyes fixated on him.

His pulse raced.

"Hi, Jake." She smiled.

He cautiously moved toward her. His heart pounded in his chest. "What are you doing here?"

Olivia's eyes sparkled with tears. "If it's okay with you, I came to take Kayla to the fashion show."

"What about your job? Aren't you supposed to be there now?"

"I put in my notice this morning and got on the first flight to Denver. I just finished talking with Dr. Dickerson. He's going to start training me next week."

Myrna and Kyle cheered from the corner of the room.

Kyle raced to Jake's side. "Daddy, ask her now!"

Jake could hardly peel his eyes away from Olivia. He looked down at Kyle. "Ask what?"

"Ask Dr. Olivia on the date."

Jake reached for Olivia's hand. He planned to take Olivia on dates for the rest of their lives.

EPILOGUE

Fourteen months later

"CAN I HOLD MADDIE, Mommy?"

The word was sweet music to Olivia's ears. *Mommy.*

"I'll be careful. I promise," Kayla said.

Jake had spread out a blanket earlier for Olivia and their new daughter. He'd gone to grill hamburgers and hot dogs.

"Of course you can, sweetie. Have a seat."

Maddie cooed and squinted into the bright July sun reflecting off the lake. Olivia gave Maddie's sun bonnet a quick tug to protect her eyes.

A month had already passed since they welcomed Maddie into the family. Two days prior to her birth, Olivia had officially adopted Kayla and Kyle. Motherhood was exactly how she'd imagined. Exhausting, but so worth every lost hour of sleep.

"I love being a big sister." Kayla took Maddie and snuggled her in her arms.

"You're a wonderful big sister, and you're a tremendous help to me." Olivia leaned back and relaxed for the first time since the party had started.

Olivia couldn't believe she and Jake were already celebrating their anniversary at the same place they'd exchanged vows one year ago. Mirror Lake held a special place in her heart. It was where Jake brought her on their first date, and it was the spot Jake learned he was going to be a father again.

When he proposed, Jake wanted it to be a big surprise. He'd asked Olivia to come over to his house and watch the sunset on her favorite bench. She'd been back in Bluebell for three weeks and they'd been spending every non-working moment together. For the first time, she declined his invitation. She'd had a long day of training with Dr. Dickerson and was exhausted.

He showed up at Gammy's house with some story about a rare meteor shower that was happening. Olivia was intrigued and decided to go with him despite her tiredness. To this day, he told the story about how she almost missed her chance to become his wife.

"Hey, how come you get to take a break?" Jake stood over her, blocking the sun. She still couldn't believe this gorgeous man was her husband and the father of her child.

He flopped down onto the blanket next to Olivia. "I thought this was our anniversary party. Why am I stuck doing all the work?" Jake joked. "I thought that big rock on your finger meant we were a team."

Olivia laughed. One thing she loved most about Jake, besides the fact that he was a wonderful father, was his sense of humor. Laughter filled their days. "But you like to be in charge of the grill." She nudged her shoulder against his.

"Daddy, after you finish cooking for everyone, can you take me and Kyle out on the canoe?"

"Sure. I'll have to grab the life jackets from the truck. Where is Kyle?" Jake looked around.

"He and Miss Myrna took Callie for a walk."

Jake nodded and took Olivia's hand. "It's quite a turnout, huh?"

"Well, that's what happens when you put

Gammy in charge of party invitations. The entire town shows up." Olivia wouldn't have it any other way. Their family and friends were a blessing.

"Hey, guys." Logan approached the blanket and removed his black Stetson. "I wanted to wish you both a happy anniversary. It's a fantastic party."

"Thanks, man. I appreciate it."

"Thank you, Logan," Olivia said.

Jake stood and addressed his brother. "We need to find you a nice girl so you can settle down."

Logan laughed. "No, thanks. I'm happy being single."

Olivia didn't believe Jake's brother. She'd have to work on that.

"Daddy, come quick!"

"That's Kyle!" Jake said and took off running.

Olivia took Maddie from Kayla's arms. "Let's go, Kayla."

"He's down by the lake," Jake called out over his shoulder. "He's okay. Gammy is with him."

Olivia, the baby and Kayla joined up with Jake. "What's going on?" Olivia looked down and saw Callie digging frantically in the sand. "What is she after?"

"I don't know. Gammy and I were walking, and Callie just started digging. I kept pulling her leash, but she wouldn't move," Kyle explained.

Jake knelt in the sand. "Would you look at this?" He reached his hand into the hole.

"It's your watch, Daddy! The one I lost!" Kyle yelled.

Olivia couldn't hold back her tears. She watched her husband and son celebrating the discovery of the lost family heirloom and thought *God is good.*

★★★★★